PRAISE FOR *US CONDUCTORS*

"*Us Conductors* stretches its arms to encompass nearly everything—it is an immigrant tale, an epic, a spy intrigue, a prison confession, an inventor's manual, a creation myth, and an obituary—but the electric current humming through its heart is an achingly resonant love story. Sean Michaels orchestrates his first novel like a virtuoso."

—**ANTHONY MARRA**, author of *A Constellation of Vital Phenomena*

"A fascinating novel! Told with grace and confidence, and in a finely wrought voice, *Us Conductors* kept surprising me to the end. I was swept from the speakeasies and artistic fervor of 1930s Manhattan to bleak, secretive Soviet Union prisons, and never once was the illusion shattered. Throughout the story, the themes of love and music sing like the pure, ethereal notes of the theremin."

—**EOWYN IVEY**, author of the *New York Times* bestseller
The Snow Child

"DZEEEEOOOoo! Just as hard as it is to make a theremin sing so it is hard to pull off a novel like this. But Sean Michaels does it. *Us Conductors* bridges body and soul, science and art, and like theremin music, it's of this world and magical at the same time."

—**ISMET PRCIC**, author of *Shards*

"Michaels's voice will pass through you like live current and conduct you to parts unknown."

—**CARL WILSON**, music critic for Slate.com and author of
Let's Talk About Love: Why Other People Have Such Bad Taste

THE WAGERS

Published by Tin House Books, Portland, Oregon

Distributed by W. W. Norton & Company

Library of Congress Cataloging-in-Publication Data

Names: Michaels, Sean, 1982- author.
Title: The wagers / Sean Michaels.
Description: Portland, Oregon : Tin House Books, [2020]
Identifiers: LCCN 2019031476 | ISBN 9781947793637 (paperback) | ISBN 9781947793644 (ebook)
Classification: LCC PR9199.4.M527 W34 2020 | DDC 813/.6--dc23
LC record available at https://lccn.loc.gov/2019031476

First US Edition 2020
Printed in the USA
Interior design by Diane Chonette

www.tinhouse.com

The Wagers

SEAN MICHAELS

TIN HOUSE BOOKS / Portland, Oregon

for T,
my companion

There's limited fortune in the world, it seems,

  or a distribution problem.

—KAREN SOLIE

When I get to heaven, they will not ask me, 'Zusya, why were
  you not Moses?'

They will ask me, 'Zusya, why were you not Zusya?'

—RABBI ZUSYA OF HANIPOL

CHAPTER ONE

Nobody remembered Theo Potiris's first joke. Theo himself didn't remember. He'd scribbled his setlist on the back of an electricity bill, folded it in fourths, lost it. What he could imagine was a room, a stage, a microphone. Loud spotlights, crummy comics, tired portraits on the Knock Knock Club's wall. He recalled the way the darkness crowded around the tables, made it seem safe to laugh. Another first-timer had brought his mother and Theo couldn't take his eyes off them: the mope in shorts and T-shirt; the mom in black blazer, skirt, her long hands wringing an undrunk daiquiri. The son had yet to go up but the mother already sensed the way this would go. The boy's smile was like a scrap of egg. He was not funny, couldn't be, any more than a cocker spaniel can paint a still life with his paw.

Theo sat alone. He hadn't brought backup, not because he feared being embarrassed (though he did fear this, comprehensively) but because he feared the opposite even more: his friends' approval, or rather the semblance of their approval—those kind white lies. When Theo went on stage he wanted to be able to trust whatever happened—to get up and tell a joke and to know without doubt, for a few faint seconds, whether that joke was any good. Whether he was. When the MC called his name, Theo drained his glass. This he did remember: hearing his name; the Malbec in his mouth. He threw down a balled napkin and rose to his feet, shuffled through the spectators and up two steps to the stage. He was twenty-four years old. He wanted more than anything to be a comedian and at last he would test the premise, unassisted. He wrapped two hands around the microphone stand. He hesitated, released his hands, feigned a minor cough. He looked the darkness in the eye. He said, "Hey, I'm Theo, I've never been up here before."

Then he told a joke. His heart was a trembling die.

They laughed.

He told another.

They didn't laugh, he told another. And another and another. And every one was a way of asking, *SHOULD I?*

SHOULD I?

SHOULD I?

:::

On a Friday twelve years later, Theo still didn't know if he should. He was swooping downhill towards a hippodrome with a hurricane at his back, the wind whipping at the flagpoles, making the divots ding, ding, ding. Red glyphs swept across the racetrack's LED marquee. Starlings whirled above him as he locked his bike to a shiny contrivance. Something about the weather had called these birds into town—unfamiliar flocks, carried against migration routes. He stood staring for a little while, listening to their whistles, ear tips pinking. It was cold. The starlings looked like a strange quick smoke, the profits of a spell.

"*Bienvenue*, welcome!" A skinny teenager had been paid to stand just inside the hippodrome's doors, shrieking hospitality.

"Thanks," said Theo, and flashed him a thumbs-up. Did people still give thumbs-ups? As he passed from the outside to the concourse he registered the change of light and so the hour—late afternoon. He didn't like to leave his Friday bet so late. He had a routine: If he won he'd go to the Knock Knock that night, tell some jokes. If he lost, he wouldn't. He liked to know the outcome early so he'd have more time to visualize his set—or to put it out of his mind. This was a tradition he had learned from his late father. Theo Sr. had considered gambling a form of existential assessment. One bet a week, for exactly ten dollars: an augury, a fortune cookie, an appraisal of where he stood with the world. "A mirror of myself," Senior had called it, pulling on galoshes one night.

"But you don't even try to *win*," Theo's older brother, Peter, complained. "You just bet."

Senior regarded his two sons. "A woman does not look at her reflection in order to make herself beautiful," he said. "She looks to see who she is."

Theo hustled past a line of digital slot machines and the drooping men who leaned against their razzmatazz. The slots players creeped him out—were the men playing the machines or the machines the men?—but the malaise left him as soon as he reached the observation deck, a concourse ablaze with chandeliers, with carpeting the colour of American dollar bills. Ecstatic voices yelled from mounted speakers.

Plate-glass windows stared down onto the track. A few dozen men and women hunched on plastic chairs, watching the race on high-def TVs, where it looked brighter, realer, than it did through the glass. Theo put down his bike helmet and grabbed a racing form from the pile on the counter. He scanned it quickly, waiting for something to catch his eye. Two races in the next forty minutes. Nancy Pants, Ghost Pine, Intensive Purposes, Nic the Smokestack . . . He had won a bet on Ghost Pine a few weeks ago. Some familiar jockeys too: Franco Segal, P.E.D. Felice, Jamal Jones—you don't forget a name like Jamal Jones. Nothing stood out in the odds but then again that was the point. Not to score a coup or to outsmart the handicap: just to pick a horse and see.

His eyes landed on a filly called Expiry Date, with 5:3 odds. Jockey: J Jones. He presented himself to a clerk and slid across ten dollars straight from his family's grocery store till. "Ten on Expiry Date," he said. "To win."

"Good luck," the clerk replied. She was about his mother's age and wore the same shade of wine-coloured lipstick. Theo didn't think that his mother had ever been to a racetrack. He never understood whether she had accepted or merely endured her husband's visits to the Dodecahedron Grill, where he met a bookie missing both front teeth. But Theo had taken strength from seeing his father approach the abyss and stare into it, then walk away. To accept uncertainty, to give the universe some power over you . . . When his father won, returning triumphant from the restaurant's tzatziki-scented lounge, his good mood sustained him through the next week. Such an easy trick, a young Theo observed. Such an easy shortcut to feeling fortunate.

"Not for children, not for children," his pop used to tell him. "Gambling's not a game. It is a duel with the possible."

"I *want* to duel with the possible," Theo insisted.

"No, sesame seed," replied his father. "It is not for children. Childhood is the only time when there are no stakes—the only time in your whole life, Theo! You will have many, many years of stakes. Perilous, high stakes. Do not hurry them."

I should bring Mom, Theo thought. One of these Fridays. Ask her if she wants to come; to watch a wager for old times' sake. He worried that she spent too much time at the store, especially since his father's death ten years ago. While other women her age enjoyed retirement, playing cards around a table at the café called Social Club, Minerva Potiris went on tallying receipts by the cheese counter, sampling every cask of honey. "I'll quit when nobody wants groceries any more," she told her kids, touching the little Casio watch on her left wrist.

Theo took his betting stub and walked away from the clerk. He glanced towards the TV: another race, two horses neck and neck. A bettor in a sports jersey took to his feet. "*Vas-y!*" he shouted, *Go!*, and Theo felt a flutter of discomfort at the desperation in the man's voice. The announcer on the PA was narrating every fluctuation in the contest between Mistake Not and Filly Cheesesteak, and Theo studied the man's face—clear eyes, chapped lips—wondering, *Mistake or Cheesesteak? Mistake or Cheesesteak?* until finally Filly Cheesesteak streaked over the finish line, a cheesesteak's span ahead of Mistake Not, and the guy in the jersey carolled in triumph. The losers around him swore in unison. How much money had just changed hands? How many fortunes made or squandered?

Theo sank into a seat in the corner and stared out the big window. The sky was blue and silver. Small clouds careered across the horizon. Horses sauntered to their paddocks. The starlings Theo had observed before were curlicuing over the racetrack. Their messages in the air seemed zigzaggier now, more up-and-down. Theo's phone buzzed in his pocket. A text from his sister:

where r you??

He tapped a reply:

Track. Back soon.

Ok need u here.

What is it?

He waited, staring at the screen. Mireille didn't reply. At that moment a voice started squawking over the PA—a new voice, different from the standard race announcer—explaining in two languages that the next race had been delayed.

emergency, Mireille texted.

What kind of emergency? he wrote back.

This was part of Mireille and Theo's dynamic: he always had to ask. Mireille was the older sister and she enjoyed her status. There were six years between them, and seven more between Mireille and Peter, the eldest. Whole epochs existed in those gaps, eras that had defined the terms of their engagement. Peter the distant paragon, fully formed. Mireille—fearless, passionate, wielder of secret knowledge. She was the one who could fold a puffer fish from paper, who extinguished candles with her fingertips. She had shown him 1-800-GOLF-TIP, where a strange man counted numerals down the line, and, one Christmastime, the ancient game of dreidel—a game of stakes, yes, over chocolate coins in gilded foil. Mireille was the only one of them to attend Sunday Hebrew school, and the only one to undergo bar or bat mitzvah, singing with her eyes shut at the tiny synagogue on Bagg Street.

Theo's own induction into adulthood centred on Super Nintendo, cake, a baker's dozen of birthday candles. But his father also arranged a different kind of ritual. At last, after an eternity of Theo's pleading, he had told his youngest yes: on the threshold of his teens, Theo could make a bet.

Theo was stoked. He saved a month's allowance and added all his birthday bounty, plus whatever change remained inside his piggy bank. Almost sixty dollars altogether, which he clutched in a plastic shopping bag as they set off for the Dodecahedron Grill. It was the day after the party, afterimages of Mario Kart still blinking behind his eyes. Theos Jr. and Sr. ate their way through two souvlaki platters and a pair of hot fudge sundaes before the gap-toothed bookie slithered up to their table. Theo avoided eye contact as the two men discussed handicaps and spreads. His father didn't really follow sports, as far as Theo knew, and had no allegiances. Sometimes he bet on a local team, but often not. "The only no-go is Boston," he had told his son. "Boston is all maniacs. I will not endorse a maniac."

Now Senior unfolded five two-dollar bills and passed them one at a time to Nikolaos. "Flyers over Flames," he said. Four eyes turned to Theo.

Theo swallowed. He scrounged the notes and coins from the bottom of his plastic bag and dumped them in front of Nikolaos. "Fifty-eight dollars and fifty-five cents," he said, trying to sound both formal and nonchalant, in the manner of grown-ups.

"For?" the bookie said.

Theo had been reading the sports section all week. "The Expos over the Astros," he said.

"Expos."

"Yes."

"You sure?"

"Yes."

"I'll give you 3:2," Nikolaos said.

Theo Sr. clicked his tongue.

"Okay, 2:1," Nikolaos said. He shifted in his coat. "We have a deal?"

Theo looked at his pop, who affected an air of studied neutrality.

"Yes," Theo said.

Senior nodded, sealing the deal. Then Nikolaos took out his notebook and a fine-nibbed pen and he carefully added two lines, one for Senior's hockey bet and one for Junior's baseball. "Enjoy your dessert," he said, and extruded himself from the pleather booth.

"Expos over Astros, eh?" said Theo Sr., when Nikolaos had gone.

"Yes."

"Sixty dollars. A big bet."

Theo swallowed. His stomach sank and he suddenly felt doomed, doomed, doomed.

"Okay, sesame seed," said Senior. He patted his son's hand. "How do you feel?"

"I feel okay," he lied.

"That's good. 'Okay' is good. You don't want to feel too happy, or too lousy. You want to feel balanced."

Theo took a deep breath. "I feel balanced," he lied.

"Me too, boy-kid." Theo Senior took a similar deep breath. "Like a spinning top."

Of course Theo lost that bet. He watched on the family TV set, stricken, as the Astros hit homer after homer, laying waste to their opponents, turning his $58.55 into empty air.

The Flyers lost too. Lingering in his son's bedroom doorway, the elder Potiris offered a glum sigh. "Sometimes, Theo, life is half-terrible."

Later, his mother appeared with a dish of honey cake. As she smoothed Theo's hair with her hand, her eyes seemed like the oldest things in the world. "You can't always pick the right team," she told him, "or you'd be cheating."

:::

Theo got back into line. The clerk with his mother's lipstick was on the telephone, taking down a bet. Her blue ballpoint scratched across the paper—*zero, zero, zero, zero, dollar-sign*. This was a very large bet. Theo inspected the upside-down racing form, trying to decipher the name that the caller was staking their fortune on. But then the clerk was putting down the phone and sliding aside the paper and asking, cheerfully, "Can I help you?" His phone chose the same instant to buzz and shudder off the counter, clattering to the tile. He stooped to pick it up.

nut emergency, Mireille had written.

He stared at the screen.

A cashew crisis?

Not an emergency?

"*Sir?*" the woman said.

"Sorry, nut emergency," he mumbled. He rubbed his face. "The announcement said my race would be delayed. Do you know for how long?"

"Which race?"

He fumbled at his betting stub, dropped his helmet, stooped again, stood. "Fifteen?"

A technical delay, she told him. At least ninety minutes. He squinted at the giant green clock, with its spinning Labatt 50 bottle. It felt like cheating to make another set. For twelve years he had been repeating the same ritual, letting one wager decide whether he'd get up on stage on a Friday night. It was like casting lots. One damn horse, not two, every seven days. Ten dollars, no loopholes—a judgment from the fates.

And so: twenty-five minutes later, back in his neighbourhood, Theo's future remained unsettled. He skirted taxis, glided through stop signs, bypassed insensible pedestrians. He was paused at a traffic light when a woman pulled up on a green road bike, a plastic milk crate bungeed to the back. The crate contained a kitten, which turned and smiled. *Meow*, it said. "Meow," Theo murmured, waving a finger. He was reminded of how much he loved this city. Not the highways and box stores around the racetrack but the untidy beauty of its oldest parts, the stalwart trees and stubborn shopfronts, the cast-iron stairways, bundled denizens, even the pitted roads. Lasters, all of them, enduring every dumb winter. He squeezed his brake grips. The kitten was still staring at him. He and this woman and her pussycat would bicycle up the hill, past the gazebo and the Cartier monument, the park gone brown from too much rain, straining up the slope, cresting the summit, then all downhill. *Lasters*, he *thought* again. The traffic light changed, and they did go up, over, down the hill, through an empty intersection. The kitten and its owner turned left at the next corner. "Goodbye, cat!" Theo said to himself, imagining a Garfield thought-bubble ballooning into the air. He felt oddly elated. He had bet on a horse on a Friday evening and that horse had neither won nor lost, not yet. He was suspended in limbo, his fortune untold. Schrödinger's black cat, borne northward on a bike.

He skipped the curb into an alley. The asphalt was sprayed with loose leaves, young ivy, vivid in its greens. How many times had Theo biked along this alleyway, dodging the same sequence of mudpiles, potholes, rain grates . . . At the speed-bump he slowed and dismounted. The back of Provisions K didn't look like anything much. Sixty-one feet of cement and red brick, two storeys and a peaked roof, a small loading dock and a ramp to the basement. A blessedly tidy dumpster, a Jenga stack of pallets, a little pat of snow unmelted in the shade. A lettuce leaf in the gutter.

Just inside, Mireille and Eric were having an argument beside the utility room: his sister with corkscrew black curls, her face streaked with feeling; Eric, her partner, his domed head bowed. Theo swallowed.

"No buts!" Mireille yelled. "You can't add a 'but' *now*. You can't just add one later. I heard you the first time, when there wasn't a but."

"*But—*" Eric said, "listen, I *do* understand where you're coming from, I just disagree, and that's *okay*, but—hold on, hold on, BUT I think you didn't actually understand what I was saying! I was *saying—*"

"Hi guys." Theo said.

Mireille's head snapped towards him. "There's a nut emergency," she said, voice low, as if she were warning that a war had broken out. "Yes," said Theo. "What does that *mean?*"

"Everywhere," Mireille said. "There are nuts everywhere."

"Okay," Theo said.

"Everywhere," Mireille repeated.

"Got it."

"You were at the track?" Eric asked, trying to lift the mood. "How'd you do?"

"I don't know yet."

"That must be tormenting for you," said Mireille.

Theo sighed. He pushed through the employee's area double-wide door and into the store. He felt a little tremor behind him, the needle of their argument lowered back onto the platter.

Everything seemed normal on the floor. The dinner rush was over and the aisles seemed weirdly desolate: a middle-aged man scrutinizing a bag of ketchup-flavoured potato chips, a little girl observing the unguarded olive cart. Across the sound system, in Greek, a troubadour sang a blues of loneliness and hashish.

Theo came from groceries. He was a child of Provisions K, the city's oldest grocery store, an emporium teeming with humans and their cheeses, families and their fruit, fish and wheat thins and paper towels. His parents had met there. Perhaps Theo had been conceived there. His first word was "milk" and, according to legend, Little Theo had said it while gesturing at a carton. Theirs was an older breed of supermarket, built in the years before frozen pizzas and fair-trade coconut chips. Low ceilings, non-fluorescent bulbs. Piped-through radio and rembetika. Creaks and jangles, crashing tills, shuffling boots, plastic thuds, whorling spools of produce bags, strangers' cotton kissing cotton as they brushed by in narrow aisles. Also: laughter by the pita bread, crying by the tuna steaks, local gossip, scooped granola, the clamorous maze of clumsy citizens and canned tomatoes, vats of Greek goats' cheese, chocolate chip cookies, fennel and plums, pork chops, aluminum foil, tamari almonds. 9 AM–11 PM, 7/52 an ambiance as familiar to Theo as the beep of reversing delivery trucks, the tang of expired yoghurt.

Back when Theo was a baby, Minnie Potiris had nursed her youngest son in every crowded section—among cereals, deli meats and root vegetables. She'd let him totter among the taco shells and day-old bread. His features then were his features still: a plump baby face, a contagious smile, dark brown eyes that shone like wet stones, giving his expressions volatility and grace. He had thick black hair. It lay wild across his brow or flew up at angles above his ears, as if his temples had been pinned with laurels. The old-timers still told him stories of those days—squeaking like a cheese curd, snapping along to Smokey Robinson. He became a kid on a high stool by the cash, swirling round and round, fingersnapping like a bandleader.

Now Theo prowled Provisions K's health-food section, past the rice-and-pickles aisle. He was almost at the bulk bins when he stepped on something hard. A hazelnut. No, many hazelnuts—there were hazelnuts everywhere, Theo observed. Beneath his shoes, hazelnuts like a spray of pebbles across a beach. And over by the spices: glossy red Brazil nuts, like chips of terracotta. Barbecue peanuts in russet drifts near the ice-cream vaults and beside the fajita kits a stretch of big, wobbling walnuts, placid in their shells.

"Nut emergency," said a soft voice.

It was Hanna, Mireille and Eric's daughter, trimming lamb chops behind the meat counter. At twelve, she was the youngest member of the Potiris clan and arguably its most gifted butcher. She was brown-eyed, spindly, wide-shouldered, a girl with wingspan—although at times she still folded up so small. Theo would catch her curled up beside her grandmother in Minnie's apartment upstairs, sharing sections of the Saturday paper, or perched on a watermelon crate in a quiet corner of the store, listening to songs on her earbuds. Hanna was kind, but the poise with which she moved, her almost spooky self-possession, could at times seem severe. She set down her knife, bloody and shining, on a white butcher's sham, and said, "The cashews are fine."

"In that case 'emergency' is a stretch," Theo said.

Hanna smiled. "Peanut problems," she suggested, and slipped her earbuds on.

Theo pressed on towards the source. When he arrived at the bulk food bins, his two nephews were making progress with a broom and an industrial-scale dustpan. His mother stood over them with her arms raised, entreating or cajoling, inspiring her grandsons to greatness. "That's it, Maurice, broom it!" she said.

Tonight Minerva Potiris wore jeans and an oversize Dans la rue hoodie. She didn't show her age; she seemed resolute, eternal, like a black-and-white photograph of Olympia Dukakis: their princess of produce, their doyenne of delivery. Minnie's expression was one of happy exasperation—elevated eyebrows, parted lips, a smile abiding in her eyes. She had always been grandmotherly, even in her youth. Grandmotherly above all: her grey hair cut short like a boy's; refined lipstick and chipped nail polish; something protective in the way she hovered.

Nudging a mound of hazelnuts with his toe, Theo said, "Did a squirrel win the lottery?"

Minnie laughed. His nephews stared at him like a pair of startled golden retrievers. Peter's sons were burly—man-sized but not yet manlike. Each was named for a hockey player: Maurice, prodigiously nosed, with a helmet of gelled hair, wielded the broom. Blake, green-eyed, with a shaggy blond mohawk, held the dustpan.

"Little Theo, always just in time," Minnie said. "Right as we're finishing up."

"What happened?"

"Maurice and Blake were filling the nut bins," she said. "They had an accident—a series of correlated accidents, actually." The boys' gazes swivelled into the floor.

"Mireille said it was an emergency."

His mother gave him a sly look. "A little panic never hurt anyone. Where is your sister?"

"In back with Eric."

A shred of sorrow rippled across her face. "Always cats and dogs with them."

"They're all right."

She shook her head. "Money's like locusts."

"Locusts?"

"Too biblical? 'Like fascism?' 'Like high-waisted jeans?' It comes, it goes. They shouldn't worry so much."

"Worrying runs in the family."

"I never worry," she said. "I consider. I mull."

He smiled. When he was younger he had taken his mother's repartee at face value. He had thought of her as a naturally expressive person, bubbly and uncontainable—saluting long-time customers, laughing at the fish-boys' jokes, scolding new hires who arrived late for work. But at night, after Senior died, she sat alone in her apartment above the store, playing solitaire or reading a historical novel, listening to *Ideas* on the radio. She was an introvert at heart, and also a subtle actress, calibrating her performances to the people she encountered in the world.

"I want to take you for a walk later," he said to her. "All these weird birds have blown in. Big gulls. Starlings."

"Vultures?" she quipped.

"Anything's possible. Maybe you'll see a toucan."

"Toucans are diurnal." Minnie let out a breath. "And I want to show you something too. Downstairs. Remind me, Little Theo," she patted his shoulder, "when we're all cleared up."

"Okay."

"Okay," she repeated. "Are you going on stage tonight?"

"Still waiting on my bet."

"A soldier of fortune," she said, with a smile. She turned to watch her grandsons at their sweeping. "Now look at those boys," she murmured. "Look at those conscientious darlings."

When Theo was satisfied that the nut crisis was under control, he continued on his rounds. He checked in on the cashiers, the delivery guys, the cleanliness of the counter behind the dairy section, where cheddar got chopped into blocks. He poked his head into the closet of vinegars, held his breath in the walk-in fridge they called the cheese pit. There were a thousand different routes Theo could wind through Provisions K—from strawberries to Swiss chocolate, challah to salsa, bitter greens to demerara sugar. Today they were all shadowed by his unresolved bet. There had been Fridays when he hadn't bet at all, but never before had he bet and bolted before the outcome. Now it felt rash, reckless. And so he checked and rechecked his phone as he tidied chocolate bars, topped up the olives. Somehow, the race still had not happened. Or had the racetrack not updated its website? He imagined Expiry Date, suspended mid-gallop. Was there a way the race could have been run, some anomalous result, which meant that Theo had become a zillionaire? He tossed blackened bananas into a garbage bag. No, there was no way. There was no way he had won more than $26.67. And he had probably lost.

Hadn't he?

Eventually his mother barged in on Eric and Mireille, still arguing in the back. "Today's special is: truce," he heard her say. She coaxed them back onto the floor and soon all six of them were working together to clean the swept-up nuts. Theo and Mireille steadied the basin of water as Eric and their nephews poured almonds and hazelnuts inside.

"I remember doing this with stones from the lake, to make them shine," Mireille said.

Theo smiled. "There's nothing more beautiful than rocks in a bath."

Minerva ran the show: *these* nuts could be soaked; *those* ones could not; the unshelled peanuts were all headed to the compost. They deferred to her authority because they were a company and she was the choreographer. Mireille teased her little brother but not too much; Theo gave his nephews avuncular encouragement. Grime floats, nuts don't, and before long Theo and Mireille were dabbing pistachios with unspooled paper towels. When the family finally dispersed it felt like the end of a concert. Maurice and Blake needed to catch their bus back home. Minerva headed to her desk to review the day's receipts while a tray of damp shells began to air dry.

Theo poked at his phone.

"What are you doing?"

He raised his head. Hanna's brown hair was mussed, curls winging like a haphazard ski jump.

"Checking on my bet."

"Don't you find out right away?" His niece's apron was covered in ruddy stains, dried blood from the butcher counter. On her it looked harmless.

"Usually," he said. He cursed at the phone's insensible touchscreen.

Customers pushed past with shopping carts crammed with cornflakes, lamb chops, smoked and sweet paprika. Hanna stood with hands clasped, waiting. The patrons barely noticed the bloodstained girl and her uncle sitting in the corner. Theo tapped and swiped and pressed and finally exhaled. "Aha," he said.

"Aha?"

"That's right," he said, stretching out his legs.

Expiry Date had finished first, trailed by Mouldy Manor and Ojingogo. It was as if a weight had been lifted from Theo's chest, and thirty dollars deposited in his pocket.

Hanna stepped aside as her uncle, newly minted, began to rearrange jars, yank packets of lentils to the front of their shelves. The rembetika music on Provisions K's PA seemed reassuring now. Theo thought about whether he should text Annette, the manager at the club, to tell her he'd like to get up tonight, or whether he should just show up. Before long, the store would close. The last delivery guys would drive away. The sweepers would sweep up whatever Blake and Maurice had missed. The cashiers would leave their time sheets and grab their coats. Theo would review his new material one last time, grab his helmet, set off. There is solace in a pattern, in the arc of probability landing where it ought.

Still, he had a little time. Maybe he'd find Minnie, take her on that walk. Maybe she'd show him whatever it was she wanted to show him. He passed the newest of the family's produce cabinets, a bank of white steel shelves with its own row of hi-tech Largo bulbs, a mounted panel spraying mist every 540 seconds. The cabinet's mound of herbs looked like a hillside—domestic parsley, imported parsley, dill and cilantro, mint, rosemary, kaffir lime leaves, thyme and sprigs of tarragon and basil, next to parcels of black and purple kale bound with string, pods of baby spinach, and a cardboard box of organic frisée. Theo remembered standing as a boy beside the herbs, eyes closed, inhaling and exhaling, imagining Greek valleys and Roman gardens, magic country.

Theo smiled a thirty-six-year-old smile. The mister misted at him. And then at the end of the row of produce, sitting in a wooden chair that had been there since another age, since the war, since long before the spritzing cabinet or the refrigerated produce section, since before Theo was born, he saw his mother. Her eyes were shut, her fingers interlaced atop the round of her belly, a perfect dreamer. "Hi, Mom," Theo murmured. She didn't stir. So much for going on that walk. He walked over to her and, very gently, touched her forearm with the tips of his fingers. "Ma?" he said. She didn't stir. He leaned in closer, to where she sat in the cold.

CHAPTER TWO

The sign on the front doors of Provisions K read as follows:

DÉSOLÉS. WE ARE CLOSED TODAY DUE TO A TRAGEDY.

The French word *désolé* is most often used as a kind of "sorry." A patron asks whether a café serves almond milk; a stranger asks a passer-by if she can spare a cigarette. "*Désolé, non.*" *Désolé* is a polite apology but there is a second meaning as well: desolated, laid waste to, undone.

Désolés, they wrote. *We are closed.*

:::

It had been almost three decades since Provisions K last closed. The store's doggedness had been a point of pride for Theo's father. It had shut its doors only twice: during the 1970 October Crisis, and then in 1992, due to a burst water main.

They did not close the store when Theo Senior died. It was a tribute to stay open.

But with Minnie, no.

No, it had to close.

They were ruined.

:::

Theo had come downstairs before dawn, unable to sleep, and had affixed the message to the glass doors. *Désolés*, in black marker. Later they'd call all the employees, tell them to take the day off. Maybe two days. They'd be mourning Minnie too. It was a heart attack, the doctor said. Painless, as she dreamed in her chair. No one had known she'd had any trouble with her heart.

Theo was still wearing the clothes he had on when he'd bicycled to and from the racetrack: jeans, boots, a baby-blue button-up shirt his mother had given him for his birthday. A shirt wrapped in tissue paper, pushed across the table. "Wear it in good health," she had said. He was ruined.

It didn't feel the way he'd imagined it would. That night he had lain in bed listening to the yearning radiator. Thin darkness through the curtains, a laptop's charging light pulsing on the bedside table. An emptiness that was wakeful, disarrayed, as if he might forget what it was he had lost. He wished Lou were there. Facing him on the bed, holding him in place with her listening.

Once he had put the sign on the doors, Theo gathered in his kitchen with the remaining Potirises who lived in the apartments above the store. He pulled fruit and cheese from the fridge, toasted croissants, gulped down a huge bowl of cereal. Hanna applied three layers of jam to each side of her bagel. Mireille sat with a single tea-spoon and an individual-sized yoghurt.

Eric ate nothing, preparing latte after latte in a stovetop cafetière.

"Did you get any sleep, Eric?" Theo asked.

"I got a few hours, I think." He smiled with ringed eyes. His earring glittered. Theo remembered when Mireille first brought her boyfriend home: the brash Egyptian with fine blue eyes, bleached blond hair, a gold stud in his left earlobe. Eric had lost his cockiness but he still had the earring, the eyes. He had exchanged his swagger for a spouse, his hair for a daughter. Theo poked a punnet of blueberries towards Mireille. "You all right?"

She frowned. "I was—" Her face abruptly lost expression, an electronic sign as it loses its signal. "I . . ." She hesitated. "I just realized: wasn't yesterday Friday the thirteenth?"

Theo thought for a moment. "No."

"No?"

"No. The ninth. Today's the tenth."

"Oh."

"It's okay," Eric said.

She shook her head.

"Do you know why you didn't sleep?" Hanna asked.

They all turned to look at her. Hanna was still eating her rainbow-slicked bagel; chewing and talking in counterpoint. "Why you *couldn't* sleep, I mean."

"Do I know why?" Mireille said.

"Yeah, like do you know what they say in Japan?"

Her mother wrapped her arms around herself. "What do they say in Japan?"

Hanna swallowed laboriously. "In Japan, they say that when you can't sleep you must be awake in someone else's dream."

Mireille smiled at her daughter for a single grateful beat.

Later, Peter arrived. He and his wife, Joanne, had moved away from the family homestead—migrating north, off-island, to a house with an aboveground pool. He was a lawyer, Joanne did real estate, and although they duly dispatched Maurice and Blake to spend time at the store, to learn the same lessons and do the same chores as their father had done, Peter had a complicated relationship with the family business. To him, Provisions K, for all its customers, for all its consequence and character, was a failure. Margins were too low, overhead too high, and the mishaps plentiful, from floods to unforeseen infestations of avocado worms. Minnie and Senior had refused to raise their markup; they had refused to cut wages; they had declined to modernize in the ways Peter demanded—especially when he was twenty-six, fresh out of law school. So he had distanced himself: the dissenting heir.

Today Peter moved blazing through all the parts of Provisions K. He was angry at the store, angry at the world, angry at the idea of a heart attack and the premise that it could take Minnie from them, so easily and unannounced. He cursed at empty boxes, slammed the doors of buzzing freezers. Flecks of pigment pricked in his cheeks, like embers flying up from a fire.

When they crossed paths, Theo felt overwhelmed by his brother's feeling, and his own sorrow seemed thin, weak, in comparison. He was just trying to get through the hours, to keep the fresh foods from spoiling, working with Eric to carry slabs of ribs and bags of calamari from the fridges to the basement freezer, tearing brown florets from the fringes of the broccoli, the damn broccoli. Idil had called on Thursday with a giveaway price and they had bought it all.

The funeral would take place on Sunday. Soon because Minnie was Jewish, sort of, in the same way the whole family was Jewish, sort of, but none of her children understood the rules for a Jewish funeral or knew whether it was what Minnie would have wanted. Their mother had approached faith as she had school lunches, or advertising. It was something to manage.

She must have learned this from her own parents, who had embraced Greek culture—and even, to some degree, the Greek Orthodox Church—as a way of fitting into the neighbourhood. Assimilation maybe, or transference. The Swirskys wanted to leave the old country behind, forging bonds less vulnerable than blood. So they became feta and eggplant experts, Easter caterers, marquee sponsors of a weekly rembetika radio show. They named their daughter for what they thought was a Greek goddess. When Minerva Swirsky fell in love with Theódoros Potiris the hexagon was hexed, and Provisions K had more or less become the thing it purported to be.

When Senior had his accident, Minnie informed everyone that he had been an atheist, that he would have wanted to be cremated. So it went. Four days later, the matriarch and her clan gathered before a reinforced glass pane as his remains were fed into the crematory. They came home with a wooden box weighing almost eight pounds. *Like a healthy baby,* Theo remembered thinking. The widow placed her husband's ashes on the mantel in their apartment, in a pale ceramic urn, and painted the exterior with a dozen black-and-yellow bees.

The day after she died, Minnie's family gathered before that same apian urn to decide whether they would choose the same fate for their mother—burn her to ash, pour her into a vessel.

"Wouldn't she prefer to be in the ground, like her parents?" asked Mireille.

"Pop didn't," said Peter.

"We can't burn her," Eric whispered.

"Let's not use that verb," Theo said.

"Wouldn't she want to be here with him?" Peter said.

Mireille wiped her nose. "Wouldn't she want to not be burned?"

"Why?" said Peter.

"Why anything?" Theo shouted, surprising himself. "Why anything!"

They turned.

He lowered his eyes, ashamed. "There's no wrong decision," he said. "It doesn't matter." But even he knew he was lying.

It was Hanna who finally settled it. She and Minnie had apparently discussed the topic—daydreaming funeral arrangements over backgammon. "She wanted to be cremated and she wanted it to be a celebration," Hanna said. "She said, 'I want to go out on top.'"

Hanna's testimony put the dissenters' minds to rest. Mireille and Eric went with Peter to a meeting at the funeral parlour. The director had dated Mireille in high school and still stopped in at the store for his groceries. A slim and serious bachelor, solemn in a black suit, buying seven hanger steaks at a time.

Meanwhile, Theo descended to the cellar. Minnie kept a desk there—a tall piece of cherrywood, with a folding drop leaf, sliding drawers. He knew she had inherited the desk, but he couldn't recall from whom. Would anyone know, now? Death doesn't just take away a person—it erases everything they knew. This desk was orphaned, too; no one could even remember its lineage.

Papers brimmed from its eleven cubbies. Pink message pads, yellowed receipts, rubber-banded chequebooks and letters. The seat of Minnie's office chair sagged. The way it moved under him, across her little square of carpet, evoked an old memory. Sitting here with her as a child? Sitting in her lap?

He began to page through the piles of paper. Correspondence, time sheets, crayoned artworks by Minerva's grandchildren. Lists from suppliers, from the years before Eric took over that job. Minnie's handwriting never changed—a thin and regal script, steady across function, purpose, across time. So light that each character already seemed to be disappearing, as if all these pages might soon be blank. Yet in the burrow of the basement, among all her papers, Minnie still seemed present. All that ink adds up to something, in the end.

He found two stapled sheets of graph paper that had been set aside. They were filled with boxes, grid lines, notes in Minnie's hand. Theo picked them up, staring at the neon sticky-note stuck in the centre, which read, "Theo."

He put the pages down after a moment. He looked at Minnie's pens in their mug. He needed to write to Lou. He didn't need to. He wanted to lie down with her. He wanted to go walking together, thawing his grief by slow degrees. She always seemed to hear him. More than any other woman he had known, Lou seemed to understand what was skirmishing inside of him. He felt no need to conceal himself with her—neither to mind his words nor to cast a glamour. He could be himself, unvarnished.

Where was she now? Walking in the sand dunes? Sitting with friends around a fire? He had known her only since the fall, and in January she had gone away. On retreat in the desert, booked before they met; when she told him about it, it sounded like she'd made it up. A four-month "clarity retreat," away from everything—disconnected, deliberately disconnected. Why does a person choose to go away? He didn't understand, not entirely, even after all her explanations. On their second date she showed him the email from the Largo Foundation on her phone. Its seal was something he had only ever seen on TV or in ads:

A tall blue *U* intersected by an oscillating line. A wriggling rise and fall and rise and fall that suggested the sea or the desert, or else mountains, or brain waves, or the fluctuations of the market.

"I think it's meant to symbolize the glass-half-full, glass-half-empty thing," she told him. They were at a bar called La Taverne du Pélican, shouting at each other over a Neil Young song.

"So which do you see?" he said.

She hadn't wanted to say.

"Half-full, surely," he said, gesturing at his own half-filled pint.

"I admire your optimism," she said.

"I admire your capacity for indeterminacy."

"I'm learning."

He grinned. "I'm not."

They had accepted her application and now she was there, living in a tent among the dunes, under brighter stars than any she had ever seen. *Dear Theo*, she had written with pen on paper, *the stars here are like diamonds on black velvet. Like Stevie Nicks lyrics.* Z. Largo's property was in an astronomical dark zone, untarnished by light pollution. *It's all candles after ten, or else we have to use these red Largo bulbs—makes my yurt feel like a darkroom. Last night a few of us grabbed cushions and sat outside. Saw straight to the Milky Way.* What would his next letter to her say? *Dear Lou. My mother died. You and she barely had the time to know each other. After you met she said you "seemed very smart." And you called her "formidable." I don't know how to show my sadness. I don't know how to embody it. I wish you were here. She left me two pieces of paper filled with names and addresses, years of entries, crossed out and rewritten. I don't even know what they're for.*

Maybe he'd send the pages to Lou, see if she could figure them out.

He looked around the cellar. Shelving and storage packed into an insufficient basement. Boxes of toilet paper, sacks of rice, a thousand fluid ounces of canned beans. Nori and fruit-leather. Theo had never known there to be any extra room down there, but now it was hard to imagine how the forklift was getting around. It could not go on this way. Or perhaps, because it always had, it could.

When he went back upstairs, drifting past the olive cart, a strange motion caught Theo's eye. The cart was a rectangular stall with a little plastic roof and nonfunctional wagon wheels. Its body was blue-black, the roof green, wheels pimento-red. In the cart's eight olive compartments, the olives were spinning in their brine. Kalamata, Arbequina, Lucques: each individually revolving in place, silent as a stone, orbiting in the same direction. Counterclockwise, Theo noted; the observation seemed both useless and uncanny. He stayed for a long time, watching the spinning olives. He had never seen anything like it. Maybe a few olives bobbing in their compartments, but never like this, spinning as one. What had set them off? What were the chances? There they were, here he was, until he wandered away, because there were things he needed to do.

:::

On Sunday morning, Minerva Potiris's children gathered behind a familiar sheet of glass and watched as their mother's body was conveyed from a hardwood table into a crucible. Theo could hear everything: the clock, footsteps, a telephone ringing down the hall. In the faintest distance, somewhere else in the building, somebody was singing "Happy Birthday."

He could not hear anything from the other side of the glass.

After the crematory door closed, the Potirises went to breakfast and then returned. They waited. Finally a woman appeared with a clipboard and Peter disappeared with her into a back room. When he emerged with the wooden box containing Minnie's remains, Theo found himself asking how much it weighed.

"What?"

"How much does it weigh?"

"Does it matter?"

Theo's face told him it did.

"Six and a half pounds."

Theo had the sensation that part of him opened, like a valve. It was almost as if he was going to laugh. But then the valve swung shut, before he had done anything, before he had even really felt anything.

On Sunday afternoon more than a hundred people gathered for a service at the Ukrainian Federation, which had offered the family the space free of charge. "Minnie always baked a honey cake for the Christmas fair," the board treasurer told Mireille. "She would paint a Ukrainian flag in blue and yellow icing. Even though she was Greek."

"She wasn't Greek," Mireille said.

The treasurer shook his head. "What a saint." The man was notorious in the community for his messy Springsteen covers on Ukrainian karaoke nights. He had a nose full of burst capillaries. "Please, seriously, it would be an honour for us."

The Ukrainian Federation building was on the edge of the neighbourhood, a red-brick cube flanked by maples. Once it had been a community centre but now the owners rented it out to anyone—rock musicians and film festivals, craft bazaars, same-sex weddings, memorial services. The Ukrainian community still held events a few times a season, usually karaoke, in a bid for their children to fall in love with one another. For Minnie's funeral they put away the laminated binders of Marvin Gaye and Céline Dion lyrics. They took down the banner reading GOOD TIMES in shiny bubble letters and the caretaker lowered the flags to half-mast.

The main hall was lined with wooden pews. Regulars brought their own cushions. The stage had a painted backdrop with grassy rolling hills and a pair of swooping seagulls. Theo's siblings argued about whether to leave the backdrop down; Peter won and harangued an orderly until the panorama got rolled up into the rafters. They placed Minnie's urn on a folding bridge table, beside a photograph of her as a young woman—a smiling girl mid-movement, with glossy black hair, white shorts and T. The urn was smooth and cream-coloured, unadorned. They filled a long table with donated flowers, lilies and mums like an Easter service, and more framed photos— images of Minnie and Theo Senior; of her and the children on a sugar-shack wagon-ride; of Grandma Minnie sitting with her first grandchild, Maurice at two weeks old, swaddled like a pita souvlaki with a crumpled little face.

Theo kept trying to imagine what Minnie would have wanted.

They had never talked about it. Talking about it would have felt like he was weakening her somehow. It was better to die suddenly. Wasn't it? He found he was shivering.

He had brought her good china to the Ukrainian Federation, for anyone to eat from. He had brought her backgammon board, so mourners could challenge each other to games, and her radio, so they could put on the CBC. As relatives arrived, he shook their hands. He kissed them on both cheeks. "It's okay," he told the cousins with screaming twins. "This is all real life, right?" He stood with Mireille at the front of the room, his arm around her shoulders. They tried to decide when it was appropriate to begin.

"Do funerals need to start on time?" he asked.

"I don't know," she said. Then: "Yes."

But they wanted to leave time for stragglers, both of them did, frozen at the front of the room with their eyes on the doors. He was so grateful to have her there—a steadying presence, awash in her feelings, as he felt dazed in his. He lowered his arm and their hands found each other. He could feel that she was near to coming apart and he wondered if she could feel this in him, too—that he was near to falling apart. Everything he wasn't keeping together was percolating invisibly inside him.

She sent a pulse through her hand to him, palm to palm. "Okay, little brother. It's time to face the music."

Peter led the memorial service as if he were chairing the national conference of a dull profession. He made stiff jokes and spent too long thanking everyone for having come. How many juries had heard these jokes, Theo wondered. How many juries had gazed at that same grey suit? His older brother applied reading glasses and read some prepared remarks about Minnie's life. She was a shopgirl who grew up on Esplanade Street and married a delivery boy; only two years of high school but she taught herself Greek and how to butcher a pig.

"She was also an excellent amateur painter," Peter noted, "and one of the history museum's most knowledgeable volunteers."

He turned a page.

"More importantly, Minerva was a wife and mother, a brilliant business owner, and an extremely proud grandmother," which was the cue for Maurice, Blake and Hanna to stand up. *Let all who are gathered here behold Minerva's progeny.* Theo, childless, realized that his brother believed him a failure. He experienced this intuition as a jolt of anger—the first time that day that anything had been able to cut through the miasma. Theo watched Peter fold up his glasses, the clicking sounds caught by the microphone. His brother's tie was too wide; it was green and brown and out of fashion. He was taller than Theo but he didn't know how to use that height. Theo imagined what he might have accomplished if he were as tall as Peter, the man he could have been—the father, the lawyer, the patriarch.

As if it was his height that held him back. Theo stared down at his shoes, black loafers flecked with particles of onionskin, and stooped to brush them off. Peter's height hadn't made him who he was, any more than Theo's height had made him into an unknown comedian managing a family business. Each of them had made their choices. Theo didn't want a mansion in the suburbs and a long commute. He didn't want to make small-talk at golf clubs and board meetings. He wanted, as he had for twenty years, to make people laugh by telling the truth, somehow, in a spotlight. To find his way before a microphone. This was the dream that had carried him through his teens. It was what sustained him after his father's death. Comedy had seemed like an answer to the illogic and tragedy of life, a clubhouse of like-minded idiots. It demanded no credentials, just to get on stage and try. When Theo first began going up the joy had shuddered through him, like a bat loose in a library. He felt an ample happiness as he told his jokes, and in the reply of the audience, and even in the pauses. He could make it up there. He could write material and say it out loud, funny—making his minutes, finding his voice, flourishing. And this is what he did, first at open mics and then bigger stages, hosting, middling, even headlining now and then. Every time he won a bet he got on stage. Anything could happen. There was the night he celebrated his birthday. The night with a mouse on stage. The first night he talked about heartbreak. The time they gave him a standing ovation and the power went out. The time the *Late Night* booker was there, her laughter like a whipcrack through the room.

Peter called Véro Lequin to the stage. Minnie's oldest friend was dressed in green brocade. Theo helped her climb the steps; he adjusted the lectern's microphone. She touched the heavy necklace at her neck.

Véro talked to them about losing to Minnie at backgammon. She talked about Minnie's special sumac-dusted pork chops. She talked about the time they went to see *Beverly Hills Cop*, two mothers on a night out, and how they vowed to never forget the moon. "It was huge and red," she said, "like an amulet."

Then it was Mireille's turn. She had wanted to memorize her speech and Theo had helped her practise, sitting in her living room, listening to her shout shit shit shit whenever she forgot a phrase. Standing at the podium now she had no patience for her tears. "When I was a girl I dreamed of becoming my mother," she said. "Actually, I still do."

Blake sang "Amazing Grace" in an unexpectedly pretty contralto.

Hanna read from Rilke. Empty branches, evensong. Then Theo got up, in his skinny necktie.

"Hi," he said. "Thanks for coming." He wasn't sure if he was nervous or afraid or something else, too delicate to name. "Somewhere, Mom has a shoebox." He glanced at his notes. "Inside that shoebox there are videotapes. They're not full-size videotapes, they're smaller than that, like cans of sardines. Maybe that was the company's slogan: '*Finally* a videotape roughly the size of a can of sardines.'

"I say that because in my family we use groceries to describe the sizes of things. Sardine cans or cereal boxes or crates of tangerines. I once heard Mom describe the snow outside as 'cinnamon-stick thick.' 'Flat or on end?' Pop asked. I don't remember which one she said it was. Whether for her, cinnamon-stick thick meant flat or on end. I wish I could ask.

"Anyway, a shoebox full of sardine-can-sized videotapes. Most of the videos Mom had shot herself. For a couple of years she yanked out the camcorder for every birthday and special event. She carried it in front of her like a baby she had lifted from the bath, like it might pee all over her any second. I had to tell her to look through the viewfinder. 'Use it like a regular camera, Mom.'

"'If I needed a coach, I'd have given you a whistle,' she replied. And she went on holding it like an incontinent grandkid."

He took a breath. "Mostly the camera was for making commercials. That was the idea—that Mom and Pop could shoot their own commercials for the store, put them on television. Mom choreographed these thirty-second bits: Mireille stacking coconuts, Peter roasting a chicken, meet-cutes beside the matches. I remember this one elaborate setup—each of us popping out from around a shelf,

Carmen Miranda crossed with *West Side Story*—and Mom directing from out of frame. 'Look at those sumptuous artichokes,' Minnie told us. 'You should seem *proud* to be holding them. You should seem *prosperous*.' That was what she wanted for herself, for us. Prosperity. It didn't mean wealth. From the Latin *prosperus*, 'doing well.' She taught me that. 'I want you to *do well*. Flourish.'

"Anyhow, Mom's career making TV commercials didn't flourish. Didn't prosper. The ad rates were too high and the footage was too grainy and eventually the camera became this relic, high on a shelf, like Mom's collections of milk glass and ancient coins. I asked if I could have it but she knew I would lose it, or trade it away to someone and claim that I had lost it—not because I was a bad kid but because I didn't have a sense of proportion, of value. I still don't, which you can tell from my suit."

He couldn't hear anything—neither his speech, his breath, nor the laughter in the room. He could only see it moving across the crowd, like a ripple on water.

"I was only allowed to use the camera for school projects, and only if I had supervision. So Mireille became my cinematographer: she supervised videos on pantry moths and British accents and the 'ancient art' of making sushi. I'm sorry, Mireille.

"When it was time for me to do something on Shakespeare's *Macbeth*, Mireille told me she'd had enough. Actually, she said she would rather be betrayed by a medieval king than tape another video. So I asked Mom—who was excited, so excited. She lined me up downstairs, in front of a wall of Campbell's soup cans. While I pretended to be a murderer, she wielded the camera. Just a standard Sunday afternoon. 'Is this a dagger which I see before me?' I asked, lifting an imaginary weapon. I was dressed in a brown turtleneck, a carton-paper vest, and one of Mireille's old skirts, which wasn't so much tartan as plaid. 'You have such handsome knees,' my mother said. She was always saying things like that. But at the time I glared at her, or tried to, with the black look of a haunted Scottish monarch. I rearranged the pleats across my patellas. I grasped again at a dagger-shaped space.

"We shot the speech once, twice, three times, five. In the beginning it was me who wanted to do it over again because I'd stammer over a word or forget a line. But then it wasn't me calling for another take—it was Mom. 'One more,' she'd say, 'one more.' She was giving me directions at first—'louder,' 'slower,' 'maybe try one without the accent?'—and then she wasn't giving directions, she was just saying 'one more,' watching me with a vividness of attention, a love or fascination that made me not want to stop. I performed the soliloquy as a hollowed-out wretch. I performed it as a vicious warlord. I performed it hard, soft, cold, hot, loud and whispering. I held my jaw tight and I held it loose. I tried to express ideas with the entire surface of my face. She was watching, listening, so hard. I'd do something and she'd nod, carefully, trying to keep the camcorder still. At times I welled up from my own murderous speech and I felt like I could see her welling up too. 'One more, one more,' and me like Braveheart crossed with Charlie Brown. It wasn't about Shakespeare or my gift for it— the note I got back from the teacher read: 'I hope you had fun. B minus.' It was about the force of my conviction—the sense that I was *trying* something so hard, *too* hard maybe. Every time I said the line again, Mom was getting another glimpse—another version—of the man I might become."

Theo looked down at his paper. He could feel something happening in his body—his chest, his eyes, his sinus cavities. A difference in the weather, as if it had begun to rain. When he looked into the room it seemed oddly uncertain, almost shimmering.

He swallowed. "Other people have talked about Mom's kindness, her smarts, her crazy spirit; the way she loved Dad and the store. Her friends. How she held the family together. But I wanted to talk about the way she believed in us. Me, you, everyone. I saw it every day. Her belief in her kids, her community. Her staff—" He caught sight of two of their managers, Esther and João, smiling and teary, near the back of the hall. For an instant he felt he might faint.

"Dad used to tell us, 'You can do anything you set your mind to.'

"'Horseshit,' I remember Mom saying once. Sharply: 'That's not true, you can't.'"

Theo gathered up his papers.

"'But you can *be* anyone,' she told us. 'Steadily, steadily: *become*.'"

:::

In the basement after the service, everyone crowded around the cup-cakes. Once the cupcake plates were emptied the crowd moved on to tea and coffee, quiche, bagels with smoked salmon and cream cheese, fruit platters with lots of tough red grapes. Theo and Eric, standing together, couldn't help but observe the reception from their perspec-tive as grocery men.

"They'll form a line for the coffee but not for the fruit," Theo noted.

"The shape of the table?"

"No." He pointed at the sesame-seed-scattered bagel station. "They're lining up there, too."

Their survey was interrupted by a former cashier, a man who had worked the weekend shifts for almost a decade. Theo faintly remembered that he might now be a doctor. He was crying—great gushing tears like squirts from a clown's flower. Theo held out a wad of paper napkins.

"She was magnificent," the man said when he had recovered his voice. "She was just magnificent."

"Yes," Theo said.

"I am so sorry."

Theo and Eric bowed their heads as they had been bowing their heads all day, as if they were too overcome to speak but really they were too overcome to speak another platitude about a woman they loved.

Theo glimpsed Mireille at the other side of the basement. She was locked in a grave conversation with Amir from the carpet store. Peter was playing the patriarch, huddling with some men Theo didn't recognize. They had a ratlike air, cunning and sleek, in shiny suits. Theo was happy to see Minnie's loved ones and also profoundly lonely, tired of treating complete strangers and lifelong friends with the same prim dignity. At one point he found himself in an exchange between Lionel, an old friend from summer camp, and Costas Vasilakis, owner of high-end restaurants not just here, but in New York and Athens. Vasilakis was wearing Hugo Boss. Lionel was wearing a raincoat and a ratty baseball cap. Lionel told the restaurateur about going over to Theo's house, eating taramosalata sandwiches in Minnie's kitchen. Vasilakis told Lionel about trying to persuade Minnie to ride sidecar across the bridge to Expo 67. And Theo kept thinking about the time his mother, late one night, patted his head and told him, "Lionel is a real friend," or the time he and Minnie had biked past Vasilakis's black sedan, parked outside his restaurant, and she told him how Vasilakis had worked as a busboy at a high-end Greek dinner club before breaking off to start his own place, hosting and cooking and waiting tables, poaching clients, serving wine and grilled octopus in a basement. Then one midnight his former employers appeared at the cellar doorway, closed the door, dropped the bolt, and fell upon him with clubs. They broke his ribs and shoulder, cracked his skull, smashed glasses, shattered plates, like a Greek wedding.

Now Vasilakis had thirteen grandchildren and a collection of ships in bottles.

Lucky.

"Your speech made me cry."

Theo turned to find a woman he had grown up with. They had in fact gone on three dates—twenty-two years old, eating vegan food at the Spirit Lounge, where the walls were covered in aluminum foil and the servers wore assless chaps. You were banned for life if you didn't finish your dessert.

"Sophie," he said. "How are you?"

Sophie was a biologist working for big pharma. On social media, her life was a series of family-related tableaux: a three-year-old sputtering at birthday candles, a six-year-old confronting a donkey.

"We're all great," she said.

He tried in vain to remember which of the nearby faces belonged to her spouse.

"You made it so funny, too," she went on. "I had to explain to John that you were a comedian. When are they going to have you back on *Conan*?"

"Any day now."

"I saw it, you know. I was still nursing Cora. I screamed so loud!" She grinned. "I was like, 'This is his big break.' How long ago was that now? Five years?"

"Six."

"I always tell people your one about the snowplows."

He couldn't remember his bit about the snowplows. "Thanks for being here," he said.

"Of course."

She seemed about to walk away but then she leaned in close, her mouth upturned, and for a moment he thought she might kiss him.

"Don't give up," she murmured, earnestly, but if Sophie had hoped Theo would smile, he did not. He believed he knew who it is one tells to not give up: that is, he believed one tells this to people who probably should. She had wounded him, or maybe he was long-wounded, and he looked away from her, over the mourners, searching—he didn't know for what.

Later, Theo took Hanna and the urn home. Mireille and Eric had elected to stay at the Ukrainian and get drunk—swallowing ouzo with their friends and the Ukrainians and assorted funeral lingerers. Peter and his brood drove home to the burbs.

Theo and Hanna came in through the store. The lights were on, they were always on, and the fridges gave off a docile hum. Every cause had an effect: Minnie had died, thus Provisions K had shut; the memorial was finished, thus the store would reopen. Though there had been moments these past two days when Theo had wanted it all to break—the freezers to thaw, the furnace to melt, the whole place to be set alight—he had the suspicion that Provisions K was like a ticking watch: tamper too much and the store's mechanics would begin to fail. They had said their flimsy goodbyes; this world was the world Minnie had left behind. Either life would resume, a thousand customers and their shopping lists, or else the remaining Potirises might find their reality wrecked, irretrievable.

Theo led Hanna towards the back of the store. He remembered so vividly the day her parents brought her home from the hospital, parading her through the aisles. Minnie had clasped her in her arms as everyone gathered beside a mountain of pomegranates, staring into Hanna's crinkled face.

Now that sesame seed was growing up. Hanna displayed a mildness that set her apart from the rest of her family. She was patient with her obsessions. For years she had bugged Theo to let her accompany him to the racetrack, at first for the horses, but in time because of other interests: niceties of racing etiquette, gamblers' math, questions Theo didn't himself know the answers to. Can jockeys bet on themselves? Who picks the odds? Do the horses get tired? Eventually he made the same promise his father had: that she could lay a wager when she turned thirteen.

Would that still happen now? Her birthday was one month away.

The two of them arrived at the olive cart. He approached it timidly, then peered into the compartments. "Did you see this?" he whispered to his niece.

The olives were still spinning, one by one, in counterclockwise orbits.

"Look," he told her.

She watched the olives, unblinking. She scratched the back of one calf with her shoe. "Weird," she said.

:::

Theo went to sleep with the urn of ashes on his bedside table, beside his phone. When he woke up the next morning, reaching for the alarm, his fingers grazed the ceramic. A reminder.

Downstairs, Provisions K was already open. Its aisles were full of customers. Stockers were loading items onto shelves. The cashiers were moving with the precision of lieutenants recently returned from leave. Theo watched the delivery guys for a little while, lumbering under cardboard boxes. He reached into the back pocket of his jeans, unfolded the pages he had found on his mother's desk. He'd realized it the night before, just as he was falling asleep—this was her charity list. Minnie's handwritten ledger of the households to which she sent free groceries, and which items she sent. *Our angel of the vegetables.* Like so much of what Minnie did, it was mundane as well as extraordinary.

"I want to show you something," she had told him.

Theo stalked the aisles with his hands in his pockets, finding nothing to fix, nothing to criticize. Orderly rows of rice cakes. Shiny jars of salsa. A summit of broccoli. Banks of freezers filled with rigid pizzas, ice cream, Jamaican patties, pierogies and bags of peas.

Theo went past the olive cart, where a customer was spooning jumbo green ovoids into a little tub. The olives weren't spinning—neither in sync nor out. Just resting, floating, very slightly bobbing. Merely olives, unremarkable.

That night he got on his bicycle and flew through the city to the comedy club. The sky was moonless, the streets were quiet.

It was not a Friday. He hadn't placed a bet.

CHAPTER THREE

In an old house by the canal, people were telling jokes. Stories of the Knock Knock Club had been passed down from comedian to comedian: that the club was originally a hospital for lepers, a nunnery, the manor of a New France furrier. That it had been used as a silent film set. *The Watchmaker* was shot here, *Vinny and Vito*, *Turtle Soup*. It was satisfying to imagine that its linked rooms had seen life and death, fervour and genius, in the years before vodka Red Bulls and 2-4-1 Wednesdays. Now the gambrelled mansion smelled of spilled drinks and subterranean mould; on cold nights it shivered like a loose tooth. Whatever it had been before Annette took over the lease, in the final years of the 1980s comedy boom, that evidence had been worn away by successive surf-swells of laughter and silence, heckling, and the chintzy strains of "Eye of the Tiger," which rolled out every night like a tide. By now the Knock Knock's floorboards sagged. Its front steps sloped. The carmine roof looked ready to slide onto the lawn.

Theo pulled up onto the grass and locked up on the club's lone shrub. It was dark. It was Monday. But there were cars at the meters, a certain buzz by the door. Two comedians were standing at the foot of the steps, sharing a teacup ashtray. Theo walked past the new kid doing the door and into the early show, where a regular had just finished her set, and as Lucien, the MC, bounded up beside her, seizing the energy of the performer's last joke. It was as if a brisk wind had blown through the audience. The MC spoke in a wonderful, ribald franglais, his hair wild at the sides but smoothly combed on top— "the 'air-do of a father oo is losing 'is mind," as he called it that night. "A father oose wife is leaving 'im and oose kids are terrible and oo thinks to himseff that 'e'll be okay if 'e jus' drags a comb through 'is 'air two more time, packs a lunch for everybody and writes a note to the kids that says 'Be good' and one for the wife that says 'I still love you' and jus' smiles, smiles, always smiles at everyone, with an 'air-do that promises 'is capabilities are greater than what 'e 'as demonstrated so far."

Lucien was Theo's favourite kind of comic, neither overly quippy nor banal. Too many comedians came canned—their gags cued up like pinballs—or else drifted at the mic, uncertain which course to take. Theo's sets would sometimes call for search parties. He savoured Lucien's patience and his discipline, but also suspected that down deep he had another reason for admiring him: given Lucien's accent, he didn't seem much like competition.

Rivalry could make stand-up feel cruel. Its hierarchies were plain to see. A cohort of amateurs would come up together, clashing at the same open mics, jockeying for the same spots, but it wasn't actually enough to be funny. The work required doggedness, and an almost supernatural limberness - an elasticity of soul - to survive. A comic doesn't just make people laugh: he bombs and bombs and bombs again while he sorts out what works from what doesn't.

Although the Knock Knock's regulars relied on each other—for small loans, solidarity, designated drives home—they envied and begrudged each other too, relishing their rivals' small defeats. Only time helped. Eventually a hierarchy settled in. Once the contenders knew who was good and who was not, they could choose exactly whom to resent.

That Monday night, Theo watched for a little while then went over to stand beside Annette. She was at the back of the room, hidden in the half-shadow of the disused popcorn machine. She didn't acknowledge his arrival. Theo waited—he wasn't sure for what, was never sure what he was doing with Annette. She was a kind of sphinx. Even after all these years, he hadn't cracked the code—whether to stand in silence or make small-talk, to laugh or crack wise, or to play hard to get. Annette chose who got up and when, but her logic was unknowable. Sometimes Theo just waved from across the room and she put him on straight away. There were other weeks that he lingered, buying her drinks, shooting the shit, and he didn't make the programme at all. One night several years ago, she promised a mid-tier set and he loitered at the rear of the club, waiting to hear his name—as 10:00 PM became 11:00, as 11:00 PM became midnight, and into the wee hours of the morning. He watched comic after comic, the bad amid the good, with upset growing in his chest; he kept trying to catch Annette's eye, shooting daggers at her. Theo *needed* to get up; he deserved to. He tapped his notebook against the tabletop, sucked gin-and-tonics through stunted straws, couldn't bring himself to applaud. As the clock-hand inched towards two o'clock, Theo's fury reached a boil. He had so much he had to say; he had so much that needed saying. He wanted to throw things. Then it was three and Lucien said goodnight and Theo had been forgotten. The feeling that swept over him, like a soft tide, was relief.

Tonight he'd been there only a few moments when Annette asked, "You want to get up?"

"Yeah."

"Late show. After Emmy."

"Cool," Theo said, acting as if he barely cared.

Twelve years of coming to the Knock Knock and it still contained a terror.

Lucien began to introduce Fuckin' Stevie. Theo decided it was his cue to stand somewhere else. He wound past a knot of regulars and lowered himself into a chair, slipping his bike helmet underneath. A stocky man sat beside him in a long black trenchcoat, his dark green shirt buttoned up to the collar. The man—Severin—had bedraggled dark hair—authentically bedraggled, sincerely bedraggled, something coaxed and pleaded with until finally it just lay the way it did, curling at the edges, gelled into place. He had a thin brown moustache. He smelled like toothpaste.

"Theo," Severin murmured.

Theo nodded to him. They sat together and watched Steve Murray—Fuckin' Stevie. He was a man with a Roman nose, long hair and fine blond eyelashes. In another age, he would have had a regal nickname—Blueblood, Lionheart. Here he was called Fuckin' Stevie, because he was always swearing. He stood at the microphone, let the room softly settle, and then pronounced one swear word after another, curse after curse, surfing the swells of laughter. It was cheerleading more than comedy—dirty cheerleading, pompoms dredged in barf. And it killed. "People will laugh at anything," Theo murmured.

"What?"

"Fuckin' Stevie."

"Fuckin' Stevie," Severin agreed. He began riffling through the pages of his notebook, a faux-leather journal that looked like it had been through a thunderstorm. Finally he sat back with an expression of defeat. He picked up his drink. "Sometimes I find myself thinking: 'I should be more like Stevie.'" He took a sip. "I find myself thinking this, and I notice this thought, and I try to look it down."

"Stare it down?" Theo said.

Severin nodded. "Stare it down."

He was from somewhere else—Armenia, Turkmenistan, somewhere like that. He didn't like to talk about it, not even on stage. That would have been the best place to talk about it, in Theo's opinion. But Severin wanted to be Leno, not Pryor. He wanted the audience to disregard his weird name, his spurred accent, the grasshoppers he clutched and sipped and that made him smell like toothpaste. He wished to be liked more than he wished to be himself.

When Stevie finished he walked past them, through the audience, heading out for a smoke.

"Good set," said Severin.

Stevie flashed a thumbs-up.

"What?" Severin said to Theo.

"Don't encourage him."

"You think he gives two shit? 'So happy you approve, Severin. Huge relief for me.'"

"Why say anything?"

"Because maybe he likes me. Maybe one day when his hack schtick gets booked for a week in Boston he says, 'Hey Severin—want to open for me?' And I go and do Boston for five nights, and see the

Space Needle, and actually get paid in real dollars, not drink tickets, while you sit here at the back of the Knock Knock being an asshole."

"The Space Needle's in Seattle," Theo said.

"Suddenly you're an astronaut?" said Severin. He shifted in his seat. "You gonna get up?"

"Yeah," Theo said.

"You do not seem confident."

"Annette said yeah."

Severin stared at his glass. He must have known he was picking on Theo, and also that Theo didn't need to be sitting here with him. He ran a finger along his moustache. "How are you?"

"Good."

"Doing new stuff?"

"Yes."

"You always got new stuff."

"I don't like repeating myself," Theo said.

"Sure."

On stage, Lucien was aggravating a table of bachelorettes. Each of the ladies wore a pair of fuzzy pink rabbit ears. Theo almost felt sorry for them. The bunnies didn't know that bachelorette parties were comedy-audience stereotypes; they didn't know they were despised as soon as they walked in the door. High on matrimony, lubricated by vodka, the women would soon begin to heckle, and the comics would not let it stand. Then it was only a matter of time before the bride began to cry, or her maid of honour began to cry, or the whole group got chucked out the club's front door. Sure enough, one of the women stood up and started shouting ripostes at Lucien. She pointed and pointed at him. On her third gesticulation Theo felt the room's atmosphere change. The fun was over. In the darkness Theo saw the slope-shouldered outline of the bouncer moving between the chairs. He had the jowly affect of a Saint Bernard. He laid a doughy palm on the women's crowded little table. They stared at him with awed round eyes, as if a moose had come striding from the woods. *"Mesdames,"* he murmured, "I'm going to have to ask you to leave." The whole room held its breath. The bride began to cry.

"Ladies and gentleman, please put your 'ands together for the funniest man in Malta, the golem of Prague, the guy 'oo puts the *el oh el* in Vladivostok—Severin Jones!" Lucien said.

Severin rose. As the bridal party made its way to the door, Severin smiled a forced smile, passing through the tables and chairs and onto the stage. He put down his notebook and drink, adjusted the microphone. He was holding the room with the whites of his eyes, the promise of the comic who has yet to say a word.

"Aloha," he said at last—his opening catchphrase, weird but not quite funny. Theo leaned back in his chair, shook his head. *Severin, man.*

Comedians' friendships are unwieldy things. When Theo had started at the club, he met two types of performers: the ones who couldn't stand him and the ones who ignored him. He preferred the former to the latter. A comic's opprobrium could actually mean anything: jealousy, insecurity, misanthropy, prickly bonhomie. These were men and women who had learned the lesson, growing up, that you show someone you like them by making a joke at their expense. Professionally speaking, making an impression was more important than making friends. "Keep kicking them in the nuts, keep putting things on the shelf," George Carlin had said. Theo's brain was full of quotes like these, absorbed as a teenager with a limitless appetite for aphorism. A zine called *BUNCHA HACKS* had opened a portal in his brain, transforming him from the sort of kid who watched *SNL* to the kind who memorized *Rant in E-Minor* and *Live on the Sunset Strip*, making pilgrimages to the video store for Alan Partridge, Andy Kaufman and the Kids in the Hall. Every couple of months, another issue of *BUNCHA HACKS* arrived from New York: twenty-four pages typed, photocopied, folded and stapled by a guy called Max Paumgarten. Paumgarten rattled on about what was true comedy and what wasn't, who made him laugh and who didn't; he wrote essays and interviewed comics and reviewed hundreds of sets at Carolines and the Cellar. His opinions formed the bedrock of Theo's comedy philosophy: that the essence of stand-up is perspective; that its secret is cadence; that the best jokes are jokes that nobody else can tell.

On stage, Severin sighed. "Let me tell you. My father-in-law is a real pain in the neck."

For a long time, all that Theo wanted was to merit his own profile in *BUNCHA HACKS*. Six years ago, at the height of his comedy success, he had received a phone call from a 212 area code. Theo experienced the moment as an apogee: the sensation of a dream become real. "I caught you on *Conan*," Max Paumgarten had said. His voice was puckish, brash. "I'd like to do a little piece."

Now Theo gazed at Severin. His friend wasn't being himself; he wasn't taking the risk. Such a hoary sequence of set-ups and punchlines—gags about marriage, bike lanes, the phrase "banana split." But about ten minutes into his set, after a bit about dishonest politicians, Severin turned a page in his water-damaged notebook.

"When I was a kid, I wore a fedora," he said. "I wore a fedora all the time, okay? I didn't leave my house without it. Like I was some

time-travelling detective. Like I was a jazz guy or something—
Charlie Parker in the body of an immigrant teenager. Everyone at
school laughed at me—my English was so lousy, I didn't know *Ace
Ventura: Pet Detective* and I didn't know who Nirvana was. But I
had this idea: maybe if I wore a fedora all day every day I would be
hip. Popular.

"Fantastic idea, yes? What is hipper than an old-style hat? When
girls see a guy with an old-style hat they always think, 'That guy is a
winner.' Even if you are a straight guy you see a guy in a fedora and
part of you thinks, 'Maybe that is the man for me. Maybe I will
change my whole life so I can hang with that guy in a fedora.' Yes?

"No, *not* yes. The fedora does not do this. Ladies and gentlemen,
let me tell you: the fedora does not do this."

Severin squinted. "Is there anyone out there wearing a fedora right
now? No? That's good." He looked at his page.

"Even though the fedora made me seem like a visitor from the land
of noir cinema, I thought it was my best feature. My old-style hat.
With its brim. With its uh, top. With its feather. I swaggered a bit,
maybe, with my fedora. I talked to people I didn't know. I ran for
school president. (I lost.) Maybe at a birthday party I offered a beautiful girl my slice of cake.

"For a long time I wore my fedora everywhere. I was debonair and
amazing. I was cool and interesting. I had only two friends—they
were losers—but that was okay, no problem, maybe they would get
hats too and we would all three be cool."

Severin took a sip of his drink. "And then one day I was on a school
trip to New York. From the small city to the big city. So many
skyscrapers and taxis and crowded sidewalks. We went to the museum
with the squid and to this restaurant with an all-day breakfast buffet,

and at night to a musical with a line of high-kicking dancers, like an animated comb. And we had free time, too. Time for me to wander around, striding the big city streets in my fedora.

"So one afternoon I was walking along this quiet street, striding, and there was this car. Long grey car, wide like a milk cow, and it was passing me and then it started to slow down. After a sec I realized it was kinda matching my pace. I looked at it. The driver was maybe in his fifties. Most of his hair gone, he had nice eyes—you know, like someone who you can tell is a good guy and means well? And he had this sideways smile on his face, and he was lowering his window, staring at me. So I halted there, tipped my head towards him, and waited. Finally in a quiet voice, he said, 'Hey.'

"I said, 'Hey.'

"And he said, 'Lose the hat.'"

That was it, the punchline. The meagre punchline. While others were wincing at the pathos, Theo, alone in the room, was laughing. He was hooting, feeling his heart happily hurt. As Severin left the stage, Theo thumped his tabletop. This was why he loved comedy, for its hilarious solace.

Around him, tea-lights flickered on the tables. Locals and tourists, mothers and sons, spouses and lovers, all seemed untouched.

Hours stuttered past, fast then slow then fast again. Theo caught some sets and neglected others, drifting around the club. "You gonna do the one about the flooded basement?" somebody asked. "Nah," Theo said. A pretty wunderkind got up, her jokes like puzzle boxes. A big lug from the suburbs, with gags about his wife and their Doberman pinschers. Towards midnight, Theo watched a woman named Emmy, one of the regulars, from a corner by the bar. He stood with one knee against a panel, felt the hot whirring of the dishwasher on the other side. She told jokes about life and just absolutely destroyed. You don't watch the comic just before you perform, not if they're any good, and Theo should have been reviewing his material, getting juiced up. Anyway he had already heard this stuff: Emmy's set had been refined over the course of entire months, seasons, line by line, pause by pause, tag by tag, so well-practised that Theo knew the moments she'd take a sip from her jack and ginger. Yet he laughed along with all the others, he couldn't help it, even as his chest filled with dread, and when Emmy was finished Lucien warbled into the microphone: "Now put your 'ands together for Theo Potiris."

Three or four tables immediately got up to leave. Nothing personal: this was the late show, it was late. When Theo arrived at the front of the room, he tried not to see the empty chairs. Brightly, bravely, he said, "If it's all right with you, I'm gonna tell some jokes now."

He opened with something about how nobody eats the shells of peanuts. It didn't really work. He tried something about his brother's suits, then about how much it physically hurt to actually write an entire letter by hand. The laughs were patchy. He considered turning that corner where you call attention to the lack of laughs but that was a last resort, it risked everything; instead he talked about the bride and the bachelorettes, even though only some of the audience had been there for the early show. "Tonight was a night she won't remember for the rest of her life," he said. This cruelty didn't feel right. Maybe he should be talking about shame, or drunkenness, or a wedding morning hangover. He tried imagining out loud the bride's vows, and then the splendour of the ceremony, half mocking, half not. He wished the bride well: "When you hold your husband on his death bed, I hope you remember getting kicked out of a crummy comedy club." There was something deeply funny in all of this, he was certain, and maybe he would find it if he kept talking.

Theo stepped over to the stool where he had put down his drink. The audience was silent. Theo raised the glass to his lips and in his peripheral vision he could see Severin and Emmy standing by the bar, wearing tolerant expressions. Theo tilted the gin and tonic until the ice cubes slid to touch his teeth. He should stop, his time was up. He should keep going, he should say the one about the flooded basement. But he couldn't bear to tell a joke these other comics had already heard; he couldn't bear to quit the stage, a comedian merely humoured. He began talking about his gambling. His Friday night, his ritual, biking to the track and laying a wager. "Every week, finally, I find out if I'm a winner or a loser. It's nothing but math. I'm a winner or a loser, nothing in between."

"How many of you gamble?" he asked them. A few people clapped. "Suckers," he said, to a bigger laugh. "We're all suckers. I'm so tired of losing."

He wiped his mouth with the inside of his wrist. "On Friday I went to the racecourse. I bet on a horse called Expiry Date." He looked out. "How much does it cost to keep a racehorse? Fifty thousand a year? Daily steel-cut oats and Kobe steak, regular massages. Trainers and agents and nutritionists. Fifty thousand *easy*. And what do they decide to call it? Expiry Date." He shook his head. "'What's something that's vaguely threatening in as low-stakes a way as possible? That's what we'll call our horse.'

"Anyway, Expiry Date and I won thirty dollars. 'I'm a winner', I thought. 'I'm inarguably a winner.'" He glanced at his shoes, still flecked with onion. "And then later that night my mother died."

They laughed, but then a silence fell. They weren't sure they had heard him right.

He went on. His tone was steady. "I mean it," he said. He explained that he had gone home and discovered that his mother had passed away. "Her eyes were closed, like she was making a wish."

Somebody laughed then—a sharp, almost wretched sound. Theo ran a hand through the tangle of his hair. He talked a little about the paramedics, the family argument about who should ride with her corpse to the hospital. He talked about the way the ambulance was the same size as one of the grocery store's delivery trucks, how he had found himself wondering how many boxes of groceries could fit inside. He talked about preparing for the memorial, the quarrel about low-fat versus regular cream cheese at the reception, which flavours of cupcakes to buy. "After screaming at each other for eighty-five minutes we agreed that the flavour we would ask for was 'a variety.'"

They laughed.

"Then there was the funeral, which is a high-pressure situation for a comic," Theo said. He fingered the mic. "Speaking of—were any of you there?" He craned his neck. "Can I get a 'woo' if you were at my mother's funeral?"

"No? No regulars?" He smiled, looked at the floor. "Well, you missed a great quiche." A breath came out of him as if he had cut himself, but his eyes didn't leave the spot on the floor. "You know what? I *killed*," he said. "My set—I mean, my eulogy"—he was still smiling that tight smile—"it was sad. It was happy. It was upsetting and also funny. People cried or laughed. They were smiling through tears. I could see it: my family, her friends. I could see it, I'm not exaggerating, right in front of me, on people's faces. I could feel it myself, *in* myself, like a bright light. Killing at a funeral. The best set of my life. For once everything landed."

At the end of the bar, a cash register began printing a receipt.

"So what do you do with that?" Theo asked. "At your mother's memorial, on the worst day of your life, thinking: 'This would crush on YouTube.' An original eulogy album. *Live at the Funeral. All Downhill from Here.* Or maybe, yeah: *Unplugged.*"

He gazed at the empty space above the chairs.

"Anyway, that's my time," he said, and he put down the mic.

"Everybody put your 'ands together for Theo Potiris!" Lucien leapt onto the stage. "Theo Potiris, our little ray of sunshine!" Theo slipped backstage as the crowd applauded, trying not to hear it, trying not to hear how much or how little, how eager or how hollow, trying not to hear it and also trying to hear it, ravenous for every separate touch of palm to palm.

:::

He listened to the next set from the dressing room. At the break, Emmy appeared. "Good set," she told him.

She led him back to his friends at the bar, bought him another G&T. Severin put his arms around him. "Sorry, man," he whispered in his ear.

Fuckin' Stevie nudged up beside them. "That scraping sound was the whole crowd slitting their wrists."

"Not a bad way to go," Theo said.

"You know, I've always said that being funny is overrated," Stevie went on. "We don't get enough *grief-stricken* comedy."

"Fuck off," said Emmy.

Theo looked around at the empty tables cluttered with glasses, the small clusters of audience members staring at him. He nodded to the comics then headed for the back door, leaning his full weight into the push bar of the emergency exit. Outside was a clear sky, a few stars. Cool air fluttered over him. Annette's Camry was parked crooked beside the crumbling brick wall. *What was that?* he thought. He walked past the car, to the street, and lowered himself to the curb. *It was what it was*, he told himself. *You didn't have anything to lose.*

Six years ago, Theo talked to Max Paumgarten on the telephone. Shortly thereafter, before any piece had run, BUNCHA HACKS announced it was folding. Paumgarten had been hired as a staff writer at the *New Yorker*. When Theo heard the news he felt at first a kind of pride—as if he too had graduated, come of age—and later a sense of anticipation—that Paumgarten might bring him with him somehow, into the pages of his new home. But Theo never heard from him again. Instead, Paumgarten wrote about pop stars, drone racers, an Indiana mayor. Theo's window closed. The dream subsided. *It was what it was.*

An owl made an owl sound, out of nowhere. Theo turned, startled, as the hoot reverberated. The shadows at the roof met in an X and he couldn't distinguish anything besides the place where an owl *might* be. Theo stared at the X-like space. He swallowed a little more of his gin.

"I'm sorry about your mom," said a voice.

She was sitting not far away, a silhouetted figure with her arms resting loosely on her knees. On the same curb, among the same shadows, facing out into the street.

"Thanks."

"You were funny."

He heard a sound he mistook for a lighter flicking open, but he realized the woman was simply scraping a stone along the pavement.

He couldn't really see her face, just jeans, boots, the matte folds of a windbreaker, her hair.

"Thanks," he said.

"Have you heard of the Rabbit's Foot?"

"No. Is it another club?"

"It's an association."

"What kind of association?"

"Professional gamblers."

"Sounds unseemly," he said.

He heard her smile. "In fact you would not believe how *seemly*. Resolutely seemly. They're methodical, humourless, et cetera."

"Boring."

"However: winners," she said.

"Ah. Lucky for them."

She shook her head. "Luck has nothing to do with it. What's the opposite of an inveterate gambler? A veterate one? The association's all mathematicians, actuaries, programmers. Systems analysts. Algorithm people. They deconstruct horse-racing and football and tennis and whatever, boil it down to its parts. Then build it up again—movements into numbers into data, as many contests as they can, so the math gets a chance to work. And they can earn their fortune."

Theo squinted at her.

"You said you were tired of losing bets, right? You could join them."

He gave a ragged laugh. "The Rabbit's Foot doesn't lose?"

She shrugged. "That's their whole thing: figuring out how not to."

"Huh," he said.

"Yeah—'Huh.'" She tilted her head at him. "You know how sometimes you'll look at something, like a box of matches, and you'll think, 'Someone's getting rich off these things.' And someone *is* getting rich off matches. Off everything. That's how it is with Mitsou. So many people making bets, all around the world, and someone's making a mint. It's her."

He wondered now if she was pulling his leg. "Mitsou?"

"My sister," she said.

"This is her company?"

"Association."

"She doesn't cut you in?"

"She and I run on different tracks." The woman brought a knee to her chest. "Maybe when my luck runs out."

After a pause, in the same tone of voice, she said, "You *were* really funny."

He looked away. "Thanks."

"Don't act so humble. You were!"

"That's the job," he said.

"Did your mom used to come to see you?"

A feeling had gradually been opening up around them, between them, an unguarded air. He could say anything into it.

"Now and then," he said.

"Did she like it?"

"She liked me. She thought the other comics were too dirty. She said, 'They talk too lightly about sex.'"

The woman laughed.

"Are you a comic?" he asked.

"No."

He remembered the owl that had made its owl sound and wondered if it would speak again into this space, filling in the silence.

She said, "Sometimes you look at the world and it's either laugh or cry, right?"

"I try to ignore it."

"The world?"

"Things I can't change."

"How Zen."

"Is that what Zen is?" he said.

"You're asking the wrong person," she said. "It sounds weird but sometimes I like to go to things alone. I always have, even when I've been in relationships. Movies, galleries, even concerts. Plays."

"There's less social pressure?"

"It's just easier to remember what *you* like. What *you're* experiencing. You don't need to worry about anybody else."

"I'm a worrier," he admitted.

"We need to stop worrying. Go dancing."

He tried to imagine her dancing.

"So you came alone."

"Yeah."

"And was it a success?"

"It would have been more fun with a friend." She laughed, and Theo laughed too.

Then he said, "Maybe I should find a new gig. Something I can count on."

"Lawyer? Accountant?"

"I'll call up the Rabbit's Foot. Ask Mitsou for a job. Tell her I know her sister."

"Better not to use my name."

"I don't know your name."

"Tell them you want to be a processor. They're always looking for processors. Maybe it will give you some material."

"Ah, *material*."

"Isn't that what comedians want? Material?"

"I don't know what I want any more," Theo said. "Except I want to catch a break."

She nodded.

He found himself telling her, "I was on *Conan* once. Six years ago. Dressing room, fruit platter, network TV. I thought that was it. Next stop, sitcom. Fame or infamy. My favourite writer called me for an interview. 'What's next for you?' he asked. 'Everything,' I said. I thought it was going to happen to me like it happened to other people, that I just needed to . . . How did you put it? Give the math a chance to work out?"

"Reversion to the mean," she said.

"But the interview never ran. The jackpot never came."

"Maybe their computer crashed."

"Paumgarten's just taking his time," Theo said. "Waiting for me to reach my season."

"Like a wine."

"Like a really funny wine."

"I'm Simone." She leaned over to him, extended her hand.

He took it. "Theo."

The sound of a faint, distant engine grew closer, then almost deafening, as its source appeared—a motorcycle turning the corner, its headlight shearing the street.

"Who's the asshole?" Theo said.

Simone rose to her feet. "Sebald!" she shouted, raising her arm. The rider spotted her, accelerating to a stop just in front of them. A hunched black motorcycle, like a Halloween cat; a rider in a daffodil-yellow helmet, his face was hidden behind mirrored glass. Sitting on the curb, Theo felt tiny, boyish. He got up too, brushed off the seat of his jeans.

Sebald took off his helmet, smoothed a hand across his scalp. He was older than Theo expected, with a face that reminded him of a portrait out of one of his childhood history books, like Archimedes—sharp nose, strong brow, a scientist's inquiring eyes. And also dark-skinned, Afro-Caribbean.

Sebald gazed evenly at him.

"Theo," Theo said finally.

"This is Sebald," Simone said. "Sebald, meet Theo."

The rider nodded. The solemnity of the gesture made Theo chuckle. He offered a thumbs-up.

Sebald nodded again and lifted his hand to his throat, touched two fingers to his Adam's apple. The gesture seemed vaguely threatening.

"He has laryngitis," explained Simone.

Yes, Sebald mouthed.

"Join us for a nightcap?" said Simone.

Theo was surprised. "I don't see a sidecar," he joked.

Simone sauntered into the road. "You could ride with me."

As she passed into the beam of Sebald's headlight, Theo examined the details of her features: straight bangs over deep-set eyes, brown hair that landed at the nape of her neck, full lips. A windbreaker hung loose around her body. He guessed she was his age, but her movements had a carelessness that reminded him of someone younger.

She kept walking, crossing the street to a different patch of shadow where another motorbike sat—a chassis in black and chrome, with a bloom of gold patina across the fuel tank. Simone knocked away the bike's side stand and hiked herself over its saddle. The engine snarled to life.

"How'd you get here?" she asked him.

"Bicycle," he said, which made her smile.

"You should come," she said.

He realized that he had forgotten his helmet inside, beside the bar or under a chair. He imagined the scene in there, wilted drunks and bitter comedians, and the gin swilled in his stomach.

"Maybe some other time," he said.

It was hard to hear anything over the two motorcycles. "What?" Simone asked.

He could have told her he had a girlfriend, on a clarity retreat in the desert. He could have clambered behind her on the bike. In the end he merely said, "I have to water my plants."

"Suit yourself," said Simone.

She lifted her helmet over her head—a piece of interlocking pearl and gold, with slashes of blood red and phosphorescent blue. The word *seldom* had been stencilled on the side of her motorcycle's tank. Sebald revved his engine. Simone flicked on her headlight and the bikes' lights were like solid beams, struts, steadying the night.

"So long!" he thought he heard her shout.

He shielded his eyes. A single star was out. The audience had laughed at some of his jokes. His mother was dead.

Theo raised his hand in a wave. "Goodnight," he called, and within a few moments the motorcyclists had disappeared, two cinders flicked away from a fire. Only their sound remained.

Selected Correspondence

Dear Lou,

This morning I saw a dog that looked like your landlord. It was a Pomeranian. It looked so much like your landlord that I did a double-take. Same hair, same eyes. Same face, basically. Same attitude. I remember when I met him. Your landlord. We were making dinner and he rang the doorbell and asked if all the radiators were working. While you went to check he stood there waiting, like a Pomeranian. I considered giving him a treat. A cookie, a little piece of apple. You came back and said, "They're fine." Your landlord shook our hands.

The dog that looked like your landlord was sitting outside the subway. Not tied to anything, just sitting, as if he were waiting for a friend. Then they'd wander uptown, catch a movie, talk about it over drinks. "I preferred his earlier work," the dog would say, "but the cinematography's still first-rate."

I like to think that the dog is a landlord and he manages a dog-scale triplex. He takes care of the lawn. He picks up the rent cheques. He makes sure the radiators are working. He chases squirrels sometimes but only if his tenants aren't waiting on anything, if he's fulfilled all his obligations.

I wonder if a dog has ever seen your landlord and thought: That guy looks just like my friend the Pomeranian.

Pomeranian, from the Old Slavic for "by the sea." Which you aren't, and I'm not, but we could be, some day.

:::

Dear Theo,

It's strange what comes back to you while you're sitting in a yurt. Song lyrics. Magazine headlines. Poetry. TED Talks. But mostly song lyrics. "Your glasses / your hideous glasses!" I can't control what comes fluttering up.

How much of meditating is about trying to stop remembering the words to "Beez in the Trap"?

Sometimes it's music I miss more than nearly anything. Other times it's banana bread. Or the Nicolai Astrup print in my bedroom. My memory-foam mattress topper. My Zojirushi water boiler, for tea on demand. Mom's jade plant, the one you nicknamed Gordon.

They say the missing will change as the retreat goes on. At first it's acute: I want this or that particular thing, from home. Pure desire. But eventually the missing becomes remembrance. "Remembrance is sustaining," our teacher said today. "A memory's as good as having."

Is it really? I wonder. Can you curl your body against a memory at night? Can a memory make you tea?

Do Tibetan monks just give everything away?

Do they throw incredible garage sales?

Are you doing okay, Theo? I think about your mom every day. She was remarkable, she loved you so much. I don't think grief is the same as missing somebody: it's not just wanting them back but wanting them to be. I wish I had had the chance to know her better. I know she lived an extraordinary life. Self-taught Egyptologist. Undefeated backgammon player. Supermarket maven. Any of us should hope to have one-tenth the life she did, the smallest measure of Minerva. We can be aspirants. (I am.)

:::

Dear Lou,

Thank you. I'm well. In the immortal words of the Provisions K flyer: "Now on sale: grapes!"

I'm still not accustomed to the time-lapse of this correspondence. Our letters are out of sequence. At first I felt like we were two blizzards snowing at each other, all these mismatched tumbling pages. That pace has slowed. It's hard to remember what I've already said, what I've already answered, what I've already forgotten. Four months you'll be gone. The lifespan of a dragonfly.

I have always been frightened of one-sided conversations. My greatest fear is that I am a punisher. That's what my friend Reema calls them—the people at bars or parties or comedy clubs who just talk and talk and talk at you, leaving no chance for escape. No exit or reprieve, not a word in edgewise. You stand there gulping your drink, draining it so you can squeak, "Time for a refill!" It's the only method for escaping a punisher: the refill. Of course it can go wrong. Mistime your move and the punisher puffs, "Good idea!" And then you are drunk and your companion is a punisher and I daresay this is hell, Lou.

My brother has officially proposed we sell the store. Mom's barely cold in her urn. Mireille feigns horror but I can tell she's thinking about it. Provisions K's too old, too crowded. Too stuck in its inefficiencies. "Let it become somebody else's problem," Peter says. Or, he concedes, if the rest of us want to carry on, we sell the building and buy something new. A shiny modern supermarket, with automated cashiers and closed-circuit cameras. A stock elevator. Wi-fi. The older generations would never have allowed it. But us? We could be moguls.

I wonder what would happen if the store was reinvented. Would I be reinvented too? The first time I brought you there, I remember I said, "Here it is, my true self." I was only half kidding. I am a beloved, ramshackle grocery store. My ramshackliness is part of my charm. I think. Unless the ram & shackle's the problem. I used to tease you about your gratitude lists. You said you were just trying to keep track.

"Keep track of what?" I remember asking you.

"Of my shit."

Do you have any answers for me? What wisdom has drifted down onto your desert plateau? Onto your "wine-black steppe"? Do you take entrepreneurial workshops with Z. Largo? Lessons on spinning one invention into an industry, one industry into another? He pivoted from superior lightbulbs to superior movie projectors, to agriculture, biotech, publishing, film. Can I at last graduate from groceries to headlining shows? Give me some advice and I'll give you some back. Two weeks, three weeks, five weeks for this letter to reach you. Two, three, five weeks to receive your reply. By that time probably Peter will have convinced us to liquidate the premises and I'll be out on my ass. Then where will I be? Working at a chain grocery store, selling lottery tickets at the cash.

:::

Dear Lou,

How are you? How's all that sand? I imagine you with sand everywhere, sand in your shoes, sand in your socks, sand under your fingernails, sand in your hair. Sand between the pages of your magazines. A few days ago I realized none of your letters have mentioned the sand and now it's all I can think about, your desert and all that sand, so much sand it becomes an afterthought, a redundancy. Sand on the ground. Sand in the air. Does it collect at the edges of your tent? Do you track it inside? Are there sand dunes in your dreams?

Thank you for the story of the cactus. Did the flowers grow back? The campus sounds cool. They should let you sleep there, basking in the A/C. Or is it part of the retreat's philosophy? Steam them lightly in their yurts.

I miss you. If you were around we could go meandering by the tracks or through the market, scatter seeds, loose change, not really doing or buying anything, looking at ferns and squashes, all the weird birds blowing in, gazing at separate things, in opposite directions, but talking. Letters don't feel like a conversation. Each of them is a dedicated, uninterrupted telling, sand pouring through an hourglass. And each is a dedicated listening, I guess. Everything seems like a pronouncement. I'd rather just go for a walk.

The walls are all still standing but something's not right. I keep expecting to come across Mom—counting blue receipts, chatting with a customer, inspecting the rye or the ricotta. Doting on her grandkids. But she isn't anywhere. She isn't even in her apartment. The absence itself feels like a presence—as if her absence is sitting in her chair, playing backgammon with Hanna, dabbing some crazy painting of a cat on a leash. Or hovering in the aisles beside me. I keep noticing the things she will never have a chance to see. I keep thinking about how we'll never have another conversation. We just can't, it's impossible, literally impossible, like wanting to talk to Heroditus or Leonard Cohen. The night she died she said she wanted to show me something. Never, she won't. All I can do is look at what she left behind and try to make up what she'd say.

Eric and Mireille are hammer and tongs. Like always, I guess, but now every day is pouring quarrels. You can hear their voices through the walls, under doors. Sometimes an argument's like siege warfare, catapults and battering rams. Raised voices, attrition, attempts to appease. Then they make up and for a few hours they're both on this beautiful, eerie high. In those moments Mireille tells me she loves me. I take the compliment and I lock it away; I try to keep stacking the canned corn or whatever. They relish their fights, in a way.

This is how they carry out whatever it is they're carrying out: advancing the store's interests, managing their family finances, parenting. The business is only so big; the profits split among us. Inflation and debt, overdue repairs. Until we modernize everything, raise prices, all of us suddenly millionaires.

But I'm making do. I'm quote-unquote practising self-care. Exercise! Fluids! Two bananas a day! Reading *Just Kids* before bed. I keep skipping the track but at least I hit the club on Fridays, do the work. I did a bit about Mom's funeral. Clumsy therapy, you called it once, my comedy. But it's more than that: it's a craft, a process, the only progress in my life. Except that high never lasts, even after my best sets. No matter how at home I feel up there—ready, alert, alive—everything evanesces after I step off the stage, into the blank night. I stew in my gumbo remembering the mistakes, all the ways I regret and resent whoever's doing better.

The most popular comic right now is a guy called Commander Big Hands. I don't remember if you ever saw him. The stage name's the whole point. He was an astronaut for real. In the mid-aughts he spent four months aboard the International Space Station—conducting experiments, liaising with the Russians, floating in mid-air. He grew a moustache. When he came back to Earth he spent a few more years at NASA then went civilian. As a civilian he became a comic. And he moonwalked to the club.

That's his shtick—he has been to space. Everything he says on stage connects back to being afloat. Eating sandwiches in space. Drinking India pale ale in space. Farting in space.

Guilt trips from his fiancée while in space, interactions
between men and women in space, you get the picture. He'll
start a joke and you'll think he's going somewhere different,
but no, he brings it right back into geosynchronous orbit (har
har) and the crowd just eats it up. They go insane. Does our
species admire any trait more than the trait of having gone to
space? The ability to transmit space-related facts from space-
related experience? It's as if he's still got moon-dust on him.
He could give a space-related sneeze and the audience would
weep with laughter. When he gets up the other comics just
despair. None of us are rivals. None of us contend. There is
nothing in all our gifts that approximates the virtue of the
space-man. We console ourselves with the thought that his
adulation is unearned, illegitimate, but it doesn't really help.
We're comedians. Our job's simple. Success isn't measured in
integrity or authenticity or kindness or charm, but in pleasure, rippling across a crowd. And everybody busts a gut
laughing at the astronaut's merest bit.

I hope I'm not bitter. More bittersweet.

:::

Dear Theo,

Lately I've been trying to retrain my fingers. I can still feel the
habits when I lay them flat on the table: scroll, swipe. CTRL-C,
CTRL-V. Open new tab. All this high-tech muscle memory, and
none of it relevant to my yurt. It's useful knowledge, you'd say.
Utility isn't everything, Theo. These days I ask myself questions
like: Is this what I want to be carrying in my body? The itch to

manipulate a web browser? To scroll and tap on a screen? I'd rather my body carried worthier impulses. What else could I carry in the places I carry smartphone swipes and copy-paste? How much more patience, self-knowledge, compassion?

So I'm retraining. You could do it too. Try. Lay your hands flat on the table, feel your fingers stretch. Palm. Knuckles. Skin. I tell my hands to forget what they aren't, and to feel what they are. To feel what I am. Aches and scars, blood pulse, tremor. Fascia tautening with age. Our hands hold traces of everything we've ever touched, a thousand handshakes and caresses. Sometimes I think about my grandmother's hands. The way they felt when she clasped my hands in hers, the strength. Our bodies aren't just shapes we're wearing, clothes we put on. They're chronicles. They're wiser than we are.

To answer the question at the end of your latest letter: no, there aren't any camels here. I mean there are camels around—Merzouga's full of them, camels for tourists and camels for function and maybe even stray camels. (I saw some milling around when we drove in—"milling," is that the right word? Loafing? Humping?) But they don't have any on the property. I think it's an animal welfare thing—see also the retreat's famous coconut bacon and cauliflower "steaks." Nobody to help us lazy humans: we do the locomoting by ourselves. When I got here I thought of it as trudging, all this trudging through the desert. But it's dunewalking now. That sounds cooler. Rarefied and meditative. A woman silhouetted in the distance, shimmering in the heat, out of focus.

Places I dunewalk to:

1) The campus.

2) My yurt.

3) An empty clearing in the sand.

:::

Dear Lou,

This morning Hanna knocks on my door after breakfast. She says, "Is there a limit on how much you can bet on one horse?" And I say, "No," and Hanna says, "Good, just checking."

And I say, "How much are you planning to bet?"

She says, "A lot."

"Remember," I say, "the thing with bets is that you usually lose the money."

"I know," she says. "Except sometimes you win."

"But usually you lose."

"Unless you're lucky."

"Even if you're lucky you usually lose. It's really a dumb pastime."

"It's intriguing," she says. She has a skateboard under one arm and a book under the other. *The Braithwaite Guide to Thoroughbreds.*

"Doing some research?"

"It's intriguing," she repeats, "that a totally random thing can still seem like a reward. As if there's a reason you won, or a reason you lost. When often there isn't."

"It's what's known as a 'crapshoot,'" I say.

"It will be my first crapshoot," Hanna says.

The crapshoot's scheduled for Friday. I promised her a bet on her thirteenth birthday. Sometimes I have regrets about this promise. Should I really be encouraging this? Should I really be helping her ~~lose~~ win money at the racecourse? Wouldn't it be better to teach her about savings accounts or compound interest? It'd be a broken promise if I backed out—but that's a kind of lesson too.

But my pop did it with me. That single bet, at thirteen, seemed like the greatest gift—a chance to stake myself against the universe. I lost, and Pop lost, and we were both in it together. So I'll take Hanna to the track. She'll lay her bet. We'll make a day of it—lunch, gambling, skate-park, ice cream sundae.

You wanna come? Cut your retreat a little short. Dig up your cellphone. Ditch Z. Largo. Slash your tent to ribbons and set the campus on fire. Lace up a camel or dunewalk to town, board a plane direct from Marrakesh to here. You'll be radiant with clarity as you step off the plane and I promise you a bouquet of something that rhymes with "decomposes."

:::

Dear Lou,

How are you? Have you stopped writing or has the Moroccan postal service just stopped delivering? I imagine a caravan languishing in the dunes. Sandlogged mailbags, paystubs, bubblepaks.

Are my letters as slow to reach you?

Are they out of order?

I admit I have not written as many as I should.

:::

Dear Theo,

I saw a desert fox today. It came right up to my tent flap, twitched its nose like a mouse. Reinforcements, I thought. Emotional support.

Sometimes being here feels like an experiment and some-times it feels like a test and sometimes it feels like an invitation and other times I don't know what it feels like, just pure experi-ence, see-through, like a sheet of plate glass.

Is it still a retreat when you keep advancing forward into it?

Writing to you, even wishful sentences seem like bad one-liners.

Three times I have picked up and put down this letter.

Maybe I can tell you about mountain pose. I remember I used to think it was so silly. "Conscientious objector pose," you called it—a yogi just standing with their hands at their sides. But I get it now. I stand and do it properly and I get it, I feel it in my body; conscientious accepter.

Dark chocolate. When you're on a clarity retreat, abstaining from the world, your tolerance goes up. The chocolate gets darker and darker. I eat 90 percent now. Two squares at a time, like an ogre.

A joke Z told me:

Why did the Zen nun fall out of the tree?

She was practising non-attachment.

Let me tell you about the conservatory, where we sit on rugs and sometimes James plays some guitar or Areta sings lieder or Z takes out his oud. I didn't know what an oud was; now I do. While all of us listen, Nikita dances a solo.

Let me tell you about makeup. I almost didn't bring any— *It's a retreat*, I thought—but in the end I spend more time putting it on here than I have at any other time in my life. At my tent's little washbasin, staring into the circle mirror.

I started wearing eyeliner when I noticed one of the other women had put some on. Eyeliner and a tiny bit of lipstick, a smudge. It wasn't that I wanted to compete with her. I wasn't trying to show her up (as if I could—she's beautiful). It was like when you see someone else is wearing sunglasses, or heels, maybe carrying an umbrella, and you think, "Maybe I should too." Or could. So a little eyeliner, a little lipstick, but for a few days I worried I had started an arms race: suddenly all the women were doing their faces, concealer and mascara, contoured everything. It wasn't what I wanted, to be here in the Sahara and worrying about my eyebrows, but the others seemed to realize that too, and just as abruptly as everything had escalated the tournament wound down. Through all of this, we never talked about it. We never acknowledged it. Maybe it was right that we didn't, or maybe we should have—I don't know what would be better, from a clarity retreat perspective. I don't think the leaders even noticed. But the point is—at the end of the day I found that I wanted to put something on. At least most days I did. Even if I wasn't planning to go out to a group sit or a lecture or an activity. Even if I was just sitting alone. I've always told myself that makeup isn't about other people, but here finally that notion isn't just a concept. I am putting it into practice. I'm not attempting to dazzle a stranger or to attract a lover or to offset my ever-multiplying crow's feet. I'm just presenting myself, Theo. Playing, painting, using these old old tools and brushes and tinctures and powders to draw my face in a different way, a new way, wherever or whatever or whoever I am today. Like telling a joke, maybe, whether or not anybody laughs. I'm using my body to say something about myself— about what's inside of me, invisible, unshown. What I mean to say is: it suits me.

CHAPTER FOUR

With their first two children, Minnie and Theo Sr. had made a point of taking time away from the store—weary hours at the playground, bedtime stories, evenings of homework at the kitchen table. The family even went on a road trip each summer: driving along the seaway in a rattling Provisions van, camping near the beach, buying cheese and apples from a shop beside a monastery. Whenever Theo heard stories of these family outings he could hardly imagine them: his parents seemed to spend every waking hour at the store. His grandparents were the ones to tuck him in. His father would only appear in Theo's doorway at some impossible, darkened hour, or Theo would wake to find Minnie beside him, leaning against the bed's hologram-stickered headboard. He remembered the weight of her hand on the crown of his head.

Theo was most aware of his parents' absence between the ages of eleven and thirteen, when they opened a second store on the other side of the mountain. He couldn't really remember what the west-side

Provisions K looked like—some misty, through-the-looking-glass world where everything was familiar and un-, the same products in a different maze. Yet he remembered his parents' absences. They were gone much more often than they were present. Neither one was there when Theo's choir sang "Danse dans ma tête" at a sixth-grade assembly. His father missed the middle-school public speaking finals, when Theo gave a speech called "Surprising Fruit Facts." Theo had a particularly vivid recollection of a quarter-final hockey game: down 6–1, sniffling behind his goalie mask. He had recently learned the word *lacklustre* and it was this that he murmured to himself, over and over, squinting through tears, blaming his non-performance on his parents' non-appearance. Although Provisions K catered the game's despondent, perspiration-scented after-party—fruit plates, crinkle-cut chips—another set of parents was the ones to ferry the supplies to the rink.

They reappeared after Provisions' second outpost flopped. At first Theo didn't understand that it was *bad* news when Theo Sr. made the announcement, frying *saganaki* on the stovetop. "Timing," Theo's father had said. "In business the secret is timing. And you don't always own the clock."

Because of their parents' constant obligations, Theo grew up as his siblings had, as Minnie had: inside the store. He mopped as soon as he was old enough to mop, stacked shelves as soon as he was old enough to stack, ran the cash or heaped pumpkins or cleaved gouda into customer-friendly wedges. During sidewalk sales he gave out free juice-boxes or doused charity hot dogs in Provisions' complimentary mustard. On the way to school, Theo often snatched a yoghurt from the fridges as a snack. Arriving home, he was recruited into Provisions' workforce. He filled customers' shopping bags, tidied away vacant baskets. If an old-timer dropped a quarter, Theo scurried to pick it up. Growing older, he was given authority over the cheese fridge and in turn the terrible responsibility of keeping it clean—scouring rancid condensations, confronting heinous fragrances. Sometimes Theo would even be called upon to manage a delivery, taking stock of the cardboard boxes full of groceries, the clothespinned addresses, calculating distance against rate of thaw. "These eight are yours, Michel," he'd say, gesturing thither. "But, Serge, you should take these ice creams."

Low-cost grocery deliveries were Provisions K's greatest pride. Av and Ruth Swirsky, Theo's *zaide* and *bubbe*, had understood delivery as a fundamental community service. Everybody needs groceries, including the elderly and ailing, the single parents and disabled vets. Theo wondered sometimes where their conviction came from. He imagined the immigrant Swirskys sleeping eight to a room in a third-floor apartment; Av peering through the banister rails as a French-Canadian kid delivered milk, potatoes, rye bread. Or Ruth, on some unimaginable morning in the old country, finding eggs on her ailing mother's doorstep.

Deliveries were laborious and costly; they were often more trouble than they were worth. They called for special staff, additional space, regularly serviced vehicles. More than once, an accountant informed them the numbers didn't add up. After one such pronouncement, Ruth started doing the bookkeeping herself. "There are some things that money-men don't count," she said.

One of the unintended consequences of Provisions K's deliveries had been the delivery of Theo Sr. himself. Answering a job notice in the window, he withstood all of Av's quizzes on city geography and finally a series of ethical questions relating to poor tippers, broken milk bottles, unanswered doors. The kid got started on a bike, delivering single fish fillets to a nonagenarian Greek Orthodox priest, couriering restaurant orders for parsley, butter and eggs. Soon he was loading and unloading vans, then driving vans, then managing the dispatch of vans. Six years after first standing before Av, Theo Sr. asked if he could marry his daughter. At the wedding, the Ukrainian Federation's ceiling was strung with dyed green twine. The bride and groom had chosen a jungle theme, inspired by their shared love of *King Solomon's Mines*.

Whenever they needed to cut expenses, Theo's parents wavered on the issue of delivery. But it pained Theo Sr. to put his own well-being first. He had learned his politics from speeches at the Workers' Hall and his conception of social justice was founded on this rhetoric—a poetry of linked arms and ardent spirits, not profit and loss. Wishfulness was what gave it its strength: the beautiful, unflagging flame of a thing that feels true. "Successful businesses do not merely have a responsibility to the bottom line," he'd say. "Remember the other lines! The ones that pass in and out through a place—these lines matter too. Customers, suppliers, neighbours, competitors, hobos famishing in the road. Lines between us. We must at least try to help the people we are near enough to touch."

And Minnie used the store's deliveries as a means of direct intervention with those she thought to be in need. Sometimes Theo gathered the groceries for his mother, arranging them in the crate, other times he pushed the cart as she moved up and down the aisles, choosing what to send: spaghetti and raisin bread, fresh corn and chicken thighs, two bars of chocolate that gleamed in their foil. It was Theo she asked, not Peter or Mireille: something had made her decide that this was a thing they would share, or something her youngest son needed to learn, since he did not have a natural inclination towards social action. She would interrupt him as he was kneeling on the floor, drawing pictures beside mounds of nectarines, writing skits near the butcher counter. They would move through the store like partners, picking out items that they meant to simply give away.

Theo's dawning self-conception was completely entwined with the proceedings of the store he lived above. If his friends came over to play they'd often ditch his apartment to roam the bustling main floor, watching strangers bagging broccoli or employees stickering candy bars, eavesdropping on Theo Sr. as he negotiated the price of haddock and tilapia, standing in spooked awe at a row of beheaded pigs, on hooks, in the freezer. Theo acted casual, a prince in his home court, saying, "Hey, Lorraine" to the curly-haired cashier or "Yo, Mo" to the tall Somalian who stocked the very highest row of shelves. He invited his friends to sample some almonds, taste a grape, or even to reach into the bin of cheese-buns and treat themselves.

Consider the boy at the beginning of his adolescence, standing in the section of Provisions that Mireille dubbed Carb Castle—a circle of towering platters laden with every kind of loaf and flatbread, tortillas and rolls and bins of pure-butter croissants. He was leaning on the edge of a flat of hot cross buns, staring at a spread of illustrated cards for a game called Wizard Kingdoms. It was after nine on a Tuesday, and the store was calmer than the Potiris residence, affording a measure of privacy that Theo couldn't find in the rooms he shared with his siblings. Beyond the section's doughy boundaries, customers paged through heads of romaine lettuce, sniffed melons. His father was trying to rearrange a turret of dented discount baklava.

He'd bought the cards from Evan Dubinsky earlier that day. Evan claimed to have an uncle who worked at the Wizard Kingdoms printing factory in New Jersey; Theo suspected his classmate was simply shoplifting, a crime he deplored for hereditary reasons. But cut-price cards held an almost irresistible allure, and he bought Evan's fenced goods whenever he had the money.

Sand Sentry. This was the name of one card, jet black, with the image of a grim, stolid creature, squat and armoured like a scarab beetle, with wings that canopied from its shoulders. The monster's face and mandibles were a flattened death's-head. *Digging, firebreathing,* read the text below the illustration. *Shadowtrace 4.* This meant that the Sand Sentry could tunnel under walls, that it could engulf several opponents at once, that it drained an enemy's shadow points four at a time. Very useful, Theo decided, but only if you were able to get the card into play: a series of symbols in the upper right corner indicated the Sentry's considerable casting cost. This monster was difficult to conjure; it could easily become trapped in your hand. Theo considered his other cards, hoping he had something that would complement the Sand Sentry, make it easier to put into play.

Theo counted the River cards in his deck. There were twelve. More than the Mines or Forests. Maybe he should discard some of his dwarves and elves and concentrate on mer-folk instead.

He still hadn't decided whether he actually *liked* playing Wizard Kingdoms. His friends were all suddenly very deeply into the game, but Theo distrusted consensus. As he saw it, each school day contained a single lunch-hour and these lunch-hours were always pouring past, one after another. Best spend them well.

When that school year had begun, Theo was under the impression that everyone was going to get into philosophy. Julie had received a philosophy book for her birthday, a beautiful leather-bound tome with gold foil lettering on the spine, and an appendix of terms in ancient Greek. *Philosophy: The Secret of Wisdom*, it said on the cover. Over August weekends, the kids studied it like a treasure map. There were colour plates with portraits of Aristotle and Kant. There was a chapter about Socrates' chalice of hemlock. Next to sections with titles like "The True Nature of Beauty" they found flow charts, diagrams, collections of what appeared to be math formulas. Then Gab persuaded his parents to buy him the same volume at the remaindered bookshop, and Mohammed Mohammed, in a wondrous fluke, found a *Golden Guide to Philosophy* in the fifty-cent bin at the library. Mohammed Mohammed's luminous older sister explained to them that they should highlight important passages, so Julie and Amberg and Gab and Mohammed Mohammed started highlighting whole swaths of their texts. Theo had the idea to rewrite these passages on cue cards so that he would have a treasury of wisdom at his disposal—concise distillations of Plato's theory of forms or Bentham's greatest happiness principle. To Minnie's considerable satisfaction, he reviewed the cards at night, while applying price stickers to Provisions' styrofoam trays of ground beef.

But then everyone got into *Wizard Kingdoms* instead.

"'It is a small part of life we really live,'" Theo murmured to himself. "Seneca."

Still, Wizard Kingdoms interested him because, unlike similar games, it did not rely on story. When Theo was younger, Peter had allowed him to sit in the corner of the room while he and his friends played Dungeons & Dragons. Theo listened as the older kids discussed gnolls, traps and platinum armour; he heard them counting out loud for hitpoints and damage; he learned curse-words from the way they hissed at their many-sided dice. But what struck him most was the storyteller: a boy with John Lennon glasses who consulted notes behind a cardboard screen and got to decide what was happening. "You come to a stone wall," he'd say. "It is marked with arcane runes." Or: "Your ice-shower drizzles the ground, turning lilacs to mulch, but seems to have no effect on the lich king." Or: "The beautiful gnome joins you at the prow of the boat. She has a blue amulet around her neck. She says, 'You must be looking for the swampman's key.'"

All of D&D's counting and dice-rolling just bolstered the tale, the players' vivid shared dream. Even eavesdropping from the corner, Theo could follow every twist. As Peter and his friends imagined themselves rogues, paladins, rangers, adventuring in the woods, Theo was a curious, silent companion, lurking at the edge of the firelight.

Wizard Kingdoms didn't allow for this. Monsters attacked monsters, magicians cast spells, but what mattered was the arithmetic of defence, damage, shadowtrace points; mostly it came down to the player and the strength of their deck. Yet even Theo recognized there could be something pleasurable in an arbitrary game: in this life of cause and consequence, here instead was a card pulled randomly from a deck, a coin flip, the collision of rock against paper or scissors. A result that was meaningless—or else arbitrarily meaningful, exhilarating, dangerous.

For about four months Theo and his friends played Wizard Kingdoms every lunch-hour, huddling on the basement carpet in the public library near their school. They drew their decks from ziplock bags, experiencing in those moments the throb of pride—at owning treasures, owning them so entirely that they could take them in and out of ziplock bags, at will. If adulthood is a process of discovering your own poverty, on the library basement's thin carpet these young people felt rich.

But then Julie got into competitive trampoline and Amberg was into making pork sausages. Theo began memorizing bits of Woody Allen records, or John Cleese's part in "The Argument Sketch." Mohammed Mohammed got into punk rock. Once he took Theo to a hardcore show at a green-gabled house in the suburbs. When Theo left early, biking home to meet curfew, they parted in the driveway. For a brief moment he thought they might kiss. He still remembered the expression on his friend's face: so filled with raw joy he looked as if he had glitter in his eyes.

Gab, meanwhile, went online. He connected by modem in the high-school computer lab, joining sundry local servers. He showed Theo a file containing entire unexpurgated *Simpsons* scripts, then a long document of 1,500 top-secret CIA codewords. *Nightingale*, *Blackjack*, *Silverdoor*, *Friendship Cove*. Sometimes Theo sat beside Gab on an injection-moulded chair, watching the cascade of grey letters across the screen, listening to the modem's chatter and howl. His friend said, "There's a whole world in here."

At fourteen Theo saw new worlds everywhere. He could study verses from *The Iliad* or quips by Groucho Marx; he could learn to play Super Mario 3 with his eyes closed and the volume up. He tried all of these things. He learned to select pallets of sweet peppers for the store by the colour and rigidity of the peppers' stems. He learned to drive. He learned to tell jokes. He learned how to love hot sauce. He got older and he changed and he stayed the same, graduating from high school, earning a bachelor of arts, working at the store, making a single bet on Fridays, falling in love, breaking up, dragging himself on stage. Stand-up became the way of telling his story as it happened: describing the worlds he found himself in (or searching for); and of course it was a way to hear other people's stories, forthright and fragile and custom-made. *The surprise of learning you and I share a secret.* He got older, changed, and stayed the same—as all of us do—watching friendships blossom and wither, stores open and close, seeing peers marry and buy homes and have children, or move away, or accomplish none of these things, peers who remained alone, writing books or painting canvases, making music, meeting clients, seeing patients, managing offices, working, trying, refining, working, trying, refining, seeing sunset after sunset until all the sunsets seemed part of one long moving painting, gold and rose and indigo, a single connected experience that we take breaks from, one day or one week at a time, having coffee or going to work, blowing out birthday candles, cycling, sleeping, until at last on our balconies or in our cars, walking between warehouses, we return to the sight of that one unremitting sunset.

Finally one October—full grown, not far from forty years old, on an afternoon approaching dusk—Theo met Lou at a children's birthday party. They were in a playground surrounded by fence and ferns just a few blocks from Provisions K, the kind of place Theo was scarcely conscious existed. You don't keep track of playgrounds until you have children; that's when playgrounds become important. Here stood a proud wooden structure with yellow painted panels, a shiny slide like a section torn off a sports-car, a sandpit and a ship-captain's wheel and weird basketball hoops that looked like plastic plumbing components. He was in the long gazebo, loitering by the snack table with the pot-lucked Baby Bels and bruschetta, when across the painted pavement and sandpit he saw a woman with springy blonde hair staring at one of those basketball tubes, forehead creased, clearly trying to work out what it was for. Her coat was open over a wide-collared black shirt; she was long-legged in jeans, with the air of a creature that can stand and stand for a long time. He had never seen her before.

Just then, a child ran into him. The kid staggered back, blinked. "Careful there," Theo said. The little girl tossed her head and ran off in a different direction. Mohammed Mohammed, now an app designer, was on hands and knees, leading a procession of kids through the park's overgrown eastern edge. Theo tried to remember the last time the two of them had really talked but got annoyed at himself for this unkind thought. He was a parent now, and parents make lousy conversationalists. These were all still his friends, and in a way his friends' children were his friends now too. Arto, Arlo, Ida, Ashby, Timothée, Charlie, Oscar, Ivy, Fergus, Misha, William, Henry, Harrison, Marguerite, Julian, Ingrid, Huxley, Ilham, Levon, Ramona, Elinor, Iza, Giles, Silas, Safi, Eloïse, Beatrice, Nori, Francis, Lumi, Hayden, Benny, Other Theo, Sara, Bertie, Jojo, Ari, Sam, Isabel, Esmë, Ivo, Efe, Everest, Addison, Rose, Isla, Marko, Aubrey, Clara, Dante, Sadie, Gabi, Nathan, Lior, Carmel, Lily, Paloma, Gabriel, Ben, Arc, Isaiah, Zeki, Holly, Max, Munro. They were short and school-age and a part of his community. *Part of my social safety net*, Theo smirked, then he wondered if this would make a good bit. He noticed the woman again, squatting at the edge of the basketball court, talking to one of Marco's boys, what was his name? Égon. She was making him laugh. Theo wondered if any of these children belonged to her.

Eventually he grew bored with the party and bade a barest adieu to the hosts, exchanging a high-five with the five-year-old birthday girl. She seemed tired of giving high-fives. Theo straightened from his crouch feeling abashed and a little irritated, he wasn't sure at whom. As he turned to go he found the woman nearby.

"I'm Lou," she said.

"Theo."

"Nice to meet you."

"Is one of these yours?"

"Hell no," she said, smiling.

Theo laughed. "I think we might be the only orphans here. Orphans? Can I say that? Or is it only kids without parents, not the other way around?"

"Not orphans," Lou said, "at least I hope not. Merely childless. Available nights and weekends."

"Selfish," Theo said.

She smiled. "Yes, we're very selfish. You leaving?"

He nodded.

"I should probably save myself too."

They walked together for a bit. Winter was coming but that evening it seemed held at bay. Squirrels rattled in the branches. The path was scattered with yellow and russet leaves. He had never met this woman and yet he had the feeling that he knew her voice—as if he had heard it across a room or in the street, loose across the air, somewhere, years ago, and then dreamed of it. Dusk moved over them with an expansive grace, like two kinds of light converging in air. It painted the water tower, the sides of trees, the cornices and rooftops, two figures as they talked.

:::

On a gusty Friday in late March, four weeks after Minnie's death, Theo and Hanna passed through a pair of gasping automatic doors.

"*Bienvenue*, welcome!" shouted a kid in a red polar-fleece vest with a miniature rendering of the Hippodrome embroidered onto the fabric above his heart.

"Thank you," said Hanna. The young people eyed each other. The greeter's Adam's apple bobbed in his neck. He gave Theo a once-over and then eyed Hanna again, taking in her size, her unselfconscious calm. A set of earbuds dangled from the neck of her white T-shirt.

"You eighteen?" he said.

"She's eighteen," said Theo.

Hanna stared at her uncle, slightly shocked. The vested greeter cleared his throat.

"This racecourse is a certified gaming house and thereby restricted—"

"I said she's eighteen. Are *you* even eighteen?" Theo grabbed Hanna's arm and nudged her through the doorway.

They carried on past the players at the slots, which held no interest for her, past the vending machines, which did, up the stairs and to the tall panes of glass above the track, sparkling with the reflection of a Z. Largo candelabra. Although the man's reinvented lightbulbs had more or less taken over the world, Theo still wasn't accustomed to seeing them en masse. Beyond the handsomeness of the bulbs themselves—copper and glass, the faintly opalescent filament—there was the quality of their full-spectrum light. All the grace and radiance of sunlight, but environmentally friendly, energy-efficient—and almost as cheap as old-fashioned incandescents.

"Wow," said Hanna, to Theo's considerable satisfaction.

There were horses below. Mid-gallop, shining, like stallions from a storybook. Gamblers shouted at the screens all around them. Announcers babbled overhead. Then came the furor of the finish line, betting stubs flying through the air.

"Not a lot of winners," Theo observed.

Hanna looked around. "They seemed to be having fun until the end."

"People hate losing."

"People *have* to lose," Hanna said. "If they don't, it doesn't work. Besides, if you like to gamble, why should the fun go away just because you didn't get a certain outcome?"

As often happened with Hanna, Theo didn't really understand.

"If you're enjoying a story, the unanswered question of what's going to happen, that enjoyment doesn't stop with the ending," she clarified. "The ending *completes* it."

"Why have an ending at all?"

"Are you kidding?" Hanna said. "The ending's the best part."

Theo peered at his peculiar niece. Her T-shirt, with the image of a palm tree, a desert island, a sun wearing sunglasses, was uneven on her shoulders. "Are you ready to make a bet?" he asked. He picked up an abandoned racing form. Hanna, he thought, needed to lose. Not to choose a decent horse, a plausible winner, and then see that pony place towards the front. Hanna needed to learn the harsher lesson: you can't count on anything, and betting's an expensive way to try.

But Hanna had picked her horse before arriving, perusing the races online. "Pinkwater," she said. She wanted to put everything on a horse nobody had ever heard of, not just to place but to win. Theo looked at the page and saw that Pinkwater was up against a group of fast horses with good records. His stomach turned. He considered reversing course, persuading Hanna to bet on the favourite, who paid two-to-one, but he steeled himself. His lanky niece glowed with juvenile conviction. She would benefit from a correction:

Hanna's adolescent sense of invincibility for a bit of her childhood savings.

They went up together to the counter. It was the clerk who had worn Minnie's shade of lipstick. This time her lips were bare. For a moment Theo felt a sense of loss. He tried not to think. "I'd like to lay a wager," he said. "A horse called Pinkwater, to win race nine." The clerk asked how much he was wagering and Hanna reached into the pocket of her jeans. She smoothed a set of bills on the counter, added a handful of change. The notes were mostly thousand-dollar bills.

"What in God's name is that?" whispered Theo.

Hanna said it was her inheritance, her savings, straight from the bank. The clerk counted the money. $13,513.53. "No," Theo said, "no, no, no." Hanna wasn't allowed to do this, he said. Hanna said "But—" and Theo said she couldn't and Hanna said that Theo had promised there wasn't any limit to the amount she could bet. He took out his cellphone. He called Mireille, told her what was happening, told her thirteen thousand dollars. Mireille said, "It's *her* money." Theo put down the phone. He made the bet for Hanna. He immediately wanted to take it back.

"I—" he said.

"It's done," said the clerk.

Theo's hands felt numb. He took the betting stub and gave it to Hanna and they walked away from the counter. "This is a lesson," Theo said, feebly. They watched on the TV screen as the jockeys led out their horses. The same scene played out in miniature on the turf below. Pinkwater was the biggest horse Theo had ever seen. He was tall and beautiful, like a stallion from a painting, white as goats' cheese, with a silver mane and silver tail, his eyes like red coals. When the race started, the other horses all hung back, as if they were afraid of him. Pinkwater streaked across the dirt. He crossed the finish line two full lengths ahead. The odds against him were 296:1, so Hanna won $4,000,004.88. The numbness had spread all over Theo's body. They left the racecourse and got in the car and it started like usual, a key in a little slot.

CHAPTER FIVE

"Sometimes I see a group of bulldozers and imagine that they all must be friends," Hanna said.

Theo did not reply. He was trying to keep his eyes on the road. He was trying to be as steady as an hour-hand; to not be crazy, to not be cuckoo. His niece beside him was holding an envelope containing a banker's cheque for more than four million dollars. The sky above the city was tinted faintly green. The sun was a pale ring. Weird weather, seemed like anything could happen. Theo clenched the wheel. A raindrop landed on his windshield and he flicked the wipers on but then no more rain came, nothing, the sun was a pale ring.

The music changed to something with bongos and trumpets, cool jazz. Hanna pushed another button on the car radio. A fanatical French announcer baying about a mattress sale. A techno remix of Rupert Holmes's "Piña Colada Song." A chiffony pop-star singing sadly about Friday nights. A hockey game.

"What are you looking for?" Theo asked.

"The Bach station," Hanna said.

"There's no Bach station."

"Not officially." She pressed another button. "There."

"What?"

"Bach."

To Theo it was just violins.

He turned on the left-turn signal and carefully turned left. This wasn't his car: he had borrowed it from the car-share service and now he felt distrustful of it, the dented Yaris, the elaborate membership paperwork. Hanna had won four million dollars and anything else could occur: miracle, aneurysm, fire. Hanna was leaning back in her seat, listening, an envelope in her lap. She wasn't even holding on to it, she wasn't even touching it, her hands lay loose at her sides. Theo wanted to tell his niece to hold on to the damn envelope, but he didn't, just checked his rearview mirror again and again, merged lanes on high alert, afraid of an accident or of getting pulled over, of carjacking—karmic retribution for Hanna's stroke of luck.

"Do you ever imagine that?" Hanna said.

"Huh?"

"That construction vehicles are friends? That they're just hanging out together?"

"No."

"Really?" Hanna sounded surprised.

Theo rubbed his cheek. "Heavy machinery, hanging out?"

His niece nodded.

"I've really never considered it."

She shifted in her seat. "Are we still going to the park?" Her skateboard was at her feet.

"No. We're going home."

A moment of silence passed.

"Are you mad at me?" Hanna asked.

"What? No. How could I be mad? Of course I'm not mad."

"Okay," Hanna said.

Theo still felt numb. The music had changed, from Bach to jazz, and a vibraphone was descending slowly from chord to chord, pairs of notes in time, one then another, enduring. It felt as if the musician was explaining a single stratum of his life, one blue layer of what he had known.

The bongos started up again and all the music's clarity came apart.

"How did you choose that horse?" Theo asked.

Hanna scratched her thigh. She said, "I had a feeling."

When they got home, Hanna and her banker's cheque disappeared at once to some far corner of the grocery store. "Tell your parents!" Theo called after her. Reluctantly, he climbed the stairs to the family's apartments. As he crossed the landing he felt a faint dread, like the queasiness after an earthquake. Certain moments change everything. It seemed perverse that Minnie's death had not been one of these moments—that his world had outlasted his mother. But this felt different. A silver-maned pony crossing an invisible finish line: Theo had a sense of knots unravelling, knots he hadn't even known were knotted, knots he hadn't even known he relied on.

He unlocked his apartment door with an unsteady hand. He looked at his mail. He let a wet washcloth sit on his face. Impulsively, he uncorked a bottle of red wine and poured himself a glass. Standing in front of the fridge he gazed at a little marker drawing Lou had made, of a frog and a lily pad.

Hanna had hit the jackpot.

On the other side of the hallway stood Minnie's apartment, still empty, and beyond that the three-bedroom family suite where Theo had grown up. It was home now to Mireille, Eric and Hanna, with a worn-out welcome mat and a mezuzah on its doorpost. Mireille had explained the mezuzah to him once, that the olivewood box contained a mystic Jewish prayer. He feigned ambivalence but in truth he found it passive-aggressive: putting up a mystic prayer scroll while others went without. Theo could put up his own but that wasn't the point. It wasn't only his discomfort around Judaism: there seemed something merciless about screwing a magic spell to your doorpost. An innocuous wooden box that asks, in rune, for you to be set apart.

But so what? Theo drained his wine. So the hell what? What was so wrong about wishing to be set apart? Didn't everybody want to be chosen? To be graced by God at the muddy racing track? Under the lights at the Knock Knock, with a booker in the crowd?

That kind, precious kid had won four million dollars.

Theo knocked at Mireille and Eric's door. He heard a sound from inside and let himself in, passing into the living room from the foyer, setting his empty wineglass on a shelf, announcing to its occupants— as well as its knickknacks, movie posters, lilies: "Hanna's a millionaire."

Eric was in the kitchen, running a vegetable peeler across a carrot. Mireille was sprawled on the couch, cradling a video-game controller. The television screen showed a warrior with rabbit ears loping through some scrub. It had a sword on its back, big puffy fur boots. "Huh?" she said.

"Hanna's a millionaire. The horse was 300:1 and she bet $13,000 and she won four million dollars."

They were both staring at him in incomprehension.

"No joke," he said.

Mireille put down the controller and the rabbit-eared warrior remained standing in place, breathing hard.

They freaked out. A synthesis of panic and jubilation. Eric didn't understand how his daughter had been permitted to wager $13,000. Mireille vowed that she hadn't understood. "I thought you said thirteen *hundred* dollars," she said. "I thought . . ." She trailed off.

"Even still!" shouted Eric.

One of a parent's greatest terrors is that they will fuck up in some significant way. And here was the sort of mistake that seemed like an inflection point, diverting their daughter from the path she was on. All of Hanna's savings, staked on a horse; $13,000 was "only" $13,000 and yet it also seemed like a gigantic amount, cataclysmic. If she had lost that, what else might she lose? The future they had laid before her like a place setting. One bet, one reckless colt, and Hanna might have been consigned to life as an unmarried eccentric, a cat lady, with bookshelves full of almanacs and Salinger stories, an oven full of heirlooms. Penniless and unfulfilled, with skateboard-induced arthritis, dying alone above a grocery store. Everybody would blame the parents.

Instead the fuck-up went unfucked. Rather than ruining her, Hanna's gamble made her rich. As Theo related the afternoon's events, he watched the dawning awe on Mireille's and Eric's faces and felt himself recoiling from their rapture, receding to some high perch. The suddenness of Minnie's passing and now the suddenness of this—the old rules all seemed broken. Anything could happen. Anything had happened. Anything could happen next.

"Where is she?" Mireille asked.

"Downstairs."

The television screen flashed into screensaver mode and for a second they were all distracted by the change. Then Mireille got to her feet. "*Malaka*," she said.

Theo helped them find her, three adults converging on a figure at the end of cashier 3's conveyer belt. Eric and Mireille stood waiting for Hanna to finish filling a customer's tote with salad greens. When she finally lifted her eyes and saw them, her face broke into a wide, radiant smile.

The subsequent uproar seemed cribbed from a kids' movie: shrieks and bear hugs, shouts, dancing, tears, hoots. Hanna's parents forgot their plan to usher their daughter upstairs. Instead, Mireille got up onto the checkout conveyer and whooped. Eric tore open a big bag of potato chips, started passing it between shoppers. Soon more bags: pop, pop, pop as they opened, filling the air with smells of salt, dill pickle, powdered barbecue. Mireille got down and now she was clutching Hanna around her shoulders, fizzing with happiness. She found a bottle of prosecco somewhere and pop this was opened too, tiny plastic cocktail glasses filled and circulated among strangers, pop, pop and more bottles yet, sparkling cider and low-alcohol bubbly, whatever liquors the government permitted Provisions K to carry. With every minute more people joined the celebration—shoppers arriving through the automatic doors, staff emerging curious from their stations. João put his fingers in his mouth and blew a giddy whistle. Shelf stockers abandoned their carts. Eric transitioned from bags of potato chips to boxes of cookies, trays of lemon wafers and dark-chocolate Petit Écoliers. The crowd passed the treats around, the news flying: *Hanna won four million*.

Theo cheered maybe loudest of all, hoisting glass upon glass for Eric's sloppy toasts. Everyone was happy for Hanna, that peculiar girl, who could be as serious as a watchtower or as friendly as a pinwheel. What had happened to her made all the staff and regulars want to clap one another on the back, yell Hanna's name, down their bubbles in one quick go, even the frail old ladies.

But eventually Theo slipped away from the crowd, along a tranquil aisle. He leaned his full weight into the swinging staff door, stomped down the stairs, then stood alone in the stillness of the cellar. Minnie's desk sat untouched. Something was spinning slowly at the centre of his heart, something hard and heavy, and he didn't want to examine it. Failure or envy. Hurt or disappointment. He just let it spin there, waiting for it to slow, waiting for it to slow, knowing that perhaps it wouldn't ever slow, that the feeling might keep revolving inside him for the rest of his life.

He shoved Minnie's chair off its patch of rug and into a set of shelves, which bumped and swayed and then bequeathed a jar of pickles. He felt a surge of satisfaction as the jar came loose and smashed on the floor. A little pool of vinegar, dill, mustard seeds. A circle of flaccid pickles. Theo heard a rustle. A figure appeared—Blake, his nephew.

Each of them stared at the debris.

"It fell?"

Theo cleared his throat. "Yes."

The teenager's mohawk was slumping in the humidity. He ran a hand across it. "I was doing the chocolate-covered raisins." He pointed through the rows of stock towards a scale, a barrel, a stack of clear disposable tubs.

Theo took down a roll of paper towels and found a dustpan and began cleaning up. Blake got down beside him. When they were done they both went to finish the raisins.

"You heard about Hanna?" Theo asked.

Blake nodded.

They continued working.

Every time Theo dipped his plastic tub into the barrel, the raisins made a sound like softly clicking coins.

:::

Springtime was stammering across the city. Stutters of sun and rain, flash frosts, then afternoons of thick, hot breezes. The strange flocks of birds had not gone away. Small blue birds with bright orange breasts, pecking at gardeners' beet-greens. Broad-winged birds with scythe-like beaks, flying circles round the steeples of churches. Inappropriate crows with slashes of bright blue plumage, ravens with uncharacteristically beautiful songs, blue jays and cardinals gliding in from the outskirts, crowding bike lanes, squatting on rooftops, battling with sparrows in the splash of public fountains. Pigeons nose-diving through basketball hoops.

There was a Hollywood movie shooting across the street from Provisions K. Its crew had dressed up a café as a neighbourhood greengrocer, parked a battered police cruiser just outside. Production assistants crossed the road to buy crates of apples and ripe bananas, or to pick up bran muffins for craft services. Theo leaned against one of the store's front windows one afternoon, observing the action through a cordon of onlookers. A bearded actor dressed as a police officer, a young woman in a houndstooth coat pleading with him, pleading and pleading until finally she bolted away from him and stole his car. Throughout this action, the director and camera operators fought an unending battle with the scenery. A cameraman would mutter something and the director would call "Cut!," swearing at her monitor. The problem was the sky, and all the birds swarming there. Gatherings of eagles, flocks of shearwaters, lifting, falling, flying braids between low clouds, darting into the frame. Their massed presence seemed otherworldly, portentous. You couldn't have a thousand birds congregating in the sky behind a character's head. It was too distracting. It was too symbolic. It wasn't realistic. "Cut!" the director would call, and they'd modify the shooting angle to show less of the real world and more of the realistically imagined one.

After watching the woman steal the policeman's car for the third time, Theo pushed off from his spot. He paused at the threshold of the store, as customers moved past him, laden with grocery bags and cardboard boxes, clutching bike helmets, flyers, fumbling with phones or car keys. None of them noticed him, but he was less sure of the employees. Esther, a senior manager, stood watch on the other side of the cashiers. Her gaze seemed to skirt his edges.

Ever since Hanna's win, Theo believed he felt a change in their staff. The family's new fortune underscored the distance between Provisions' owners and its personnel, the labourers and the millionaires. This gap had always been there but it hadn't seemed so vast, not with most of the Potirises living above the store, working day jobs within it, spending hours in the cheese pit shaving mould from mozzarella. So long as no one was getting rich, the distinction between them seemed like a matter of roles and responsibilities. Theo preferred it this way—living his life as if class were a conspiracy that happened to other people. It felt different now. One of the delivery guys made a joke about getting a raise. The next day a different delivery guy made the same joke. Theo chuckled through clenched teeth.

When he mentioned this to Mo, the night manager didn't laugh. "Up to you," Mo replied in a careful tone.

However it wasn't up to Theo. An across-the-board raise required the approval of his siblings. Peter proved surprisingly open to the idea: Hanna's win had loosened something in him, some long-lost generosity. He just thought it made more sense to wait until after other, grander plans had been put into place—a new location for Provisions K, using Hanna's money as collateral. The notion seemed crazy to Theo, but he played along—"Maybe, maybe"—as if he too dreamed of shutting the old store down, relocating the fruit and vegetables.

Mireille was harder to pin down. She and her family were constantly out and about, basking in the glow of new possibility. "Our daughter won a jackpot," Eric told Theo. "We might as well do some jackpot-like things." First it was pianos: Hanna said she wanted to see some, so Mireille took her to the Steinway store, where they wandered among chèvre-coloured baby grands. Next the three of them went hoverboard shopping, taxiing from boutique to boutique to evaluate various models. When Hanna returned, near nightfall, she glided through Provisions K on a whirring silver platform, her expression grave.

Before long, Hanna and her parents were embarking on a series of helicopter trips. Every morning, Theo observed their departure from a hiding-spot near the shopping trolleys. Black town car; bow-tied driver; off to a helipad. *A helipad.* Where the hell did the city have a helipad? The trio flew across the Seaway, went skimming up the mountains; after a fourth excursion they came back in matching jumpsuits, surnames embroidered on their chests.

Other indulgences included: (for Mireille) diamond earrings, an autographed Rolling Stones record, weekly at-home massage treatments; (for Eric) a thousand-dollar cookbook, with recipes for squid à l'orange sanguine and liquid nitrogen coleslaw; (for Hanna) night-vision goggles. Theo finally cornered Mireille in the supply room, where he made a case for raises in the corner beside the brooms.

"Give everyone a raise?" Her expression flickered.

"We can afford it now. Or at least afford the risk."

"Who can? The store's a money pit, Theo."

"But Hanna—"

"Nothing's changed."

"*Everything's* changed."

"Hanna won a bet," Mireille said.

"Actually, technically, *I* won a bet."

Her face darkened. "Don't think that thought."

"It's true."

"That thought will eat you up, little brother."

He went to answer, stopped.

"You're Hanna's uncle," Mireille said. "Be that."

A blush lifted into his face.

"If Provisions can afford to give everyone a raise then of course we should," Mireille said. "But the store *can't* afford it. You know that. Maybe if we moved. Remix, reset, hopefully do a little better. In the meantime, Hanna's good luck doesn't belong to anybody but her."

"Fine," Theo said. He rubbed his face with both hands, leaning back against a column of cardboard boxes. As they crumpled under him, Theo was slowly, inexorably, lowered to the floor.

"You okay?" asked Mireille.

"Yes."

She left him there.

Luck is not a virtue, Theo reminded himself. *You do not win a bet because you ought to.* Yet the arbitrariness of Hanna's good fortune

seemed to lend it even more force—as if it *must* have been earned somehow. And so the corollary: Why had such luck never come to him?

Theo did not want to covet his niece's winnings. He did not want
to covet anything that was hers. He had never even wanted to be rich:
a modest wage had always seemed sufficient. He saved up for holidays; he was indifferent to helicopters. Yet he could not now shake the
slippery, wicked idea that he was the one who deserved a break, not
his niece. Her luck was not founded on anything: it did not come
from years of hard work and equitable dealing. Theo's parents had
devoted their whole lives to the store, running themselves ragged,
bending over backward for the welfare of their staff, and what had it
brought? His dad had been hit by a taco truck as he was crossing the
road. Minnie had died in her chair.

Theo got up. His mother would have told him not to think these
thoughts. She would have told him not to question the legitimacy of
luck, whether good or bad—just to acknowledge the role it plays in
life. Take what's unearned and turn it inside out: imagine it as an
obligation, a debt to be repaid. But Minnie had never won four million dollars. This was what galled Theo most. Why not a different
lucky break—something more keenly longed for, or longed for longer?
For Minerva to still be alive. For Theo Sr. to have missed his date
with death.

For any dream more yearned-after than a thirteen-year-old
millionaire.

Theo felt ungracious and he felt unkind. As evening fell, he went
to the front of the store. A photograph of the family was mounted on
foamcore near the entrance, from Provisions' fiftieth anniversary. *I
want my mother back*, he thought, staring at the young clan. *I want
my father.* Their slow senescence, a ripe old age. He remembered

taking the picture that day. He remembered the film shoot just days ago, how the film crew's lighting panels had blazed across the pavement outside. Strange birds still jockeyed on the horizon. *I want my own score*, he thought. It surprised him to hear himself admit it. It didn't even matter if he deserved it. He wanted it. He wished for it, heart straining. There was nothing he wanted more. A big break, a fortune, a fluke in his favour. *Please, please.*

Hanna was somewhere in the store, near the back, doing homework or dividing meat. Theo didn't want to chance upon his mystic, lucky niece. What a vicious fact: someone else's good luck, despite all your longing.

That night, Theo went to the Knock Knock Club. *Settle your heart*, he thought. *Go and do the work.* He made his way through the crowd and straight to Annette. *You're the funniest man in the world*, he told himself. He told Annette he would go on next, or soon; that he needed to get up, right now, this hour, tonight.

She sent him on stage after René, a timorous redhead, and Theo went without hesitation, without a thank you. He passed through the audience's dark shapes and up on to the stage and when he came to the microphone he discovered he did not know what he wanted to say. He wanted to be magnificent and vulnerable, irrefutably present. All the bright lights looked like vacant circles, haloes. The ball of the mic smelled of dry sweetness, old cake. "I had a rough day," Theo said, with a little smile hanging on the edges of his mouth, the suspicion of a grin, an expression that says that this is an unfolding and funny thought, and yet he felt no change in the room, no shift or even acknowledgment, just empty air and the sense that, like him, the audience was waiting for something. They were waiting for him.

The word, *bombing*, it's not a description of what you *see* when a comic bombs. The catastrophe's so tame: a comedian tells jokes and nobody laughs. The bomb is the sensation in that comedian's heart, ineluctable and plunging, and the desolation that follows him out of the light.

When the set was over Theo pushed past the emergency exit and walked out onto the raw concrete behind the club. He felt impotent, stupid, alone. The night was stilled and pearly. For twelve years Theo had been telling himself the same story: that he was putting in the work, heading somewhere. But where? There were no motorcycles here tonight, no sitting figures. Instead a word on his tongue, *orphan*. No one who mattered to him had even seen him trying. He walked to where the Knock Knock's back alley met the road, the sound of distant laughter following him like a haunting. After a little while he took out his phone. He brought up the browser. He had done this many times since the night he sat here with a stranger.

He entered the words "the rabbits foot."

He waited.

A phrase at the top of the webpage, gold as new treasure.

Contact us.

CHAPTER SIX

Simone had been correct. The Rabbit's Foot was always looking for processors.

Theo, perspiring, wasn't certain whether he ought to be excited. He had called the number the following morning, cross-legged on his duvet. The person who answered was terse and professional. Yes, they had some vacancies; yes, he could come in. They gave him an address, an appointment, and sixty minutes to arrive.

He had expected something glamorous, mysterious. Instead the office was in a plaza near the motorway, squat and flat, across from a field of weeds. Signs advertised the offices of a community radio station, an artisanal salsa lab, an improbably confident ribbon manufacturer (*The "Best" since 2015!*). A long-languishing bowling alley trembled at the end of the lot.

Suite 500's buzzer was unnamed on the intercom. When he hit it, the lock thunked open and Theo took the steps two at a time, bicycle helmet under his arm. The staircase ended at the fifth floor: a heavy door, shiny black, with the numbers 5-0-0. Theo hesitated for a moment and then left his helmet in the stairwell, on the second-to-highest step. He ran his hands through his hair.

The door revealed an open-plan office that seemed to go on forever. The light fell evenly over glass desks and flatscreens, cyan-tinted water coolers, men and women in voluptuous, translucent office chairs, their workstations divided by short blue partitions. Nearly everyone he could see, as many as a hundred people, was wearing headphones. Nobody was listening to their own typing, clicking, scrolling; heedless of the clack and whirr, they consigned these sounds to him.

"Yes?" The man behind reception had taken off his headset.

"Theo Potiris. I have an interview?"

"An interview?" The man had a birthmark across his chin, like an ink spill.

"For the, uh, processor gig?"

"Oh, you're here to take the test. Use the terminal under Mr. Peanut."

Theo looked around. There were a few free workstations in the row nearest the entrance. The last of these, next to the wall, sat below a large black-and-white poster. A peanut-shaped biped leaned on his cane, winking through a monocle, under a bold heading that read, *MR. PEANUT FOR MAYOR.*

"There?" Theo asked, pointing.

"Yeah."

Theo went and sat down. The screen came to life as soon as he pressed a key.

THE RABBIT'S FOOT

Processor Screening

build 4.1

(Spacebar to begin.)

Theo shifted in his seat, trying to get comfortable. He spacebarred.

The test was in fact a series of tests, each one incorporating its own tutorial. At first the tasks were simple: count the number of white circles in a green colour-field; press a key when an animated figure crosses a dotted line; identify the pentagon in a series of hexes. Next came a segment focused on spreadsheet skills. Theo was already adept, an expertise acquired through years of bookkeeping, but even if he had not been the exam might have been okay, since the software explained exactly how to obtain the result it wanted. He looked up from the computer at a clock. About twenty minutes had passed. No one was paying him any attention. The dog-eared corner of Mr. Peanut's poster quivered in the exhalation of Suite 500's ventilated air.

The third and final section of the screening test required the user to study video footage from sporting events. Whereas the earlier segments had relied on text prompts, now the terminal instructed Theo to put on a pair of wireless headphones.

He did, and a woman's voice began speaking: "Processors are interpreters. They interpret between two languages: the language of human life and the language of software. The first of these vocabularies consists of sense data, perceptions, clumsy human judgments. The other is made up of clean, quantitative data. This is our work. Converting what you—the aspirant processor—discern, into what our system—the Model—understands."

The woman's voice was undecorated and almost severe. She did not need to be liked or to spark the listener's interest. She sounded middle-aged, a native speaker; the way she emphasized certain words—*quantitative, discern, the Model*—gave the impression that she completely understood what she was saying, that perhaps she was not even following a script.

She continued, "Here is the first example. A tennis match. Click the mouse whenever either player strikes the ball with their racket."

Theo did this. With every click, a numeral in the corner of the screen increased by one.

"Serves should not be counted the same way as other strikes. Instead, indicate a serve by pressing the *S* key on your keyboard."

Then: "The only events that matter are the events in the match that are designated as significant."

And, "When a player misses the ball, press the spacebar.

"Try to press the keys or click the mouse as soon as possible after the event occurs. The more accurate you are, the better your screening score.

"Good. Continue processing the match until you hear a long, uninterrupted tone."

So Theo learned to process a tennis match. He clicked the mouse button and touched the spacebar and pressed *S*. His hands found the most efficient finger positions without his ever needing to think about them and after a few minutes he found that he was not watching tennis at all, not in the traditional sense: he was watching the two players—it was Nadal, it was Djokovic—without admiring or considering them. All he was seeing was the movement of the ball and the instants when the ball was met or missed, or served.

A tone sounded, long and low, like an engine catching. The video flickered and was replaced with a racetrack. Greyhounds. Theo couldn't remember ever having actually seen a greyhound race. It seemed like a trick, that these lean, eerie mammals should be configured at a starting line and made to compete. "These are greyhounds," offered the voice. The image freeze-framed. "Click once on each greyhound." Theo did. The starting pistol was fired, like an inner tube popping. The greyhounds leapt into life, fervid and absurd. *Dogged*, Theo thought, and then the video paused again. "Click once on each greyhound." Theo did, squinting to make out the blur of their contours against auburn earth. The race resumed. Then another pause, the same instruction, and on and on until the fastest dog nosed across the finish line. Freeze-frame. "Click once on each greyhound. This helps the Model to distinguish the competitors from their environment."

From greyhound races the screen transitioned to basketball, with keys to press for dunks or fouls. "*A* for a *successful* steal, *Z* for an attempted steal." The voice explained what a "steal" meant; the software didn't require a familiarity with the sport or its rules. The rules, in fact, seemed irrelevant: to process a game you didn't need to follow it. Once real life had been processed into events and time-stamps, ones and zeroes, the algorithms could do the rest, deducing the ways these numbers fit together. Perhaps steals presaged losses. Perhaps a greyhound's subtle movements could forecast its future powers. It didn't matter whether the Model *understood* the rules or strategies of basketball, tennis, racing: just *this* is a basket and *this* is a serve and *this* is a purebred nosing over the finish line, and what are the ways that each of these things lays bare what will happen tomorrow?

A long, low tone, like a ship's groan. The basketball game snapped off, leaving the words "Screening complete."

Theo waited for the woman in his headphones to say something. She remained silent. Eventually he got up, removing the headset. It felt strange to do it unbidden. All through Suite 500's broad office, he saw now, processors were processing video. There were screens with dog races and screens with horse races and screens with race cars and soccer players and gymnasts, and in front of them men and women wearing headphones, clicking, watching, waiting, touching *A* or *Z* or *P* or ; if the events demanded it.

"I'm done," he said to the man with the birthmark on his face.

The man looked up. "What?"

"The screening. I'm done."

"Oh." He craned his head around. "You were on number four? Under Mr. Peanut?"

"Yeah." Theo clasped his hands.

"All right," said the man. He pressed some keys. He had kept his headset on and this bothered Theo. Didn't Theo deserve the man's full attention? Was he trying to send him a signal? And then the thought occurred to him: at this very moment, while Theo stood with clasped hands, the receptionist might be in the act of processing *him*, using keystrokes to record *his* actions and reactions, and to predict what might come next. *Press C if the applicant coughs.*

Theo unclasped his hands.

"Okay," said the man, "you scored an 85."

Theo was pleasantly surprised. "That's good, right?"

"It's out of 130." The man noticed Theo's disappointment and added, "But it's not bad. It's within the bounds of tolerance." He consulted a chart. "If you can start today, I'll put you under Mr. Matisse."

Theo assumed he was referring to another poster on the wall, a print of *Goldfish* or *The Dance*. But after his silence was taken for assent the man picked up a telephone receiver and enunciated into it, "Mr. Matisse? I have that processor for you."

He saw Theo staring.

"Fifteen dollars an hour," the receptionist whispered, "excluding lunch."

:::

Mr. Matisse turned out to be a reedy man in slacks and a button-up shirt, with a grand pile of corkscrewing hair. He was young, with the tanned/clammy mien of an elite postgraduate student. He seemed thrilled to encounter Theo. "A rat for the maze!" he exclaimed. "Just kidding. It's more of an analytical warren. A series of caverns. You learn your way around. Come this way. A maze is by its nature confusing, no? Or else it ceases to be a maze. A labyrinth must be labyrinthine. Yes? No? Perhaps I'm wrong. Something to think about. Don't step in the recycling bin."

As Matisse conducted him through the rows of terminals, Theo began to distinguish a mild shabbiness to the office, the sense of a place that was installed in top condition and then neglected. Chair wheels whined, partition walls were frayed, screens hunched on their mounts. A couple of nineteen- or twenty-year-olds sat murmuring at a conference table, huddled over what looked like a phone book. They didn't look up as the others passed by. Matisse halted at an unkempt desk. He motioned for Theo to sit.

"Your throne," Matisse said.

Theo hesitated; he had assumed this was Matisse's workstation.

"Do you have a name?" Matisse asked. "Or do you prefer to make one up?"

"Theo."

"Pleasure. I'm Roberto. I go by 'Matisse.' It's my surname. I do appreciate Matisse's canvases but the moniker is honestly earned, not an affectation. May I join?"

"Sure?" Theo said, confused.

"Thank you. I will fetch my chair."

Theo lowered himself into the voluptuous, translucent chair. He would call the store at lunch, he decided, and get Esther to take care of his chores. For now he surveyed the workstation. A computer, headset, keyboard, mouse. A pad of foolscap and a dull orange pencil. Rummaging through the desk he found a few more pencils, pens, a half-erased eraser in the shape of a raspberry. The drawer at his knee concealed empty Kit-Kat wrappers and an over-saturated photograph of a man and a woman. It appeared to be, but was not necessarily, the sample photograph that comes with a frame. A solitary one-panel comic had been thumbtacked to the partition on his right: an anthropomorphized key having a conversation with an anthropomorphized lock, asking, "You busy Friday?"

Finally Matisse returned with his own voluptuous, translucent chair. He threw himself down on it. Men and women all around them continued working without looking up from their monitors—horse races mostly, baseball, soccer, someone processing what appeared to be synchronized swimming.

"To be perfectly candid, I wasn't expecting you," Matisse said. "Dolores said it would take at least a week for me to be assigned any processors. 'You can't rush incoming,' she said. But lo and behold, fifteen hours later, here you are. Hello and welcome. How are you liking it so far? Of course you don't even know the story! The fact is: you are my very first processor. The first! Hello! Welcome!

Believe me, I'm as nervous as you are. Most likely even *more* nervous. Why should you be nervous? You shouldn't be nervous! Processing is passive, procedural. It does not require independent thinking. At least it shouldn't! If you're thinking independently, you're doing it wrong. 'We can't have the processors getting creative.' Isn't that the case in so many industries? Isn't that a late-capitalist status quo? 'Ask the bricklayers! Ask the—' Oh, haha, that's pretty good."

He was looking at the comic with the lock and key. "Is that yours? Yes, well, it's yours now! Right? I tell you: in a perverse way, it's nice to be back at the ole 500. I spent the past four months auditing the Dublin systems. Half of that chez Dolores, mind you, but two full months on the Emerald Isle. Something weird in their greyhound spread. But we found it. It just takes patience. 'Doctor, we need some patients!' Sometimes I postulate that this is the most important criterion for this job. The capability to sit with a problem. To roost until it hatches. As Jackson Pollock once said, 'The truth will never divulge itself but the falsehoods will.' For a little while I encouraged the other specialists to call me Pollock, until one of the code guys took it for a reference to fake crab. I suppose Matisse makes more sense. It is, after all, my name. But sheesh: his paintings are so easy to adore. I would prefer an artist whose work was more abstruse. Those are the greatest, are they not? When the story's a little harder to work out? Defer narrative and representation: devise a work that functions at the level of apprehension. A chasm, a mirror, a burning bush. If there's any logic it should be the logic of dream. Tea?"

It took Theo a few beats to recognize that this was a genuine question. He knew this type from comedy clubs. He was okay with it. "No, I'm good," he said.

Matisse yanked a courier bag from the back of his chair. "I keep a thermos," he explained. "It's green. The tea, not the thermos. Haha. I discovered this tea in Hong Kong last year. Have you ever been? The Rabbit always puts us up at the Palace of All Workers' Aspirations. It's a fancy hotel—goose-feather pillows, chrysanthemums in vases, a Rodin in the lobby—but the tea at the bar's like bathwater. I think it's deliberate, to compel the tourist class out of the hotel, into the streets. Down the hill you find one of the city's oldest tea markets, rows of stalls with baskets and bags and barrels of teas, popcorn *genmaicha* and black *keemun*, twisted saffron bundles, emperor's buds, orange-blossom and Fujian white and the *cagada*-like pellets of divine, aromatic oolong. A paradise. And scales everywhere—if you have an interest in scales, as I do, you could wander the tea market just for that, a history of weight and measures, perfect little instruments, some that collapse like Swiss army knives to hide in a tea-seller's coat. So you go from tea stall to tea stall, drawing deep breaths, inhalations not aspirations—am I boring you? It's not necessarily that I talk a lot but when I'm interested in a subject I try to exhume it totally. The other side is that when I am working I find I plunge myself into the material. I *dive*, you understand? Captain Nemo, Jacques Cousteau. Did he actually climb into the submarine or did he stay in the boat? No, of course Cousteau went in the submarine. I've seen the films. YouTube. It's not my fault. I'm a millennial. I appreciate the term because it assigns me an era, situates me in time. Pliocene, Neolithic, Post-Impressionist. I fit within a taxonomy. What about you? No? Were you born before 1980?"

"1981," Theo said.

"Ah, *near*-millennial," Matisse declared. "Cusp. Picasso in his Blue Period. Blogs? Yes. Emojis? No. How many fingers do you use to type?"

"Listen," Theo said, "are we supposed to be working together?"

"Oh, sure," said Matisse. "Sure we are."

And so it unfolded. Roberto Matisse recounted and digressed. Roberto Matisse showed Theo the ropes. Over the coming days, the Rabbit's newest recruit learned the why, how, whither of this role. He watched tape and processed it. He clicked and counted, weathered Matisse's soliloquies. Whereas most of the Rabbit's processors worked in isolation, obeying the instructions that came from their headsets, Theo had a real live boss. Experimental research, skunkworks; Matisse was on a mission and Theo was his subordinate. He processed what Matisse told him to process, using schemas that Matisse had designed, investigating the inklings that Matisse had dreamed up, months prior, before Dolores sent him over.

"Who's Dolores?" Theo asked, after the umpteenth mention.

Matisse began to laugh. "The Dolores is a place, my man. It is headquarters, the Dolores Building, the edifice in which everything of import occurs."

Even from Simone's description, Theo hadn't expected the organization—the association—to be so vast. Matisse's job title was "specialist," way up the org chart from the processors, but he still seemed a long way from leadership. The group's upper echelons—attorneys, data scientists, software engineers—worked at the Dolores and other offices off-site, far from the processors' suite. The scale was bewildering, as was the Rabbit's Foot's tone: studiously legal, meticulously bold. It earned its revenues by placing winning bets, in bulk—thousands a day—with bookmakers across the world. Not a single one of these bets was placed by a human being. Every decision was made by an immense and complicated computer program, a network of predictive algorithms, housed on an encrypted server. "The Model," said Matisse. "She's the prettiest woman on the catwalk."

The Model decided what bets to place—which horses or greyhounds or one-hundred-metre dashers to back. The Model decided how much to bet and when to take a pass. Assembled line by line, module by module, over years, it was the association's crown jewel and its hidden advantage, the source of all its edge. The Model knew that right-handed pitchers were more likely to strike out left-handed batters. It knew that teams that won a lot were more likely to win in the future. It knew the age at which tennis players, or thoroughbreds, begin to fall off. It learned these principles, and unimaginably more complex ones, by parsing the data, running the numbers. The Model also *contained* the numbers, all of them, in a gargantuan codex of sporting statistics. The bulk of these statistics came from proprietary sources: on-base percentages and home run rates from official MLB databases, racing records from bookmakers, prospect rankings published in the trades. The next data set came from processors: workers reviewing video, tallying whatever they were told. They also helped the Model to learn to help itself: training the software to see the things they saw. Therefore Theo at his terminal, distinguishing greyhounds from the dirt.

Most of Suite 500's processors had been repeating the same tasks for months. Perhaps the Model had uncovered that the length of a basketball player's stride had a bearing on the odds of his team winning their game. A processor would be assigned to watch the matches, pausing and playing, clicking footfall to footfall, repeating the same operations every day, or most days, for weeks on end. Piece by minuscule piece, the Model gained confidence in what was likely to happen. It calculated odds for every wagerable event and whenever these odds exceeded the bookies'—even by a small amount—the Rabbit's Foot's software automatically placed a bet. Volume mattered most: a coin-flip you can predict even 50.1 percent of the time, over thousands and thousands of tosses, across millions and millions of dollars, turns pocket change into fortunes.

"Here's the trick," said Matisse one lunch break. "Win more than you lose."

Matisse's big idea was weather. Employees of the Rabbit's Foot were always trying to find new sources of edge: it was the way to earn standing and to get a big payday. If one of your findings was incorporated into the Model, you'd receive a proportion of the corresponding winnings.

"You mean me, too?" Theo asked.

"Processors don't count," said Matisse. He gestured out at the glassy-eyed workers. "You're the cannon fodder. To cash in, you need to have come up with the idea. Most of the time it's a linkage we hadn't noticed yet, something hiding in our statistics. Maybe certain soccer clubs should avoid taking corner kicks. Or teams play better when they're wearing red uniforms."

The other approach was to find something useful that nobody was counting. "There is a literal infinity of attributes to observe in the world." Matisse was twirling cold soba salad around a plastic fork, shedding peas and cranberries and shards of tempeh. "So how do we know which ones to record? The knife, the fork, the lunch? The number of calories? Of bites? Of colours in the bowl? It's an act of discernment, curation. The painter and his subject, choosing colours from a palette. The scientist and her hypothesis. One choice among an infinity of choices—just so for the gambler trying to ascertain what's significant."

Theo said, "So you thought to yourself, 'Weather!'"

"I thought to myself, 'Weather!' and I convinced Mitsou to let me give it a shot."

Theo paused in his banana-peeling. "Mitsou?"

Matisse pitched his fork into the garbage. "Mitsou San Marziale," he said. "Mistress of the Model, queen of the gamblers, Our Lady of the Numbers."

Simone's sister. From Mitsou's office on the Dolores Building's thirty-sixth floor, she oversaw the association's wins and its losses, the division and multiplication of stakes. She had made her first fortune predicting two of the Final Four in the 2004 NCAA basketball tournament, using a computer system that grew up into the Model. "She was a one-woman Computer Group, an ingénue Ranogajec," Matisse insufficiently explained. "They say she grew up fiddling with Markov chains, stochastic calculus. Romping Bayesian and non. Dogged. Self-taught. Everyone was like: 'Holy shit!'"

After years of loyal service, Matisse had won the Lady's permission to pursue his interest in the impact of weather on sporting events. No more missions to Dublin or Hong Kong, no more all-nighters scraping Olympics data or squishing the bugs in the Model's rugby sevens code: Mitsou had allocated him a single junior processor and three months to ascertain whether heat waves and rain clouds could be baked (or soaked) into the Rabbit's predictions. Did weather nudge gaming outcomes? Could it help predict them? "We're sprinting through as many meteorologies as we can," Matisse said.

Theo's main job was logging the weather conditions on archival sports tape. Every morning he biked away from Provisions K, sat at his computer (headphones on), and turned his attention to mud on racetracks and sunshowers on baseball diamonds and the rare, semi-apocalyptic hailstorm on a soccer pitch. Sometimes the apposite question was whether an arena roof was open or closed—skimming a broadcast for overhead angles. For two days he watched tennis. For three he weathered NASCAR. Then he spent an interminable week of fact-checking international weather databases, evaluating the accuracy of their hourly local temperatures. A chime would bell in his right ear, followed by a message superimposed over some field of uniformed athletes. *Dataset states "VERY HOT." Press [Y] if appears correct, [N] if erroneous.* He'd watch until he witnessed a nonaerobic rivulet of perspiration, a player removing his cap and shaking his head at the sky. Then he'd press *Y*, and the game would change to another, with a new chime and a fresh inquiry. *Dataset states "AVERAGE COOL." Press [Y] if correct, [N] if erroneous.*

"Average cool," Theo murmured to himself.

After work he'd cycle back to the store, folding unannounced into the fray. He'd check that the specials were restocked and the pushcarts squared away. He'd touch base with the fish-boys and the section managers, Esther and Mo, and the white-coated curators of the cheese pit. He'd speak with Mireille, if she was around, though usually she wasn't. He avoided the basement, his mother's untidied desk. Bit by bit, day by day, as Theo made his presence in Provisions K less critical, the store's lieutenants took over.

I'm chasing a bigger return, he told himself. Never mind the hastiness of his career-change, its worrying resemblance to a midlife crisis. Never mind that this gambit didn't seem sensible—an international gambling ring, $15 an hour. Of course it didn't seem sensible: the best bets rarely do. But looks can be deceiving, as most successful gamblers know. There's no reason to put it all on red except, intriguingly, that there's a chance to win.

:::

Theo was standing at an overlook when his phone rang. It was a Sunday morning and he had decided to bike up the mountain, a half hour each way, taking advantage of cool air and honeyed light. It would be hot later. Now, looking out over the city, he felt sweaty, satisfied, a fully functioning human being. His bicycle was leaning against a guardrail and the scrubby bushes behind it were studded with berries. Luscious or poisonous he wondered, luscious or poisonous, luscious or poisonous.

His phone rang; some convoluted number. He answered.

"Hello?"

"Theo?" said Lou.

He forgot at once the berries, the bushes, the sky, the view, the polished disarray of his hometown. "Lou?" he said into the phone.

"Yes, hi."

"I can't believe it. Are you okay?"

"I'm fine. I'm still here."

"Where?"

"Morocco."

"The retreat."

"The retreat," she agreed.

"I thought there weren't any phones."

"There's one, a landline at the campus. For emergencies."

"Is this an emergency?"

"Not like that. I wanted to talk to you. It's good to hear your voice."

"It's good to hear yours," he said.

"You sound okay. You sound well. I thought about calling when your letter . . . I'm so sorry about your mom."

"Thank you. Yeah, I'm okay."

"Are you at the store?"

He moved his phone to the other hand. "I'm on the mountain. It's the weekend. I mean, I have a new job—did you get my letter?"

"I don't think so. I don't remember anything about a new job."

"I'm doing forecasting," he said. He tried to describe the Rabbit's Foot, calling it a lucky break, a lucrative opportunity. He did not tell her about the commute, the cubicles. He told her it drew upon his untapped skills. Theo had been talking for some time when he registered that she was not saying much herself. It was not like her.

"Lou," he said.

"Yeah?" she said.

"What is it?"

She didn't reply at first.

She said, "I'm extending my stay."

"You're not coming home?"

"Not yet," she said, in the same cautious tone. "Maybe at the end of the summer."

"'Maybe'?"

"This is a lot, Theo."

"I know," he said, though he didn't really know.

"Will you keep sending me letters?" she said. "I read them all."

It was only after they hung up that he considered whether Lou sounded different than she had before she left. Whether she sounded sad or happier, or more equivocally changed. Had there been someone else in the room? He found he could not remember precisely the way she used to sound, before she went away, when they had walked by the tracks or lain together in her bed.

CHAPTER SEVEN

Theo's first visit to the Dolores Building took place at the beginning of his second month. The new job had already begun to feel routine, even with Matisse's trail mix of digressions. The work itself had little to recommend it. What sustained him was a sense of prospects, potential. His future wouldn't always be tied to Matisse's.

"Theo Potiris," he'd tell himself, "you are more than you seem."

And so he took considerable interest when Matisse invited him along to headquarters. Although Matisse could tap into the Model from his desktop terminal, it wasn't possible to upload files. Just as Matisse's computer required at once a twelve-digit password and a real, brass key (with Rodin's *Thinker* on its chain), the Rabbit's fresh code had to come to the Dolores in person. "Our adversaries are everywhere," Matisse claimed, "waiting in the shadows."

Theo lifted his eyebrows. "'Adversaries'?"

"Competitors," he replied. "Cheaters. Jockeys of Trojan horses. Poachers of code. What the Vegas bookies wouldn't give for a little slice of our cake." He saw Theo's expression. "Don't get any ideas."

Besides, Matisse missed the Dolores and he was eager to show it off. Which was how they found themselves in a taxi headed downtown. The driver had constructed a diorama on his dashboard, above the vents and dials and the ticking, glowing taxi meter. Felted jungle, plastic trees, a cellophane koi pond fluttering with the turns. Matisse gave directions—left here, right there—sending the car on a roundabout route. "Never mind the exact address," he said. "It's the black-and-white one, like a six-sided die." Theo was surprised to discover that he already knew the building. As they took a last corner, the Dolores rose like a pale column. Its tinted windows evoked the dots of a Dalmatian—drawn white blinds, bare black panes. He had passed it countless times, never knowing its name, never remarking the way it stood apart from the rest of the skyscrapers. Whereas its neighbours were dull grey concrete or glossy green glass, the Dolores was its own majestic thing.

High above their heads, birds still billowed between the city's buildings. Others squatted on the asphalt or pecked at sidewalk crumbs, tufted and cooing. Several species were familiar or -ish—gulls, pigeons, Canada geese—but others had been carried here from somewhere tropical. The cab driver wove between the landed birds, cursing; when the car came to a stop, Theo stepped out onto a splash of radiant birdshit. He followed Matisse through a revolving door and into the building's grand lobby, ash-white marble etched with veins of black feldspar, fool's gold. They showed their hologrammed passes at reception and joined a crowd at the elevators. Every time the doors parted on the way up, Theo caught a glimpse of a different reality. Rows of glassed-off computer servers on floors four and six; men yelling into phones on nine; a wood-panelled feel on floor thirteen, its entrance marked "Elections." Each department was identified on the wall opposite its elevator bay. A stencilled logo in fine white paint, cloudlike on powder-blue: a woman's forearm and hand, outstretched, letting something go, reaching or revealing. "The Rabbit's Foot" was inscribed in slender cursive, along with "Accounting" or "Failsafes" or "Legal" or, on floor sixteen, the Olympics' five intertwined rings. Many of the floors were sparsely populated and overall the skyscraper seemed a luxury, with much more space than the Rabbit needed.

"Is Mitsou around?" Theo whispered.

"Top floor," replied Matisse. "The penthouse. Thirty-six."

Being near Mitsou made him remember Simone. Despite what she had implied about her relationship with her sister, Theo kept imagining her through the elevator's open doors—a figure in the distance, down a hallway, inclining towards a water cooler. Or sauntering towards him, heedless, something in her hands.

On the nineteenth floor, Matisse and Theo got off the elevator and proceeded through a network of offices and cubicles, potted bonsai. "*That's* the guy who came up with expected possession value," Matisse hissed, pointing at a man at a computer. "*That's* Matt Fenwick. *That's* the lady who handled passing metrics for FC Barcelona." Eggheads, prodigies, superstars of sports analytics; to Theo they were just middle-aged drones with so-so posture. Finally Matisse presented the USB key to a woman at a desk with three computers. "*Grazie*," she said.

"*Prego*," he replied.

Theo said nothing, only smiled like a man who has brought you a plate of tiramisu.

Back in the elevator, behind its closing doors, Theo hesitated at the controls. His index finger was hovering above the topmost button: 36, rimmed in light.

So many people making bets, all around the world, and someone's making a mint.

Matisse pushed *G*.

:::

That night, after Theo arrived at the front door of his apartment, he turned. He didn't know what made him turn. A subtle fragrance, a shadow, a draft.

He gazed along the corridor. Dimly lit and silent, like a movie theatre after the day's final screening.

His mother's door was ajar.

The only sound was of cars outside, beyond the walls.

Theo went over to the door, and touched it with the tips of two fingers. The gap was wide enough for a cat, for a hopping red robin.

He slipped off his shoes before padding inside. An old habit.

Change on a dish just inside Minnie's door. A vase of dry pussy-willows, tall as children. Theo stuck his balled-up hands in his jacket pockets, ready or nervous or simply taking care. There was a lamp on in the living room. He continued past Minerva's umbrella stand, her framed poster from the Degas exhibition. He knew the ballerina's expression by heart.

A cardboard box sat on the carpet, full of milk glass Minnie had purchased at a garage sale. No one had ever put it away. "Hello?" Theo called.

His brother-in-law stood by the window. Eric was wearing slippers, a sweatshirt for Algeria's national soccer team. A steaming mug of tea rested on the dining table beside him.

"Theo."

"Doing some stargazing?"

"I'm just . . ." Eric shook his head. "I don't know."

"I get it," Theo said.

Eric glanced away. "Mireille said something the other day. How grief doesn't make sense at a distance. You can't read it or understand it. Grief's wordless. What's there to say? To talk about? 'I feel this way,' that's all."

"'Suddenly I feel this way.'"

"Suddenly I feel this way." Eric picked up his cup, sipped. "It goes away and then it comes back. Like a stray dog."

Like birds, Theo thought. *Like seasons.*

He found he was looking at the black-and-yellow urn on Minerva's mantel, the one with his father's ashes.

"We haven't seen you in a while," Eric said.

"I heard you were in the Galapagos."

"We got back a week ago."

"Gambolling with turtles?"

Eric smiled. "Tortoises. Hanna wanted to buy one."

"Did she?"

"Almost," said Eric. He sat down in one of Minnie's big uphol-stered chairs. "Next time we should all go."

Theo lowered himself onto the ottoman. "Groceries don't stop," he said.

"Esther can take care of things. Anyway, what about you? Where have you been?"

"I got a desk job."

Eric made a face. "That doesn't sound like you."

"I'm a new man. Spreadsheets, algorithms, popcorn in the break room."

"Where?"

"Forecasting," Theo said.

Eric set down his mug. "What does that mean?"

"Seeing into the future." Theo hoped this would seem tantalizing, mysterious, but out loud it sounded childish. "Estimating what will happen."

"For some company?"

"Basically," Theo said.

"Grocery trends?"

"Sports."

"You don't know anything about sports."

"Correct."

Eric leaned his head back on the cushion. "Well, that explains why we haven't seen you."

"I check in."

Eric closed his eyes, opened them. "We've decided we want to move."

Theo stared at Eric, as if daring him to close his eyes again. "Move what?" he said carefully.

"The store. Find a new location, take out a mortgage, move."

"What about the old store?"

"Sell the building. Or lease it."

Theo swallowed. "Close the store."

"*Move* it. Find somewhere with more space. More flexibility. Up to date, sustainable. Where it can last."

Theo laughed. "Last?"

"It's your call, not mine. And Mireille and Peter's. But the three of us have talked a lot. The state Provisions is in now, it's hard to imagine passing it on."

"Passing it on?" said Theo.

"If Blake or Maurice—"

"Or Hanna."

Eric shook his head. "Hanna's not going to be a grocer."

"She might."

"We've been talking to Amir Homayoun," Eric said. "He's closing the carpet store. That whole space is up for grabs."

"When were you going to tell me?"

"Mireille's been trying to get ahold of you. You're never here."

"She could call."

"You don't pick up the phone."

"Maybe *I* want to run the store. Keep it exactly as it is, keep it going, until I have a heart attack in the potato aisle."

Eric looked at him. "Well, do you?"

Theo hesitated. He felt like a counterfeiter who has taken out a twenty-dollar bill and can't remember if it's the real one or the copy.

"I guess it depends on the forecasting business," Eric said.

"Yes," Theo said. He tried to imagine Provisions K unmade and remade somewhere else. Clean and resplendent, organized, highly profitable. He looked at the mantel mirror and the artifacts arrayed beneath it. Ancient Roman coins, a ceramic Nefertiti, baby photos of Minerva's grandchildren. A matchbox-sized Parthenon, from a holiday in Athens. The bee-bedazzled urn.

After a moment Theo said, "Do you remember what Minnie kept saying after Pop died?"

Eric smiled. "'A taco truck?! A stupid taco truck!?'"

"Ha, that too. We should have had T-shirts made."

"'Life is so short.'"

"Life is so short," Theo agreed. "And she'd say it with *so much* force. *'Life is so short!'*—like a complaint. Or at least I heard it that way. But now I understand it was advice, or a warning. Life is short, carpe diem. If you don't seize them, the days could get away."

"They're already getting away," muttered Eric. "The days are flying by."

Theo sank his toes into the rug. So many hours spent in this room. So many pots of tea, plates of cookies, birthday parties. He remembered the walls overlaid with decoration—banners, streamers, plump balloons. Wrapping paper ruffled on the floor. None of it left now, not even a trace of the sparklers' smoke.

"Do whatever you want with the store," Theo said. "I'll go along with whatever the rest of you decide."

:::

When Theo left the apartment, Hanna was standing in the hallway. She had her arms crossed, elbows clasped like a country pastor.

"What are you doing?" she asked.

"Shouldn't you be in bed?"

She yawned. "I'm going to buy a turntable for playing records."

"Right now?"

"Tomorrow. For records, not CDs."

"Do you own any records, Hanna?"

Theo wasn't sure whether his niece was considering the question or contemplating her reply.

"I will buy some once I have the turntable," she said.

"Oh, okay."

She remained there, standing like a witness as he went to his front door.

"People miss you," she said.

"'People'?"

"Downstairs."

"Our customers do? The staff?" He pushed his key into the lock, felt its pins crisply catch. "There's more to life than people missing you," he said. As he pushed the door, he tried to smile at her, briefly, the way you'd give someone a blossom you picked impulsively from a garden. He reached for the light switch, thinking: Life is a contest between connection and detachment. Thinking: We spend a great deal of time binding ourselves to other people, in practice or in concept, hand in hand or across whole oceans. And we also spend time stepping back, breaking free. Some people favour connection while others favour independence; or one could say, some favour love + dependency and others, freedom + loneliness. Perhaps all of life's decisions are just versions of these calculations.

This is what he thought.

When he turned to shut the door, Hanna had gone.

:::

As summer inched closer, Matisse's research converged on sports that were (A) played outside; and (B) required players to stand for long periods in open air. For the moment, his exclusive focus was sunshine. "It's not that a wet pitch or a muddy golf course doesn't have an effect, but that effect doesn't usually favour one side," he said. "Nobody works on their rain game. But the sun! The heat! Some players *are* more accustomed to its rays. Some players weather the weather a little better."

Baseball, soccer and cricket each called for players to remain in the open, unsheltered, for withering stretches. Particular players, and

players from particular places, seemed impervious to high temperatures. Others plainly suffered—the data showed it even if their faces
didn't, with evidence of deteriorated play. By taking into account the
players on the pitch and the sun above their heads, the Model could
improve that little bit at predicting the outcome of a match.

When the data backed up the hypothesis, Matisse was exultant.
"Hello, sunshine!" Matisse shouted at his screen. "I knew you were up
to something!"

He still needed to hammer out the kinks, fine-tuning their algorithms with thousands of simulations. He'd gesticulate at a graph,
some crooked parabola. "Look!" he instructed Theo, though Theo
didn't understand whether what he was looking at was good news or
bad. Usually it was good. If all went well, the weather module would
be tested by the wonks at the Dolores and eventually integrated into
the Model's byzantine math. "And that's a grand slam," said Matisse.
"That's a hat trick."

Theo grinned. "And then we retire to Malibu?"

"Then we keep going," said Matisse. "We do another thing."

In anticipation of this next phase, Theo had begun processing a
new set of data—golf games, marathons, sports that weren't as obviously affected by weather but where heat and sunshine might likewise
privilege certain competitors. Leaning back in his chair, as the processors to either side of him processed goal-kick after goal-kick, Theo
watched a golfer tee off towards a Barbadian green. *Dataset states
"AVERAGE WARM." Press [Y] if correct, [N] if erroneous.*

Early the next morning he visited Homayoun Carpets. He had
cycled past it a million times. With a peaked granite portico and
Corinthian columns, the store resembled a ritzy mausoleum. Amir and
his family had expanded the showroom over a period of decades, taking

over storefronts, raising the ceilings. Their walls had held carpets with red Afghan roses, Tuareg eagles, fractal patterns from the souks. It was all gone, now. "They're moving to Miami," Eric had explained. Theo surveyed the store's empty windows, the sun-bleached outlines of departed stock. It was strange to imagine these carpets in people's homes now, on floors across the city. Left behind were vacant white rooms and abandoned chandeliers and, according to Eric, ample ready cellars, a relic of a bootlegging operation in the 1920s.

What would happen to the old place? Theo wondered. "Six months to transition, then we move out," Eric had said. Theo detected the influence of his older brother in Eric's phrasing. A tea importer was apparently interested in the space. "David something," Eric said. A few scruffy millionaires had proposed opening a "start-up incubator," whatever that meant. A Pennsylvania poké impresario wanted to expand his empire. Why not all three? Theo thought. Let them do it all, tea and apps and Pittsburgh's best poké in the building where his mother died.

"Don't worry," Eric had said. "We'll keep the apartments."

Theo got back on his bike.

He had been dispatched to the Dolores, this time solo, with new information on how the Model should incorporate weather data into its baseball, soccer and cricket bets. Matisse hadn't wanted to go. "I hate being a tourist," he finally admitted, and sent Theo with a USB shaped like the figure from Edvard Munch's *The Scream*. Users had to plug in the screamer's head.

The USB required a password and the password stayed with Matisse. "Not that I don't trust you, but I don't trust you," he said. Theo thought about that as he cycled down among the skyscrapers, through squalls of swallows. His work with Matisse was not a partnership: only one of them would earn a commission if the idea panned out, or lose it all if their code was stolen.

The Dolores Building was puzzlingly short on bicycle parking. Theo circled the block, searching for an unoccupied stand or meter or even telephone pole. Near the building's southeast corner he glided past a square of elevated pavement on which sat six stationary motorcycles. They were evenly spaced, like permanent paying residents, regulars. A sturdy, futuristic BMW F800GS; a rearing KTM Super Duke; a 2009 Ducati Sport, crimson and lunging; a custom black Norton, the word "seldom" on its flank—Theo froze at the sight. He stood astride his bike, staring for a full minute. Finally he wedged his Peugeot twelve-speed beside Simone's '74 Commando, locking his bicycle to itself. He considered for a moment and then removed his helmet, threading its straps around the lock, closing the buckle.

Inside the building he again passed his ID to the sentinel at reception.

"Floor thirty-three," said the guard. "QA."

As Theo turned to go, lifting his hand from the counter, he found he had cut the end of his finger on its cleft marble edge. A gemlike blood drop gleamed.

He wiped his hand against his jeans. A little shaken, he followed a pack of workers into an elevator. It leapt upward, plasma in a vein. From *G* to three to nineteen, and to thirty-two, where most of the occupants disembarked. Theo realized only then that he had not selected his floor; only two of them were left in the elevator, Theo and a woman. His eyes lit upon the control panel, where a single button was illuminated. It was dimly pink, the pink of light through rose quartz. A glowing 36, the stand-alone penthouse floor, Dolores's very summit.

Theo swivelled to stare at the woman. She was already considering him. Meeting Mitsou made Theo remember vividly Simone's half-darkened features. Her older sister had the same broad face but in smaller proportions, lines at the eyes, a neat ponytail of mostly grey hair. She wore a powder-blue shirt under a fitted navy coat, all sharp corners. A necklace of green jewels. She was heavier than her sister, pretty yet also severe, proud. All of this he took in in seconds, yet it was still too long to look, and Mitsou's gaze had sharpened with every moment.

"Yes?" she said.

"Nothing," he said helplessly.

But the elevator had arrived at the thirty-sixth floor, and its doors moved aside to reveal a disorienting grey view. It was hard to understand what he was looking at. A blank wall? Open space? No: a colourless colour-field of sky through a window, a measureless expanse like unexposed film.

"Sorry," he said. "I forgot to choose my floor."

"I can see that. Who are you?"

Theo swallowed. "Theo Potiris. I work at Suite 500."

She gave no response.

"With Roberto Matisse."

Mitsou eyed him. "You're a processor."

"Yes."

"You don't work *with* Roberto, then. You work *for* him."

The doors began to close and Mitsou's arm snapped out to block them. "How is that project?" she said.

Something was nagging at him, hearing Mitsou's voice. At last it came to him—she had recorded the voice-over for the automated processing exam.

He tried to smile. "I've got the preliminary, uh, stuff, here . . ." He fumbled the screaming USB from his pocket. "I'm delivering it to—" he furrowed his brow—"thirty-three. QA."

"Fine," she said. She paused at the threshold of the elevator. He felt fixed in place by her gaze. "Tell Roberto he should be delivering any data himself."

Theo lowered his head.

Again the doors began to close; this time he was the one to stop them. "I know your sister!" he said, a little feebly.

She turned.

"Simone," he said.

A smile shimmered across her lips.

The elevator had begun to complain, making a sound like an inconvenienced metal-detector. Mitsou began to walk away. He tried again: "I'd love to become more involved with the company."

"It's not a company," she shot back.

"With your association."

She faced him again. "The system's simple here. If you'd like to receive a piece of the action, you need to contribute a new idea. Do you have any new ideas?"

In the window behind her, a seagull had suddenly swung into view. It seemed as if it was being hoisted up and down on a string.

After a moment he said, "I know a lot about groceries."

She pursed her lips. She was one beat away from losing interest.

"Wait," Theo said. "You could bet on them, right? On supply and demand?" Mitsou's face showed no sign and Theo hurtled on. "Prices go up or down, obviously. It's a market. But if you can work out which items will cost more next month, and which ones will cost less . . . That's money, right? That's edge? You can predict demand based on time of year. Or weather! Or fads. Chia seeds, kale, *blah blah blah*, right?" Mitsou seemed like the kind of person who would spurn the idea of superfoods. "You can see what's going to happen before it happens, you can make bets accordingly, you can—I can—"

"Groceries," she said gently.

"Yes."

"A wager, for instance, on the value of chocolate before Christmas?"

"Yes," he agreed, gratefully.

"Or on South American pineapples."

"Yes."

"Or pork bellies."

"Yes."

"Mr. Potiris," said Mitsou, "I am not a day trader. I am not a speculator playing the financial market. I am not even a grocer." She knocked on the elevator door. "All I am is a gambler who prefers not to lose."

Theo didn't have a comeback. He tried to hold her gaze. As the elevator doors began to close the seagull still floated there, like a wraith.

Theo did eventually make it to floor thirty-three, where he presented the drive to a man at QA. He tried to avoid looking at the USB stick's shrieking face. Then he plunged down through the skyscraper's central elevator shaft, shivering in the air-conditioning. Finally he was back outside, where it was raining so softly it was almost imperceptible. Theo felt a little nauseous. He took out his phone. The screen shone waxenly at him. No messages, no calls.

He walked round the building to the place where he had locked his bicycle. The motorcycles were still there—the black KTM, the '74

Norton that said "seldom." Now that he had found it, Simone's bike seemed to hold a power. It was a clue, a lead. She was here somewhere.

Theo sat down on the curb, a small distance away. *I won't wait very long,* he told himself. *Just in case. Just to see.* He stared at the stand of machines. Before too long a peacock ambled close, one of the downtown's exotic visitors. It was on tiptoes, pecking at crumbs near Theo's feet, iridescent tailfeathers furled and low. It gleamed. "Hiya," Theo murmured.

Then Sebald appeared. Theo suppressed the impulse to spring to his feet. He was astonished to see Simone's friend, but then why was he so astonished? The man's motorcycle was sitting right there, a few steps from the Norton. Theo almost said something. He almost waved. But already Sebald was lowering his helmet visor and already his bike had come alive—snarling engine, shining headlight. And something else had stopped Theo too: Sebald's humourless expression. His grim gaze.

As the motorcycle roared, the peacock fluttered away.

Theo watched them go.

He had seen where Sebald came from. It was not the Dolores Building.

The sign read, LE BLACK CAT. A short awning over sunflowers, rows of terracotta flowerpots, white plastic birdcages tied together in groups of two or four, up and down the wall, like parcels of ghosts. The smoked-glass windows were covered with vintage posters, faded ads for concrete, birdseed, snow-blowers, decades-old photographs of grinning families, foremen with hard hats and crossed arms. The door was at ground level but the business extended into a half basement. Peering through lower panes, Theo could see narrow aisles, rows of shelves spilling over with tools, rope, electricians' supplies.

According to its ageless, hand-painted sign, Le Black Cat was a
"Hardware Store/Diner." "Hamburgers, pizzaghetti, poutine, beer,"
bragged the crooked letters. Theo could not at first see any evidence
of food, let alone the illegitimate progeny of pizza and spaghetti;
finally, crouching with his hands around his eyes, he glimpsed a
couple of tables wedged among the shelves, jammed beside masses of
plywood panels, coils of copper tubing. They carried lustrous ketchup
bottles, napkin dispensers, plastic cups full of cutlery. Sitting at one
of these tables, with her back to the window, was Simone.

Theo got up from his crouch. Having actually discovered her, he
felt a little like a creep. The nausea he felt earlier had transitioned into
something more slippery and grinding. He walked away from Le
Black Cat, towards his bicycle. He unfastened the U-lock, pausing
only when he realized that his helmet was missing. It wasn't on the
ground. It wasn't beside any of the motorcycles. It had disappeared.
Theo felt a bizarre concern for it, as if the helmet were a lost child, a
lonely friend. He squinted through the downtown's different dark-
nesses and lights. This was the moment when he was approached by
a man in an overcoat.

Selected Correspondence 2

Dear Lou,

So I got arrested.

You thought I was respectable.

In fact I am lawless. Ungovernable and wild.

I was at work. Not at the office, which I've described to you, but at company HQ, rubbing shoulders with the upper crust. A month and a half on the job and I'm already on the move. Soon I'll be statistician-in-chief. They'll call me "the Grocer."

The meeting was over. I was about to head back north. As I was collecting my bike, a policeman emerged from the shadows like some beckoned spectre. A tall guy in a camel overcoat, a real Colombo type. Colombo? Columbo? Not Sri Lanka, Peter Falk. The downtown's dark blues, then a man at my elbow, saying, "Je vous en prie."

When I replied in English he switched to that. He had coiffed black hair and a pencil moustache like he was from central casting. A moonstone on his wedding ring. "Would you please come with me?" he said.

"What?"

"Would you please come with me?" he repeated. Then he showed me a badge.

I looked all around, like maybe there was a crime scene I had missed, some police tape, a riot, victims. Nothing doing. The city was busy and indifferent—red light, green light, hot air puffing out of grates. All these weird birds still cooing in the alleys. "Is there a problem?" I asked. He said, "Yes, perhaps, yes," and this seemed like such an odd thing to say I followed him to his car.

It had a flashing light on it. That's how you could tell it was a police car. We turned the corner and he pressed a button and set off the incandescent flash of red and blue. There's something dreamlike about it, isn't there? Something plugged into the subconscious, ruby and azure. Whenever I see those colours it always feels faintly as if I'm having a vision. The lights were coming from one of those car-top boxes, with a wire that trails back inside the driver's side window and plugs into the cigarette lighter or something. The car wasn't a proper police car, but a big old Buick, a boat, brown as a treasure chest. When we got to the car he said, "Please get in." I was so bewildered that if I hadn't had my bike to consider I think I would have simply obeyed. But I pointed at the handlebars and said, "What about this?" Then I said, "Wait, no—what the hell is going on? Are you really police?"

"Yes, I am Inspecteur Sovrencourt," he said.

The accent, the overcoat, the matter-of-fact impression of his clear round eyes—he wasn't physically intimidating, he was suggestively intimidating. And he seemed absolutely, completely a detective, a man who solves mysteries. "You're a detective," I proposed, just to make sure.

"Oui," he said. "Please come with me."

What mystery could I possibly be a part of? I locked my bike to one of those knotted grey metal pieces that shoots from a wall and has something to do with electricity.

"Before I come with you you need to tell me what's going on."

"Yes, yes," he said.

"Am I under arrest?" I asked.

"No," he said, and somehow this lulled me into getting inside.

Before I knew it we were driving. There was the hiss of his police radio and underneath that the murmur of a presenter talking current events—tax bills and primary challenges, ornithologists' debates—all the news I've stopped following.

"Hello? Sir?" I said. "Seriously, what's happening?"

"You are wanted for questioning."

"I am?!"

A voice came crackling over the radio and the detective grabbed the receiver and crackled something into it. I heard the word "Theodore."

"My name's Theo," I said.

"Yes."

"I mean it's Theo, not Theodore. Theo Potiris."

"Yes," he said. And we pulled into a police station.

He brought me inside and signalled to the cop behind reception—pointing at me, at a form on the desk. The cop nodded and began writing something down. Sovrencourt led me into an interrogation room.

"Wait here," he said.

I helplessly lifted my hands. I sat behind a metal table. I checked the clock before realizing it was in fact a no-smoking sign. I could hear calypso music from under the door. "I'm a spaceman," sang the voice. "A spaceman from the moon!"

I got up and walked around the little room, reminding myself I wasn't under arrest.

When the detective came back he carried fizzy water in two foam cups. The hissing carbonation played against the faint calypso in an interesting way, and I realized then that I was dazed, not thinking straight.

"It's my birthday," he said.

"What?"

"It's my birthday today," he repeated. "I am here spending it with you."

"Happy birthday?" I said.

"Thank you. Now, Theodore: let us talk." And he asked why I was downtown, what I was doing.

"It's a free country," I said, but he gave me such an amused, skeptical look that I just went ahead and told him it was for work.

"Where do you work?"

"The Rabbit's Foot?"

To be honest by this point I figured that the association was what this was all about. Like I told you, I think they're above board. I get payroll stubs—they deduct tax and benefits. But let's face it, how legit could they be?

"The Rabbit's Foot?" repeated Sovrencourt.

"They're . . . gamblers?" I said.

"Gamblers?"

"Legal gamblers," I said, after a pause.

"Oh yes," he said, as if he had just remembered.

I cocked my head. "Is that why I'm here?"

The detective's hound-dog frown seemed to say, "I can't see why it would be." But he did not reply. He wrote something down.

"Are they breaking the law?"

The detective dismissed the question with a wave of the hand. "Please go on."

"Go on?"

"Continue," he said.

So I went on, explaining that I had gone into a building for a meeting, to deliver some documents, and then I had come out and found that my bike helmet was missing. "Is that what this is about?" I asked, incredulous.

"No," he said.

I told him I usually worked uptown. That I was on my way back.

"Oh yes?" he said. He kept saying things like that, coaxing me to keep talking, tugging all kinds of digressions out of me. He made me ramble, like I was improvising on stage. I certainly wasn't scared, or even mad. Sovrencourt seemed solitary, harmless. He seemed curious, he smiled at my jokes. He kept scratching his little moustache with the end of his cheap pen. It was like being stuck in an elevator with a sympathetic audience. And yet every time I remembered why or how I was there, that I had been picked up by a cop and brought to a police station, my confusion bubbled over.

"Look, am I under arrest?" I asked again.

"Should you be under arrest?"

"No!"

"Then why would you be under arrest?"

"I'm—what's happening here?"

The detective placed his pen on the pad. "Theodore, what can you tell me about illegal imports?"

"My name is Theo," I said. "What do you mean 'illegal imports'?"

"Surely you understand me."

"Importing illegal items? Or importing legal items illegally?"

"Yes?"

Then it hit me. "Is this about the cheese mafia?"

"Ah," said Inspecteur Sovrencourt, leaning back.

"I don't have anything to do with those guys," I said.

Then Sovrencourt leaned forward. "No?"

Lou, maybe you already know about the cheese mafia. Maybe you heard the rumours at dinner parties. Maybe it's something you guys talk about between meditation sessions at your retreat, as you sit with luminaries on the wine-black steppe, listening to distant camels' gumball chewing. Honestly you might know more about it than I do. Because I do not know very much. What I know is what I told the detective: Our city is said to have a cheese mafia. A Gouda gang. A network of individuals who import or manufacture cheeses and then insist that merchants buy them. Restaurants, delis, grocery stores—the Camembert Camorra forces every-one to order their cheese, eat their cheese, crumble their cheese over toasted almonds and caramelized beets. If you don't stock the cheese mafia's dairy, the story goes, they'll lob a milk-bottle Molotov through your window. If you don't grate it over your restaurant spaghetti, they'll leave a bullet and a cheese curd in your mailbox. There are powerful cheese-related gangsters with strong opinions about where you should acquire your cheddar. So the story goes.

"I have nothing to do with that stuff," I said.

"No?"

"I've never met a cheese mafioso, never spoken to one. We've never been shaken down . . ." Suddenly I flashed to some men I saw at Mom's funeral, a rat pack snickering with my brother. "Do you mean at the Ukrainian Federation? I'd never seen those guys before in my life!" I crossed my arms on the table. "Honestly, I'd be happy if you were investigating this stuff!"

He was writing something down. "Oh yes?" he said, lightly. But if he was trying to goad me, there wasn't anything to goad. Provisions' dairy section goes unmolested.

We sat in silence for a little while. I checked the clock again before remembering it was a no-smoking sign.

"Can I go?" I finally asked.

Sovrencourt stood up. "Perhaps later." He said it like this was theatre, like he was reciting a line from a play. I tried to laugh. But he was as serious as a hornets' nest and as he left the room I felt as if I was hearing the door slam shut even before it closed. The snick of a mechanism and its lock.

Eventually a stocky deputy let me use the phone and I called Peter. His tone was of disbelief—at me, not the police. My brother's natural inclination is to assume that I am a hapless screw-up. After the phone call I sat for what felt like hours, running over the day's events and what Sovrencourt had said, thinking back to past dealings with feta distributors. The detective didn't return—eventually the same stocky deputy who had brought me the phone stuck his head in to say that my family was here. I could go.

Hanna was waiting in the station lobby, grinning. Her shoes were untied. "Is there bail to pay?" she said.

I looked at the deputy.

"No," said the deputy.

"I brought ten thousand dollars," said Hanna.

"There's no bail," I said. I thought: *My thirteen-year-old niece is the richest person I know.*

"Oh, well. They're waiting in the car."

Sovrencourt emerged to hold the door as I exited the station. "I will be keeping my eye on you," he said in a dry voice.

"Sure," I said. "Why not?"

Peter and Joanne drove us home. Peter kept asking me what I had done to attract police interest. "There must be something, Theo." But I just sat with my head flat back, eyes closed, feeling half-dead.

"Theo," said Joanne, "is there anything you want to tell us?"

"No," I said. "I am as the pure driven snow. Just unlucky."

"Snow isn't unlucky," said Hanna.

"That's right, Hanna," said Joanne, as a heron passed ghost-like before the windshield. "Snow is just weather."

They dropped us off outside Provisions K and Hanna and I trudged upstairs to her apartment. Mireille was on the big

Turkish carpet playing a tennis video game that required her to imitate actual tennis swings, volleying an invisible ball. Eric brought a tray with mint tea and Coca-Cola, figuring one of these beverages would cure whatever ailed me. Standing beside the TV I explained what had happened, or tried to. Mireille continued playing tennis. Each imaginary hit caused a loud ponk and I kept flinching at them, as if Mireille were pelting me with aces. Eric started to laugh. I laughed too, for a bit, but stopped. Mireille kept swinging.

"Maybe it's karma," Eric said. "Your lover's in the desert; you lose your helmet; the police arrest you for no reason. Ever wonder if it's just karma, bad karma, come home to hatch?"

"To roost," I said.

He rolled his eyes.

"I don't believe in karma," I said.

Mireille's tennis game ended. She stood panting. She said, "Maybe karma doesn't believe in you."

CHAPTER EIGHT

Theo returned to the Dolores Building a little before ten in the morning. He had walked the whole way, over the hill, eyes on the horizon, distilling his thoughts. At the edge of the commercial district he stopped at a convenience store, bought a bottle of fizzy water. He drank it in one long go, minuscule bubbles tumbling through green plastic.

His bike was where he had left it, locked to the convolutions of an electrical meter. The Dolores's door was like a heavy, revolving metaphor. At reception he said he had a meeting with QA. The officer examined his ID, reviewed a ledger. "You're not listed here."

Theo beamed at him. "That's why I need to see quality assurance."

The guard snickered, gave his badge one more glance. "Okay," he said, "go on."

The thirty-sixth floor smelled like orange peel. The sky outside the windows showed a blue that went on forever, decorated with a hundred elaborate white clouds. Theo passed silently under the inset lighting, over rich black carpet. The receptionist's desk was vacant—just a waiting area with low glass tables and leather sling chairs, a vase of tall poppies, a slightly open door. Painted on its surface, in the same white hand as the Rabbit's other signs, were the words:

Mitsou S. Marziale
Director

Theo knocked.

She was *not* happy to see him.

"Are you here to sell me some cereal?"

Theo cleared his throat. "I've got something for the company."

"It's not a company."

His first instinct was to gulp. But the performer in him recognized the faintest tremor in the way she held his gaze, a nearly imperceptible glint. He took a breath. "Let me make us both some money," he said.

"Sit," she said. Her desk was enormous, teak and rosewood, covered in stacks of paper folders and spiral-bound manuscripts. Bookshelves occupied an entire office wall—not decorative volumes, but dog-eared and bookmarked books, books that looked read. *Fancier Fancy Stats, A Bone of Fact, How to Grow a Server Farm, Principles of the New Radio, The Kelly Criterion, The Braithwaite Guide to Thoroughbreds* . . . Mitsou's laptop was closed. Navel oranges filled a fruit bowl. She picked up one of the oranges and, as Theo took his seat, one more. She lobbed one at him—he caught it square in his hands. "Go," Mitsou said.

So he went.

His pitch began with the word "destiny." She had begun to peel her orange; he could smell it. "Balance," he continued. "'Karma.'"

"No such things," she said.

"Which is why there's money to be made."

The idea had come to him near dawn, as he lay like a shipwreck in the mess of his bedsheets.

People believed in destiny. They believed in balance, in *deserving*—"karma" in its crudest sense. Theo had spent years of his life in disappointment. Whole seasons, whole years: disappointment in himself, his work, his accomplishments. He knew that sting so well; he was sick of it, sick and tired, almost despairing. Furious at the lie.

He said, "Children are told that life's not fair but they're also taught that good people are rewarded. That assholes get what's coming to them. We're taught to love an underdog. 'If you just work hard.' 'If you have a good heart.' But underdogs usually *lose*. That's why they're underdogs."

Mitsou nodded an acknowledgment. "People are irrational."

Theo began peeling his orange. "As I understand it, the Rabbit's Foot makes most of its money by looking at data nobody else is looking at. Finding new stuff to count, or intriguing relationships between the stuff you're already counting. But instead of only paying attention to what happens inside the games or races, what about something that *isn't* on the field? That only exists in the imagination of the dumb public?"

She narrowed her eyes at him. "'Karma.'"

"Suppose the stats call something a 50/50 toss-up between two teams. They're equally matched. But one's a team of sweethearts, or they haven't won a championship in a hundred years, or they lost their last five chances, or their coach beat cancer, or they're from a city that got ripped by floods or hurricanes or a financial crash. The statistics still say it's 50/50 but the public won't behave as if it is. All sorts of people will bet on the team that *deserves* to win, as if deserving has anything to do with it."

Mitsou put down another thick stub of orange peel. "They believe justice will win out."

"They're blinded by what they wish to be true. Who wants to root for the soccer player who bites his opponents' ears off? For the team that cheats, deflating their footballs? For the horse owned by a war criminal? You'd rather bet against them."

"But people do still bet for the favourites, even when they're shits."

"But not *quite* as many as ought to. Right?" The orange's bright smell filled his nostrils. "The odds will be distorted by, uh, karmic expectations. By what hopers hope *will* happen."

"And we would take advantage of the gap between what the numbers predict and what the gamblers' hearts are telling them."

"Yes."

"That's the edge," Mitsou said.

"That's the edge."

After peeling her orange, piece by piece, Mitsou had produced a handkerchief from somewhere and was using it to wipe the flecked pith from her fingers. "But bookmakers are not so foolish," she said. "The Vegas line doesn't give a pony better odds because its owner is Mother Theresa. They calculate their odds based on statistics, facts, data—and then they collect off the mistakes of a credulous public."

"Right," said Theo, unsteadily.

"The Rabbit's Foot are gamblers. We're not bookies. We place our wagers with others. We bet *against* the line. How would we win their money?"

"Well," Theo began. But he didn't have anything else to say. He tried to pretend he was merely groping for the best way to word his reply. The charade lost its substance when he said nothing else.

Mitsou chewed on an orange segment. Was she still thinking? Was she trying to make him squirm? His confidence had left him in a puff. Another big swing, another wild miss. He knew this sensation so well: a speech delivered and an audience gazing back, apparently unmoved. Theo's attention drifted to a cello case in the corner, beside a stool, and then to a framed portrait over Mitsou's shoulder. It showed a stern woman sitting before an expanse of floral wallpaper. She and the wallpaper seemed to be biding their time. The signature was *Vincent*, each brushstroke discernible.

Theo absent-mindedly deposited his orange peel on the edge of Mitsou's desk.

She stared at it—the peel, a single uninterrupted spiral.

"Hm," she said.

She lifted her gaze, appraising him anew.

At last she leaned forward, elbows on the desk. "I am not being entirely fair to you, Mr. Potiris. I spoke of the Vegas line, their calculated odds. But there is also parimutuel."

"Perry Mutual?"

"A type of bet, available from certain bookmakers, in certain contexts. It's a different game altogether. In parimutuel betting you are not attempting to beat the house. The bookies don't set the odds—the market does. Even when the contest is a 50/50 coin toss, if more money's being laid on heads, the odds shift accordingly. The payout for heads gets smaller. The bookmaker doesn't bother trying to out-think the public—they earn their piece regardless, by taking a share of each bet. A rake, win or lose."

"So it's just you against Larry in Tucson."

"Or Kiki in Hong Kong. Against everyone else who has also laid a wager. We could buy and sell against those positions, or perhaps— yes, your technique might predict certain market elasticity . . ."

Theo took a breath. He risked a grin.

"However," Mitsou said. She had pulled a knee to her chest. Her chrome office chair was soundless as she reclined. "We have no idea how many contests would fit the description—large numbers of people betting against an 'undeserving' favourite."

"Probably fewer than one in twenty," Theo said. He had thought about this. "But *some* of them. *Some* proportion. And they'd be many of the biggest, most contentious events."

"The Super Bowl. The world heavyweight title."

"Yeah."

"In parimutuel, your potential winnings are limited by the size of the pot. The more popular a contest, the more it is possible to win."

"That's good, right?" Theo said. He felt as if he had just finished telling a long, effective joke.

Mitsou reached for another orange. "Mr. Potiris, I'd like to offer you a promotion."

Before noon, Theo and Matisse had been reassigned to the Dolores Building. If Matisse was piqued that Theo's scheme, hatched in secret, was the one to change their circumstances, he concealed his feelings well. They came as comrades to the Speculative Analysis department, home of the Rabbit's grand experiments, its bigger-picture thinking. Each man was awarded a new title: Matisse rechristened a senior specialist, Theo a junior assistant specialist. "You have eight weeks," Mitsou told them: if Theo's idea didn't work then he, at least, would be sent back to languish by the bowling alley. In the meantime, Matisse agreed to set aside weather and turn his attention to this. They would collaborate as partners, sharing all the spoils. The two men's desks were back to back, in a cubicle on the eighteenth floor. *This is my shot*, Theo thought, looking around. The view was onto traffic.

Immediately, Matisse began coding simulations, analyzing data. He called them "karmically weighted contests"—games or races where bettors believed there was a "just" result. Theo was slower to start. He didn't know how to begin. He had brought the lock-and-key cartoon from Suite 500 and he sat staring at it, wondering, now that he was here, what should happen next. It was strange to have an end in mind, without any sense of means. This was his shot, yes, but the process seemed diaphanous. He didn't have Matisse's technical skills, he couldn't parse the datasets. He wasn't even sports-fluent, capable of reeling out opportunities to test his hypothesis. Could he name a single hurdler? A quarterback? Let alone a *sinful* hurdler, a *saintly* quarterback? Which squads had deserved to win the Tri Nations Cup? What *was* the Tri Nations Cup?

As hours became days, Theo scoured the internet for inspiration. He sent whatever he found to Matisse; Matisse infrequently responded. Theo had expected to be reignited by this enterprise— opportunity! stakes!—but instead he felt nearly useless. He bumbled through Wikipedia, reading up on obscure competitions: the Iditarod, the Futsal World Cup, the Mondial la Marseillaise à Pétanque. He wheeled around on his swivel chair. He was distracted by social media. He stared at a barren document, created in an optimistic moment, filename: *BOLD_NEW_IDEAS.docx*.

Theo was sure he wasn't working hard enough but he didn't know what to work harder *on*. It was the opposite of Provisions K, where there was always another inconsequential task to complete. Although Theo was happy to have a break from those minutiae, leaving the store to its other custodians, he was still puzzling out his role at the Dolores. A contest's unjustness didn't show in the way its balls bounced. Everything was subtext and context, the framing of the game.

Theo simply tried to do his best.

Sometimes he rearranged the pushpins on their cubicle wall.

He sipped water from paper cones.

Matisse would spin around to lecture him on machine learning or iced tea.

And finally, one evening after such a workday, Theo walked into Le Black Cat.

:::

The front door made a beautiful and janky sound as it closed behind him, like someone had pitched a baseball into a Christmas elf. Le Black Cat was deep and crowded, filled with shelves, brackets showing, on which hundreds of shoeboxes overflowed with particular bolts and nuts and screws and washers of itemized size. Shoeboxes full of key rings. Shoeboxes full of sandpaper. Shoeboxes swollen with squeeze-bottles of grease. There were whole ramparts of shoeboxes—every shoe long gone, off in the world to cushion the foot of a child, or the foot of an athlete, or of a hard-working schoolteacher, or else already a hand-me-down, or garbage, or each component part transformed, inch by inch, stitch by stitch, into new and expedient materiel.

Anyway: a lot of shoeboxes.

Theo threaded his way past them, under dozens of suspended hammers, chisels and conifer-shaped air fresheners, swinging semi-decoratively from hooks. He jostled a lean-to of brooms. The store smelled like sawdust and cherry gum and, more faintly, like gravy. Ageless soft rock wafted over the aisles like muslin. One employee was pouring a shoebox of nails into another shoebox of nails; another was scrawling notes on yellow post-its, adding them to a collage above the cash. Somebody was cutting a key. Somebody was sawing plywood. Theo almost tripped on a shoebox containing a package of dressmakers' pins, a can of plum tomatoes, a VHS of Tom Cruise in *Risky Business*.

In the back, where the disco lighting fixtures cast tired rainbows across the shelves, the gravy smell was stronger. Customers sat huddled around plastic-coated tables, grazing on hot dogs and fries, sipping beer from small glass mugs. An elderly waitress topped up coffees, relinquished frothy pitchers. Hockey highlights swished across a ceiling-mounted TV. Theo heard Simone before he saw her: the end of a sentence and a short, clipped laugh. He wouldn't have said he remembered her voice but he did. He turned a corner and her glance flicked up. Her elbows on the tabletop.

"It's the comedian," she said.

She was sitting with an older man in a polar-fleece vest and faded blue jeans; he had a big grey beard, bright eyes, inarguably a little bit Santa Claus. When he saw her looking he turned; they were like a pair of birds, heads abruptly raised.

"Oh!" said Theo. "Hey! Simone, right?"

The man narrowed his twinkling eyes, but Simone smiled. "Correct." She addressed her companion. "I met Theo at a comedy club."

"Who was telling the jokes?"

"He was."

"How're the hot dogs?" Theo said.

"Inadvisable," said the man. He took a sip of beer.

"The fries, however," said Simone.

"The fries are redeeming," the man admitted.

She nudged the chair beside her. "Care to join us?"

He sat. Simone's companion seemed surprised by her invitation. "This is JF," she said. He offered Theo a doughy hand.

"Long day at the office?" Theo asked.

"Something like that."

Simone touched her frosted mug. "You? Shopping for divots?"

Theo grinned. "Did you know I'm working for your sister?"

The two of them straightened.

"My sister?" Simone said.

"Mitsou."

She nodded carefully. "I hope you haven't given her all of your money."

"She's the one paying *me*," he said. He pointed back the way he'd come. "I am a denizen of the Dolores."

"Really?"

"I took your advice. I called and asked for a job." He craned and plucked a black brush from a box of black brushes, felt its bristles. "Last week I got promoted."

"Shit," she said. "I'm honestly impressed."

"I thought I might run into you."

"Not chez Mitsou."

She began pouring him a beer.

"I thought you were a comedian," said JF. "Why are you wasting your days at the Rabbit?"

"A reformed comic," Theo said. "Possibly even retired."

"Really?" Simone said.

"You start to feel foolish at a certain point."

"Telling jokes for a living?"

"What's the cliché about insanity? Doing the same thing over and over and expecting a different result?" He shrugged, looked around. "This place is amazing."

"I remember when this city was *made* of spots like this," JF said. "Beautiful dive bars. twenty-four-hour diners, ninety-nine-cent pizza and bars selling pigs' knuckles. I've spent so many hours here I don't think I even really *perceive* Le Black Cat any more. It's not a place I go to sit and drink—it's my resting state. It's where my mind goes when it wanders."

"Your natural habitat," said Simone.

"And where I empty my bladder," he said, getting to his feet.

Once JF was out of earshot, Theo asked, "How did you guys meet?"

She seemed amused by the implication. "We work together."

"I don't think you told me what you do."

"You're probably right." Her expression was sly.

"Am I supposed to guess?"

"You could try."

He evaluated the woman beside him. "Are you teachers?" he said finally.

She rolled her eyes. "Try again."

"Journalists?"

"No."

"Architects?"

"No."

"Administrators for a dance troupe? Some kind of interesting scientists—biology? Marine . . . Marine something? Wait—doctors!"

"No."

"Jewel thieves."

She smiled. "Getting closer."

JF rejoined them.

"Professional mimes. Stockbrokers."

"Do we look like fucking stockbrokers?" Simone asked, aghast.

JF poured out another beer. "Do we look like *mimes*?"

"You run a business together," Theo proposed.

Simone inclined her head. "I suppose you could say we run a business. Couldn't you?"

"I don't know about 'run,'" said JF.

Simone waved down the server, a pink-cheeked matriarch who barely acknowledged Theo's existence. They ordered coffees and another basket of fries and Theo asked for an all-dressed hot dog, which meant ketchup, mustard and a funky, nearly medicinal sauerkraut. Talk of sauerkraut turned to yeast and bread, and to JF's childhood in the boondocks. His parents lived up north, on a farm dedicated to breeding tiny animals. Shetland ponies, pygmy hogs, miniature alpacas with scat like chocolate almonds. "For petting zoos," said JF. "They're still at it."

"But you came south."

"I needed faster internet."

"I knew it: you're app developers," Theo said.

"Now you've hurt his feelings," said Simone.

"I was lying anyway," said JF. "I'm too old to have come panning for broadband. When I came to the city it was all Cobol, SCSI, green text on CRTs."

"Hitting rocks together to make fire."

"Hard disks and floppies . . ."

"Do hackers ever retire?" Simone asked. "Or do you just keep going until you forget your passwords?"

"I've got it, you work in an old-age home," Theo said.

"She's a professional troublemaker," said JF. "Let's leave it at that."

Both of them were interested to learn about Theo's other métier, the grocery business, and the way he had parlayed those skills into a gig with a multimillion-dollar gambling ring. He found himself at once overstating and understating his abilities, painting the portrait of a humble, resourceful jack-of-all-trades. Theo felt unusually tentative in his storytelling, as if the conversation were a test he could pass or fail. Simone seemed to recognize his nerves and she drew him out, smiling at his digressions, even an occasionally dismal joke. Still, there was an edge to these companions which he never quite met: a sense of atten-tiveness, a sort of visceral conscientiousness that outstripped his carry-ing capacity. More than once, Simone mentioned politics—the latest Washington scandal, another protest in the streets—and each time Theo tried to jam the conversation back to things he knew about, expiry dates or microphone stands or how to off-load a truck.

"A forklift? You have an actual forklift?" JF said. "I know that store. I've shopped there. I never imagined you had a forklift."

"It resides in the cellar. Or out back."

"It's shy," Simone said.

"It's biding its time."

She laughed. And Theo felt a swell of pleasure.

:::

Nearly a month went by. Breezes came and breezes went. The skies were blue and open. In the countryside, kernels of corn assembled in their cobs. Every morning Theo took an elevator to the eighteenth floor. Every morning he woke his computer and entered the same password, *calamarirings3*. According to Matisse, the work was going well. He had identified fifteen sporting events where the odds seemed to have been distorted by what bettors hoped would happen. "Numbers don't lie," said Matisse. However, it wasn't enough to have a proof of concept, recognizing these matches in retrospect: the Rabbit's Foot needed to be able to spot them coming, days or weeks ahead. So the senior specialist (Matisse) continued plugging away, his fingers clattering across the keys, while the assistant junior specialist (Theo) uselessly browsed the internet and filed reports and pretended to be working harder than he was. Sometimes he'd claim he had a meeting to go to and just wander through the building, prowling the stairwells, encountering the neighbours. He ascertained which of the eighteenth floor's potted plants were plastic. He ate lunch on the Olympics floor's wind-raked outdoor patio, chewing a croissant purloined from Carb Castle, looking out onto downtown. He located the Dolores Building's meditation room, a padded cell filled with rugs and beanbag chairs, and he contemplated curling up there with a notebook to write some jokes. But he wasn't writing jokes any more. He was done with that, *finito*.

To certain observers, Theo might have appeared bored, but he wasn't bored, exactly. Boredom requires a degree of self-knowledge. It is not enough that an activity be tedious (i.e., without momentum) or aimless (i.e., without direction): for it to be *boring* the doer must recognize he is being dulled. Theo was too restless for that. He interpreted the emptiness he was feeling as a marker of his indolence, or his inadequacy. Here was an opportunity to finally achieve something, earning his fortune, and would he squander it? No, he insisted. Slowly, surely, he would find his feet. He would warrant Mitsou's trust, reward her confidence, cut through the reeds to a clearing. And then he'd be happy. Then he'd have arrived.

So he endured. He kept up appearances. He arrived at the Dolores near dawn and every afternoon he waited out his partner, malingering at his computer until Matisse finally turned around and said a version of "Sheesh, blimey—time to call it a day." Theo extended a well-practised goodbye—sympathetic, preoccupied—as if he could see no end to his own unfinished business. Once Matisse had scrammed, Theo loitered for at least ten minutes before following in his superior's footsteps, to and down the elevator, exit downstage.

Then he'd cross the street to Le Black Cat.

Theo told himself he was trying to decompress. A beer and some conversation with a few new friends—winding down the day as he had in his twenties, before he somehow fell out of the habit. The drinking was never serious: a small, sloshing pitcher, then rounds of black coffee. *It's reassuring to feel a tiny bit more degenerate*, he wrote in an unsent letter to Lou. *I missed the pallor of beerlight reflected on faces. I missed the slippery clatter of certain kinds of laughter.* But he knew that as he ducked under the brooms and buckets, threading through the aisles, the silhouette he was searching for was Simone's. When she was there they'd sit together talking, swerving at each other. Sometimes the day's current events were like a veil across her eyes, a worry and a fury and a sadness that seemed ineluctable, "What did the president do now?," except that for Theo it was eluctable—he cut through it with ambivalence and nerve, the sting of a sawtooth joke. He changed the subject to nearer things, weird birds. Banter rebounded, mugs clinked, music played. Sometimes it was as if Simone appeared by magic from a secret corner of the store, a hidden compartment. When she was absent, Theo would feel himself hesitate—whether to sit down with JF all the same, or to sit alone, or simply to turn and leave. And in that hesitation something like guilt clenched him, small and leaden. He would make himself think of his girlfriend, if *girlfriend* was the right word: with her head half-hidden on a cushion; in the sunset-soaked playground where they met; at that Danish Christmas bazaar, hunched over a polystyrene plate, lifting a dill and lemon-laden *smørrebrød* to her lips. Lou had seemed like the answer to a question he had been asking for years but been unable to put into words. She was beautiful and hilarious and resilient and mystic and steady. She was intrepid, thoughtful, easy to be with. The way her arm landed across his back, secured him there. The way she bicycled towards him on his birthday, steering one-handed, balancing a strawberry-rhubarb pie. The way she stepped out of her jeans and onto her duvet, knee first.

So he had sent love letters to the desert. And she had written back. Maybe the letters she wrote weren't love letters; maybe they were. They hadn't known each other this way before, trading missives in the mail. Maybe this was just the way she was in writing, reasoned and circumspect. *Bloodless*, this was the word he had landed on and once he had landed on it he was unable to forget he had found it. She had not written him in four weeks, since just after her phone call. He had not mailed a letter in three. It was June now; she had said "the end of summer."

Theo had asked her not to go to Morocco. "Change your mind," he said.

"I can't just *change my mind*," Lou said. "I agreed months ago."

They had taken their bikes to the wholesalers' flower market, where Lou had an account. A long ride through Little Italy, past Roberto's with the lemon and hazelnut gelato, to a former shoelace factory where suppliers brought trucks of buds, blossoms, teetering bamboo. Lou had been coming for years and everybody knew her; it made Theo feel proud, as if he was dating a celebrity. Although he was a veteran of the city's fruit and vegetable markets, the flower sellers seemed softer, gentler of voice. They wore brighter-coloured clothes. There were rose vendors with handkerchiefs tied around their necks, suave men in silk ties selling irises. Each of them greeted Lou like a sister, a daughter. They said things in French and Italian, appraised her companion. Theo gamely small-talked, tried his best to charm as he trailed Lou through the lawns section, the ferns section, the section of the market devoted to different blends of earth. "Soil's the worst," she confided, "such a tedious fucking pain in the neck." The smell reminded Theo of lakes.

It was grimy and beautiful in there, the aisles littered with fallen petals. When they arrived at the cut flowers, Lou darted from bin to bin, assembling a bouquet, and when she presented it to him it almost made him cry. Not just the gesture but the bouquet itself: pink and paper-thin lisianthus, sturdy green sage, whirling sapphire dahlias. An arrangement of flowers that seemed to say something about him, and her, and the ties between them. Lou had started her career as a florist, years ago, before she got her horticulture degree. Theo tried to imagine her gathering a bundle of pussy-willows at eighteen.

Change your mind, he thought to himself. *Change your mind*, he willed in a message to the woman he had been sleeping with for six weeks. He didn't say it aloud until they were at dinner—at a restaurant that served hummus warm, with pomegranate seeds. The bouquet lay under his chair.

"Oh, Theo," she said, not without some anger. She wanted him to be excited about what she was about to embark on. She felt so lucky to have been chosen, and the retreat seemed to hold so much attraction for her—as if it would solve an enigma, a secret question she was asking. He didn't want to rob her of that pleasure or that hope; he just wanted a chance to see this through, uninterrupted. She made him feel kind. She made him feel funny. She made him feel that his character had fewer blemishes than it did, that it was enough to simply be—enough for her and thus also enough for him somehow.

He didn't want her to go.

"We can write each other letters," she said.

"I hate writing letters." He was embarrassed by his petulance.

"I don't believe you," she said. "You're the letter-writing type."

When he didn't answer, sensing the hurt in him, she softened. "When's the last time you handwrote a letter?"

He said he couldn't recall.

She rolled her eyes. "Try," she said.

So they sat there, each of them with a half circle of pita bread. He tried to remember when he had last written down the word *sincerely*, signed his name underneath. He remembered the postcard he had written to his mother from York, in England. That was years and years ago. She kept it magneted to her fridge. "We walked on the walls yesterday," he wrote, "there were wild herbs everywhere, little birds." Surely he had written postcards since then. Surely he had written someone a letter. A relative. A lover. But he couldn't remember. You write a letter to a lover and this retrospectively becomes a letter to an ex. What is one to do with old letters? Old gold, he thought. It is difficult to throw away anything that once seemed precious.

"Hanna," Theo said finally. "I sent Hanna a postcard when I went to New York last year."

When you're in love, you weigh your doubts against your desire. You stare into another person's eyes. A tea light flickers. Is there a sign to tell you you're on the right track? Indicators to watch for, variables to isolate? Time had taught Theo that lust can lie. A thing that seems like love can lie. Anything you feel can fly away, on a plane.

"At least every two weeks," Lou had said.

Now it had been three.

Theo had gradually encountered the rest of Le Black Cat's regulars. A handsome voice actor who sat alone, reading plays by Harold Pinter. Two brothers who jostled for checkmate, mercilessly trash-talking. A married couple who ran a law firm; they specialized in divorce. A pretty poetry student from the university, who alternated between glasses of club soda and glasses of red wine. There was a dishevelled, portly millionaire, his ash-grey hair tied in ponytail; his best friend, a dancer, had grown up with him on that very block, before the row houses had been razed for skyscrapers.

There were also two others, Black Cat occasionals who finished their drinks and left whenever Theo arrived. The first was Sebald, whom Theo had met that night at the Knock Knock. If he had recovered his voice, he wasn't showing it off. He'd get up from Simone's table at the first glimpse of Theo, nod to each of them, then vanish down an aisle.

The second was a woman whose name Theo did not know but whom he had twice seen arguing with Simone.

"Who was that?" he asked her, after.

"My shadow," said Simone, and changed the subject.

Both of these people seemed wrapped up in whatever it was that JF and Simone were wrapped up in. "We're colleagues," Simone would say, and nothing else. Despite the hours she and Theo had spent together, Simone remained tight-lipped on the matter of her profession. The little he knew he had gleaned from chance disclosures: that they worked nearby, and kept erratic hours; that JF worked with computers; that they had travelled together, and shared hotel rooms; that they had known each other for fewer than fifteen years. Sebald was wearing coveralls once, as if he were a factory worker, and then the next time a crisp suit, as if freshly returned from the courthouse. Sometimes Theo had the sense that he was unwelcome at Le Black Cat, disturbing some boundary, but Simone never said anything. The others either deferred to her or disappeared.

Perhaps they were members of a high-stakes sales team, Theo speculated. Peddling nuclear reactors to China, security systems to casinos. Casinos had come up more than once: JF told the story of earning a small fortune, years before, "cavorting among the gaming tables" with his boyfriend, each of them in "marigoldish" jeans. Then he and Simone exchanged a look, and again someone changed the subject.

Clearly they were well-to-do. The signs were subtle—Sebald's occasional cufflinks, JF's brand of smartwatch, the label stitched to Simone's leather jacket. They had a tab with Le Black Cat's kitchen; it wasn't long before they were paying Theo's bill. Simone refused to take his cash, told him not to worry about it. Yet neither she nor JF had come from wealth and Simone, in particular, seemed hostile towards the one percent. She reserved specific vitriol for heirs and heiresses, trust-fund kids, the structures of income inequality. It was difficult to imagine her in a professional setting. She had an abandon about her, a crudeness almost, that overran decorum. Also: they all drove motorcycles.

Maybe they're consultants, Theo thought to himself. That word, *consultant*, seemed to encompass anything. Simone could be an artist, a criminal, a mercenary, a corporate fixer. She could be anything, and at the heart of it perhaps Theo was happy for it to stay that way. It's very easy to fall for all of someone's unanswered questions; the harder work comes after a reply.

Finally, on a Thursday, Theo arrived late to an unusually quiet Black Cat. Matisse had lingered at the office and so it was after 8:00 PM when Theo finally crossed the road to the store, yanking open the fucked-up jangle of the door. He headed straight to the diner section, worried that Simone had gone. But then he spied her, alone at a table beside the spirit levels, with a book.

"Hey."

"Hey."

"Long day?"

"Long day."

"Happy solstice."

"Where is everyone?"

"Fair question."

"Maybe there's a sporting event. A presidential debate."

"I think it's just a beautiful summer's night. And we're in a basement."

By now his eyes had strayed to the volume in her hands. "*The Labrador Sea*," he read aloud.

"Do you know it? It's for work."

"I've seen people reading it. Is it any good?"

"Too soon to say."

"I wish *I'd* brought a book. We could sit here reading in the dark."

"If you tilt your page towards the disco light, it's not so bad." He leaned in as she demonstrated. "See?" she said.

He looked at her. Long eyebrows made Simone's face particularly expressive, almost sly. Yet she guarded the progress of her feelings: her expressions remained unshown, concealed, until the moment they changed. Here now he was trying to observe such a change, the tremor of anything unfolding.

Maybe she was feeling what he was feeling. Uncertain and bold. The unspoken suggestion of a wish.

"Stay for another drink?" he asked.

"Yes," she said.

They drank whiskies together, and the force of that earlier moment dissipated. Mary Margaret O'Hara sang across the radio, then came a duet by John Prine and Iris Dement, and before long Simone and Theo had ordered another round, a bowl of salted peanuts, he asked for mixed nuts but the only nuts were peanuts; they were laughing. More whiskies, then espressos, little glasses of tap water.

After a while he said, "Should we go somewhere else?"

"What did you have in mind?"

"Apple-picking?" he said.

"Ha. Some whale-watching, while we're at it?"

"Find some bobsleds, go bobsledding."

"Did you know I was a pole vaulter?"

He laughed.

"I'm serious! I was a pole vaulter. Sydney Olympics."

He wore his smile like a shiny medallion. "Uh huh."

"Changed my life. Didn't make it past the first qualifier. So it goes." She was smiling too. But her expression fell away suddenly. "I'll be right back," she said.

She vanished down one of the aisles, towards the bathroom. Theo sat motionless for about half a minute. Then he took out his phone and paged to a browser, thumbing in Simone's name + "olympic pol-evaukt." It autocorrected and stalled and then to his astonishment there she was, Simone at twenty-one, long-haired and serious, sixteen years earlier. Theo gaped. He stared in the direction she had disappeared and down again at his screen. Camera flashes were going off behind young Simone San Marziale. Rippling tresses floating in the air. The pole was bent at an incredible angle and her body was partly airborne, faintly impossible. Her toes pointed towards the ground. Her chin was tilted up, facing something out of frame, her mouth pulled tight and brow furrowed, eyes glittering, a statement of speed and concentration, nakedly expressive and yet also completely masked, divulging no secrets.

"Let's go," said Simone. She had reappeared with a big shoulder bag, a motorcycle helmet.

He put away his phone. He reached for his coat.

He was on his bicycle, pedalling wildly. She was on her motorcycle, its engine roaring.

"Where we headed?" she shouted.

"The canal?" he called back. "The river?"

"A forest?"

"Where would we find a forest?"

"How about a bridge?"

They spilled over a rise and rapidly downhill, green light after green light, too many green lights to count, some of them all-clear and others only barely, changing to amber as they dove underneath, barrelling past billboards for flour and roses and brand new houses. Theo felt ridiculous cycling next to her—ridiculous and also sort of mischievous, sort of free. He could zigzag and braid on his old

Peugeot. He could feel the wind ripple along its frame. She leaned ahead on her faded machine, pumping the engine to make him laugh. As they turned a corner he glimpsed a seagull atop a stop sign, that wry beaky grin. Then another stop sign, another seagull; another stop sign, another seagull. "That's the third seagull I've seen like that!" he shouted. He looked up and saw a shooting star.

Further on, there was a submarine sandwich joint called Theo Sandwich. She pointed at it as they passed. Five blocks later, across a grimy orange shopfront, beside the cartoon logo of an elephant-turned-vacuum-cleaner, a place called Electro Chez Simone. Theo shook his head, dinged his bell.

"What are the chances?" he yelled.

She pumped the gas again and rumbled ahead.

Eventually they came to the water. The bridge's gigantic concrete struts were like leaning towers. Sodium lights blanched the night-time, casting yardage of illumination then the dim turf beyond, pebbles and garbage and gardeny meadows of chamomile. A spiked black fence separated the city from the river; from where they stood they could faintly hear the current. It smelled like a rushing fountain, all ozone. Then it smelled like apples, suddenly, as if a breeze had lifted up across an orchard. Theo felt only a very little bit drunk, at his edges. He stood over his bike and Simone stood over hers, a little way off, helmet visor raised, gazing at him.

He pointed. Three men were clustered together where the sloped asphalt met the bridge partition. All were painting. Two with spray cans and one with an actual brush, wide-bristled, leaving maroon curls on the wall. A faded Freddie Krueger was eating pizza on a mural nearby, cheese-strings sluicing between his claws. There were obscure tags and signatures. There was a bad sunset and a grotesque, beboiled Pope. The three graffiti artists were at the very beginning of a new work, something in a different style.

Theo lowered his bike to the pavement and padded over to Simone. Just as he reached her a car passed by, on the road above them, and a shred of light grazed the objects on the ground. "Hey, look at that," he said. He stooped and held up a ten-dollar bill.

In the half-light Simone's smile almost seemed sad.

"Looks like the next hot dog's on me," he said.

They stood together as a painted frame appeared on the wall. The maroon lines were a ribbon, an animal; no, some kind of 3-D cryptogram.

"What do you think it is?"

"You should ask them," he said.

"I'll flip you for it."

He laughed. "Okay."

She wore a cunning look as he dug a quarter out of his pocket.

"Heads you go, tails I go," he said.

"Sure."

The coin seemed to vault and float and turn and turn, and then it landed in his palm.

"Best three out of five?"

She rolled her eyes. It didn't matter: tails again, then tails again, and Theo threw up his hands. "Fine!" he said. He was smiling. He pressed the quarter into her fist and began the climb up to the painters.

"What are you painting?" he called.

They turned.

"The thing, what is it? It's nice." Theo had to scramble to make it up the last part of the slope, where it grew steep. The three men eyed him as if he were wildlife—a squirrel, a skunk. He was still catching his breath. "I've never watched anyone doing, uh, this. Before."

"It's a desert," one of the spray-painters said.

Theo scanned back and forth across the image. "Huh."

"This is Ode," said the other spray-painter. He was pointing his thumb towards the brush-painter.

"Theo," Theo said.

The first spray-painter seemed irritated, furious even, that his partner had prolonged the conversation. But Ode didn't seem to mind. He was lanky, with droopy eyes. He wore a long white T-shirt and low-slung chinos. His square, sagging moustache resembled his chosen painting implement.

"You heard of him?" asked the more friendly of the spray-painters.

"Who?"

"Ode."

Theo shook his head. "Can't say I have."

The first spray-painter made a frustrated sound.

"Well, you're lucky," said the second one. Ode still had yet to say anything. "Ode's from Spain. He's only here for twenty-four hours. He's the best there's ever been."

"You don't say?" said Theo.

Ode bowed his head, eyes closed. Then he turned and went back to painting dunes, dragging his brush across the wall.

Back at the bottom of the slope, Theo told Simone what he had learned.

"What did he mean, 'the best there's ever been'?"

"The best graffiti artist. Street artist. I guess?"

"Ever?"

"Ever!" Theo declared. Suddenly he felt so happy.

"'Ode,'" said Simone.

"Yes."

"Like, 'she owed me money'?"

"Like 'an ode to someone.' A poem, a tribute. I think."

"You think."

"Well I didn't ask."

"So it *could* be 'owed.' As in money."

"I guess."

"Or a mispronunciation of 'odd.'"

"Odd?"

"Ode."

"I guess."

"It could be any of those things," she said, as they watched the three men paint a desert on the wall.

Simone and Theo sat down together, on a bench, in the hot night. She had a flask of dry brandy, moonshine, some eye-watering elixir. "Just a sip," she said. They talked about painting walls, making art, writing jokes. Brushstroke by brushstroke, Ode's image took shape on the bridge strut. His desert looked astonishingly real, almost porcelain. The sand gleamed. The task of the other two men, the ones with spray cans, was to draw the air. They drew it in translucent layers, cloud by cloud.

"I feel as if the painting already exists, and they're just uncovering it," Theo said.

"As if it were waiting for them."

"A joke can seem that way. Like a rare bird: look what I found."

"Really? Aren't they more like inventions? Things you work out on your own?"

"But it's not like there's a particular problem you're trying to solve. You can make a joke about *anything*. Infinite possibilities, infinite ways of talking about them. You don't necessarily choose some-thing—you stumble on it."

"'Eureka!'" said Simone.

"Even *that* seems too much like discovery. There was this great piece once in BUNCHA HACKS, about how good comedy is just *seeing*. Seeing the world as it is, or yourself as you are, or the way other people feel about something but haven't found a way to say."

"But then *you* still have to find the right way to say it."

"Okay, so it takes a *little* invention," he said, smiling. "I used to take the whole process so seriously. I had this Wednesday-morning ritual. I'd go to the fruit and veg market, check on orders for the store, then hike out to a little café—this Italian place with mint-green walls and soccer on the TV. And I'd write. Drinking macchiatos, scribbling in a spiral notebook, as if I was a . . . As if I was for-real. A real comic. I'd look over and I'd see someone at another table—a poet, a musi-cian, everyone with their own notebook, their own expression of enlightened consternation. Fakes and for-reals. I'd write whole bits there, at the coffee shop. It was good stuff, sometimes." He made a face. "But as the years went by, I didn't go as much. I'd just write things down wherever. Or I'd try to remember. I improvised more."

"You got more confident," Simone suggested.

"Or more lazy," Theo said. "I don't know. You have to *practise* seeing, I think. If you let a habit dwindle, if you let it fade away . . ."

"It fades away."

He pressed his lips together. "I hated repeating a joke."

"How'd you ever get better?"

He considered this. "I think I didn't."

This almost made her laugh.

"Just desserts," he said.

She lowered her legs from the bench. "Do you know where that expression comes from?"

He frowned. He had never considered it before.

"'Just desserts,'" she repeated.

"Fair desserts, I guess? Receiving the dessert you deserve?"

"The suitable cake. The appropriate sundae." Simone shook her head. "It's not, actually. It's not 'desserts' like that. It's a different word, antiquated; pronounced like 'desserts' but spelled with one *s*."

"Deserts."

"But pronounced 'desserts.' It's *what you deserve*, from the same root."

"'Just deserts.'"

"You get what you deserve."

He looked up again at the mural. "Do you think you really do? How long should you wait? At a certain point you wonder where you're headed. If you're headed *anywhere*."

"Some roads lead to dead ends."

"*You* made it to the Olympics."

She settled back on the bench, her arms folded around her. "Sure, that felt like a destination. Then I competed, and I lost. So what next?"

Theo fell silent.

She said, "You're supposed to try again, right?"

"I suppose."

"I didn't."

They sat for a while.

"I was always searching for signs," she said. "'Should I keep trying?' 'Am I good enough?'"

"'Will it be worth the trouble?' Sometimes it's wasted patience. There's nothing waiting at the end."

"Maybe what matters isn't patience," Simone said, "but desire."

Theo looked at the ground. Another passing car, another shred of light grazing another part of the pavement. A second ten-dollar bill. Theo shook his head, stooping. "Speaking of signs," he said.

"What's the sign say?" she asked.

Up above them the desert was finished and beautiful and all three painters had disappeared.

"'Life may yet surprise you,'" he proposed.

Moonlight moved across a wall.

Simone smiled. "It may."

:::

Nothing else is like cycling at night in summer. Nothing else is like the feeling of a moonlit wind, the scent of swift, green-leafed, dark-flowered air.

Theo passed chains of shining telephone poles and roads that led into darkness. He felt all his weariness leaving him block by block by block. He and Simone had still not encountered a single red light.

Theo called out to her: "Nights like this, I adore this city."

"What?" she shouted from her Norton.

"Nights like this—"

She gunned the engine.

"Nights—" he repeated.

"I don't need to hear the rest," she yelled. "I love any sentence that begins that way."

She sped on ahead. He felt the breath in his chest, hard swells that seemed to rise into his shoulders and roll down through his arms. So fast across a straightaway, fingers over the levers of his brakes; he could stop whenever he wanted to; he could stop if he wanted. He dodged a giant pothole and already Simone was swinging round the corner ahead, taillight like a ruby. He shifted gears. He sped round the corner after her, a ten-dollar bill in each of his pockets, the solidity of the pedals palpable through the soles of his shoes, like objects pressed into your hands.

Finally they came to a red.

Theo caught his breath as cars with darkened passengers whisked through the intersection in front of him. Theo thought this thought: *Cars are like rooms, I guess. We could be in any of those rooms.* It would have been something to write down, if he were still writing thoughts down. *Cars are like rooms.* He shook his head.

Simone took off her helmet and rested it before her. She was looking at him with a new expression, a lightening. Her hair was mussed where the helmet had sat.

"I'm going to regret this," Simone said. The side of her face looked as if it had been roughly kissed.

Theo answered slowly, "You're going to regret what?"

"What I'm about to do."

There was a long silence, and the light turned green. Her eyes seemed to be searching his face for something.

"I'm a thief," she said.

It felt as if a part of him was overflowing. "A thief?"

"All of us are," she murmured. "We steal luck."

:::

They were sitting on the curb.

Simone took a jar from her bag.

"Luck," she said.

The moon was like an open window.

She unscrewed the jar's lid and set it down beside her. She took the smallest pinch of something from inside the jar and then she took his hand and she opened his palm. She released some luck into it.

It was like sand, thin and glittering.

"I don't understand."

"I know," she said.

"Is this a joke?"

"No."

"It's not a joke."

"It isn't."

He stared at her, hard. She stared straight back.

"Luck's just chance," he said.

"Yes."

"Probability."

"Yes. But also, sometimes," she nodded towards the little handful of sand, "it's this."

"Sand."

"It isn't sand." She set the open jar between them. "Luck flows through the world—odds and chance and happenstance. But think of magnetic forces—swirling out through space, or throughout the world, everywhere. Think of magnets. A thing, a substance, that manipulates these forces."

"Luck," he said.

"What you're holding in your hand looks like sand but isn't," she said. She reached over and took something else out of her bag—a tall wooden cup, burled walnut or cherrywood, the sort of object that's given for a present. "It's stranger than that. Iron in a horseshoe, metal rivets in a car: there are materials in the world that interact with forces we can't see."

He could feel the little dune of luck resting on his palm.

"Coal can give us heat. Uranium can make us sick. But what you're holding is sensitive to human will—to wishes, all our wishes."

She reached into the cup and withdrew six white dice, which she showed him.

"This seems like a magic trick," he said.

"I'm not a magician." She put the dice back in the cup and shook it, covering the opening with her hand. It was a sound like rolling bones.

"I . . ." he said.

She stopped.

He shook his head. "Go on."

Simone rattled the dice once more and took her hand away.

Six white dice.

Each of them showed a side with six pips.

"They could be trick dice."

"They're not."

"What are the odds of that?"

"Not that far-fetched, actually. Six sixes. One in six to the order of six. So about one in 47,000."

She covered the cup again, shook. They were looking into each other's eyes. When she stopped she showed him: again each die was showing a six. "That's twelve sixes now," she said. "One in two billion."

She collects the sand from his hand, returning it to the jar, and gave him the cup. It was smooth and light and it felt good in the hand. He examined a die, feeling its plastic edges on his fingertips.

When he shook the cup he heard the rattling bones.

Six, six, six, six, six, six.

"It could still be a trick," he said.

"I told you, it's not a trick. You remember all our green lights?"

Lines appeared across Theo's brow.

"This is the dice test," Simone said. "It's sort of like a Geiger counter. We use it to find luck, or to check if a cache is real, or if the luck's still working."

"Why wouldn't it be working?"

"Luck gets used up. Every time it's applied to something, it loses a little of its power."

"This test doesn't count?"

"It counts," she said. "We try not to run a dice test too often."

"Only when you don't know."

"When we don't know. But if you keep on testing the same batch of luck, keep on asking it to interact with the world, gradually the luck will winnow away."

"It disappears?"

"It just stops working," she said. "The magic goes, but the substance stays. Then it's just sand."

Theo stared at her little jar of luck. "So some of that's already spent?"

"And some's unspent," she said. "The two things look the same."

"It's as if diamonds stopped being diamonds once they had been worn."

"Luck's much rarer than diamonds," said Simone. She stood up. "It's the rarest of all."

:::

Later, standing at their bikes, he asked, "You can just use it for any-thing? Win at bingo, hit a homer, meet a long-lost friend?"

He did not know how to stand, where to put his hands. And Simone too seemed to be wavering in her poses. She hesitated. "It's inexact." She lowered her head and a wall of hair fell free; he could see only the bottom half of her face. "With luck it's always so fuzzy. How much you need, how much you're spending. Even piling it on, noth-ing's guaranteed. Once in however many thousand shakes, one of those dice might land wrong. Maybe too much of your stock's already spent, exhausted. Maybe you nudged the chances to 99:1 but hit the unlucky 1 in 100. A handful of luck won't let you win the lottery. But a trunkful, a roomful, a vault—maybe then."

"A vault?" said Theo. "Who's got a vault?"

She led him back the way they'd come, away from the water, over an underpass, under an overpass, up the hill, past parks with invisible leaves, late-night lovers on benches, swans in their ponds, airborne skateboarders, Theo trailing the clouded silhouette of Simone and her motorcycle, its loud sound.

Eventually he realized where she was taking him. Now it was rain-ing, a light rain, and Le Black Cat seemed different from when they had left it.

The shop was closed, all of its lights extinguished. The downtown's glass and asphalt and fixtures and façades seemed slackened by the rain and the late hour. And Theo, too, felt unwound. His muscles were tired, his butt sore from cycling. He stood with her as she unlocked the door.

"So you own the place."

"We lease some space," she said.

He noted the way she said "we."

He followed her through the darkened aisles, shelves and shoe-boxes, past the tables where they'd sat together, and then past the staff room, the kitchen, even the minuscule bathroom and its hand-drawn sign.

They came to another door, a locked door, with three deadbolts. Again she raised her keys.

This door opened onto a staircase. Simone flicked an unseen switch and they descended beneath a blazing Largo bulb, its fila-ments like golden handwriting. At the bottom was another door, this one much heavier—something from a bank. A keypad. Simone punched in a code, paused. A rose-coloured light passed across her fingertips. "Smile," she said, gesturing over their heads. A black lens watched them from the ceiling.

The luck-burglars' hideout was a narrow corridor of offices, four desks. Unlike the dilapidated store, the space was clean and new, unspoilt. Fresh drywall, nude wood, Sputnik-like light fixtures that could have been stolen from a Soviet lab. Steel surfaces twinkled. A horseshoe had been nailed to a wall but mostly the decoration con-sisted of portraits, sumptuous oils in gilded frames, of men and women with felt hats, frilled collars, resting with greyhounds or sceptres or bowls of torn rose-petals. One or two in almost every room, bare personalities reigning from the walls. She saw him admiring them.

"They're Danish," she said. "This duchess with an art collection, and a mountain of luck in her greenhouse. Sebald couldn't help him-self; he grabbed a whole crate."

"Right," said Theo. His fatigue dulled any unease. These were just rooms; this was just a lair of thieves. A few computer monitors, piles of books, potted cacti, satellite photos in an array. A map that spanned an entire wall, with string and coloured pins. One of the offices had stacks and stacks of French newspapers. "This is all yours?" he said. She didn't answer. A wooden jewellery box rested atop a filing cabinet; he prodded the lid with a fingertip, peeked in. It was a box full of leaves.

No, four-leaf clovers.

"Should you be showing me this?" Theo asked quietly.

"No," said Simone. She turned to look at him.

The hallway widened into a small meeting room. Its plywood conference table had been covered in scratched messages and Sharpied initials, loose graffiti. A sheaf of blueprints was unscrolled across the surface, showing some kind of big house or pavilion. A lemon tree stood at the table's foot, planted in what looked like an old aquarium. The tree rose almost to Theo's chin. It was flourishing somehow, in this sunless basement.

Simone went up to the tree and unscrewed one of its lemons. The movement was so unexpected that Theo almost laughed. Then she removed another. A careful twisting motion, as if she were threading a lightbulb from its fixture. She paused. "Look somewhere else," she said, tucking a band of hair behind her ear.

The rustle of "lemons" being removed from their branches.

"Okay," she said. When he turned back, five particular lemons had been taken from the tree of counterfeit lemons and there was a high-pitched tone, another noise like a dropped stone. The wall behind the tree became unmoored and Simone eased the opening a little wider, signalling for Theo to come with her. He followed through the secret door and into a limitless room.

Not limitless. It took a moment for his eyes to adjust to what he was seeing. The room was small. It was only a little larger than the basement's other rooms, and yet it was an unending chamber, glimmering with inset halogens, orange gleams like little embers. The ceiling was mirrored, the floor was mirrored, and the other surfaces, all mirrored, and the walls, mirrored, and the walls, the walls, the walls, and even the mirrored door behind him. Theo stood face to face with kaleidoscopic hundreds of himself, with infinite Simones. "This is . . ." he said. He did not know what to say.

Simone lifted something, a gesture that seemed to repeat forever. It was a lid, the lid of a mirrored box. Uncounted Simones lifted the same lid.

Inside the box lay two long rows of mason jars.

"Luck?" said Theo.

"Yeah." She lifted one out. The powder inside looked dull, harmless. Theo could make out another row of jars underneath, yet another under that.

She closed the box and unclasped a panel covering a different section of the mirrored wall. This too revealed a row of jars, and jars beyond that. "There it is. Our loot."

"It's all stolen?" He tried to say this with a trace of mischief.

She shrugged. "You can't make your own."

"I feel like I'm inside one of those Yayoi Kusama installations. Mirrors forever."

"If you take out the mirrors the luck starts seeping out."

"Like a gas leak?"

"*Things happen*. The luck begins to apply itself to the world." She closed the panel. "Mirrors are a kind of insulation. The way lead works with radiation, or a Faraday cage against lightning strikes."

"Whereas broken mirrors . . ."

" . . . don't do shit." She smiled. "Seven years' bad luck, right? We've chosen marks before by tracing large purchases of mirrors. And all the big manufacturers— Gladstone, Verité Industriel—are owned by Hustler families."

"You call them 'Hustlers'?"

"Luck collectors."

With the panels closed, Theo felt as if he could sense the dust in its jars. Hidden engines, tiny turbines, clinking against the atoms of the air. It made the hairs on his arms stand up.

He said, "So are you gamblers?"

"What?" She was standing nearer to him now. "Why would you think that?"

"The Rabbit's Foot . . ."

"Oh no, Mitsou wants no part of this. Luck's too fickle. Too unpredictable. She does well enough with numbers. We'll make a bet now and then, for petty cash, but casino games are more reliable than sports. Luck works best on *objects*. Horses are harder. You could waste a whole barrel on a football game."

"So what's it for?"

"What's what for?"

"This luck?"

She hesitated.

"You're not using it to make money. You're not hoarders. Are you saving up for something?"

"I shouldn't have shown you this," she said. The words hung there, and the longer they hung there the more untrue they sounded.

She stared at her hand, lying against one of the closed panels, and after a moment she began again: "There's a theory," she said. "If you accumulate enough luck, if you collect and steal it, gather it together . . . Eventually the luck will start to multiply." She raised her eyes. "Little by little, particle by particle, by accident."

"Forever?"

"Forever."

He followed her out of the secret room; she closed the door.

"And then what?"

Simone seemed surprised by his question, as if the answer were obvious.

"Then we'll have enough."

He stood near the scentless lemon tree, beside the long table and the hidden room, beneath the old diner/hardware store and the city's downtown streets, beneath the day not yet dawning.

"I want to help," he said.

Only her eyes showed that she had heard him. It was as if the shade of them had changed: from an old brown to one that was like new wood, unfinished. "So join us."

AN EXCERPT FROM
"PARSIMONIOUS DOWSERS: TOWARDS AN UNDERSTANDING OF THE PROPERTIES OF LUCK"
L. L. SEBALD

(The Contemporary Review of Tychology, vol. 5)

. . . Which is not to contend that the enterprise is completely otiose, or irredeemable. Strides have been made, both by solitary researchers and—alas, less frequently—through a public model of scholarship. Setting aside the era of Greenwood and Caron-Dumas, most of the scholars have worked in isolation, without the bolstering of peers—or even the encouragement of rivals. Furthermore, doubtless to the dismay of Oldenburgistes, almost none of the research has undergone peer review. This journal, and publications like it, strives to remedy these matters. Yet it must also be said: in spite of the field's decentralization, its near-geological pace of advancement, our community has enjoyed considerable cumulative progress.

In recent years, a growing debate has centred on methodology: whether tychologists should focus their energies on empirical data collection or on the advancement of theoretical work (see: Pagnucco, *CRT v.1*; Letters page, *CRT v.2*). It is my view that the challenges particular to Luck—primarily its scarcity—nullify such arguments. Pending a breakthrough with respect to origin, production or preservation of Luck's raw material, our sphere is ill-suited to the qualitative/quantitative clashes that characterize similar domains.

Correspondingly, while the scarcity, utility and exchange values of Luck encourage theoretical or historical methodologies, it is important that real-world incentives not overwhelm the advancement of empirical inquiry. Man cannot live by fish alone. With so many questions unanswered, the past is not the only oracle available to us. Mysteries can be illuminated here, in the present, by what sits in mirrored boxes before us.

For example, a clear-headed application of the scientific method has been able to substantiate speculation: Luck and common sand are indeed essentially indistinguishable. Each is a heterogeneous granular material composed of particles of as many as hundreds of different rocks and minerals, predominantly silica (quartz), but also commonly limestone, feldspar, gypsum, mica, man-made substances like sea-glass and plastic, and vegetal material such as cork and wood fragments. Researchers have not isolated any substance that is necessarily present in Luck but absent in beach sand, or vice versa, nor have they identified any significant difference in the constituent proportions thereof. Moreover, years of experimentation have demonstrated the impotence of conventional diagnostic tools: X-ray technology, nuclear magnetic resonance imaging, electrical impedance, chromatography,

Raman spectroscopy, and more, are all thus far unable to differentiate between Luck and the stuff of seasides and deserts. Luck is sand; except it isn't.

Interestingly, Luck's unique properties do not appear to survive major temperature, pressure or state changes. Although the material reacts to these physical forces in the same way as sand (cementation, vitrification), the resultant stuff is inert, lacking the original material's distinguishing attribute.

That notorious, astonishing and slippery attribute is naturally at the heart of any tychological inquiry. Empirical approaches have proven particularly effective at understanding—or even occasionally manipulating—it. Take our most commonly used evaluative tool, the so-called Dice (or Chang) Test. The utility of this technique rests not only upon its simplicity, but also upon its obvious mathematical sturdiness. Together, these qualities are (usually) felt to compensate for the test's failure rate (1 false positive in 46,656). The same principles have also allowed for the development of even more accurate tests: see our review of G. Smith's ClockDrifter app in *CRT v.4*.

We have also been able to measure, at least in relative terms, the degree to which Luck makes one lucky. Loïc's monumental discovery of a tychological constant transformed the field; his successors' successive modifications have brought us to where we are today. Our historical forerunners in the Order of St.-Tropez, or among the Janissaries of the Silver Minaret, would have been staggered by the existence of an equation like the following, which allows us to describe the interaction of a quantity of Luck on a given probability (where K represents Loïc's

Modified Constant, p is the natural probability of a given event, and p' is the probability after the application of m grams of Luck):

$$p' = 1 + \frac{p - 1}{e^{Km}}$$

They would also have been grateful for our empirical certainty on a number of issues that they were unable to advance beyond a rhetorical frame:

(1) that the more unlikely an event you hope to influence, the more Luck is required;

(2) that although Luck can act across long distances, its results improve with proximity; and

(3) that certain categories[1] of events require more Luck than others.

Experiments have also established that Luck's probabilistic influence deteriorates with use. This dwindling—or "winnowing away"— of power can only be slowed by limiting the Luck's exposure to other objects, people and probabilistic events. This is most often accomplished through the use of mirrored surfaces and containers.

Unfortunately there are other areas where scientific rigour has been unable to improve upon knowledge passed down

---

1 Outcomes involving plants, for instance, are more "expensive" than outcomes involving only inanimate things. As Riudsepp showed in her monograph, the hierarchy continues: plants; most non-human animals; dolphins; large primates; a single human being; two human beings; three human beings; *et cetera*.

through generations, its origins long lost. While it is unclear how Luck "chooses" which events it acts upon, we do know this "choice" can be influenced by human will. We do not know how, why, or whether Healey's famous analogy—comparing the bond between Luck and humans to the one between ferrous metals and magnetic fields—correctly applies. But even here, persistent inquiry has reaped unexpected dividends: not only is Luck's influence verifiably modulated by variables like physical proximity and mental concentration, but also, we know now, by its current ownership (see Khan, this volume).

Findings like these, sudden and bewildering, underline the potential before us. In a field where the most fundamental principles seem like acts of magic, much of this magic has yet to be uncovered. Furthermore—and crucially—much of this work can now be pursued at home or in an ordinary laboratory. No need to wait for antediluvian eye-witness accounts or unfurled papyrus scrolls. All that science requires is its method—hypotheses tested and re-tested. Alongside the delectable conjectures of Molleson's Camelot theory, or Gélinas's newly ascendant ideas concerning Luck and ambergris, there is room for patient, humble experimentation.

Whether Luck was ever grown or forged, whether there was one great mine or one thousand, or whether this substance still feels like something brought from another world (Narnia or Tlön, Philip Pullman's dreams of Dust), what matters most is that it is here before us still. Everything we know about it is a testament to our predecessors' collective curiosity—but also, I hope, a motivation for the work that's yet to come.

CHAPTER NINE

When morning came, Theo was still underground. He woke slowly on the tattered couch. There was a smear of illumination from the hallway, pinlight gleams from computer LEDs, just enough for him to discern the hodgepodge of the office and the occluded rectangle of the doorway. He remembered only hazily the end of the night, a sense of closeness but caution. Simone had suggested he crash on the couch; she went to lie down on a futon in the room next door. If she had proposed they share the futon he didn't know what he would have said. He thought of Lou. He let out a long breath.

Then he noticed the woman with the gun. For a moment he mistook her for Simone. She had the same wiry build, the same screen of bangs across her brow, a chin like the point of an axe. She was standing just inside the door, the gun at her side held loosely, easily, as if she were accustomed to the pose. It was not a large gun. He had time to have this thought, *It is not a large gun*, before the woman demanded, "Who the fuck are you?"

He recognized her now. "My shadow," Simone had said.

He swallowed. "I'm Theo."

"Well, that clears everything up."

He shifted on his cushion.

"Hold it," she said.

He said, "Simone's next door."

"Simone?"

A chill went through him. Something caught in his throat. "She brought me here."

The woman examined his face with a dark gaze. At last she shouted, sharply, "Simone!"

Silence. Perhaps Simone had not stayed after all, perhaps she had woken and departed. Fear began to stitch Theo's ribs.

"Simone?" he called roughly, in turn.

Finally, distantly, an answer from the other side of the wall. She emerged in tousled clothes, framed by the doorway.

The woman with the gun glared at her.

Simone rubbed her face, blearily. She said to Theo, "I see you've met my other sister."

Her name was Suzy. Once the gun was away and the lights were turned on, Theo discovered that he had been sleeping in her office. He wondered if it had been a kind of test. The room was a clutter of cables, notebooks, empty glasses, flatscreens, as well as cactuses, dozens of cactuses, in small pots. The walls had been plastered with taped-up images of fortresses—Carcassonne, the Red Fort of Agra, and many more obscure. The citadels and succulents shared a kind of affinity, as if every potted cutting was its own small stronghold.

Within the hour, the group's two other members arrived: JF, the blue-jeaned Santa Claus, and long-limbed Sebald, ever mysterious—the only one who kept his office locked. Sebald was dressed like some kind of security guard—slate-coloured slacks and a pale blue shirt with chest pockets, empty epaulets.

"Do you guys have a name?" Theo asked.

"No name," said Sebald.

The No Name Gang sat around the conference table, appraising him like members of a jury. "He looks like a cop," said Suzy.

"In what universe does he look like a cop?" asked JF.

"He looks like a cop's idea of what a hardworking joe would look like. A middlebrow bohemian."

"Ouch," Theo said.

"Tell me a joke," said Sebald.

Theo sighed. "Seriously?"

They were waiting.

"I really don't—"

"Perhaps you *are* a cop," said Sebald.

Theo gave him an even look.

Simone was grinning. "Go on then."

Theo shook his head. "Why did the Buddhist fall out of a tree?"

Only JF seemed ready to laugh.

"She was practising non-attachment."

"He quit the comedy business," said Simone. "He works at the Rabbit's Foot now."

"I want to join you," Theo said. "I'm honest. I work hard."

"We're thieves," said Suzy.

"Not *that* honest," Theo amended.

She reached over and prodded one of the lemon tree's false lemons. "We don't need him."

"You don't think we could use another body?" demanded Simone. "Another person?"

"We've been fine so far."

"What about Colorado? Or Belfast?"

"It's not worth the risk."

"We're close now, Suzy."

Sebald arched an eyebrow. "Isn't that precisely the concern? That we're close?"

"And now you want to cut some bozo in?"

"Hey, now," said Theo.

"What if he betrays us?"

"Who would I betray you to!?"

"He won't betray us," said Simone. She regarded her companions. "You've always trusted my judgment."

Theo felt their eyes on him, appraising.

Suzy got up, chair scraping. "All right, scram," she told Theo.

"I—"

"Just wait outside," said Simone.

He did, outside the door. Face to face with a Flemish grimace.

Through the wood he heard them talking, voices batting back and forth.

JF was the one to come and get him. He was smiling. The others had resumed their positions, like councillors round a table.

"Welcome," said Simone.

"*Provisionally*," said Sebald.

What they had decided was: they would do a job together, see how it went.

Suzy was reclining in her chair, hands clasped behind her head. She extricated an arm, pointed with a thumb and index-finger pistol. "If you screw us, *stronzino*, I'll kill you."

Theo nodded. He drummed his fingers on the doorframe. "Is anyone else hungry?" he said.

:::

So they ate breakfast together. "I don't eat," Suzy claimed, but even she relented. Le Black Cat's diner seemed transformed by the morning, or else by Theo's knowledge of what lay beneath it. The grandmotherly server treated him with newfound tenderness: her approval felt like an affirmation that all of this had really happened, the luck and the hide-out, Theo's enrollment into a gang. A coffee refill had never meant so much. When their orders arrived, cheap cutlery scraped across plates. The mood lightened, and lightened again. Suzy tore sections from a morning-glory muffin. Theo had a hundred questions.

:::

Mitsou, Simone and Suzanna San Marziale were born one by one in stubborn, sun-stamped Sicily. The girls' mother, Françoise Malo, was a dancer from Trois-Rivières. Their father, Sandro San Marziale, was an importer of children's toys and a small-time stakeholder in the local Cosa Nostra. Sandro was famous for his linen suits— *Sandro chiaro*, they called him, "pale Sandro," as if his suits were a second skin.

The couple met when Françoise's dance company appeared at the Teatro Massimo in Palermo. Backstage after the show, among the platters of melon and oranges, and carafes of inky wine, Sandro was the only man with a flower in his lapel, a rose so red it looked as if it was bleeding. As soon as he glimpsed Françoise he removed the rose, pressed it into her hands. "You are the most beautiful woman in the world," he told her. "I knew it before I even saw you. In the darkness, before the lights came up, just from hearing your footsteps."

"That's a good line," she said.

"I think I am in love," he said.

"We don't even know each other."

"This is always how the story starts."

Françoise—round-cheeked, long-limbed, secretly arthritic—found that she preferred Sicilian sunshine to Trifluvian blizzards. Once Sandro had proven his love, flying twice trans-Atlantic to woo her, she quit the company and returned with him to Sicily, installing herself at his villa—wedging her suitcases among the crates of spinning tops, Lite-Brites, *Giacomo*-in-the-boxes. They were married. They had three daughters. And then Sandro, whose criminal ambitions had kept pace with his family's growth—from low-level *picciotto* to more like upper-mid—was found floating facedown in a community swimming pool. It might have been taken for an accident had he not been wearing his suit.

Françoise returned with her daughters to the land of her birth. She raised them in a city of wintertime want and springtime lilac blossom. She forbade them children's toys. Instead the girls played with sticks and stones, pen and paper, their mother's solar-powered calculator. And Françoise did not go back to dancing, but to school, drawing funds from undisclosed (sun-stamped) sources. By the time her youngest daughter moved out, and until Françoise took early retirement and moved to Florida, Signora San Marziale *née* Malo counted her days as a professor of actuarial mathematics. "I liked dancing," Françoise told her daughters, "but I prefer to see the future."

At least at first, the actuary's daughters showed none of her pragmatism. Mitsou, the eldest, became an artist. Her métier was conceptual: live performances blending original music with demographic data, like orchestral infographics. In Suzy, the youngest, Mitsou's work provoked rattling awe and abrading envy. She followed her sister to art school, invented her own conceptual practice. Whereas Mitsou made stats into installations, Suzy preferred to wreak havoc: vandalizing memorials, sneaking into city hall to stage dance-ins. Her only documentation was Polaroid.

As for Simone, she vaulted on poles. Until Sydney and its qualifiers, when everything screeched to a halt. She came home with a bruised rib, burnt out.

"So I became a sculptor."

She registered Theo's surprise; he could see it made her melancholy.

"Like, bronzes?"

Paper. Glue and folded paper. Both of her sisters were already doing so well, were already so happy—Simone followed them into it—making small, intricate objects; hewing to no particular style. She made abstracted alley cats, frozen clock faces, hyper-realistic Olympic podiums. But the work mattered less to her than the idea of the work: "I wanted to be a sculptor more than I wanted to actually sculpt." She hated sitting in her kitchen with an unfinished piece, adding parts, taking other parts away. She wanted to skip to the finished work—to the show and its opening, the little article online. "The outcome was more satisfying to me than the doing. And I know that because after I gave it up I never missed it."

The sisters never showed together and they generally moved in different crowds. Mitsou was adept at grant applications and agitating for gallery commissions. Suzy's provocations had a rowdy younger following, especially around New Year's and Halloween. Simone's work became popular online, where photographs of her paper tigers began to appear on amateur art blogs. Then everything changed, with news that came by thunderbolt: the Lightning Prize, sponsored by Lightning Gas & Energy, not the country's biggest art prize but a very respectable third or fourth, announced its finalists. Every year, a blind jury selected six nominees. This time the shortlist included all three San Marziale sisters.

"SISTER ACT," bragged the local paper. Yet the siblings' smiles faded greyly into the newsprint. They were too competitive to celebrate.

"I don't know which I dreaded more, that none of us would win— or that you or Mitsou would," said Simone.

"The latter," Suzy growled.

The matter reached a crossroads when Françoise San Marziale summoned her daughters to an uncharacteristic Friday-night dinner. They trooped to her leafy, tall-ceilinged brownstone. Its uncluttered rooms were almost unrecognizable from their childhood. Françoise had long ago replaced the particleboard furniture where they ate green apples and peanut butter: now the women sat at a polished maple table eating salade niçoise.

Françoise told her daughters that she had an aquarium full of luck.

"The story was that a man named Montecarlo gave Papa the luck to thank him for a job," Simone said. "He told him how to use it but Papa didn't believe it was real, and he never tried, but it got shipped across the ocean with the rest of his stuff when we moved. One trunk among many. Maman claimed she forgot all about it until that spring, during a purge of the basement, a.k.a. throwing out her children's most precious keepsakes."

The luck looked like sand and it was stored in what appeared like an aquarium. The container seemed well made but oddly light and, unlike most aquariums, it had a lid. Much more peculiar was the aquarium's enclosure, a mirror-lined box of black lacquer, engraved with the words Touchwood of Louisiana, 1949. The sisters were skeptical, as their mother had been too, but then again: the results were already in. Françoise described the way she had lugged the container to her sitting room, plopped it on the table, and wished for her daughters' careers to get luckier. The Lightning contenders were announced five days later.

"I told her, 'So you think the only reason we were nominated was that you sat here and stared at this box of sand?'" Simone said.

Theo's brow softened.

"And she said, 'My love, not the *only* reason.'"

Assuming that the Lightning jury's deliberations had indeed been influenced by thirty-year-old Sicilian magic, the question became: Now what? Should Françoise keep wishing? Might this luck indulge a three-way tie? Or would these circumstances spell the sisters' doom—their serendipity split three ways, precluding any one of them from collecting the prize?

"The box isn't God, Maman. There's no point praying to it," Suzy had said. But she was only feigning indifference. Unlike Mitsou, who rolled her eyes (dramatically) and left early, empty-handed— "Correlation not causation," she sneered—Suzy and Simone lingered late, debating who should take the heirloom home. Françoise settled the matter as war-weary parents usually do: she told the sisters to share it. (Biweekly.)

Neither of them knew what to do with the luck, exactly. They didn't know if they could touch the sand, or take it out of its aquarium. They didn't know whether to keep the box open or closed. It was as if Aladdin had a lamp but no clue he should rub it. The sisters simply lived with it, hoped at it, pleaded for it to work its wiles.

Some days they kept the box of sand in its silvered enclosure, other times they plunked it on a bedside table or beside the ripening avocados in their kitchen. They hadn't yet learned that luck's influence is hindered by mirrors, that mirrors are a way of keeping it in, but they soon observed its bewildering effects. During the weeks it sat chez Suzy, she accidentally got pregnant, her landlord forgot to collect the rent, a long-lost cat returned, her barren magnolia tree exploded shockingly into bloom. When the luck was with Simone, she was selected for jury duty, cashiers gave her too much change, three birds shat on her head, and her cat, too, came back. As the Lightning announcement grew closer, each sister found excuses to hang on to the luck a little longer. They didn't think about their work; they didn't make sculptures or stage interventions: Simone and Suzy just thought about their father, his friend Montecarlo, and whatever this stuff's strange physics might be.

Finally the day arrived. In Fort McMurray, a panel of judges gathered like choristers around a microphone. Simone and Suzy watched from the former's apartment, casting sideways glances at the aquarium on the floor.

Mitsou won. The prize jury lauded her work's "interplay of total vision and complete commitment . . . San Marziale's creations seem as if they are uncovering proofs for human appetites, for wishes themselves." Lightning wired her a sum of $25,000, plus $10,000 in credit towards domestic electrical services.

Mitsou used the money to stake her first big bet, on a horse called Brave New Waves, at the Preakness Stakes. By the following spring, she was calculating the odds for college basketball.

Suzy quit performance art. After four weeks of doldrums she gave up her lease and packed up her things, loaning her cactus collection to a friend. She boarded a plane to Palermo. In a black moleskine journal, at the top of page one, she had scribbled a man's name. *Montecarlo.*

Simone quit sculpture. After twelve weeks of doldrums she gave up her lease and caught a Greyhound south to New Orleans. In a red moleskine journal, at the top of page one, she had inscribed the name of a company. *Touchwood of Louisiana.*

Two years later, Suzy and Simone would form the No Name Gang.

Nobody knows if luck is more like water or more like wine. Nobody knows whether it was invented or whether it was found. The thieves explained to Theo that what they knew was that you will not find it on a beach, or at the bottom of a canyon. It does what sand does not do: it turns fortunes. "Some people still think there's a mine for it somewhere—that it's a rare substance you can dig for," Simone said. "Someone else—Sebald found this theory online—thinks that there was this alchemist in Worms, in Germany, who produced it in his lab. That all the luck there is is left over from the twelfth century."

Or stranger rumours. That all the world's luck was stolen from Jesus's abandoned tomb. From inside the Kaaba in Mecca. That it was gathered from King Arthur's crypt; from the sea-bed of the Bermuda Triangle; from the summits of the Himalayas; or that it's the treasure of El Dorado. Some collectors believe Newton invented it, or a scientist in Japan—and that's why they bombed Hiroshima. Maybe Amelia Earhart was smuggling luck on her plane. Or she was trying to get some back.

"Maybe it's from the moon landing," Theo suggested.

"No," said JF. "We know it's older than that."

Wherever it came from, the supply was limited. The supply was small. If it were a renewable resource then people would not be so remorseless in their pursuit of it. They would not be so desperate or so cruel.

:::

It wasn't until late in the evening, on his way home, that Theo saw all the text messages from Matisse. He had missed one full day of work and fourteen texts. A few of them were variations of *Wherefore art thou?* and *U OK bud?* and *maybe you were kidnapped* but most were just rippling expanses of question marks. Pausing at a stop sign, he tapped a response. *Sorry sick*, with a death's-head emoji. *Hopefully better tomorrow.*

Within seconds Matisse sent his own emojis back, tulip tulip tulip. Theo didn't know what that meant.

Cusp, he thought.

In the morning he biked down the hill and found himself again in the Dolores's sardined and dawdling elevator. Crushed against a wall, Theo stared at his reflection. Was his face the same as it had been? He took a deep breath and let it go. He was wearing a ratty yellow backpack, one hand closed around each strap. Sebald had given him the backpack, as well as its contents, and it was too small for him, as if borrowed from a kid. Theo stared into his own appraising gaze. There was a quiver there, he could see it. "Knock that off," he whispered.

The hardest part of stealing luck, it emerged, was working out who had luck to steal. Like diamond thieves looking for a really big score, Simone and her confederates could pass whole seasons scouring the planet for marks. Often heists came in clusters: the Gang would devise a new scheme to uncover Hustlers, collectors of luck; they'd rob them one by one; and then return to the drawing board.

Unfortunately, Hustlers didn't keep directories or register at city hall. They rarely publicized their holdings because, if they did, they didn't hang on to them for very long. Instead, most collectors kept their luck underground, away from rivals' and robbers' prying eyes. Although there were exceptions—famed Hustler dynasties like the Gladstones of London and the Batcheats of Buenos Aires, or Tokyo's Teruteru Company, whose security was legendary—most collectors were reluctant to be identified. So the thieves had to be creative, canvassing storage facilities for unusual holdings, combing estate-sale catalogues for infrequent heirlooms, wandering through cities with rattling dice tests. To Theo's surprise, there *were* a handful of message boards where Hustlers discussed luck—the largest of them in Mandarin. Although their users were anonymous, they slipped up sometimes, said JF, "or you can embed something to scrape IPs."

The Gang's longest-running scheme related to antiquarian books. More than a century earlier, the scholar and Hustler Loïc Caron-Dumas published two pamphlets on luck and its properties, *Traité sur la chance manifestée et ses caractéristiques physiques* (1889) and *Autres études sur les effets, ambivalences et insuffisances de la chance manifestée* (1890), among the only known works on the subject. The Gang didn't own either volume ("just the PDFs"), but for years they had maintained eBay listings that purported to sell them, recording the mailing address of every prospective buyer. Eventually Sebald took this concept even further, creating the *Contemporary Review of Tychology*. Published online, the journal presented scholarly articles on the social history and natural properties of luck. Most of its visitors took it as a whimsical fiction—one of the internet's many weird, tinfoil-hatted dead ends. But for those who knew luck's secret, stumbling across the *Review* was like finding the Rosetta Stone, and they pored through Sebald's writings—which were largely, though not entirely, factual. A handful of armchair academics, idle Hustlers in hilltop villas, began to contribute their own research, which Sebald duly published. The Gang's computer servers logged each of the *Review*'s visitors, and particularly its contributors; JF traced their locations; and eventually, whenever possible, they burgled them.

Still, Simone told Theo, "The easiest way to locate luck is to look out for people who are lucky. Just keep your eyes open. Pay attention."

There was the Floridian golfer with his eleven holes-in-one. (Suzy found the cache in a corner of his guest bedroom, under a caftan.) There was the politician in Guernsey who won multiple elections by single votes. (In the guarded paddock of a broken-down stable.) A South African prospector who went scouting for rhodium. (Shelves of luck in a poured concrete hangar.) And a Sri Lankan dowser with a knack for striking oil. (Bank of Kandy safety deposit boxes.) For a little while Sebald had a run on raiding treasure hunters—trawlers of shipwrecks and diggers of dunes—who had been curiously successful in their quests for priceless relics.

Yet what lucky people loved above all was to gamble. And at the end of his first breakfast as a member of the No Name Gang, Theo learned one of the reasons they had inducted him into their ranks.

"You're gonna get us the Model," Suzy said.

"I am?"

"You are," said Simone, crunching an ice cube in her teeth.

It wasn't because they wanted to pit luck against math. The reason the thieves wanted the Rabbit's Foot's algorithms was to help with their triage. They wanted to be able to look at the results of the Triple Crown, March Madness or the Champions League Final and see whether, when someone had earned millions on a wager, their wager made sense. Was the result comprehensible? Or was the outcome lucky beyond reason? On a list of winning bets, which ones were fishy and which were just smart?

At that point, Theo told them about Hanna.

"Occasionally people *are* just lucky," Simone admitted. "The world's full of people who rolled a timely die." Some were mathematical prestidigitators (like Mitsou) or flukes (like Hanna). But the more a person's lucky streak strained credulity, the more it seemed too good to be true, the likelier it was that somewhere, in a cellar or a tower or a secret compartment, that lucky so-and-so had a strongbox filled with sand.

During the Gang's earliest days, when it was scarcely even a gang, Mitsou had let her sisters use the Model to test potential marks. Over time, big sister became less generous. Mitsou had too much to lose by lending out her software. "She's squeaky clean," Simone said. "And we're criminals."

Caught up in the thrill of luck's magic—and under Simone's steady spell—Theo was able to put the group's lawlessness out of his mind. Their project was grander than comedy or the Rabbit's machinations: this was sincerely special; this was a grand prize. By joining the Gang it seemed like anything could happen—could and *would*, like a wizard's adventure. He needn't stand on stage and reveal himself, dreaming of applause: he could chase this real, rare wonder, all around the world. Lou had her desert, her enriching miles of sand; now he had his sand, too, or would, so long as he could prove his worth.

This was what had returned him to the Dolores and its humming eighteenth floor. Theo moved through the corridors with strumming nerves. When he turned the corner to their cubicle, Matisse was bent over his keyboard like *Peanuts'* Schroeder at his toy piano. Theo ran his tongue over his lower lip. It was as if everything was just the same. No bike ride, no hideout, no luck. Just a guy a little late for work.

Matisse's chair squeaked as he straightened. "The kraken wakes!" he exclaimed.

Theo allowed a smile. "Did you miss me?"

"Like a mongoose misses his snake. What was it? A case of the oysters? Bubonic plague?"

Yes, no, maybe; Theo waved the question off. He didn't want to lie any more than he had to. "Anything happen here?"

"Our Lady of the Numbers dropped by."

"Mitsou?"

"Yesterday." Matisse propped his battered high-tops on the desk. "She insulted my shoes."

"Those ones."

"Yes."

"I'm sorry."

"It's okay. She told me we could unfork, push to server."

"Matisse, those words don't mean anything."

"Our algorithms. She approved them! Well, the first two."

"Already?" Theo was genuinely stunned.

"By the end of today, karmically weighted contests will be waltzing with the Model."

Theo plunked into his seat.

"Don't act so excited."

"I'm just surprised."

"*Felicitaciones.*"

"I don't think I ever really expected it to work."

"And check out our commission," Matisse said. He pulled the keyboard into his lap and tapped out some commands. The cells of a spreadsheet fluttered across the screen. "The field's still relatively narrow. Our conditions are semi-rare, and then there's also the limitation of parimutuel markets; and localization, too—so far the bot's only scraping English-language chatter, and *that* constrains things. But its IDs are pretty reliable!"

"Right . . ." Theo felt oddly fragile.

"Still, taking the average daily—or maybe weekly makes more sense. Anyway, if you—yeah, there . . ." Theo's consciousness had floated up a bit and he was staring at the comic pinned above his monitor. He had never noticed how happy the lock looked, and how happy the key.

"The Rabbit's standard rate is five percent," said Matisse. "Five percent on whatever the improvement on their return. But that's not nothing, not when you're gambling with seventy-five million dollars *o lo que sea*. The association ain't broke! I take forty percent, you take sixty, and that means . . ."

"Just for me?"

"Yeah, for you, weekly. Zero, carry the four. Maybe six ten?"

"Six ten what?"

"Six hundred and ten dollars a week. 30k a year? Give or take?" Matisse saw Theo's face. "What is it?"

Theo squinted at his colleague. "Say that again?"

"Thirty thousand dollars. For you. Ish. Per year. Hopefully. With caveats."

"Thirty thousand dollars."

"Ish!" Matisse scratched his chest. "Nice bonus, right? If I can roll out some more of these processes it'll bump up some, too. It's not fuck-off money but these things add up. Pancake stacks. Mille-feuille. Keep coming up with stuff and it makes a tidy little living."

"That one idea was worth thirty thousand dollars a year?"

"Your share. So far."

"And if I left the company . . . ?" Theo began.

"It's not a company."

"The association."

Matisse peered at him. "Are you—?"

"No."

Matisse maintained his scrutiny, which was very direct and very steady.

"But just to say . . ." Theo said.

"It's a bonus. A commission paid forward into ongoing work."

"Right," said Theo.

"So, no, you don't keep collecting it if you 'leave the company.'"

"The association," Theo said.

Matisse picked up his thermos of tea and sipped from it. He glanced, pointedly, at Theo, before turning his back. He clicked his computer awake. "You be you, my man."

Theo swivelled to face his own screen. He typed the word *calamarirings3*.

Each of them sat at their computers, without speaking.

I could stay, Theo told himself.

He could stay and earn a salary, plus the bonus, and more to come, a mille-feuille of commissions.

Prospering. Using his brain.

He could sit in this cloth room, entering passwords. Maybe he'd even learn to code.

Buy a fancy apartment and a nice car, a racing bike for weekends.

Go on holidays with Lou.

Grow rich on ingenuity.

Bold new ideas!

Theo rested his hand on his mouse and dragged it around, high-lighting and unhighlighting an icon representing a silver trash-can.

Was this what a big break felt like? Somewhere down the hall, somebody was playing "Put the Lime in the Coconut" on repeat.

At exactly 11:11 AM, Matisse got up from his chair. Theo jerked upright and opened a new browser window, leaned into his screen as if he had found something fascinating there.

"Time for oolong," Matisse said.

"Sounds good," said Theo.

"Want some?"

"Always."

Theo opened his email to find a note explaining the Rabbit's Foot's new in-house policy on email subject lines.

Matisse padded towards the break room.

For ten seconds, Theo did nothing.

Then he reached towards his feet, where Sebald's backpack was slouched. He zippered it open and kicked across the carpet to the opposite terminal, elbowing aside Matisse's chair. The screen was still on; moreover, Matisse's brass key was still plugged into the workstation, *The Thinker* hanging sullenly on its chain. Theo mini-mized the other windows and clicked a symbol he had seen Matisse click a hundred times before. A blue-and-salmon panel opened up, with a handful of words in tall Helvetica Light:

THE RABBIT'S FOOT

Model (global)

build 58.17

Enter password:

Theo took out an object from the backpack. It looked like a black plastic hamburger bun, with a silver cable. He plugged the dongle into the computer. Its beep reminded him of a hiccup; an LED glowed gold.

Theo's heart was beating like a tambourine. He felt like James Bond, if James Bond's heart could ever beat like a tambourine.

Simone had drilled and drilled these steps with him, repeating them like a nursery rhyme. "Enter the password when the light goes gold," she said.

Theo reached back into the backpack. He withdrew its only other item—a small rectangular box, like a deck of cards. Theo flicked a tiny copper clasp and slid away one of the case's panels. The inside of the box was mirrored. Carefully, like a jeweller with a pouch of diamonds, Theo spilled the contents of the case into his palm. He dropped the case back into the backpack, as Simone had implored him to remember, and then brought his hands together, rubbing them, coating right and left with a thin layer of powder.

Now came the implausible part.

Theo took a deep, shaggy breath.

He closed his eyes and placed his fingers above Matisse's keyboard. He still didn't really believe it.

He randomly pressed some keys.

No, not quite randomly. He had been coached by JF: "Your average 'strong' password is seven to eleven characters long, with two numerals." Their assumption was that Matisse's password would be strong, but not too strong—the middle caution of a perfectionist.

Theo's digits tickled the keyboard while in his head he carried the abstract notion of touching between seven and eleven characters, and two numerals. ("And remember the shift key!")

Luck dusted his fingertips.

He didn't know what he had typed, but when he looked up there was a row of black circles in the window's password box.

••••••••, like symbols for a new moon.

He hit enter.

The box gave a little tremor.

Wrong password. Try again.

(You have two attempts remaining.)

"Fuck," Theo whispered, but he was also feeling a curl of amusement. "Try again." As if the Model were goading him on.

Matisse could return at any moment.

Again Theo closed his eyes.

"It might take a few tries," Simone had said. "The ol' password trick's not luck at its most reliable." He remembered the way she laughed, a lock of brown hair falling free at her ear.

"So it might not work at all," he'd said.

"How about, 'So it might work.'"

"So it might work."

"It might. It's a glass half-full."

So Theo tried again. A dumb dance of blind fingers, his pinkie on shift, like a kind of automatic writing.

He looked up.

••••••

This time the black circles seemed like an ellipsis, a story awaiting its next act.

Six characters, one fewer than suggested.

He touched enter, a little sand-timer icon appeared, the password window flipped around and he was staring at a multi-panelled interface like something for air-traffic control, with a quilted spreadsheet and hurrying lines of text and pixellated vectors moving across a shining, cross-hatched grid. "Welcome, Mr. Matisse," said the banner at the top of the screen.

Theo blinked. There was an anticlimax to it, one computer-screen simply changing to another. But what was strangest was that he did not even know what he had typed. His fingers had fumbled to a secret and he didn't know what it was. Matisse's password—was it Nemo84, or r0thko, or teaP0T? What was the code Matisse murmured to himself when he and it were all alone? Theo didn't know, and wouldn't. He was just some thief.

The thing that looked like a weaponized hamburger bun beeped, sounding like it had choked on something. Its LED was flashing green: it was already finished, the back door installed.

Checking over his shoulder, Theo yanked out the dongle and stuffed it into his pack. He quit the Model software, reopened Matisse's other windows, pushed back across the cubicle to his own desk. He let out a breath.

Matisse reappeared not thirty seconds later, his thermos under his arm. In each hand he held a napkin with a slice of elaborately iced cake, like two tiny unmade beds.

"Hey," said Theo.

Matisse paused at the edge of the cubicle. Did Theo see him glance at his computer? Did he see something flicker across Matisse's face?

Had Theo forgotten something?

Matisse's screen was plain and illuminated, it looked the same as it had.

Of course its Rothko screensaver had not come on.

"Someone in machine learning had birthday cake," said Matisse, handing him a piece.

"Thanks."

:::

Come evening, they left the office together. The elevator slid like a drop down the Dolores's spine. Exiting the lobby, Matisse held open one of the building's heavy metal doors. Then Theo held a door for him. There were puddles on the ground, like so many mirrored pools. Matisse and Theo stood staring at a slow, solitary pelican, which stared in turn at them. The bird was loitering under a streetlight, as if it were waiting for a bus.

"They say the birds have something to do with climate change," Matisse said.

The pelican noticed someone's red, uneaten apple. It seemed amused by it.

"I heard it was tides," Theo said.

He adjusted the backpack on his shoulders.

"Well, see you tomorrow," he lied.

The creature looked up at them. It was like a look between fellow audience members.

Theo found himself waiting for Matisse's reply.

The pelican was now nudging the apple with the cherry-coloured stripe of its beak. It kept rolling, and rolling away. Matisse wouldn't meet Theo's eyes.

Finally, his ex-partner said, "I'll see you around."

Theo didn't hang around downtown. Once he had handed off the backpack to the Gang he begged off on supper, left the diner, biked home along the rain-glossed roads. Outside Provisions K he watched a food-truck barrel past, running the red. He noticed a parked police car across the road, without anybody inside. He went up to his apartment, messed up his grilled-cheese sandwich—one side burnt, the cheese unmelted—but he ate it anyway. When he went to bed he couldn't sleep. Part of him wanted to circle back, undo, but the greater part of him didn't have the stamina for it. He logged onto Sebald's electronic journal, read old articles. He looked at online listings for bicycle helmets. He dreamed, when he finally dreamed, of various betrayals.

:::

The following morning he skulked into Le Black Cat, worried that someone from the Rabbit's Foot would recognize him on the street. He found the Gang gathered around the battered conference table: JF with a laptop, Suzy with her phone, Simone with a cryptic crossword and a thickly peanut-buttered slice of toast. Sebald was using a matchstick-sized tool to repair his wristwatch, its components arrayed on a piece of suede.

"So there's bad news," said JF.

"There's always bad news," said Suzy.

"Not always," said Simone.

"Usually."

Theo felt queasy. "Did it work? The back door?"

"The script's running fine—top job, young Padawan. Thanks to you, we're scampering like field mice through the Rabbit's Foot's server. But. The bad news is Miss Summers."

Simone and Suzy lowered their heads to their hands.

"Who's Miss Summers?" asked Theo.

"Our mark," mumbled Suzy.

"We had hoped," said JF.

"She's a millionaire," Simone said. "Lives in Hobart, Tasmania. Very successful bird-watcher. Lucky with her birds."

"Too lucky."

"We thought too lucky," JF agreed. "She caught Sebald's eye because she had discovered, what, *three* new species?"

"And nine subspecies."

"Sebald reads all the birder journals," Simone explained.

"It can be pertinent," he said.

"Anyway, three new species and nine subspecies. But she made her money betting on dogs."

"Greyhounds," said Sebald.

"A serious high roller—big bets on big races, big bets on small races, all sorts of wagers on other people's pups."

"She ran the Tasmanian Greyhound Racing Authority," Sebald said.

JF cleared his throat. "Yes, so—here's the thing: her bets check out." He sighed. "We're looking for people who regularly *beat* the odds—who win lots of wagers the algorithms can't explain. Summers didn't do that. She's smart. The dogs she bet on the Rabbit liked too. It doesn't look like luck; it looks like she does her homework."

"What about the birds?"

"Petra Summers went on 190 separate birding trips last year. Over the course of a lifetime, maybe identifying three species isn't so implausible."

"And nine subspecies," said Sebald.

Suzy slumped back in her seat. "So she's not a Hustler? She's just a fucking expert?"

"Are the hotel rooms refundable?" Simone turned to Sebald. "Did you already pay that boat dealer?"

"Indeed," said Sebald.

She shook her head. "And we spent all that time getting the architectural drawings."

JF leaned forward, propping his arms under his chest. "So that's the bad news," he said.

The others paused in their poses, turning to look at him.

JF was grinning.

A pause like ten pennies dropping.

"Is there good news?" Simone asked.

"Theo," said JF, "have you read a book called *The Labrador Sea*?"

CHAPTER TEN

In 2013, Penguin Random House acquired international publishing rights to *The Labrador Sea*, the debut novel by Fogo Island novelist Daniel Merrett Leys, in a bidding war. The author reportedly received an advance in the high six figures.

In a press release accompanying the announcement, Ayesha Lewisohm, the acquiring editor, called *The Labrador Sea* a "radiant and magical adventure . . . studded with jewel-like prose." The plot was the story of a journey: "One man searches for his beloved, across a mysterious sea," and had something to do with the skeletons of saints.

The Labrador Sea appeared in early 2015. It was at first only a modest success. There was an approving review in the *New York Times Book Review*, something more equivocal in the *Telegraph*. *The Labrador Sea* was overlooked by the *London Review of Books*. In Merrett Leys's home country, the *National Post* profiled the author as a "global literary phenomenon," emphasizing his "nearly-million-dollar advance." Merrett Leys told the interviewer, "I consider myself very fortunate that anyone would be interested in this story of long-ing and sea foam."

The Labrador Sea went on to receive Canada's lucrative Tim Hortons Prize. More surprisingly, it was named as a finalist for the US National Book Award and for the Man Booker. It won the latter, to widespread astonishment—bookies put Merrett Leys's odds at 100:1. This recognition opened the floodgates. Over the next sev-eral months, *The Labrador Sea* and its various translations collected at least twenty more honours, according to the author's Wikipedia page, from Vermont Reads! to the Borges Medal to France's Ordre des Arts et des Lettres. The book was instantly an international bestseller.

None of this was necessarily unusual. *The Labrador Sea*'s prog-ress had followed a well-worn trajectory. "Statisticians call it crowding," said JF. "Humans are social creatures—they don't want to seem deviant and they don't want to be wrong. So they tend to huddle around the same things. When a consensus begins to emerge, there's a network effect—especially regarding taste. Things snowball fast."

It was what happened next that brought Daniel Merrett Leys to the No Name Gang's attention.

He won the lottery.

Literally: about a year after his novel came out, the author of *The Labrador Sea* bought the winning Swamp Magic ticket for Atlantic Canada's ExtraMAX 649. He was presented with a cheque for $65 million.

"What serendipity," said Simone. She'd been the one to notice the news online. "That's a lot of happy accidents for a single middle-brow novelist."

Experience had taught the thieves restraint—the investigation into a potential mark often didn't pan out. During one disastrous, rain-soaked episode outside Belfast, Sebald was arrested after breaking into the home of an (unusually fortunate) Egyptologist. (What they had identified as a hoard of luck was in fact a library of rare salts.) Over the past two years, there had been three instances when reliable information led to empty vaults, as if the Hustlers in question had sensed unwanted attention from somewhere and whisked their luck away.

In the case of Daniel Merrett Leys, the group's enthusiasm waned when they uncovered his history with a local bookmaker. Contrary to expectations, the novelist had mostly lost money. The wagers had begun a few months before the lottery win. He had placed three large bets, two on basketball games (which he lost) and one on tennis (which he won). Inconsistency like this was inconsistent with the profile they were looking for: the hallmark of Hustlers is winning. "Canada's answer to McEwan" might just be a talented scribe who bought the right ExtraMAX ticket.

Now JF inched forward on his chair. "Here's the thing," he said. "I checked Merrett Leys's bets against the Model. None of them make sense. His wagers were all on massive long shots. The Rabbit's math says he didn't have a chance in hell of winning. So why waste his money?"

"Because he's a wealthy idiot?" Theo said.

Or maybe, JF proposed, Merrett Leys intended to manipulate the outcomes.

True, the Toronto Raptors had not overcome the New York Knicks. The Nuggets didn't squash the Hornets. But late last night, alone in the basement's crepuscule, JF went back and watched those games. To his tremendous satisfaction, each of the contests included a host of player collisions, weird bounces, botched free throws. "And although the favoured team won, both outcomes were way tighter than they had any right to be."

"As if the universe were nudging it the other way," said Simone.

"As if someone lucky was fucking around."

JF was a patient investigator. Perhaps Merrett Leys had been experimenting with tactics. Perhaps he hadn't applied enough of his supply. Perhaps he was a victim of what Sebald called "probabilistic diffusion": team sports like basketball contain too many probabilistic events, diminishing luck's impact. Whatever the reason, the writer seemed to have learned from his mistakes. JF nodded towards Sebald. "Maybe he started reading your journal."

For Merrett Leys's third and final bet, six days before his lottery gambit, he did not choose a team sport. He wagered $10,000 on Elliot "Stingray" Jacobson, ranked 155th, to beat Ollie "Budgerigar" Alary, ranked 139th, in an early round of the Memphis Open.

"Well, that's fucking random," said Suzy.

"It gets stranger. According to the Model, their match ought to have been a blowout. It was crazy to bet on Jacobson. Budgerigar and Stingray had faced each other eleven times before, and Budgie won every game. It wasn't just 139th seed versus 155th: every piece of data put Stingray at a loss. Yet Merrett Leys had a hunch?"

His hunch was correct: Stingray won. (It was a short-lived upset: he lost his next match.) Merrett Leys collected a purse of almost a hundred thousand dollars.

The following Friday, at the Fogo general store (known locally as "BJ's"), Merrett Leys purchased his lottery ticket.

"I guess he figured it out," said Theo.

"He figured it out," agreed Simone. "And between the book deal, the Booker and the lottery, this guy's stash of luck must be big as a schoolbus."

By the end of the morning, the Gang had decided to rob Daniel Merrett Leys. Watching the four thieves spring into action, Theo understood at last what it was they actually did down there.

Suzy began by making calls—yakking on a landline beside her cacti and fortresses, with a Missy Elliott CD cheerleading from the corner. Simone's little sister had a gift for social engineering, prying information from banks and officials and even their targets' neighbours, disguising herself as a concerned relative, a friendly busybody, a big-city journalist on a story. She was the one to discover that Merrett Leys had left Fogo Island. Thereafter the trail went cold: all she could learn was that Merrett Leys "had moved to Asia."

The next part fell to JF. He worked amid a mountain of computer hardware, blue cookie tins of wires, alligator clips, nuts and bolts, and also jars of actual nuts—peanuts and almonds and macadamias, dry-roasted—which he chomped throughout the day. It was his specialty to plot the blueprint of a target's life online. Alias to alias, MySpace to MetaFilter to Instagram to Reddit, a fibre-optic layout of Daniel Merrett Leys's world. Work like this could be like playing pin the tail on the donkey: you acquired only the broadest, blindest picture of a life. Progress relied on breakthroughs—one chunk of metadata clicking into another, recipient to sender, location to location, the answers pouring out. An initial social media account left a breadcrumb trail to another, then each of these aliases could point to something else.

JF found a message board for expats in Taiwan and a member with a username resembling one of Merrett Leys's old email addresses. The user had only begun posting last year. Little by little, the Gang filled in their blanks. Merrett Leys had bought a property on the outskirts of Taipei. "Recommendations for people who can install sprinkler systems?" @finite_jest asked online. The forum recommended two different contractors; Suzy grabbed the phone and called them, pretending to be Merrett Leys's bookkeeper. Soon they knew not only which contractor had taken the job, but also the address where the sprinklers were installed.

Simone was responsible for the thousand-yard view—the sequence of events that would take them from Le Black Cat to Merrett Leys's front door. Her office seemed at once tidy and lived-in, like an architect's studio, with its wall-sized map and bright white futon, a vermilion Afghan carpet, bookshelves full of tabbed and depleted notebooks. Sebald, meanwhile, took care of the group's logistical needs. He proceeded with nearly wordless efficiency—collecting equipment, testing supplies. He was a brusque, fantastic dogsbody, coming and going with a helmet under his arm, bearing oxy-fuel torches or stinking vials of ethanethiol.

To Theo's surprise, he did not entirely feel out of place. Working beside Simone, he found that planning a burglary was not so different from prepping for Provisions K's December rush. The component tasks were mundane—making lists, assembling spreadsheets, trawling for answers on the web. The main distinction was subtle and mildly occult: whenever any of them was engaged with a sensitive task, Theo noticed a box of luck nearby, like a stray pack of cigarettes—glinting in a pocket or on the corner of a desk, one panel open to the air.

Despite his sleight of hand on the Dolores's eighteenth floor, Theo did not expect to be so quickly initiated into the Gang's operations.

He got the sense the others hadn't expected this either—that they'd intended a longer audition. But the fact was they liked him. Theo was accustomed to collaboration, cooperation; he was good at reading people, and responding to sudden circumstance. As wary as Suzy or Sebald occasionally still seemed, they were also disarmed by him. He saw it plainly in their faces. Sometimes it was easier to trust someone than to doubt them, a kind of gift you gave yourself.

At the same time as they were plotting against Daniel Merrett Leys, the No Name Gang also wanted to restructure their own luck reserve. Theo was impressed to learn that the cache behind Le Black Cat's lemon door was just one of several. The crew had hoards all over the city—in safes, under the floors of sheds, concealed in attics, even a few coffins, Simone said, buried in a park up north. By dispersing their loot they made it less likely they'd lose it in any one fell swoop. But their caution was also inconvenient: without bringing it all together, a dragon's powdered hoard, they'd never know if they had enough luck for it to begin to replicate.

The theory was Sebald's, based on experiments he had conducted in the (to Theo still-shadowy) years before the group formed. According to his research, large quantities of luck caused strange fluctuations in the places around them. Given that luck could guide the flutter of a coin in the air, it wasn't surprising that it could nudge the course of an electron. Bring together silicon and oxygen molecules and maybe a new grain of luck would appear. Multiply the phenomenon to scale, and a chain reaction could set in—the so-called Domino Point, named for Sebald's favourite way to spend a Sunday morning.

Theo bought a big whiteboard, like the one in the basement of the store, and drew up a grid of tasks and needs. He surveyed the calendar, set deadlines. It reminded him of what he had once enjoyed about managing the store: making decisions, adapting to circumstance, finding the best solution to whatever problem was at hand. Theo had stopped even dropping in on his staff: the others took up his duties as if they had just been waiting to be asked. *They must think I'm telling jokes*, he thought. *They must think I'm laying bets.* He avoided their questions, and Hanna's glances from behind the butcher counter. He looked forward to starting each day with Simone—collecting action items on sticky notes, colour-coded for priority, arranging them on the wall. "Pass me a blue," she'd say, and he'd fling a marker like an arrow to her breast. "What's the name of that apartment broker in Da'an?" he'd say, and she'd answer before he finished the sentence. Working like this was gratifying, a process of snags and solutions, crises and inventions, tinged with something else—excitement or anticipation or maybe it was desire. Theo felt Simone's attention like a spotlight on his face. Since Lou's departure, since Minerva's death, he had not known how much he yearned for the nourishment of another person's eyes on him, paying attention. He became the most dashing version of himself, crafty and fearless, earning what he won. He told stories; he made her laugh. He hid his doubts, his fears—every part of himself that might not gleam.

One day they put on wigs. Simone took Theo to the casino, inviting him to place their bet at the roulette table—$10,000 on red ("or black, if you prefer")—giving him some luck to carry in his back pocket. In her fake blonde tresses she looked like a character from a movie, a harmless waif. Theo was wearing a wig of the same flaxen hue. "We look like cult members," he whispered. She laughed, they doubled their money, they doubled it again, and afterward they went to get roti by the canal. Sitting beside him on the picnic bench, she pulled the wig off her head. Her real hair fluttered into her eyes. She made him keep his on. Before she carved into her roti she slathered the outside with two packets of hot sauce, as meticulous about it as if she were icing a cake.

Between chews he asked, "You do this every couple weeks?"

"Whenever we run out of ducats," she said. She licked her plastic knife. "It's the easiest way to top up our bank account and it doesn't even take much luck."

"You just can't bet too much or the casino gets suspicious?"

"Or the casino can't afford to pay you."

Theo marvelled, shook his head.

"A roulette wheel only needs a bump. Whereas the odds of winning the lottery are really small. You can drain your whole luck supply, doing that."

He asked her if she was troubled by this possibility—that Merrett Leys had already spent his luck.

"Nah." She speared a piece of potato with her fork. "This guy knows what he's doing. He's pacing himself." And if the writer had enough luck to gamble on long shots like literary prizes, lotteries, then who knew how much he was sitting on. Who knew what was hidden in his home?

When they were finished, Simone and Theo went to the movies. Movies, plural: Simone saw one and Theo another, in a different cinema. "You'll see," Simone said. "Once you go solo you never go back." At first he understood where she was coming from. Although it wasn't his first time going alone to a film, there was a certain entertainment to knowing Simone was nearby, experiencing something separate. But the feeling didn't last. He had picked an indie comedy, an adaptation of Mike Steeves's *Giving Up*—dark and witty, the story of a man's endless mysterious life's work and his wife's escapades with an obstinate stray cat. Theo soon wished he had a companion there to experience the pleasure of shared pleasure. Instead he stared through the darkness, at the screen, thinking his own thoughts.

When he emerged she was waiting: the new James Bond had let out ten minutes earlier. They rode the escalator to the top floor, crossed the confettied carpet to a fire door that she pushed open, unseen, alarmless. They stepped out together under the sky's last light, onto a roof.

"The end is always the best part," she said. "The gunfight, the chase, the ridiculous set piece."

"Don't you prefer something a little subtler? More realistic?"

"Realistic? There are spies in real life, too. Bad presidents, bigoted cops. There's violence. The only difference is that in real life it's usually incremental. A steady tick, tick, tick. It makes me impatient."

"For an explosion?"

"Sure, for an explosion."

"Someone dangling out of a helicopter."

She grinned. "Or from the back of a motorcycle."

"Basically you're a revolutionary."

"I guess I am," she said.

They crossed the pebbled tarpaper to the edge of the roof, stared down at pedestrians, jaywalkers, shopping bags like clutched florets. "People are too frightened of running round corners," Simone said.

:::

On a rainy afternoon, Theo took a seat behind JF's computer. The others watched, arms folded, as he navigated to the homepage of a free email service.

"There," JF said, pointing at a blue button.

Theo clicked to create a new account.

Even though it had been his idea, it still felt strange: "Max P. Paumgarten," he typed, when it asked for his name.

"No stopping us now," said Simone.

Theo began composing an email.

:::

At the same time as they were plotting their moves against Daniel Merrett Leys, Theo was also working with Suzy to find a better location for the Gang's luck. It wasn't entirely a collaboration. When Theo asked for the coordinates of the group's current holdings, Suzy said, "Let's take it slow, okay, buddy?" So Theo meandered through the city in search of a prospective new home—somewhere spacious, secure and big enough to unite everything in one vault. Better yet if the location was inconspicuous, fading into the landscape, making it easy to come and go unremarked.

At first he explored the city's industrial parks. The flat blankness of the buildings seemed to convey a sense of security. Suzy disabused him of the notion. "Quiet's the enemy," she told him. The more deserted a place, the easier it is to rob. Neighbours were better than locks, she explained. If you really wanted to keep something safe, put it in the middle of the action.

So Theo steered back towards the city centre, or through the city's many centres, past an arena still echoing with victory chants, the mountain and its belvederes, down pitched bike paths and into the choked grid of the downtown core, under Chinatown's gilded arch, through the Village and its suggestive shop-windows, neighbourhoods with hedges

and yards, alleys spilling with fallen blossoms, crabapples; past the playground where he had met Lou, past elderly couples holding hands on
benches, rollerbladers rollerblading, LARPers besieging one another
with duct-tape weapons, an angel balanced on a monument's grey granite spire. Not far from Provisions K he parked his bike outside the block
of tall buildings that had once been garment factories, brutalist structures that now housed dozens of artists' studios, fashion workshops,
porn sets, start-ups. There were cargo bays for giant trucks, freight elevators for hauling shipments; the building's polished concrete corridors
teemed with the steady hum of unlinked activities. The Gang could
lease a space here. They could fill it up with luck and no one would ever
know. On an upper floor, Theo looked out a panoramic window and
onto the old neighbourhood. A familiar skyline, its knots of trees, a mess
of duplexes, triplexes and their cast-iron stairs. He could make out the
awning of the Dodecahedron Grill, the fluorescent-shining YMCA, a
crowd of regulars outside Social Club. In the distance the marble shoulders of the Oratory, the ring-shaped pond of the park whose name he
could never remember, where kids went ice-skating in winter.

He went back down to his bike. He had had an idea and he pedalled towards it.

Theo's niece stood at the precipice of the loading dock, watching her
uncle and a couple of strangers manipulate a crate onto Provisions'
new forklift. The crate kept catching on the corner of the left fork and
Suzy kept swearing—loudly, brazenly. Hanna was riveted. Finally,
unable to restrain herself, she called out a suggestion: "Just turn it a
little clockwise!"

Suzy glanced at the girl on the pier. "Who's the kid?" she muttered.

"My niece," Theo replied from behind the controls.

"She okay?"

"Yeah, she's okay," said Theo, annoyed. "I told you—everybody here is okay. No one cares."

"'Soil samples,' you said."

"Dull as dirt."

"And yet apparently worth collecting?"

"I told them you're anthropologists. Archaeologists. You gotta store your stuff somewhere."

"The basement of a supermarket; why n—*Fuck!* " The fork had sheared the bottom of the crate, throwing off splinters. Theo winced and dialled back the angle. He had never really gotten the hang of using a forklift, and this was a different model, with unfamiliar controls, purchased for Provisions' new location. He was trying as best he could while also trying to ignore Suzy and Sebald's scrutiny. He was, after all, steering the Gang's luck into the basement of his family's grocery store.

Theo had argued the proposal on its merits but he had also made a show of lying to his siblings—an opportunity to demonstrate his loyalty to the Gang. The parties' first meeting took place beside a coffin-sized box of avocados, as shoppers wheeled around them. "May I introduce my friends, Dr. Suzanna San Marziale and Dr."—Theo hesitated—"Sebald?"

Eric and Mireille did not conceal their skepticism. The alleged professors were like a pair of huddling alley cats, waiting to slink away.

It took a few more talks to agree on all the terms. Sizable as they were, the cellars under Homayoun Carpets didn't go on forever; Eric had to make sure there was lots of room left for the store. Suzy wanted permission to install her own security system. But the family knew they could benefit from the extra tenants, especially during the second location's first year—the amount of money the scientists were proposing to pay just to store their soil was three-quarters astronomical.

Opening the new Provisions was proving more difficult than the Potirises had hoped. After they had gone ahead and taken over the space, there were weeks of unforeseen repairs, holdups with permits, the uncovering of issues with the water supply—all this before even trying to install the new walls, refrigerators, shelving, storage units, sprinklers, conveyor belts, points of sale. They needed a butcher counter, a cheese pit, their own Carb Castle. Memories of the failed west-side Provisions K, overseen by Minnie and Theo Sr., sprinkled them like spray from a vegetable mister. For the time being, the original Provisions remained intact and in business. There were no plans to dispose of the apartments.

To his siblings' confusion, Theo was still staying out of it. He had become a thief.

At last he coaxed the forklift around the corner and down the ramp into the basement. Suzy and Sebald followed to Theo's right; Hanna trotted on his left. They guided the crate past elevated wooden platforms, bales of insulation, counters for packaging prepared foods. A refrigerated storeroom stood with door ajar, not yet chilled. They continued on, deep into the underground.

The Gang had built their treasury at the back of the basement, well away from where Provisions' staff would (one day) roast chestnuts, parcel kale. As they approached, a set of blinding motion-sensor spotlights snapped on, ten white-gold rays. Theo and Sebald had worked together to put up and reinforce the storeroom's walls, interspersing sheets of carbon fibre, mirrors and stainless steel. Installing the interior mirrors, two nights earlier, Theo had felt like a sorcerer. Even just carrying a sheet of mirror—under starlight then underground, through darkness—seemed like a sort of trespass, an act of magic. JF put in cameras, pressure sensors, pneumatic locks, a biometric sensor like the one at Le Black Cat. It was all for climate control, Theo told his siblings. None of them, so far, had thought to question him. They just seemed happy to see him around.

Theo steered the Gang's first container through the storeroom's doorway. He lowered the crate onto the silvered ground and reversed away; Suzy began removing its mirrored panels, unveiling jars and jars of what looked like sand. This was the first of nine intended deliveries. When they were finished, a thousand jars would sit together here, holding space, making chance, sensors underfloor ready to register the most minute change of weight.

Suzy kept turning to glare towards the storeroom's door. It occurred to Theo that she was trying to guard it. From his teenaged niece.

"Don't worry about her," he said again.

"Sebald caught her checking out the mirrors."

Theo rolled his eyes. "She's a kid. Why wouldn't she be curious?"

Suzy sniffed. When he had guided the forklift out she closed the door behind them, sealing it with her thumbprint. "When I was a kid I knew to mind my own business," she muttered.

"To be perfectly honest," Theo said, "I don't believe you."

He clambered down from the machine. Hanna was sitting in half shadow, her back to a generator, earbuds in place. He knelt beside her. "How are you doing?"

Hanna took out one earbud. He could hear the faint sound of sitar.

"Your friends kinda seem like dicks, Uncle Theo."

"They're just very private," Theo replied.

"With their soil samples?"

"Wouldn't you be? If you had lots of precious soil samples?"

Hanna took a long time to consider this. "No," she said.

Theo didn't head back to Le Black Cat that night, nor did he head straight home. He imagined writing to Lou: *Haven't heard from you in a while. I'm a robber now.* Instead he stopped at a bookstore, a tall room of caramel-coloured wooden tables and endless shelves. Books by Lynda Barry and Jacob Wren and Karen Russell, set on plinths, had beautiful crimson and cerulean covers. Cookbooks leaned on comic books. Hustvedts nuzzled Austers. A moomin smiled from a calendar. Theo ran his hand across a dust jacket's soft, embossed dromedary, then flipped through a collection of incomplete cartoons, each of its last panels unfinished.

One of Z. Largo's magazines faced outward in the rack, advertising *New Ways of Seeing!*

After a few minutes, Theo went to the fiction section and selected the volume that rested between Herman Melville's *Moby-Dick* and Gustav Meyer's *The Golem*. He paid in cash.

Outside, he crossed the road to a café. He ordered an espresso. The game was on, noisily on, and its noise filled Theo with a sense of purpose. He opened to the first page of *The Labrador Sea.*

THE LABRADOR SEA

Sylvan woke to find the rain had stopped. Maybe the end of the rain is what woke him. Sometimes silence is itself like a sound, a presence in the room. He got up and went to the kitchen. For the first time in thirty-one days he could see the willow from the window. Thirty-one days of ceaseless rain and now finally silence. The boughs of the willow looked heavy as rope. The earth around the tree was flooded and muddy. The grass and ferns seemed glitched, lying wrong. Sylvan flicked up the flame under his kettle.

By afternoon the clouds had cleared. The flatland around Azay-in-Curtain didn't seem like highlands but they were highlands nonetheless. It was a half day's drive to the nearest edge of the plateau, where Azay's plunging grey cliffs, its "curtains," enclosed it. Its elevation meant that the rain didn't stay in the ground. It vanished, drained away.

By the end of the third clear day, the fields were dry. Sylvan went and sat under the willow. He was carrying the saint's femur; he balanced it on his knee. The bone looked like a piece of driftwood, an object tossed ashore by waves. He touched it with his index finger, watched it wobble. Tomorrow he'd go into town. The road would be passable. He kept imagining that Lou would appear, ambling between the boles of the pines, bending her head under the willow branches. She'd have a burlap bag over one shoulder, bulging with butter, oranges, eggs, rabbit meat, cod, maybe a bar of nougat. And over the other shoulder, the leather satchel that she used to carry her half of the saint's bones. What a storm, she'd say, and he'd answer, Aye, and then he'd run to her, and take her bags, and after putting everything away in the house they'd lie down together in the soft blue light.

He set out at dawn. It would take half the day to reach Azay-in-Curtain—if he didn't stop at Lily's or Porter's, or for something at the Mill. But he would need to stop: he needed to know if they had seen Lou. Sylvan cursed himself—for the hundredth time? the thou-sandth?—that he had not asked the Mechanic to repair their car when she last came through. He remembered the argument with Lou. The problem wasn't just the cost: the Mechanic refused to let anybody watch her work. Why should we pay for a repair if we can't also see how it's done? Sylvan had said. Lou replied, It's the choice between having a working car and not having one. Lou knew more about cars than he did; he got angry that she wasn't as upset as he was at the Mechanic.

Now the car sat in the rusted-over shed, permanent as a tree. Sylvan walked past it. He carried two saddlebags. They contained a repair kit, a bedroll, a tent, some food, two changes of clothes, a flashlight, a pistol, a book of Shortreed's poems. The saint's remaining bones were in their embroidered bag, golden thread on purple velvet, which he had laid on the top of the first saddlebag. He wanted to be ready for whatever happened. For whatever *had* happened. To Lou.

She'd left on the twenty-seventh day. They chose that day because it was the saint's day. That much they knew: it was the saint's day; maybe it would be lucky. It had been raining for three and a half weeks and they had not gone out, exhausting everything in the larder and the root cellar, doing jigsaw puzzles on the big table, drawing portraits of each other in their respective notebooks. Lou sketched plans for an apiary. Normally they kept all the saint's bones together, on a wooden board under the kitchen window, where they'd stand and watch the rain come down, try to see the willow through the water. The world was washed out, invisible. Sometimes he'd rest his hand on the pile of bones and pray, or they'd pray together, as they had been taught to do. But the saint's magic rarely worked on weather. The rain kept falling, the larder got barer. They finished all their puzzles. On the morning of the twenty-fifth day of rain he noticed Lou staring at a map of Azay-in-Curtain in the front of a book about pigeon games.

You want to go to town? he asked.

One of us should.

Or both.

Or both, she agreed. We'll have to walk.

That's all right.

Is it?

You stay here. I'll go, he said.

Your leg.

It's all right.

No, let me go. Tomorrow, if the rain hasn't stopped.

We can go together.

Maybe if it stops. If it stops, we'll hop on our bikes. Otherwise one
of us should stay here, to look out for flooding.

It never floods here.

It's never rained like this, Sylvan.

In the end they delayed one more day. The saint's day will be better,
Lou told him, and he did not have any reason to doubt her.

Their bicycles rested together against one of the old apple trees. They
could have rested them on the pine fence—the fence was just there—
but they had gotten in the habit of using this old apple tree. The
orchard had stopped producing fruit a few years ago, they didn't
know why. The trees didn't even flower any more, though their
branches were still covered in pale, tilting leaves.

A cardinal stood on a fence post—gazing at Sylvan, gazing at their
bikes. Its eye was like a black bead. Sylvan put down the saddlebags
and lifted out his bicycle and gave it a shake. The tires were all right.
He looked at the other bike, Lou's bike, and its lolling front wheel,
and a sudden fear gripped him.

He swatted at the cardinal. Go on, he said.

The road was only just dry enough. Its mud was hard; it was like
cycling through chocolate. He could already feel the pain in his right
leg, like a hornet's sting. It had been like this all summer. At first he
thought he had simply pulled a muscle while tending the garden, but
it hadn't gone away. Now it throbbed with every push.

There were all kinds of weird birds on the road. Sitting in the
mud, or flying in arrowheads above him, or perched on the maples
and chestnuts that led away from the property. Geese with curved
beaks, raspberry-coloured jays, puffins and songbirds. Something

like a condor. Something like a hummingbird. The storm must have carried them in, or trapped them there, or they came for the worms the rain had brought up from below. A large ebon shape circled above him.

Sylvan had left a note on the kitchen table. *Dear Lou,* it read. *I went to town to look for you. I hope you're all right. Stay put. I'll be back tomorrow. I love you.*

P.S. I brought the rest of the saint's bones.

It took almost two hours to reach Porter's. The crofter was on the roof of his farmhouse, replacing the sod. One of his girls was just coming down the ladder. Pop, she yelled.

I see him, Porter said.

Sylvan dismounted. He wheeled his bike towards the foot of the ladder.

Porter was squatting at the edge of the roof, above the straight line of the eavestrough. His ginger hair seemed to glow in the sunlight.

Some rain, huh?

Yes, Sylvan said.

Porter's daughter had disappeared into the house.

You seen Lou? Sylvan asked.

Porter considered. Maybe a week ago? It was still pouring. He raised his head, concerned. She not turn up?

No.

Hm, Porter said. He was wearing pale, paint-scuffed coveralls. Yeah, a few days before the storm broke. Morning. On her way to Azay—but it was raining so hard, we took her in, dried her off. Ate the last of the ham. Porter raised his eyes. She said you'd run out of supplies.

Almost, Sylvan said.

Hm.

And then she carried on?

She did. She was in a hurry.

Did she say anything else?

She told me to check in on you. Sorry I didn't.

Sylvan gave a dry laugh. That's all right.

We had our hands full here.

I know. Sylvan climbed back on his bike. All right, thanks.

She'll turn up, Porter said.

Past Porter's, the woods got thicker. The road felt more like a path *through* something. Dark birds cheered from the periphery. The pain in Sylvan's thigh felt like an echo of a sound he couldn't make out.

At one point he stopped to drink from his flask of water, and to piss.

Back on the road, he imagined what other notes he'd leave her, if he could. *Dear Lou,* he'd write, *I saw some foxes and they were so unexpected that they seemed like tricks of my eye. One of them stood with its paws in the ditch, just letting the water run over them.*

Dear Lou, I was thinking about a conversation we once had, about how the world changes. We were talking about whether it changes all at once or bit by bit. It's bit by bit, you said, obviously it's bit by bit. I said, I think you're probably right. We were both pretty certain of this: that the world changes bit by bit. It seemed so obvious. This was before all the rain. I know it was just rain but someway it pulled me loose. Nothing seems so obvious any more.

Dear Lou, When we get home I'm going to finally fix the rocking chair. I'll get out that book, and my tools, and before long it will be like new.

You'll be able to sit in that chair all day if you like, doing crosswords, drinking hibiscus tea, like people used to do when they retired.

Nobody was home at Lily's. The property around her place was half-wild, overgrown with sandgrass and loosestrife, great swaths of brambles. Machines were hidden everywhere—tractors, draggers, busted trucks, old mowers, even chainsaws in a jagged mass. Lily let the greenery grow up around them. She fixed this collection at her own pace, slowly, acquiring damaged machines faster than she restored them. Lily gathers things to her, Lou once said, after Sylvan had criticized her. I wish more people were protectors.

Now Sylvan wove his bike between the piles of brush and iron, looking for signs of Lou. The house, a low-slung cottage, was completely dark. The glass in the windows looked like sections of black mirror. He remembered they had debated asking Lily to repair their car instead of the Mechanic. We'd never get it back, Lou had said.

Sylvan found two footprints outside the building's side door. Just two—they led towards a swirl of torn-up, muddy ground and tire tracks. Nothing else to find. He wasn't actually certain they were Lou's. What did Lou's footprints look like? Did her boots leave any distinguishing marks? He couldn't remember. He remembered she had brown boots with thick woven laces, black gum treads. She had bought them from Mikelson's. The two footprints might be hers, he could imagine her stepping from the side door into the mud here and then away, but he wasn't certain.

Then there was a sound. Faint at first, gradually louder, a giant arriving through the woods. Lily's truck came roaring round the bend, smoke plumes pouring from its stacks; it frightened the birds from their trees. She didn't notice Sylvan until she had stopped and thrown open the cab door, jumping to earth, a solid, beautiful woman in thick woollen scarves, with a gaze as sturdy as a good bridge.

Now it's you, she said.

Now it's me? he replied.

She had already stomped off to the back of the truck. He followed. She yanked down the tailgate and clambered up.

I just said goodbye to your Lou, she said.

Just?

Well, a few days ago.

Since the rain stopped?

No, it was still raining. Standing in the truck bed, Lily hauled a motorcycle upright. You must have known she was coming.

Yes.

She was wet as a dog, poor thing.

Did she seem all right?

She seemed all right, given the circumstances. She stayed here two nights. Finally she was getting so anxious I agreed to drive her the rest of the way.

Sylvan gingerly put down his bicycle. Anxious?

That she'd be late.

He halted at the foot of the truck. Suddenly he could feel the cold of the place—the damp of the leaves and soil and clotted moss, the chill rising up from the wet birches, the abandoned machines.

Late for what?

His voice didn't sound like his voice.

This time it was Lily who stopped. For the ship, she said. I thought you said you knew.

Knew what? he said.

Listen, I really don't want any part in it.

Knew what?

It's not my place to get involved if two grown—

She said she was going to catch a ship?

Lily considered for a moment, working her lips. I drove her to the Mermaid and Coral. I just thought it was—well—I don't know what I thought. With these things you never know.

She didn't say why she was going?

She didn't say.

You didn't ask?

Lily sent him a stern look. Saying nothing, she finished steering the motorcycle from the back of the truck and into the road.

She said she was going for supplies, Sylvan murmured.

Lily dug a key out of her pocket. She twisted it in the motorcycle's ignition and the engine didn't catch, but the bike's headlight snapped on: white pearl, empty eye. A beetle crawled onto his boot.

Sylvan sat in silence for most of the drive. It seemed strange to be up so high off the road, moving at such a clip. The seats in Lily's truck bounced on little springs. He felt like a doll, some kind of marionette. His thigh ached. Hot air breathed out from square, grey vents. For a little while she played the radio. A guitar descended slowly from chord to chord. She turned it off. Bah, she said. His saddlebags were with his bicycle in the back but he had taken out the velvet bag and laid it at his feet. Dim shapes were visible through the drawstring's opening.

Lily wore one of her saint's finger bones like a talisman round her neck.

They passed out of the woods and into the open pastures around Azay-in-Curtain. Horses nosed at clover. Sheep huddled in their meadows. There were fewer birds here but more flowers—roses, snap-dragons, jagged pink astrantia. Briars curled around the mile mark-ers. The rain had been good for the plants. The road turned to pitted asphalt. They passed travellers on foot, cyclists, horses and wagons. A few cars putted behind them. Slowly the town came into view—first the fallen western wall, the Rothfels Windmill, the mustard-yellow tents of the livestock market. Houses began to line the roadway, with pale blue and chalk-white facades. They passed the old abbey, the tannery, Saint Jordan's square. Beyond all this lay the library, teeming Centre Street, the chicken alleys and fallen clock tower, Saint Katherine's gardens, city hall, the promenade, and then the port, its docks and pier, Khan Fish & Chips, the Salmon's Crown, the Mermaid and Coral, and a hundred anchored motorboats, tugs, sail-boats, clippers, windjammers, frigates.

Beyond them, the sea.

CHAPTER ELEVEN

Their plane flew low across the water. Dawn had scarcely lifted and the shoreline seethed with surf, as if a war were being waged. The aircraft landed with one light bounce, like a lid falling shut. Theo raised his head and saw Simone looking at him.

"What?"

"You were asleep," she said.

"You were watching me?"

"I was waiting to hear what you'd tell me."

"Reason for your visit?" the agent asked.

"Holiday," Theo said.

She waved him through a set of shatterproof glass doors.

They waited for Suzy at an outdoor café near one of the airport exits. The air outside was so warm, so close, it felt like someone had come up beside Theo and placed their hand on his cheek. Sebald remained standing while the others sat on flimsy, four-legged plastic stools. Theo sipped from a cup of black tea. In his left hand he held a bun studded with shards of green onion and pieces of hot dog. The Chinese characters on the paper bag, the cup, didn't feel quite real— as if they might be misunderstandings, mistakes. He wasn't sure whether he was going to eat any of the bun or whether he was just going to hold it, as evidence of something.

Suzy pulled up in a big burgundy cube truck. She threw open the rear doors and they tossed their bags into the empty cargo area.

"Any trouble?" Theo asked.

"Not a peep," said Suzy. "Not a whisper."

The truck folded through the city like a curl of smoke. Taipei was a metropolis poured around hills and valleys, crisscrossed by bridges, clouded with swarms of mopeds. It seemed part of morning's machinery, as if the city and its mechanisms had come up with the sun. Roads rose. Motorways crossed and curved like a pile of ribbons. Peering over Simone's shoulder, Theo glimpsed breakfast counters, factories, cedars and bougainvillea, shacks and skyscrapers, bulging water towers, butcher stalls, shimmering malls, murals, palaces, the peaked red roofs of shrines. Classes of schoolchildren swirled through painted gates. Dragons threshed on rainbow gables. Phosphor-tinted billboards announced the names of corporations while flags and flagpoles cast long, rippling shadows across the plazas. Theo's wrist rested on his thigh and Simone's wrist rested on her thigh and their two wrists almost touched.

:::

They pulled to a stop on a quiet block. A brazier rested on the sidewalk, flames darting at its scorched iron edge. A shopfront's grille waited behind it, half-open. All the nearby businesses were one-room garages with tool benches, engine stands, scooters laid down on sheets. They ducked past the sooty fire and under the grille, into a long showroom. The air had the peppery, magical smell of incense.

"*Ni hao?*" said Suzy. Watching her move through the space—coiled, wary—Theo was reminded of another morning, a gun in Suzy's hand. He had not thought of it in weeks and a tremor passed swiftly through him now. His eyes were gradually adjusting to the dimness. The store was as narrow as a subway tunnel, flickering with orange candlelight, crammed floor to ceiling with religious paraphernalia. Little granite dragons sat beside preening marble lions, stone tongues outstretched. Buddhas reclined in countless poses—serene, jolly, vigilant, bemused. Unhoisted chandeliers, handmade wind chimes, torn-open cardboard boxes of bowls, plates, vases, offering trays, incense holders, moon tiles, powdered incense, wooden flowers. Plastic bouquets, with glittering chrysanthemums. Painted silks and cotton tapestries—farm scenes and saints-on-clouds and elaborate, mystical battles, with tigerheaded knights and upraised spears, horses leaping across ravines. Theo almost tripped over a bag of charcoal briquettes.

Deep in the back of the temple supplies shop, sitting among the shadows, was Roie. At first it looked as if she was surrounded by bars of gold, like a clerk at the centre of the US Treasury—her desk enclosed by orderly row upon row of parcelled joss paper. Her black hair fell to her shoulders. "You're late," she told them. She finished tying a string around a set of golden pages. This bundle of ghost money, like all the others, would eventually be thrown into a fire.

"Our flight was delayed," Suzy said.

Although they'd eventually see Roie's real smile, rich and wide and almost silly, at this moment she offered only a perfunctory one. "It doesn't matter."

She had not yet lifted her face, and Suzy remained frozen—head tilted, jaw crooked—until she did. Then their eyes met, held. Theo recognized story hidden in the way their gaze glinted.

Roie was their fixer. She herself collected luck, but nobody had explained to him why she was an ally, not a mark. Roie was a thief, presumably; they had agreed she would receive a cut of their spoils. But there was something more here than honour among thieves. All that Simone would say was that Roie had met Suzy in Sicily.

She wore a big wool sweater and faded boot-cut jeans. Her sneakers were neon orange. She followed them back outside, grabbing a silver children's push scooter from where it leaned against a wall. "Bring the truck," she said, and led them round the corner and down an alley. They had to stop to tuck in the truck's wing-mirrors. At the end of the alley lay a ravaged lot, fringed with dogwoods, that backed onto a warehouse. Roie had taken out her phone, was saying something in Taiwanese; a few seconds later, three women emerged through a rusted steel door. Suzy straightened; Theo wondered for a moment if she had brought her gun. The women wore black turtlenecks, high-waisted blue jeans. Each of them raised a hand in greeting.

Roie saw Theo looking.

"My daughters," she said.

They hauled open a scrolled gate, revealing the Gang's equipment. Sealed steel cases, locked boxes full of gear, shipped under separate cover. Together they loaded the supplies into the truck.

Once the way was clear, the women vanished through the doorway. They reemerged in cars: two small coupes—one mauve, one lavender—and a sleek town car. Simone took the mauve car; JF took the lavender; Theo got into the black sedan; Suzy and Sebald remained in the truck.

Roie climbed in beside Theo. One of her daughters was disappearing down an alley on her scooter. The others had retreated into the warehouse, closing the gate behind them.

Roie pointed down a laneway and the truck pulled out, and they all advanced together, as a column, into the rest of the day.

Theo turned on the radio. A woman was singing about work. The beat was lifting, blurred and blue; it reminded him of a trembling barometer. "Work, work, work, work, work," she sang, "work, work, work, work, work," and then the words became unclear, something he couldn't quite decipher.

:::

They had rented a large house in an area west of Da'an Park. The convoy turned off Xinsheng South Road and down a narrow lane, rattling past veering cyclists, students with schoolbags, one tawny alley cat. Most of the buildings were three or four storeys high, with shops or restaurants on the ground floor. Everything was closed apart from a pharmacy and an open-air fruit store—Roie explained that the shops here wouldn't open until nightfall. A pair of middle-aged women stood hosing down a patch of pavement. Jade plants kneeled with tea trees in terracotta pots. As their car eased past a minuscule playground, Theo watched an old man boost a boy onto a balance beam.

The house had once been the home of Roie's great-uncle, who had earned a small fortune importing ink. Now it stood empty, behind an anodized aluminum fence, its yard overrun with climbing ferns, Cherokee roses, an old arbutus with its bark sloughing off. The pond, sleek with oil, looked like it might have once held koi. Cool air wafted through the car's open windows; everything smelled like blooms and undergrowth.

They proceeded down a ramp and into an underground parking lot, where they left the vehicles. The building above was an agglomeration of eras and renovations, its sloping second and third storeys late additions stacked atop a Japanese-style cottage. Each room was decorated in curious, ink-splattered wallpaper, like grand-scale Rorschach tests—remnants of the importer's unsuccessful foray into interior décor. The bedroom floors were so uneven that Theo's watch would slide off its table in the middle of the night. Doors left open slammed shut. The attic had been redone most recently—a single spacious room under the roof's white incline, its beams left naked. A long dinner table. Rice-paper lamps. A bay window looked out across Da'an Park: tracts of flowers, basketball courts, groves with winding trails. The seething city sprawled at each of the park's edges; hanging high above it, glimpsed through clouds, stood the shrouded spire of Taipei 101.

It took most of the day to unpack. Maps went up in the attic, alongside wall-sized diagrams. Their equipment they arrayed in the living room, among the chairs and chesterfields, atop tatami mats. Heaps of black garments—lycra, mylar—like dropped gowns. Flares and flashlights, energy bars, many-pocketed vests. Marine-grade backpacks, air rifles, limp rope ladders. A bona fide grappling hook, which

Theo would pick up and twirl, feeling its heft, marvelling. There was a wooden box filled with stones—heavy and pitted, carefully curated, like schisty grapes or fingerling potatoes—and a locked and mirrored trunk holding dozens of smaller mirrored containers, some as big as pounds of butter, others like decks of cards.

Down the hall in the kitchen, the fridge contained a yoghurt tub full of C4 plastic explosives. A set of vials rested beside it, labelled by hand: PEPPER, VALERIC ACID, SKUNK, ETHANETHIOL. There was also a carton of milk. Theo had stocked the pantry, but the Gang would end up eating every meal away from their base. Too many delicacies were for sale in the alleys around the house: hot soy milk in the morning, with *yia tou* sticks, like gangly churros; bento boxes at lunch, or rice balls stuffed with egg and pork floss, scallion pancakes, pork and wood-ear dumplings. At dinnertime they roamed together through the night market, munching on squares of spicy taro, slurping from cardboard bowls of beef noodle soup, chewing battered tendrils of deep-fried squid, which shivered, ghostlike, on skewers.

There was one more item of note, pressed flat under the coffee table in the den. It was a large and curious object, of indeterminate dimensions—pebbled, rough and shiny, sharing certain similarities with the Gang's collection of rocks. Except this thing was huge and soft, like a large, deflated life raft or a piece of humped, grey-silver garden equipment. Theo would kneel beside it from time to time, squashing its edges, pressing the vinyl back into shape.

They hadn't been there long before they went to stake out their target. The group had brought a drone—a propellered machine like a flying tea set—and three of them drove with it to Taipei's outskirts, near the base of Yangmingshan's mountains. They laid it gingerly on the ground then sent it whirring across the treetops. From JF's laptop they watched a camera feed of roads, ditches, the jungle's virescent canopy, and suddenly a pristine overhead view of Merrett Leys's estate. Theo felt a shiver up his spine. Until now they had been using satellite images. Now all at once Merrett Leys's house seemed real, seemed close. Trees swayed. Figures ambled across the driveway. Water gurgled from a spring. So near the jungle, the neatly mowed lawn appeared grotesque. It spanned the property, lush and emerald green, linking the guardhouse, the rose garden, a Georgian-style mansion, and a third building: the tower, squat and solitary like a chessboard's rook. "There it is," murmured Simone, for the novelist's tower had occupied the centre of their attention for some time. A structure of uncertain purpose, set far away from the road, wired with more security measures than the house where the writer slept.

"It's bigger than I pictured," said Theo.

"It's just right," said Simone.

Mostly the drone confirmed what they already knew. Twenty-foot walls enclosed the estate on all sides, closing it off from the city and from the jungle. Entrance was by way of an electric gate, with a guardhouse just inside. Merrett Leys's security had a sight line onto the house and the tower, plus at least twenty-five cameras, while razor wire curled along the top of the wall, nestled among the moss and flowering ivy.

"Can you get closer?" asked Suzy.

"No," said JF.

"There, on the wall."

"If we get any closer we'll get picked up by surveillance."

"What about zoom. Can you zoom?"

JF adjusted the view, magnifying a section of wall. "What am I looking for?"

"There," she said.

"What?" said Simone.

"Right there."

"I don't—"

"Under the wire, there—see? Stumble sensors."

"What are stumble sensors?" said Theo.

The image zoomed and refocused on a small stretch of masonry. Something or somethings were tucked like coins among the pillows of moss, under the glittering cutthroat coils.

"Fuck," said Simone.

"We must have missed them," said Suzy.

"Or they're new."

"Fuck," repeated Simone.

Theo said again, "What are stumble sensors?"

The image telescoped as JF zoomed out and began steering the drone along the full length of the wall, tracing the dotted line of inset discs.

"Can we disable them with the rest of the network?"

"We can't disable anything before you get over the wall."

Simone hesitated. "Theo could do it?"

"As part of the grand tour? Sneak away to hack security?"

"What are stumble sensors?" Theo asked, one more time.

JF lowered his hands from the keyboard. "They're vibration sensors. Pressure, motion—tech to guard against someone climbing over that wall."

"Like we were going to," said Theo.

"Like Simone and I were going to," said Suzy.

"Could I disable them from inside?"

"Suzy's right—we can't risk letting you get caught."

"There'd be policemen there in minutes," said Suzy.

"Why are you always so concerned about policemen?" said Simone.

"Because it's policemen's *job* to *catch* people like us."

JF sent the drone swooping up and away. "So what's plan B?"

Suzy sighed. "Me and my big sister go fucking swimming."

:::

After sunset that evening they took a gondola to Maokong, all of them bobbing upward on a wire. The mountain valleys lay below, invisible. All they could see were the headlights and taillights of cars, like orderly fireflies, and then the massed fluorescence of the city behind them. Theo felt an intimacy here that he had not felt in any of the Gang's other hideouts—not under the hardware store or in its vault or in any room at the ink importer's mansion. Their glass chamber floated upward, open to the world. Each of them could look out into the darkness or into somebody's face, vivid, warm under Largo bulbs. Sebald was gazing at something far away—a satellite or a star. Suzy was studying a map of Maokong town and all its plantations. JF was staring at the nimbus of the city as it receded behind them. Theo was looking at Simone and Simone was looking at Theo, with a lopsided smile. "I can't believe I'm here," he whispered. The rest of them raised their eyes.

After a long silence, Simone said, "Don't mess it up."

:::

Two days later, JF directed the drone back to Daniel Merrett Leys's property. It moved more unsteadily this time: their copter was not designed to carry much more than its own weight.

Here and there as it flew, high above the lawn, the drone released a succession of objects. Stones like schisty grapes and fingerling potatoes tumbled to the grass.

In the afternoon, Theo sent another email from his Max P. Paumgarten account.

Hey Daniel, he wrote, *Hope we're still on for tomorrow. I've been drinking so much bubble-tea I feel like I'm floating.*

The following morning, the drone went up again and dropped more rocks.

At the same moment, a wine-tinted truck was rolling towards Merrett Leys's gates. The vehicle had large graphics on its sides: a logo with a starfield, a globe, a grid of dotted lines. Above a two-toned illustration of a plum blossom, the Han characters read, "National Astronomical Service."

"Do you have an appointment?" asked the guard.

"We are from the government," Roie said.

"May I see your identification?"

Sebald, in the passenger seat, sighed. Like Roie, he wore a clean blue uniform, with a patch on his shoulder that showed the sparkling logo of the NAS. He picked up a clipboard and unclipped two ID cards; he passed these to Roie, who passed them to the guard. Each of them made a show of their impatience.

The guard examined the cards.

There was a small black box in Roie's chest pocket, about the size of a pack of cigarettes. It was open.

"We'll need to search your vehicle," the guard said finally.

The guards found nothing. There was nothing to find. The van was admitted and, sometime later, L. L. Sebald and his co-conspirator met Daniel Merrett Leys.

At around 8:00 PM that night—many hours after Roie and Sebald bade goodbye to their host, many hours after he had told them, "Thank you for this information, it was so pleasant to meet you," and the guards had again searched their truck, and again found nothing, because there was nothing to find—it was time to rob the author.

Daniel

Daniel was nervous. Usually his nervousness manifested as writing, as pacing, or as the consumption of espresso. He had always found fiction easiest when he was nervous, as if anxiety improved the volume and velocity of his creativity. Some writers find their work leisurely, serene, or a kind of old-fashioned labour. For Daniel it was like coping with a rash. It was a relief when it abated.

Tonight he was not writing. Instead he was trying to relieve his nerves by reorganizing his belongings. Real estate agents call it "staging," as if the objects in a house are the actors in a play. You are the playwright, Daniel supposed, and your life is the play. He was well aware which of his possessions occupied the lead role, however, and he had no intention of taking Paumgarten anywhere near the Presidio.

Accordingly, Daniel was staging the most banal, domestic parts of his existence. He had refreshed the fruitbowl. He had concealed all the boxes of tissues. Now he gathered up the stray phone, tablet and laptop cables, tossing them with his multivitamins into the catch-all drawer. He agonized over which magazine(s) to leave on the coffee table in the living room (the *London Review of Books* and *Largo Home*, he decided). He dithered over the music in the stereo. Although his housekeeper had been through that day and the whole house was spotless, even the tree branches dusted, Daniel worried that it might seem *too* spotless. He decided to set out a half-filled glass of sparkling water. He spilled some almonds on a kitchen counter, reconsidered, cleaned them up, set out a bowl instead. He put away the *London Review* and *Largo Home* and replaced them with *Thrasher.* Opening the refrigerator he took a deep breath. White wine, soy milk, soft tofu, passionfruit, eggs, pudding, red ribeye steaks, a tray with gherkins, olives, sliced Chinese sausage and saucisson sec. Some old parmesan at the back, its rind flecked with green spots. Eva had made a big Caesar salad for yesterday's dinner; Daniel wished now that he had asked her to make extra so it could be sitting here in the fridge, covered in plastic wrap, evidence of his robust and healthy spirit. At least there was the charcuterie platter. Would Paumgarten even look in his fridge? It was hard to say. Certainly Daniel would not invite him to do so. Would Paumgarten examine it without asking, during a pause, when Daniel wasn't looking? It would be the crossing of a line, yet perhaps precisely the sort of line a journalist might be inclined to cross, if that journalist were writing the profile of a celebrity and if the contents of that celebrity's crisper seemed like they might offer insight into the celebrity's broader, ineffable being.

So Daniel decided he ought to toss the pudding. And maybe the cheese. He had made the decision but not yet begun to act upon it when he received a notification on his phone. Somebody had arrived at the gate. Assuming it wasn't the astronomers circling round for another gander, it was—he checked the clock—yes, Paumgarten was on time. Daniel closed the fridge and went to the window, parted the lace with two fingers. A chameleon lolled at his feet. Outside, a panther-black sedan had pulled into the guard station. Daniel's phone buzzed again.

"Mr. Max Paumgarten here for his 8:00 PM"

"Thank you, Mr. Wu."

Daniel watched Mr. Wu say something to Mr. Yu, at the car window. Yu nodded. Both men walked around the vehicle—one clockwise, the other counter-—peering through its windows. The guards were good at their job. Mr. Wu rapped on the trunk and Daniel briefly considered ringing Wu back, telling him to waive the screening. He didn't want Paumgarten to think the subject of his profile was a security-crazed nut. But Daniel did not call, because he was indeed security-crazed, and the risk of criticism did not outweigh the risk of allowing a nefarious party onto his estate.

Meanwhile, in the front seat of the car, the man who called himself Max Paumgarten yanked the trunk release. The trunk's open lid obscured his view of Mr. Wu, who was peering inside. Wu was short and stocky, with pockmarked cheeks. His eyes—quick, large, handsome—gave his face a certain power. The compartment seemed empty. He used his fingertips to lift the trunk's spare tire. He did not examine the bulky vinyl cover pressed around and under the spare.

Mr. Yu—taller than Wu, with a blanker, unreadable face—was still at the driver's side window. "Welcome, Mr. Paumgarten," he said. "You may park by the entry."

Paumgarten's smile concealed a long exhale.

Inside the house, Daniel let the curtains fall shut. He stepped away from the window. Just then a loud noise went off—an engine shriek—and when the writer looked out again a cloud of black, incense-like smoke was drifting up from the car. The sedan had advanced only a few feet past the guards' station and was halted there, helpless. Paumgarten got out of the car.

"Shit," he said.

Daniel watched the guards emerge and stare, like bewildered tourists.

"What is it?" one of them asked.

"I don't know."

"You can fix?"

Paumgarten spread his palms. "I'm a journalist."

They stared some more. Behind them, the electric gate shuddered shut.

By now Daniel was standing framed in the house's front doorway, a hand shielding his eyes. He was conscious of first impressions; he hoped his pose conveyed a mixture of calm and curiosity. "Is everything all right?" he called.

"Mr. Merrett Leys?" said Paumgarten.

"Daniel," Daniel said. "You must be Max."

"I must be. Look, my car, it's—"

"Broken."

"Well, I guess. I'm sorry about this. It's a rental."

They both gazed at the sedan in the manner of men who are baffled by automobiles. A short distance away, Mr. Yu and Mr. Wu were also still gazing. In the place of bewilderment, their faces showed irritation, most of it directed at Paumgarten. This did not abate when Paumgarten got back behind the wheel, trying to coax the vehicle into motion. The ignition cycled uselessly. No one noticed the three broken wires hanging slack by Paumgarten's knee, beneath the steering column. No one, that is, except for the driver himself, who had been the one to break them.

"No dice," Paumgarten said.

"Should we call a tow?"

"I guess so," Paumgarten began. "The rental company—"

Merrett Leys held his phone aloft. "I have a mechanic in town. Let me text him."

Paumgarten began to protest.

"Don't worry—it won't cost you anything."

The journalist calmed. "I should just really contact the rental company before we do anything . . ." Then, as Daniel had not stopped thumbing something into his device, he added, "I guess we'll postpone our talk?"

Daniel raised his head. "Why would we postpone it?"

"I'll have to go with the car. Who knows when I'll be done. And I know you're so busy . . ."

Daniel was about to say that he wasn't that busy, but he caught himself. "I suppose you're right."

"Maybe—" Paumgarten said.

"What is it?"

"Maybe we could hold off calling the tow? Until after we speak? That is, if you don't mind this smoky hulk in the middle of your drive."

"You've come all this way," Daniel said carefully.

"You wouldn't mind?"

"Of course not," said Daniel, who had his back to the gritted expressions of his hired security. "I would hate for your journey to have been wasted. Anyway, where are my manners?" Abruptly he made a gesture he had spent the afternoon mentally rehearsing—extending his arm so that his open hand took in the sprawling brick house, the laden and burnished plum trees, the red maples and the green lawn, turning slate in the twilight, and the rambling rose garden that stretched to the tower on the far side of the estate. "Welcome. Welcome, welcome. To Rongshu Wu, the Banyan House. It's so nice to meet you."

"The pleasure's mine," said Paumgarten. "Here. I brought you some bourbon."

So Daniel allowed a black-haired man, a former comedian temporarily calling himself Max Paumgarten, into his home. Paumgarten's car remained in the driveway, dark and solid. In a curious coincidence, the vehicle's stalled shape happened to obstruct the view from the guards' clean white cabin to the ivied, turreted folly that Daniel called "the Presidio."

Daniel's guest did not look around as he followed the author into the house. He kept his head down. He did not gaze up the hill at the Presidio, or across it to the gardens, or into the dwindling violet of the evening sky where something dark was darting, whirring. It was roughly the size of a tea set.

Daniel began by giving Paumgarten a tour. One of the things he'd most liked about the *New Yorker* profile of Zadie Smith was the way Paumgarten made her home seem like a reflection of the novelist herself, an index of her depths. Daniel was proud of his house, confident in it. Whereas at times in life he felt inadequate—as if he were less of a person than he pretended to be, not just less talented but less fully formed—his home in Taiwan was everything he wanted it to be. Its rooms were evidence of his wealth and good taste, proof of his distinctiveness, and unlike his previous home, on Fogo Island, Rongshu Wu possessed an additional aura, conferred by its setting near Yangmingshan National Park and, of course, by the banyan trees. Daniel felt an exquisite pleasure every time he revealed the interior to a guest.

"Good grief," Paumgarten whispered when he glimpsed the banyans.

Daniel rocked back on his heels, gratified.

Paumgarten shook his head. "Did the house . . . ? Was it built like this somehow?"

"The trees came of their own accord," Daniel said. "The building was derelict after the war. The banyans gradually took over."

Although Paumgarten knew the premise of the Banyan House, he had not been able to imagine it. The surprise showed on his face.

"The structure itself is almost 150 years old," Daniel said. "Much of the brick is original. It was built as the home of a camphor baron, famous for his rose garden. And for his camphor, I guess. When he died, there was trouble with the executors and so on. The roses grew wild. Maybe the banyans were already growing here, below the foundation, or else they spread from the jungle. It wasn't until the 1940s that they took over. They burst through the floor, scrambled up the walls. A set designer finally bought the property in the seventies. She tore out some walls, built those beams to support the heavier boughs. An admiral took possession in the late eighties, a pineapple-cake tycoon after that, and then, last year, me. I rebedded the roses, redid the windows"—he gestured—"and some other little things, like raising the ceiling in the study . . ." He pointed. But Paumgarten still hadn't diverted his gaze from the centre of the room, where the first extraordinary banyan tree rose and outspread, its trunk as thick as a subway pylon, branches that extended at almost horizontal angles, fragile and sturdy, bowed and yearning, propped on roots that reached towards the bamboo floor or from it, a myriad of sinuous supports, like ropes or chains, dividing the space and embroidering its walls, patterning the whitewashed brick. They penetrated the house's panels and joists, dipped through doorways, under masonry, braiding through the other banyans that had also pushed up through the floor and suffused the building, pervading its maze of rooms.

Paumgarten turned a full circle, awed. "It's like you live in a forest."

"Yes," said Daniel. "In spring we get birds."

Paumgarten had taken out a notebook and begun writing something down. Daniel experienced a bloom of intense satisfaction.

They spent the next hour exploring the ground floor of the house. Daniel showed off the library, dining and billiards rooms, his corals gleaming in glass cases. He pointed out his kitchen and its humming refrigerator, keeping his distance. He led Paumgarten past the copy of *Thrasher* magazine.

"You skate?" Paumgarten asked.

Daniel was breezy about it. "Sometimes."

They made small-talk. About the banyans, about Paumgarten's flight to TPE, about the shamrock-green and china-white corals, about living in such an old home and keeping it tidy, about collecting too many books, about keeping chameleons as pets, about Daniel's relations with his neighbours, about not having many neighbours, about the weather. About a movie poster for Apichatpong Weerasethakul's *Uncle Boonmee Who Can Recall His Past Lives*. About banyan weevils and the prevention thereof, about Taiwanese breakfasts, Taiwanese lunches and dinners, about ice hockey and Daniel's ambivalence thereto, and about writing. "Is that where you write?" Paumgarten asked, gesturing at a small teak desk.

"I write everywhere," Daniel said. "I find it's important not to discriminate."

Eventually they sat down, each man on his own plump leather chesterfield. The charcuterie platter sat between them, next to Paumgarten's whirring dictaphone. They had actual snifters of bourbon.

A huge bay window looked east, into the darkness of the estate.

"Do you like living alone?"

"I get a lot of work done."

"Are you working on something now?"

"A lady never tells," Daniel said. He reconsidered his quip. "I mean—yes."

"What's it about?"

Daniel paused. "A noodle maker," he said finally.

"A noodle maker?"

"That's right."

The fronds of the banyan wafted in the periphery.

"Winning the lottery must have . . . disrupted your routine."

Daniel jammed a cushion under his elbow. "Yes and no. Writers have to be resilient, don't you think? Anything can happen in a day. You mustn't let life distract you from your pages."

Paumgarten nodded.

"Funny story actually." Daniel got up and crossed the room, picking up a ziplock bag from a table. He brought it to Paumgarten.

"Do you know what these are?"

"Rocks?"

"Open it."

The journalist did and at once pushed the bag away. "Ugh—what's that smell?"

"They're meteorites," Daniel said, taking back the bag. He reached inside and pulled out one of the pitted, metallic rocks.

"Why do they smell like that?"

"It's something to do with the minerals. Off-gassing from re-entry. Sulphur? I mean, I don't really know. They landed right here."

"On the house?"

"Around the property. Just over the past week! A whole spray of meteorites. There are probably more outside. It's not that unusual apparently—a conflux of conditions, geographical, meteorological, astrophysical, and then for a few days one spot gets pelted with shooting stars."

"How random," said Paumgarten. He examined the rocks through the bag.

"Like Mr. Wu said: 'Auspicious!' Some government astronomers picked it up on their radar. This morning they came round to explain. As you might expect, you have to be careful about fires—meteoroids can come in quite hot."

"Are they worth anything?"

"I imagine so."

"Even with that smell?"

"Maybe it fades? Or you can wash it off? The astronomers who came took it all very seriously. They laid out the rules. I'm entitled to keep everything smaller than eight inches across."

"So if a putrid space-basketball comes flying through your roof, you've got to hand it over."

"Unfortunately."

Paumgarten shook his head. "Daniel, you lead an unusual life."

Daniel waved his hand. "It's a state of mind." He suppressed a grin. This was going well. Perhaps the meteorites would become the story's lede? He felt he was conveying an appealing mixture of openness and mystery. Above all he wanted to seem intriguing: for Paumgarten's article to paint him as thoughtful, writerly, a beguiling character with sombre insights. A sense of humour, yes, but not too much humour. Serious-minded. He took another swallow of bourbon. Paumgarten did appear to like him. That was half the battle. The writer hadn't really asked anything about money, which was a relief, as the issue of money seemed tacky and mildly embarrassing. It made him feel *underhanded.* He had won the lottery; what else was there to say? What else would he ever choose to say?

"I wanted to tell you I loved *The Labrador Sea*," Paumgarten said.

Daniel stared into his lap. "That's kind," he said. He did not, could not, know whether Paumgarten was telling the truth. He hated this and accordingly hated such compliments, the cruel opacity of them. The only thing worse than someone hating his book was for someone to lie about loving it—and the doubt this sowed, sick and swirling. Whenever anybody told him they liked the book he was dogged by a suspicion they were lying. Their words (their tone, each syllable's subtlest micro-inflection) reversed through the bundle of his brainstem, souring reality. Perhaps his novel wasn't bad, but he knew each one of its failings. They came to him like old friends, long time no see! They fluttered up every time he opened the screen of his laptop, hoping to write another page. The Booker win and the approbation his novel had subsequently enjoyed had not, as he had hoped, cured him of this self-excoriation, but amplified it. Was he not now even more of a fraud? Was his admirers' praise not now even more embellished?

Paumgarten's eyebrows furrowed.

"What?" Daniel said.

"You seem stricken."

Daniel expelled a hollow laugh.

Paumgarten considered for a moment and said, "I'm not blowing smoke up your ass."

Daniel looked into his drink. "I wouldn't know if you were."

"Do you think I'm lying to you?"

"It doesn't matter," Daniel said. He wanted to sound nonchalant. "You do the work for its own sake. Not for other people's approval. You must know this from your own work."

Paumgarten seemed unsettled by this. "Yes."

Daniel gathered himself to his feet. "Let me show you something." Now that darkness had fallen, the air inside Rongshu Wu had changed. It was cooler, moister. The rooms' rice-paper lamps cast their light in shallow overlapping circles, like ripples on the surface of water. Paumgarten followed Daniel between the banyans' prop roots and under a hanging bough. The interrupted lamplight gave each of them jaguar spots. They passed through a doorway and into a snug room, where halogens shone white. Their spots had disappeared.

The items nearest the door were comics and graphic novels, perched in shatterproof display cases. Daniel's first editions of *MAUS* and *Fun Home*, *Tintin Goes to Dawson City*, *LOSE 1*, *Hair Shirt*, an autographed copy of the *Love and Rockets* debut. He had the yellow Quimby the Mouse/Sandman crossover, some original Fletcher Hanks, Moebius's *Dune* sketches. He passed all this without comment and halted at the end of the room, where there were no more books or comics. The cases here contained what looked almost like CDs: round, hand-sized discs, with circular holes in their centres. Some of the objects were made of variegated stone, others seemed translucent, glass-like.

"Fossils?" asked Paumgarten.

"They're jades."

These weren't the jade-green of jade-green crayons or the jade-green of jade plants, deep and vegetal. Nor could they be compared to flea markets' cheap, jadish junk—elephants and medallions on a collapsible plastic table. The objects were white-green or silver-green or aquamarine, their colours almost slipping, as if perceived through water.

"They're called *bi* discs," Daniel said. "From mainland China, Stone Age. People made these things for literally thousands of years, millennia, across a huge geographic area, spending unimaginable resources to do so." He lifted a case lid and took out one of the discs. He was always surprised by how heavy they were.

He placed it in Paumgarten's hands. "No one knows what they were for."

"Not currency?"

"No, they didn't trade them. They hoarded them, buried people with them. Relics, storehouses of power. Empty rings. Or imaginary doorways."

Paumgarten held the disc up to his eye, blinked through it. The jade had been carved with an interwoven pattern, like braided grasses.

"Hundreds of people devoted their lives to these things," Daniel went on. "*Why?* Was that worthwhile? Or a waste? They thought they needed them, they were *sure* they did. A story they told themselves. And about these other objects too—*cong* tubes. Archaeologists find them beside the bis. Jades as well, but rod-shaped. Not discs—wands."

"How many of them do you have?"

"I have some bis," said Daniel. "They're very hard to acquire. I keep saying that one day I'll stop collecting bi discs and I'll start collecting congs, the inverse, not the empty rings but the solid centres."

A pause passed.

"Is that what the building's for?" Paumgarten asked.

"What building?"

Paumgarten cleared his throat. "I saw it when I came in. The silo thing. Is it for your collection?"

"That's just storage. Landscaping equipment."

Paumgarten raised the bi again, looked at Daniel through it.

"Where were we?" Daniel said.

Back on the chesterfields.

"Where do you get your ideas?" Paumgarten asked.

"When did you write your first story?"

"Did you always want to be a writer?"

He continued refilling Daniel's glass of bourbon.

"How did you convince yourself to keep going?"

When Paumgarten got up to urinate, the outside night loomed in. Everything on the other side of the windows seemed held in place. As if nothing could possibly happen there.

Later, each of them was sitting on the floor. Daniel had his back to one of the banyans' roots. Paumgarten was a couple of feet away, leaning against the lower section of a chesterfield. His dictaphone whispered on the rug.

Daniel said: "To tell you the truth"—he drew up his knee—"you're drawing a false dichotomy. Yes, it requires luck to get published. It requires luck for your book to ever be read, for it to win a prize. Luck to win a draw. All of it's luck. And at the same time none of it is. Have you ever been in love?"

Paumgarten said, after a moment, "Of course."

Daniel put down his glass. "Did it 'just' happen or did you also make it happen? How much of one and how much of the other?" He didn't wait for Paumgarten's answer. "I wrote a book. The best book I could. I did the work, page upon page, and I put it into the world. Everything follows from that."

"The lottery?"

"I bought the ticket," Daniel said.

"But surely that's—"

"It's of a different order. It is. But there are not just two categories of things, things that are earned and things that are not. The reality's woollier. Is a coincidence pure chance or evidence of a connection? Often it's both."

Paumgarten pressed his lips together. He looked into his notebook, turned a page. "It's funny you should say that."

"Funny?"

"Your book had all these coincidences. With my own life. Bicycles and motorcycles. Strange flocks of birds. Letters to a woman named Lou."

"Lou? Really?"

"I've been writing all year to a woman named Lou," Paumgarten said. A sadness had come into his face. "I've started hating them. Letters. One-sided and strange."

"They're a useful device."

"They're always hiding something." Paumgarten raised his head. "Are you offended?"

"Of course not," said Daniel. "Perhaps I lean on them too much." His finger traced along the carpet, a river in blue thread. "No letters in my next book, I promise."

"At least not between lovers."

"All right."

"Great. Then I promise to buy a copy."

"My agent will be relieved!"

Paumgarten began to laugh. But Daniel watched a different thought pass across his eyes, stilling him.

"Do you think you'd write anyway?" Paumgarten asked. "If you didn't have sales? If no one cared?"

"If nobody was reading?"

"Yeah."

Daniel closed his eyes for a second. "People always treat that question as a sort of secret weapon." His tone was forthright but his body language was almost embarrassed. "A knife that might stab to the artist's heart, revealing his frailty, his insincerity, his ego. But it's actually the opposite. When you ask that question—you, Max from the *New Yorker*, 'What if no one read your work?'—the answer wells right up. It feels more certain than ever. Visceral, natural, obvious. I know it immediately: I'd do it anyway."

Do I really believe this? Daniel wondered.

I do, he thought.

He straightened. "Your question's still important. But it isn't *profound*—not to me, no offence. Where it resonates is as a matter of commerce. When nobody reads your work, how can you live? How can you pay for your meals and your mortgage, your air fare, flowers for Mother's Day? That's the way the question matters. If you happen to be broke. If every day of writing brings a whole night of doubt. *Why am I wasting my time on this? I can't justify it. I can't afford this labour. What if no one reads it?* If no one reads it, will you be all right? Will you be able to carry on—physically, materially? To keep the heat coiling through the radiators?"

He intended to stop there—that line about radiators, a borderline-excessive literary flourish. However Paumgarten was watching him with such untempered attention—an attention that seemed both ample and unfilled, like a sort of vacuum—that after a few seconds he continued talking.

"If you can *afford to* carry on, then the question's easy. If money's no worry—if you're solvent or comfortable or rich, if you've won the lottery, if you're able to sustain, self-sustain, idle away—then never mind if anybody reads your pages. Never mind that. Fuck it. Some days it might matter but other days it won't. And it needn't. What's *really* important becomes clearer. Words splashing onto a page, like rain from nimbostratus. The puddles they leave. The skinny rivers. What's *really* important is the feeling a book rouses as it's finding form, chapter by chapter, and how you feel when it's done. Each moment is different, but each is sustaining. At least on the good days. On those days, when I'm lucky, the desire to write feels as forceful as any feeling I've known—lust or loneliness or grief. 'Will anyone read it?' I don't consider that. What I'm thinking is: 'A comma here?' 'A period?' 'A lustrous word or a plain one?' 'What kind of tree should be growing there, in this story, spreading its branches above their heads?'"

Both of them were staring at the boughs.

"Huh," Paumgarten said.

Daniel worried suddenly that this speech had been jejune. Why was he making such lofty statements? Did he believe everything he was saying? He didn't really know. He wanted to believe it. He would act as if he did; there was power enough in that. One set of lies to make up for another.

Paumgarten looked at his watch. "A noodle maker, you said."

"It's a metaphor for making art."

The dictaphone made a sound like a lock being cut. The two men exchanged a look. Paumgarten reached over and took out the little cassette.

"That's my last tape."

"Old school," Daniel said.

"Yes."

They lapsed into quiet.

"I forgot about my car," Paumgarten said.

"It's outside."

"It's fucked."

"Just leave it."

"No, I'll call the tow."

"Just leave it. It's late."

"I can still call." Paumgarten swallowed. "I think I'm a bit drunk."

"Where's your hotel?"

"The Grand Oriental."

"I'll ring you a cab."

"The car—"

"Forget it until tomorrow."

"You don't mind?"

"No."

The room held their silence like ashes in an urn. One of Daniel's chameleons had moved soundlessly, inch by inch, onto the sill of the bay window. It was the same slate grey as the glass and the world outside, nearly invisible; Daniel perceived it only because he was so practised at discerning them, his chameleons. Beyond the lizard and the window lay his estate. There were some distant blue-toned flashes, like the flickers of will-'o'-the-wisps. Fireflies perhaps, or guards on their peregrinations. Daniel forgot the flashes as soon as they had faded. Living on Fogo there had been so many weird, faint glimmers: spirits shifting on the seashore. Yangmingshan held a different share of mysteries. Rongshu Wu was peaceful, its old joins trembling in the tropical breeze. The Presidio was secure, locked with steel and software, reinforced concrete. Daniel was sitting with a journalist, a great journalist, who would tell his story and in the telling cement it, make it real. He needed this, because he knew what he had done to get here, the cheat of it, and he craved anything that would liberate him from this true and dishonest story, as if there were another story that could redeem his fictions.

Paumgarten rolled over and started getting to his feet. "I think it's time," he said.

"I'll call that cab."

Paumgarten bent and picked up the dictaphone, slipping it into his shirt pocket.

They went outside to wait. Daniel still wasn't accustomed to the heat of Taiwan's summer nights, the way it didn't really subside. Each of them was surprised by the deafening mechanisms of the insects. All the evening's other sounds were indistinguishable. They proceeded past Paumgarten's stalled black car, Mr. Wu's stern face behind the guardhouse window. Mr. Yu must be on patrol. The estate's gates parted.

They stood together on the hard-packed dirt.

"My Lou stopped answering," Paumgarten said.

It was pitch black and they couldn't see each other's faces. "Your Lou . . ." Daniel said. In the fresh air he did not feel as drunk as he had, not even with the drone of the cicadas in his ears, and he did not feel certain what to say to this man about his Lou, or whether to say nothing. He found he was running a calculus: Would Paumgarten resent him later for this moment? For his own vulnerability, or Daniel's silence? It would be so easy for the journalist to punish him.

"Maybe her letters got lost," Daniel said.

But when the taxi came, Daniel wondered if he was actually drunker than he thought. In the bright lights of the car he said, "I hope you got what you needed," and he didn't understand Paumgarten's bitter laugh, a laugh as if Daniel had said something regrettable, something tragic.

"It was what it was," Paumgarten told him. "See you in the morning."

:::

Once Theo left the house, Daniel Merrett Leys spent twenty-one minutes fixing himself a bowl of cereal, eating it, and paging through an old issue of the *New Yorker*, plucked from a stack, looking exclusively at the comics.

There was a cartoon about a lock and a key. "You busy Friday?" asked the key. It was wearing a necktie.

He turned the page without smiling. All around him, even in the rooms he was not in, the banyans fanned.

Bi discs shimmered in their velvet.

A glass of water, long-deserted, let go of its last bubbles.

An unmarked octo-prop drone crouched on Rongshu Wu's roof.

A car sat in the drive.

Mr. Wu, who had returned from his rounds, reclined in the guardhouse with Mr. Yu. From time to time, each of them glanced at the green-tinted midnight on their screens. A control panel showed eighteen untiring LEDs.

Mr. Yu riffle-shuffled a deck of cards. Mr. Wu watched him do so. The gates were locked as tight as mirrors.

Cameras stood wide-eyed.

A light flicked out. Merrett Leys had gone to bed.

Mr. Yu turned over a queen of spades.

Not far away, in the long grass near the bank of the creek, Simone and Suzy rose to their feet.

Theo, in a Grand Oriental hotel room, took his "dictaphone" from his pocket, put it down beside the TV.

JF, at the ink importer's house, clicked an icon on his computer and pressed enter. A progress bar appeared.

For the briefest instant, the images wavered on Messrs Wu and Yu's screens.

Simone breathed in the jasmine air. She felt warm—that odd, dull, wetsuit warmth. The ground had turned to mud where they had been crouching. She brushed grass and grit and soil from her haunches, listening through the churn of jungle sound for a voice in her earpiece.

"*On y est,*" JF said finally. It was a scrambled channel. "You can go."

For now they had only disabled the video surveillance. Merrett Leys had given Theo the wireless password; the trojan in his dictaphone had whirred away; after several hours the camera system was compromised. The guardhouse monitors were no longer live: like the men's card games, the footage repeated in permutating loops. The drone kept its bat's-eye view, lest Wu or Yu embark on patrol. Simone and Suzy stalked across the lawn. Although they had left their dive masks they still wore bulky waterproof packs; night-vision goggles gave their faces a curious resemblance to crickets'. The passage they had used, underwater, was too narrow for them to carry much; the current was too strong to swim back the way they'd come.

The pair went immediately to the rear of the guardhouse. In the gloom of its northern retaining wall, they picked the lock on the outdoor utilities compartment. The internal panels used combination locks: these they simply guessed, each woman with one hand on a packet of luck.

Once they had access to the electronics, Suzy connected a thermostat-sized control box. They waited open-palmed, like insecty supplicants, for its LEDs to align; the pinlights blinked, like pips on a die. Working remotely, JF powered down the estate's high-gain antennas and deactivated the alarms' alert system. Suzy moved away, up the hill to the tower—her progress hidden by the bulk of Theo's car. Simone, on her belly, inched towards the rental's trunk.

Suzy took thirty minutes to scale the tower's wall, ten more to pierce the ventilation grille on its roof. The arc of her oxyacetylene torch was a light like lightning as it crackles in its cloud. Simone had returned by then from the driveway, dragging the vinyl shell concealed beneath Theo's car's spare tire. Passing across the lawn, unsilhouetted under a moonless sky, Simone was a sleek black spot. Or else she was not. Suzy watched her sister through the infra-red: a figure dragging an object into the rosebushes, hauling it singlehanded, like an enchanted hunter with the carcass of a bear.

Simone deposited the unmade meteor a little away from the tower, tucked among the thorns.

:::

As the night wore on, the burglars penetrated each of the Presidio's locked chambers. The sisters descended its spiral staircase, working side by side. First a room full of cash, stacked bills in plexi boxes, which they left undisturbed. Next a room of heirlooms—furniture, photo albums, candlesticks and jewellery. They ignored this too. There was a room with every edition of *The Labrador Sea*, spiral-bound drafts and editors' notes, and another with acid-free boxes of back-issue comic books, series Merrett Leys had been collecting since his teens. Some of the doors had key codes, combination locks; these they serendipitously solved. Others they cut, with odourless oxyacetylene.

Finally, about halfway down the tower, they reached a chamber with double-kited walls, Mas Hamilton locks, a giant bank-vault door. Infrared beams, overcome with lead film bags. Proceeding patiently, painstakingly, the sisters breached the room's defences and entered its hall of mirrors. Packed among the reflections, in hundreds of suede bags, waited a material like glittering sand.

"Thank God," whispered Simone. It was not a tower full to the top with luck but a bonanza all the same, among the largest caches they had ever found.

They heaved out the sandbags a few at a time, carried them to the roof, hoisted them off the side. They landed softly in the verdure.

Their drone was the lookout, still as a gargoyle. Whenever Mr. Wu emerged on patrol—as he did at times—and whenever Mr. Yu came out—as he did, too—JF chirped a warning in the women's ears.

Mr. Wu sang as he walked. A tuneless quiet song.

Mr. Yu did not sing. He counted every step.

But it was Mr. Wu who heard them. Simone and Suzy were crouched in the rosebushes, hefting sandbags towards the object

Simone had retrieved from Theo's trunk. There's no concealing certain presences: they're conspicuous, unassailable. Mr. Wu came all the way to the edge of the thorn-swirled garden. His sandals imprinted the soil. Perhaps he heard a rustle, a snap, their steady breathing. Perhaps he simply felt them there. He pointed his flashlight at the tower—the building's unbroken brick, its sealed front door. He pointed it at the security camera—a serene black globe. His flashlight skimmed the bushes, gilding the sandbags, but he did not see the sisters. *An animal*, he thought.

Simone, lying facedown in earth, wore explosives on her back.

Suzy, beside her, felt a worm lift and loop beside her cheek.

Eventually Mr. Wu walked on.

The sun rose, and everything became precarious.

The thieves were more visible now, exposed under Yangmingshan, and they hurried to finish their work. At his workstation, JF sipped a sixth cup of tea. Theo was dozing, dreaming, in a tousled king-sized bed. Merrett Leys was sleeping too. They had to act before the night-watch left at 8:00 AM, replaced with fresh new eyes. Already the San Marziales had taken down the rope ladder. They had lowered their goggles, the top halves of their faces flushed, damp, like little kids', and were standing in the roses, vibrant blooms of *chi can hong xin* and pale Souvenir de Malmaison, stuffing sandbags into the shell. It was soft and expandable, elastic, lined with mirrored foil. As cargo filled it the vessel got larger, larger, until it was itself as big as a room. The shell was pebbly, with a textured exterior—smears of gallium, bands of heat-scored rock and grit. A coating of pale charcoal. Set among the roses, it looked like a great, deflated boulder.

Once the main task was finished, Simone used a footpump to fill the rest of the shell with air. Suzy cast about with her torch, burning back the briar, touching white flame to roses. Soon a scorched circle surrounded their false, fallen meteor. They took the C4 from Simone's waterproof pack—harmless-looking packets, like rare cheeses—and began to plant it in the earth. Wires led from the explosives to a contraption on Simone's belt.

The last step was clean-up: sweeping for footprints, gathering equipment, using a spray-bottle to douse the area in skunk juice, pepper and valeric acid. When they had prepared the stones for the drone, they had only needed a few drops; here Suzy dispersed fetid spritzes of the stuff.

"Those poor roses," Simone said.

The worst part was the way they did not wither. As dawn broke, the reeking mist hung like dewdrops. Flowers freshly kissed.

:::

Theo was in a taxi, staring at a four-inch plastic crab. The crab stared back. It had shiny eyestalked pupils and a cheery, guileless smile, a carapace painted the same fire engine red as Provisions K's sign. It stood on the driver's dashboard, its claws open and upraised. In friendship, Theo thought. It wobbled as they climbed the road to Rongshu Wu.

Theo's phone buzzed.

All set, read the message from JF.

You're on.

Theo turned the phone facedown on his lap. He was hung over. No, he wasn't particularly hung over. That was just an excuse. Before going to bed he had stood in the hotel bathroom drinking glasses of lukewarm water, hydrating, rinsing away his deceptions, washing down the role of Max Paumgarten. Theo had wanted to go to sleep as himself.

Now he was on his way back to the Banyan House, the same role resumed. "Paumgarten," Theo murmured, feeling the name on his tongue. He couldn't shake the feeling that he was doing Daniel harm. He had liked him. Immediately, without effort, despite the writer's anxieties and ego, despite the way he tried to bluff through certain answers. Despite his long-winded speeches. In a lifetime spent at comedy clubs, Theo had known a lot of talkers. Daniel was agreeably strange, thoughtful, his frailties showing. He had allowed Theo into his home, a liar into the living room, and he had been generous.

The crab grinned at him.

This is what it is to be a thief, Theo thought. *You thieve.*

The gates to the property were closed. Theo paid the driver and disembarked, bade a silent farewell to the dashboard crustacean.

He pressed a button on the gate's intercom. The estate seemed different in morning light. Through the gate's bronze bars: the brown ribbon of the driveway, a splendid scribble of roses, the tower like a distant chesspiece. Theo's sedan still sat stalled before the guardhouse.

A voice crackled across the intercom.

"Hello. Max Paumgarten back again for his car."

"One moment."

It took more than one. Theo waited, waited, shuffled in circles as Mr. Yu tried to rouse his employer. While Theo waited he listened for any sign of the Gang's clandestine work. Nothing. The fence glittered. He could see the house's stained-glass windows, half-moons high up. Perhaps that was Daniel's bedroom. Perhaps it was the room where he had shown him the bis. Perhaps it was his private cinema, his library, the billiards room, his elevated, temperature-controlled wine fridge. Theo's heart tightened. The writer and his treasures, his hoard. It was envy, envy at its loosest, unrooted. There was no single aspect that Theo yearned for—it was Daniel's prosperity in general, his success in general, the way the world was generally open to him and whatever he might choose to imagine. The writer hadn't earned any of it. The state of his life, the colour of it, was founded on a lie. Daniel's riches and opportunities, his fame. The camphor baron's house and the twisting banyan trunks. His kindness. Theo stared at the swirls his footsteps had left in the dust. Daniel did not even deserve his wisdom. All of it he had stolen.

Mr. Yu's voice rippled from the grille. "Welcome," he said, and the fifteen-foot gate rattled aside.

Theo strolled up the drive, hands in his pockets.

He and his friends would steal some of it back.

Daniel stood on his steps in a robe, not so different from the previous evening. He is a charlatan, Theo thought. He's a sham.

"Hello!" Daniel shouted.

Theo raised his hand in greeting.

As he did so, something exploded in the yard.

:::

The rose garden was on fire. Smoke was climbing up in columns, as if somebody were drawing inky fingers through the sky. Daniel ran cautiously at first but then with increasing urgency once he glimpsed the scene. He turned to make sure Paumgarten was behind him.

Blackened petals had been ripped from their stems, sprinkling the crater like the remains of a wedding. Flames glittered among the blossoms, amaranth pinks and fool's-gold blonds, curling the blooms. The scent was like honeycomb, until the wind changed. Daniel covered his face with his sleeve. The meteor stood at the centre of the wreckage, burnt and weathered, a boulder as big as a shed, with fumes that curdled the air, wilting the grass.

It hadn't been an explosion, Daniel understood now. It was the sound of landfall. He was coughing at the stench, the smoke, tearing as he marvelled, wide-eyed. "Can you imagine . . . !" he shouted.

Paumgarten shook his head.

"A meteor! A shooting star!" Daniel whooped. "Look at the size of it!" His laughter was muffled by his terrycloth sleeve. "Does it ever stink!"

"Sulphur, you said?"

"More like a garbage fire!"

Daniel glanced towards the Presidio. It seemed unscathed, safe. He went back to marvelling, exchanging half-hidden grins with Paumgarten.

"How did you sleep?" he eventually asked.

"Like a lamb," Paumgarten said.

"I can't believe you're here for this."

"If it weren't for my second-rate car . . ."

Mr. Yu had appeared, out of breath. Mr. Wu could be seen back near the house, labouring to carry a hose.

"Hey, be careful with that." Paumgarten was pointing at Yu's brandished fire-extinguisher. "Shouldn't we let it burn off? Maybe there are chemicals that would react to the spray."

Yu ignored him, taking aim at the smouldering roses, releasing toots of foam.

"It could be radioactive, right?" Paumgarten said. "We should all keep our distance."

The group retreated. As the morning poured in, the meteor looked ever more ravaged, shining.

From down the hill: the sound of an engine.

They turned. Daniel saw Wu, swathed in garden hose, turn too. "Did you call your tow?" he asked Paumgarten. The vehicle was just visible through the gate—halted now, idling. Its driver leaned on his horn.

Not a tow. A cube truck, the wine-red colour of young Beaujolais.

"That's the astronomers!" Daniel said.

He took a few steps down the lawn, signalled for Wu to go and let them in. "Cripes, they're fast!"

"The government?" Paumgarten said.

Daniel gazed towards the giant reeking stone. "You have to concede," he murmured, "the thing is bigger than a basketball."

A few minutes later, the National Astronomical Service's burgundy truck rumbled up the greeny slopes and all the way into the rosebushes. When Wu shouted a complaint, a woman leapt from the cab—one of the officials who had visited yesterday. She replied with her own invective, waving him back. Three more women sprang from the cargo area, and then the other official, the black man; all wore the crisp blue uniforms, NAS patches on their shoulders. The three women donned surgical masks, then swarmed towards the meteor.

"Did any of you touch it?" the man demanded, in English.

"No," said Daniel.

"Good. Please stay back."

The young women circled the rock, stamping stray flames. They produced cables, laying them across the area. All of them wore turtlenecks under their coveralls.

"Is it dangerous?" Daniel asked.

"Yes," replied the man.

His partner had snatched away the fire extinguisher and was barking at Mr. Yu.

"Will you just take it away?" Daniel said.

"Also yes."

Paumgarten, with a tone of incredulity: "The whole meteor?"

"The whole meteor*ite*," said the man.

"What bullshit," said Paumgarten.

With cables securing the thing in place, the women had fitted its circumference with a set of pneumatic jacks.

"According to Article 41B of the Republic of China's Statute on Aerospace and Astronomy Research," said the man, "the NAS lays claim to any landed astral matter above twenty-five centimetres in diameter, whether or not said matter is located on public property."

Mr. Yu said something in Mandarin.

The other astronomer growled a reply.

"Is there any compensation?" Paumgarten asked.

"There is no compensation," the man said.

"That's insane!"

Daniel flashed him a look.

"No, I'm sorry," Paumgarten went on, "some priceless astrological treasure lands in this man's yard and you're entitled to tear in here and whisk it away? To some lab?"

"Yes," said the man. "To some lab."

"Please clear from the area," said the woman, hustling them back.

"It isn't right!" said Paumgarten.

"Max . . ." said Daniel.

"Please clear," the woman repeated, taking Paumgarten's arm. He shook off her grip.

"Sir," said the man.

Daniel and Yu were now exchanging glances. Paumgarten was flushed. He kept forgetting to keep his sleeve across his face. "Where's your warrant for this?"

"Have you been drinking?" Daniel asked.

Paumgarten shouted, "They can't just stroll . . . Hey!"

The workers' jacks, wedged under the meteorite, had lifted the object off the ground. The boulder teetered, steadied.

"Can your truck really carry it?" said Daniel. "How many tons must it weigh?"

"Most meteorites this size are hollow," the man replied. Quickly this fact seemed borne out: the trio of women had balanced the boulder on a dolly and were guiding it across the grass.

"They're just *taking* it," said Paumgarten.

"Max, it's fine," hissed Daniel.

They heaved it up the ramp.

"Hey, stop!" Paumgarten bellowed. He lunged towards them and then was jerked straight back as the man from the NAS seized him by the collar. In a swift movement, and with unexpected violence, he used a plastic cuff to secure the journalist's wrists behind his back. "What the fuck!" yelled Paumgarten.

"You are hereby detained under the authority of the Statute's recovery and protection clauses," the officer said.

"Sir—" said Daniel.

The man loomed towards him. "Yes?"

His partner hoisted the fire extinguisher.

Daniel shrank back. "It's just he didn't do anything wrong."

The woman pointed towards the Banyan House. "Please wait inside."

Daniel gazed at Paumgarten, helpless. Paumgarten gazed back, then turned to the lanky NAS leader.

"Now," the man said.

The truck was creaking with the weight of its freight.

Petals were everywhere.

The sun was shining.

Mr. Wu finally arrived with the hose.

"*Now.*"

Fifteen minutes later, Daniel Merrett Leys finally reached his lawyer. It was to be a very confounding phone call. The thieves' luck-stuffed truck was already roaring out the gates of Rongshu Wu. The counterfeit meteorite trembled on the cargo floor, its vinyl dimpling as they barrelled from dirt to asphalt. Two of Roie's daughters sat around the stinking booty, seat belts buckled; the other was opening a slit on the side of the meteorite, helping the San Marziale sisters out. Theo sat up front, wedged between Roie and Sebald. With a loud, vaguely dental snap, Sebald severed the zip around Theo's wrists.

"Thanks," Theo said.

"I hope I did not cause you much discomfort," Sebald said.

The truck tumulted down the mountain, into the city. Roie had turned on the radio—some kind of Taiwanese children's choir, their voices sharp and raucous—and Theo's mind was whirring like rewinding tape, visualizing the scenes that had led to this moment. After weeks spent planning with Simone, the starfall and its aftermath had seemed unreal, a dream come to life. Now he imagined everything he had not witnessed: the sisters' eel-kicking underwater journey; their tiptoe and skulk; a darkened hand tossing a grappling hook—up, straight up, somehow undescending. What had the view been like from the tower's parapet? How much luck had they found?

The truck rattled through the gates of the ink importer's house and down the pebbled driveway to the lot. JF was waiting for them, perched on a ladder, extending dragonfly-green bottles of bubbly. While Sebald and Theo bounded towards him, cheering, solemn Roie crossed behind and hauled up the trailer door. Her daughters appeared: kicking off their astronomers' coveralls, retying their sneakers. One of them stooped at a wing-mirror, refreshing her lipstick; another kneeled beside a thermos and poured out cups of tea.

At first Theo didn't see the San Marziales. Their silhouettes were lost amongst the detritus at the back of the truck—the giant slow-crumpling meteorite, the putrid fumes, bits and pieces of gear. Then Suzy stepped out of the fray—exhausted, filthy, uncharacteristically fragile. At the edge of the cargo bay, Roie all but caught her. When they kissed it seemed rough and almost rueful. Watching them felt like trespassing. Until they separated: then the women stood radiant, like smiling playing-card faces, jacks or queens of spades.

Maybe seeing this affected what happened next. Or else maybe it was simply the look on Simone's face when she appeared, dishevelled, dirt-smudged, reeking, grinning, so much more worse for wear than he expected. When she jumped down from the truck he took her in his arms. To his surprise she kissed him on the mouth. Soft lips, clicking teeth.

Soon everybody was holding a cup of cava in one hand and a cup of oolong in the other. Theo and Simone toasted cup to cup to cup to cup, drank two times. JF and Sebald dragged out an industrial fan, propped it at the mouth of the truck, to try to disperse the smell. The fan was shoving Simone's hair around. After a few minutes she scampered up the trailer hitch and knelt in the shadow of the strange, fraudulent boulder. She undid the fastenings and the vinyl sloughed open, showing its mirrored interior and dozens of sandbags jumbled inside. Sandbags, holding something that wasn't sand.

Still, the No Name Gang had a rule: *check the dice.* No matter how certain your score, test the goods. Simone raised a wooden cup. All of them were watching. She rolled the bones, shook, threw. The dice test showed six times six equals thirty-six pips, and all the thieves exulted.

:::

An hour after takeoff, the airplane cabin was quiet, lights low. Men and women reclined with open mouths, dry tongues; others lay catlike, curled towards the walls. Theo was unnerved by flying first class. Air travel ought to be a makeshift, incommodious hurtling. It shouldn't be like a night in a dulled and peculiar hotel.

The meteorite made him uneasy too. They had hosed it down, negotiated a cargo rate, checked it in under a fake name. Flying through the air alongside a shooting star, even a fake one, seemed a little like asking for it.

How did I get so superstitious? Theo asked himself. The answer was this: by finding out that luck is real.

Suzy and Sebald were snoozing in the row ahead of them, JF snoring in the row behind. Theo and Simone had watched *Top Hat* together—each on their own tiny screen, with its own crummy headset. It was like and unlike their time at the cinema(s). "I always watch old movies on planes," Simone had told him. "Makes it feel like an education. Like I'm getting something done up here." They timed it "3-2-1" so they were laughing at the same pratfalls, awed by the same softshoe.

Afterward, Simone took out a folder. A creamy piece of carton folded in her lap.

"What's that?"

"We found it in the tower. With the luck. In a safe."

She withdrew a letter. One page of heavy linen stock, formatted like a wedding invitation or a municipal declaration—a block of text with four massive margins, centre justified. The typeface looked familiar, Times New Romanesque, but not quite that, like a younger version. The fulcrum of the capital *L* reminded Theo of a gilded, half-open hinge.

The letter was dated four years earlier.

Dear Daniel,

Let me first say how happy I was to meet you in Ichiro's olive grove. Some nights I acquire a vivid sense of the softness of the world—how easily the boundaries between things blur, disparate entities coming together. It makes me excited but always a little frightened. You and I spoke of islands, the way they're defined by their edges. "What is an island without its water?" you said. Sometimes we require walls, despite all our dreams of softness, permeation. We must be true to ourselves.

Listen to me, the two-bit sage. Again, it was a pleasure talking with you—a fellow collector with interests besides collecting.

I wanted you to know that my invitation remains open,

should you ever change your mind. I already harbor portions of
several other friends' collections. It is a way of diversifying risk.
It gratifies me to do this for kindred spirits, fellow travellers.
Safeguards are easier en commun; even then they aren't easy.
Maybe they are the hardest part of our pastime.

    Good luck with your book.

"What's 'Ichiro's'?" Theo said.

"Ichiro Teruteru. Probably. The eldest son of Akio and Hikaru
Teruteru."

Theo looked at her blankly.

"They're like the Rockefellers of luck."

"Someone sent this to Daniel?"

She nodded.

"Who?"

"I don't know."

"Huh."

"There's another one."

Unlike the first letter, which had been sent to Merrett Leys's old
home on Fogo, the second used his address at Rongshu Wu. It was
dated nine months ago.

Let this letter serve as promissory note: (i) acknowledging the
receipt of approximately one tonne of pure, unwinnowed
chance; and (ii) entitling you to its return, in full, upon request.
The costs of transportation shall be borne by you. This property will be held by me until a mutually agreed upon time, such
agreement not to be unreasonably withheld or delayed. In the
case of loss, your chance shall be replaced at my own expense.

Reasonable protections will be made against winnowing-away.

This note is non-transferable.

Each document ended with the same valediction, and the same signature:

Until our roads next cross —

Brightly,

"Is that an *M*?" Theo asked.

"Or two *N*s?"

"Mysterious."

"Yes."

"A luck collector."

"Yes."

"Who keeps luck for others, out of the goodness of his heart . . ."

"Or her heart, yes."

Theo reread the letter.

"Sounds like a trick."

"Maybe so. But on whom?"

CHAPTER TWELVE

Autumn had landed in the city, leaf by crinkled leaf. One day would bring a cold, rattling wind, the next it was Indian summer, with sunsets softer than icing, kids spraying water pistols in the alleys. Theo stood at Provisions K's loading dock and watched one such campaign, four friends in cheerful melee. Dousing each other, wasting away the evening, the boys seemed happier than they had any right to be.

Inside, the aisles were dusty, quiet.

"Hey, Mo," he said, catching the manager's eye. "Where is everybody?"

"It's always like this now," Mo said. "Since number two opened."

Number two. "Provisions L," the fish-boys called it. The bright white brand new location, in the former Homayoun Carpets building. A shiny supermarket roosting above the No Name Gang's hoard.

Busy as a burglar, Theo had not been assiduous in following the new store's progress. He had dozens of unread emails from his siblings, threads with subject lines like *Going Forward?*, *Stock Transfer??*, *Lighting Grids???*—correspondence which it had never been in his nature to ignore but which by now ignoring filled him with an irresponsible, unforeseen elation. He had answered Eric's calls about the basement storage site but scarcely anything else. *Let them have it*, he told himself, while he plotted his Taiwanese treasure map.

Still, he hadn't been prepared for how unsettling it would feel to return home and find things changed; nor for how he'd feel to learn that Lou was still wherever she was, changing however she might. And no word from her for him. *Perhaps she will be home*, he had told himself, back from a nine-month absence, bearing love and clarity. A stroll along the tracks, a reunion over hummus and pomegranate seeds. Instead, no sign, no letters. And here—a store without its crowds. Provisions' customers had been what gave it life. Without the hubbub the old store now seemed waning. *Like visiting a relative in hospice*, Theo thought.

Provisions L was just as unrecognizable. Central air! Kombucha taps! Freezers that did not faintly smell of taramosalata! Most of their clientele seemed to have flocked to the new location, wooed by higher ceilings and wider aisles, the store's clean and citrusy whiff. A pair of automatic cashiers loomed beside a display of cut roses; Theo watched, stunned, as a kid whisked through with a two-litre bottle of Coke. The customers here seemed happier, and also somehow less interesting.

Theo had arrived there for a family outing to the history museum—an annual tradition. Every year on Minerva's birthday, she'd lead them on a tour of the Antiquities exhibit. Theo met his siblings, their spouses and children under Provisions L's lolling GRAND OPENING banner; the eight of them then subdivided into van-cabs and made

their way downtown, gliding towards and past the Dolores. The taxis
were Hanna's idea. "Every year you complain about the parking," she
said, meaning the adults. Since Minerva had died, every ritual seemed
up for re-examination, so they took the two cabs and then meandered
up the museum's front steps, past a man in a Spider-Man costume
dancing to Otis Redding. They crossed through the turnstiles and
Theo felt his heart sink—the sight of the exhibit's fake arch, its poly-
ester ivy, the model of Plato with arms held aloft. Minnie would
assume the same pose to lecture them on happiness. He couldn't
remember what she'd said. No, he could. He mumbled the words into
the atrium: "'Happiness is not an animal . . .'"

Peter and Mireille finished the quotation: "'. . . it is a rustle in the
grass.'"

"Plato," said Theo.

"Plato," agreed Mireille.

"I googled that line once," Peter said. "I couldn't find any evidence
that Plato ever said it."

"So who did?"

Peter shrugged. "Mom."

"You think she made it up?"

Peter didn't answer.

Mireille patted the plastic Plato on his shoulder. "The first time we
went to see you do comedy—I remember she was wearing the biggest
earrings, like lacy birdcages—she turned to me and said, 'He just says
whatever he wants!'"

Theo gave a thin smile.

"Maybe you learned it from her."

Theo squinted across the museum hall. He met the gaze of Julius
Caesar, a clay bust on a plinth. Cleopatra was resting nearby, her eyes

on Theo's, staring at him with an air of steady encouragement. He looked away. Hanna stood with her father, making a pencil rubbing of Greek characters. Maurice and Blake had each found a pair of the exhibit's VR goggles and they turned in slow circles, ogling fifth-century Athens.

"I wonder what Mom would have thought of it," Theo said.

"The exhibit?"

"The new location."

Mireille nodded. "I think about that every day." She must have been able to read his face; her eyes flashed a kind of warning. "I think she would have appreciated the improvements."

"The changes," Theo said.

"Yeah."

"And what about the *old* store?"

His sister hesitated, then said. "It would have made her sad."

"We're in a transition," said Peter. "Till Christmas."

"Why keep it open at all?"

"Nostalgia," said Peter. "Foolhardiness."

"It's postponing the inevitable," Theo said.

Mireille rounded on him. "*Now* you're taking an interest?"

"Are you kidding?" said Theo. "Pull the plug already. Put the place out of its misery."

This stopped her short. His brother and sister wore contrasting expressions: satisfaction; unease. Theo shook his head, gazed at old coins behind glass; he tried not to see his own reflection, the hair wild atop his head. "The first Provisions will limp along as long as you let it. It'll never die."

"I'm happy you agree," said his brother.

"Just do it."

Mireille's lips were pressed together. "You're sure?" she said. The look she was giving him was one he knew from childhood—the same look she gave him when he had skinned his knee or busted his toe, when he was trying to keep from crying. It spoke of concern and patience and responsibility. Theo clenched his jaw. "Yeah, it's time," he said. "Maybe I'll open a souvlaki stand."

"Don't be so dramatic. You have your new thing."

"Forecasting," enunciated Peter. Theo could hear the mockery in it.

"That's right," Theo said. "Beats boxing groceries."

They walked together to a display of columns. *Doric, Ionic, Corinthian*, he thought. They could see Hanna on the other side of the display case—tilting her body left and right, drifting through the exhibit on her hoverboard. Eric and Joanne were meandering towards the gift shop. Peter's sons were still in their simulation: they appeared to have encountered ancient Greek ice cream. Theo watched the boys lap at empty air.

"Well, that's that," Mireille said finally.

Theo brought his hands together, a restless clap. Peter looked at him. "'It is a small part of life we really live,'" Theo said. "Seneca."

:::

Homecoming had brought other disappointments. After they stashed their plunder in the storeroom under Provisions L, JF stood by the closed door with an instrument in his hands, monitoring the treasury's weight, its barometry. The needles didn't waver. Suzy whispered a curse.

"We are close," Sebald promised.

"Maybe we're not," said Simone. "We don't actually have any idea."

Sebald shook his head. He raised his folded-over notebook, full of spidery calculations. "We are very close. Happily ever after."

The San Marziale sisters trudged away, locked in conversation. Theo watched them go. It had occurred to him recently how little he knew of the group's long-term intentions. Would they divide the spoils after the Domino Point was reached? Dissolve the Gang, retire? He had a vision of a bundle of fireworks, a very long fuse; or of that bundle mid-flight, just about to explode. He imagined all the phosphor falling and standing with Simone at the centre.

If they were as close as Sebald thought, the writer's IOU was an insult, a dare. Some of Merrett Leys's luck had escaped them— another whole tonne of it, tucked in the coffers of whomever he had met in an olive grove. The thieves in their hideout were determined to find it, out of pique and pride and also bare curiosity. Who was this mysterious benefactor, safeguarding the fortunes of his or her fellows? How much luck did this person hold?

Suzy was the lone skeptic. "Sounds like a trap," she said, quite reasonably.

"You're paranoid," Theo said, assuming the role of persuader. He didn't see the way this stirred Suzy's misgivings. Why was Theo so sure, she wondered. What else had he and Daniel discussed beneath the banyans?

Suzy's unease didn't prevent the crew from presenting Theo with a gift to mark his first successful mission. Since it was clear they'd still need more, they allowed him to take some luck home: a mirrored container of the stuff, a novelty too novel to neglect. That night he stayed up until 3:00 AM—flipping coins, daffily marvelling, texting photos to Simone of tails after tails after tails. He couldn't help himself. She finally told him to cut it out.

Don't you like a winner?

Let me know when you start losing.

Half of it he put away beside his bed, in one of the Gang's deck-of-cards-sized boxes. The other half he carried with him wherever he went. It brought about many lesser displays of good fortune: patterned whirligigs of dust bunnies, strangers' dogs who (all) adored him, exact change when he reached into his pocket. Robins shat on his shoulders. Luck was a little like falling in love: it was hard to tell which wonders were bona fide and which were just coincidence. When Theo went with the Provisions' buyer to the produce market, just for old times' sake, they found not just bumper crops of red-dyed pistachios, like salty garnets, and massive Cortland apples, but pound upon pound of low-priced, semi-miraculous peppers. Each of the red, green and orange peppers contained a smaller capsicum curled inside, like a bulbous, fragrant pearl.

Once, accelerating downhill past the park, Theo watched a fast-approaching traffic light turn red. He thought the kind of half thought you know deserves more thinking, yet already he had released his brakes, closed his eyes, flown on in. It was lunatic and dumb. It was a sharpened, abject thrill. Partway through the intersection he peeked, one-eyed—saw the bumper of a car he had narrowly missed, clutched his handlebars in awe as he skidded through the space between two buses. Everybody was honking, horrified, panicking, veering, cursing him through their windshields. Theo simply glided, then picked up speed.

It didn't take long for the container in his bag to get sapped of its magic. He had never been more glum to see a coin showing heads.

Bad news, he tapped into his phone, under a photo of the upturned quarter.

Simone replied, *Don't take it personally.*

It bewildered him that she could be inured to it, the wonder of the stuff. So many years of lucky rolls, impossible odds—what would it feel like to be so charmed, for one's wagers to have turned reliable? He relished their moments of convergence—landing on the idea of the meteorite, or at the party after the heist. But Theo and Simone had not kissed again, or even acknowledged their kiss. She treated him like a confederate, not a hero. She'd hang out with him, laugh with him, until her attention turned elsewhere. His mind pitched with thoughts of Lou, gone across the world, and the crosscurrents of his desire. Whenever he talked to Simone about luck he tried to woo her back to his way of seeing: the particular marvel of where and who they were, what they were collecting. This extraordinary stuff, supernaturally fleeting.

"But *all* riches are fleeting," she said.

"No, actually. Most riches stay put."

"Until the flood, the robbery, the divorce, the bankruptcy. Then what do you have?"

"Regrets," he said.

She didn't laugh but she smiled. This felt like a victory. *Let me remember this*, he thought. *Let this be something I get to keep.*

The longer they searched for Daniel Merrett Leys's benefactor or benefactress, the more powerful he or she appeared. They had nicknamed him "M." Simone pursued the direct route—tracing Merrett Leys's recent travels, visitors to his home. Roie surveilled his actions in the aftermath of the robbery: Did he fly abroad? Did he receive any deliveries? The answer to both was no.

JF went underground, skimming the dark web, lurking in private chat-rooms. Sebald met undisclosed contacts in undisclosed places. None of these efforts brought answers. It was like stalking a ghost.

"Maybe Theo should try," Simone suggested. "He has fewer preconceptions." But Theo's dilettantism didn't furnish any epiphanies. Neither did his beginner's luck. Despondency began to bleed into Le Black Cat's underground rooms.

"Does Ichiro Teruteru even *have* an olive grove?" Suzy asked one day. "He's Japanese."

"The family owns an estate in Italy," said JF.

"Outside Grosseto," said Sebald.

"They export," said Simone. "I've seen them in shops."

The Teruterus, Theo learned, were a special class of Hustler: one of a handful of dynasties whose reserves of luck were so vast, and went back so far, that they could lead a kind of public life. Families like these formed a lofty elite, with its own social circuit and calendar. Akio and Hikaru Teruteru had led the Teruteru Company for almost fifty years. Their eldest child, Ise Teruteru, was married to Antonio Batcheat—whose family was of similar stature in the New World. Their youngest, Satchiko, was known for a stint in Hollywood— writing and producing a drama called *Bumble Bee*, which had flopped at Cannes but cleaned up at the Academy Awards. Not long after the Oscars, she retired from the industry—retreating from Beverly Hills back to Okinawa, and other sweet-scented safe havens. The olive groves of Teruteru.

Ichiro was the middle child, and the one who led the least public life. He had attended Cambridge, studying physics. He seemed connected to Silicon Valley. He would sometimes be spotted in the front row at Paris or London Fashion Weeks.

Once or twice before, the No Name Gang had considered pursuing the riches of a family like the Teruterus, but the logistics were always too challenging. Such families had been resisting bandits for generations; the Batcheats were descended from them. Each understood it was not enough to be lucky—one had to be savage as well.

Simone and Suzy, for all their nerve, were leery of opponents like these. If that was who had written to Merrett Leys—if M were Ichiro's cousin Mahime Teruteru; or Lady Margo Gladstone; or the formidable patriarch of an Ankaran clan, Meier Billurcu—the sisters were inclined to let the matter drop. "You don't pick a fight with a five-hundred-year-old tomcat," said Suzy, "unless you've got lots more than nine lives."

Perhaps the novelist from Newfoundland had befriended a member of this old, ruthless order. Perhaps he had not. Perhaps M was a Swiss banker, a socialite, minor royalty from the yacht club. Perhaps it would be the easiest score of the Gang's careers. As Theo's companions dug for distant leads, loose evidence, trying to track the recent transits of Mahime, Margo or Meier, Theo imagined himself simply asking Daniel—unravelling this knot in the easiest way, an interviewer and his answerer. Except that Daniel must now despise him. This fact rested on his heart like an ancient jade bi. Daniel would know by now that Theo had not been Max Paumgarten. He would know he had been lied to in his own home, by a thief. And while Theo could (or should?) have left this wound alone, one morning he found himself opening the email account he had created for Paumgarten, found himself staring at two notes from Daniel Merrett Leys, sent ten days apart. The subject line of the first was, "Please." The second was, "To my betrayer." Theo could see the first few words of Daniel's letter: "You are a black-hearted deceiver, a—"

He closed the tab.

:::

A bird had nested in Provisions K's ventilation. They said it was a pigeon but they knew it could be anything. No one had seen it. "Rats?" asked Theo.

"Not rats," Mireille said, gunning down a video-game giant. "Esther said she heard some coos."

Some coos. Theo let the words play on his tongue. A good line on its own. The setting of a scene. Another man might have turned it into a punchline.

Esther was no longer working at Provisions K; she had been transferred to the other location. The story of some coos might have been apocryphal, an account misremembered or concocted. It *might* be rats rustling in the flue. It might be a squirrel, a blackbird, a pigeon.

Theo was up on a ladder. Hanna was holding it steady.

"How's school?" Theo asked.

"Fine. How's work?"

"Fine."

"What do you actually do all day?" Hanna asked.

"Rescue pigeons."

"Only when you're here."

"I travel the world as a professional thief."

His niece rolled her eyes. "Are you at the track?"

"No." He was removing a screw from the corner of the shaft's protective grille. "I haven't been to the track since you won."

"You have to know when to hold them," she said.

"You have to know when to walk away, and when to run," Theo replied. He passed Hanna the panel.

The shaft before him lay dark and perfectly still.

"You said you didn't care about winning."

Theo took a deep breath. "I was lying." He stared into the unempty darkness. He didn't know what to do next. "Pass me that mop," he said.

Hanna did, watching him with a mixture of curiosity and concern. Theo clumsily reversed his grip and was about to jam the mop into the ventilation shaft when he paused.

"Can I ask you a question?" he asked.

"Yes," said Hanna.

"I was thinking about your bet."

"Yes."

"Do you . . . own sand?"

"Sand?"

"Maybe you got it at a garage sale? Or on a strange beach? A quantity of sand?"

"*Sand*?" she said again.

Theo closed his eyes. "Yes. In a jar. Or a . . . a box."

"No," said Hanna.

"You just picked that horse."

"That's right." Hanna was staring at him, confused.

"Okay," he said.

For one more moment they stared at each other. She started to laugh; and he laughed too, persuaded by her laughter. Hanna's serendipity still mystified him but as they stood together he realized he no longer envied it. What he felt for his niece was instead a loose, almost ridiculous happiness.

"You don't have to worry, Uncle Theo," she said. "I've invested the money."

"Oh yeah? Mutual funds?"

"Vintage magic tricks," she said.

He cocked his head.

"The old kind. Edwardian, Georgian. From the wars. 'Vichy'? Is that how you say it? McEown's Wallpaper trick. Sam Lord's Castle. One of Tetz's Mystic Portrait Sitters, from eBay."

"These are investments?"

"Yes. Over the past thirty years, the rate of return on small-run vintage magic tricks has vastly outpaced the markets."

"I see." Theo was still standing on the ladder's second-to-top step, holding the mop like a majorette. "Tell me you play with them at least."

"Of course."

This cheered Theo some more.

"Do you want to see?"

Hanna searched under her butcher's smock and withdrew what looked like a silver dollar.

"L'Ange Rapide," she announced. "Watch carefully." She threw the dollar in the air. It spun, caught the light, called back all of Theo's recent tosses. But when it landed again in Hanna's palm it was a wand: black, white-tipped. Then Hanna cast forward with the wand, pointing, and the wand had become a drooping piece of rope. "Abracadabra," she said, tying it in a knot.

"Well, shit," Theo said. Hanna opened her hands and it was gone.

"That's quite the trick," said Theo. He was in fact at a loss for words.

Hanna sneezed and wiped her nose with her wrist. "It's from 1944," she said.

"Same as your grandma." Theo plunged the shaggy mop into the shaft. He felt it nudge something, and felt the something move, then braced himself for pointed teeth, claws. But nothing came, and then something did, massive and unfurling, a plumed macaw that made Theo rear back, tottering, as it trumpeted or whistled or shrieked, shaking itself free of the flue, wingtips scattering nest-stuff, squiggles of rainbow feather-down, scraps of onionskin, russet-coloured flower petals. The macaw smelled sweet and faintly acrid, like burnt sugar. It was scarlet and viridian, with outfanning splendour. It somer-saulted into open air, half-footed and half-winged, then it was truly flying, wings in widening span, flap flapping beside and around them and then sailing across the shelves, above their heads, dully reflected in coffee cans and shiny packs of dried miso. The macaw now flew silently, unnoticed, above the shoppers. Maybe they felt its wings flap, reached absent-mindedly to smooth a nudged parcel of hair, mumbled along with "Mr. Blue Sky" on the Provisions PA. Theo, on the ladder, and Hanna, beside it, watched. In its way it was a wonder that exceeded any others. Unbidden, uninvited, just the accident of life. The bird made its way to the front of the store, where it drew a collective yelp from the cashiers, then carried sleekly on to the store's automatic doors and out them, into a soft rain.

Theo swallowed. Hanna sneezed, then whispered: "Wasn't pigeons."

They tidied things up together, gathering the spilled refuse. Then Hanna wriggled a short way into the ventilation shaft, spraying it down with soapy water. It was foul-smelling work but quickly accom-plished. The macaw's nest had been meagre, perhaps even polite. *A good tenant*, Theo thought.

When they were done, Hanna and her uncle tramped up the stairs to their apartments. Theo stopped in the hall, among the welcome mats and leaves. "I wanted to show *you* something," he said. He had only just decided. Was it because they had shared in that tufted wonderment?

He took out the thin sheaf of papers.

"What are they?"

"Can you figure out who wrote them?"

Hanna held the letters with the tips of her fingers, blinking. Theo waited for her to ask him about "Daniel," about "Ichiro," about "chance" and "winnowing-away." Hanna finished reading one, then the other. "Is this a test?" she asked finally.

"No."

"The stamp," said Hanna, passing the two letters back. There were no stamps, of course there weren't, but as Theo took the pages and smoothed his thumb over the corners Hanna had been touching he discovered there *was* a stamp, a different kind of stamp, a shallow and invisible indentation. A letterpress-like impression, at the top right edge of each page. A kind of watermark.

Theo raised the letters to his face.

"You didn't notice?" Hanna asked, confused.

A large *U*, like a tall cup, traversed by a peaked line, like a wave. A vessel half-empty, or else half-full.

Not an *M* for a signature but a *Z* kissing *L*.

"Z. Largo," said Hanna.

Selected Correspondence 3

Dear Lou,

This might sound odd.
But I'm coming.

CHAPTER THIRTEEN

Three motorcycles poured across the steppe. The sand and scrub were moonlit, dark rust-red; the silhouetted rocks and wormwoods, shaggy tamarisk, seemed like salvage. *Wine-dark steppe.* The words arrived on Theo's lips and tongue, floated there, as his sidecar bumped and slammed and shook, the whole steel frame of it shuddering. Who was it who had said it? Simone's motorcycle engine was thundering in his ears, but he could feel the touch of each syllable in his mouth, *wine, dark, steppe,* and the tremor of the recollection at the back of his head. Was it Shakespeare? No, he remembered then. Homer. And not steppe. Sea. The wine-dark sea. *How could Homer's sea be like wine?* scholars had asked. Perhaps the sea has changed colour. Perhaps wine has.

Their shadows sped towards a red horizon. To the northwest, across the mountains, lay untidy Marrakesh. To the east, across a ridge, stretched the Sahara. But for now there was just a single steady path, their vehicles flying along it. Simone was at the front of the procession, its leader. Theo led too, in his way—cramped in her side-car, helmet smashed down to his ears, clutching metal, craning to squint at the figure beside him, her pearlescent blue and crimson helmet, its visor closed—and at the riders following behind. The moon was like a hole punched through the sky. Clear white light; tire-tread on bare road; engine snarl; desert. Across that ridge, Lou.

There was luck in their saddlebags.

The No Name Gang had landed that afternoon. Marrakesh airport was like a hotel crossed with a rippling deck of cards, all glass and white lines. Theo had expected it to be dusty. Instead all these towering windows, the bands of daylight like pieces of curtain. Someone from the rental agency met them at arrivals. His hand-lettered sign carried the name they had used for the booking: *Seldom.* "Miss Seldom, Miss Seldom, Mr. Seldom, Mr. Seldom . . . ?" he asked.

Yes, they answered. *Salaam.*

Sebald grabbed a cab. The rest of them went with the agent to a chainlinked lot filled with bikes. Theo signed a form. The others pointed. Theo was resigned to their plan, prepared for it—or thought he was. Still he winced when Simone selected the ivy-green Ural with its headlight like a piece of abalone shell, its beetly beat-up sidecar.

"C'mon," she said, "it's cute."

Like a child, Theo folded himself beside her. The keys were in the ignition.

"Comfy?"

"Snug as a crab in his shell."

"This was *your* idea."

"And it is now my regret."

They waved goodbye to the agent and vanished one, two, three, into the wondrous, lawless streets of Marrakesh.

"Shit, shit, shit, shit, shit, shit, shit," hissed Theo, as Simone swerved through traffic. They overtook a woman in a yellow truck, its bed full of dates; they overtook a man on a moped with a dog on his lap. *Arf,* said the terrier. "Arf," Theo murmured back. Mostly the other drivers passed them, the regulars dusting the travellers, until the column of thieves peeled off from the city and onto open road.

They weren't sure of what they were doing. Z. Largo was a man of many houses, a man of extraordinary means. He could be hiding his luck anywhere: in his mansion in Palo Alto, his condo in Macau, his pied-à-terre in the 7e arrondissement. Or even further afield: a numbered vault, an unmarked mine, the secret catacombs under Salt Lake City?

However, Theo had a hunch, and the Gang trusted hunches. He told them he had a friend who was in the desert with the creator of the Largo bulb. "A friend"—these were the words he used. "Her name's Lou," he said. He did not tell them he had written Lou fifteen letters since January, when she had left the city, or that she had not replied since August. He did not tell them how many times they had slept together, or how many times he had told her he loved her. The answer to this last question was: only once. He said his friend Lou was on a "clarity retreat" with the inventor of the Largo bulb, the Largo smartbell, the publisher of Largo Magazines, the father of the molecular irrigation boom, former voice actor, angel investor, electrical engineer, rescuer of marooned Malaysian soccer teams, activist and guru, chair of Largo Studios, the author of *Good Light* (a *New York Times* bestseller), and sole trustee of the Largo Living Foundation.

And so they had come with him.

Passing battered cafés where men sat on humped stools, sipping mint tea, watching Leicester City play Réal Madrid.

Passing a gangly tree with goats in its branches.

Passing co-operatives selling carpets, untended stands offering handpressed argan oil, homemade almond butter, agates, honey.

A village with just one shop, advertising rare stamps.

A village with two shops, one selling oranges and another guns.

A river gorge where a donkey stood lashed to a platform, tears in its eyes.

Then finally the desert.

They reached the edge of Largo's property in the middle of the night. The billboards had come first: towering in Arabic, French and English, forceful black on white:

MERZOUGA/LARGO DARK SKY RESERVE
DIM HEADLIGHTS NOW

As Theo saw the words, Simone touched a switch on her dashboard. At once her headlight dimmed to something softer, nearer. Around him, beside him, the other riders followed suit. It seemed like overkill. The moon was like a floodlight, and there were no stars.

To their right stood a shining fence. And beyond the fence, glittering like drifts of snow, a thousand dunes.

They drove on until they reached a place called Hotel Argo. Theo was grateful to stop, disentangling himself from the sidecar, standing shoulder to shoulder with Simone. Spending time with her required a constant renegotiation of his body: what to do, how to be. It was better to be standing than crouched at her right heel. Or maybe not better, but easier. He spent so much energy policing the way he was with her, fearful that at any time she could lose interest. A constant performance, like holding a rose between his teeth.

Sebald was not there; he would join them later. The rest of the No Name Gang surveyed the hotel—three floors of white marble, like an oversized layer cake, within a huddle of slouching palms. Its name was written in neon across the flat roof—cursive letters in sizzling azure, raised high, either a violation of or an exception to the Dark Sky rules. Theo couldn't help but ask himself whose handwriting it was.

At reception, Simone glanced at Theo, gestured with her chin towards the counter's silver bell. He rang. When the concierge emerged, in luxurious pressed pyjamas, Theo was the one to give his name, to sign the forms.

He distributed keys. The travellers—weary, jetlagged—dispersed to their third-floor rooms.

Theo was tired but restless, a river full of eddies. Whenever he looked at his phone and its un-updated time he felt unmoored, half-real. He left his room and wandered down the hall, past Simone's door; wanted to knock, didn't. But then her door opened anyway, as if she had heard his thoughts. She had her bag over her shoulder. You're beautiful, Theo thought.

"Hello," she said.

"I couldn't sleep."

"I didn't try."

"I didn't try either," he said.

She said, "Let's go look at the moon."

The floor's tiles were full of mazes. They rode the elevator without speaking, moved invisibly through the tidy, darkened restaurant. A patio door opened onto the deserted terrace. Wireframe chairs leaned against dull chrome tables, with furled umbrellas. The moon seemed big enough that someone could lay a ladder against it, climb up.

Sitting at a table, Simone produced a bar of dark chocolate, a bottle of raki. She tore the foil and each of them took a chipped square.

The raki tasted cool, distant, lunar.

"Do you think this will work?" he asked.

"'This.'"

"Tomorrow."

"Probably not."

"Ten to one?"

"A hundred to one. A thousand."

"That we'll find it?"

"That we'll find it, that we'll be able to steal it, that we'll get away."

Theo nodded thoughtfully. "A thousand to one isn't so bad."

She smiled.

"Suppose we find his treasure chest of luck. Ten treasure chests. We seal it under the store; we step back and wait. And Sebald's theory holds."

"Dominoes."

"Unlimited, overflowing luck."

"Okay, suppose," said Simone.

Theo hesitated. "What are you going to do with it?"

Simone narrowed her eyes.

"Divvy it up, make hay while the sun shines? Go our separate ways? Or is there a play that comes after?"

Simone wiped at a wet spot on the table. Moonlit, it looked like a thin spill of mercury. "What would you do?"

"Do I get a share?" he said.

She didn't answer.

He shrugged. "Travel the world? Buy a house on the Riviera? Run for president?" For a second an image flashed before him: lights, a microphone, a thousand-seater room. "You could all retire. Maybe JF launches a moon lander. Suzy finds true love. Sebald sets up, I don't know, a private island? Moves into a giant submarine?"

Simone's expression was cryptic.

"What?" he said.

"We're not splitting it up."

"Not ever?"

"We're going to give it away."

He stared at her. "I don't understand."

Again she flicked at the spill of water. "What don't you understand?"

"Who are you going to give it to?"

"To people who need it more than us."

"Ah," he said. He didn't mean to sound let down.

"You thought we'd just cash out? That was your idea? Another band of millionaires basking in their good fortune? We could have done that years ago, Theo, put it all on black."

"Of course not—"

"The world is *fucked*. The purpose of all this burglary is not to replace one set of hoarders with another. *Someone* has to do better than that. *Someone* has to start rebalancing things. We need this luck so that we can deliver it somewhere else."

"Philanthropy," he said.

"*Revenge*. The lucky are always getting luckier." She took the bottle from him. "Time to remove some thumbs from some scales."

"A band of Robin Hoods—travelling the world, righting wrongs?"

"You say that like it's silly."

"It's not silly. It's . . . implausible?"

"More implausible than stealing luck? More implausible than magic?"

"No," he said.

"No," she agreed.

Their gaze met and—after a grave beat—they both chuckled. "I want in," he said, but her answering smile, like her laugh, was less rowdy than his. Something was hiding in it, disappointment or maybe caution. Theo understood this, but he was also determined to overcome it. "Seriously: I can't imagine any better way to spend my days."

"I'm happy to hear it."

"It's true!"

"I believe you."

"The redistribution of fortunes."

"That's right."

He drew and let out a breath.

"It's late," she said.

All of a sudden Theo felt soft at the edges. "Yeah," he said, and they stood together. He wanted to reach for her, to tell her he would follow her wherever she led him. She was gazing out at the road. Towards the highway, the desert, the fence that separated the two. Just then a silver suv shot past, abrupt as a memory.

The thought was like a flash: *Lou's out there.*

Simone turned. Her eyes were as steady as jade.

"What?" she murmured.

He tried to clear his mind—met her gaze, smiled.

"Big day tomorrow," he said.

The untroubled sand seemed to go on forever.

In Japan they say that when you can't sleep you must be awake in someone else's dream.

No birds in the air, no falling stars, just the chatter of old bugs.

:::

When the two of them emerged the following morning, the sky was blue. They wore their helmets. Theo squeezed into the sidecar and Simone started the engine and they steered together out of the lot, onto the highway. The entrance to Largo's property was just a mile down the autoroute, past another billboard for the Dark Sky Reserve. This one wasn't as explicit as the others: instead of trilingual text, a note about headlights, it was dominated by a drawing of two closed eyes.

A split in the fence; a right-hand turn. Theo's legs were out before him, like a passenger on a fairground ride. His fingers were knitted. His clothes were clean, he had wakened early to iron his shirt. It was cotton gingham, white and blue, he used to wear it a lot last fall, in his old life, before Lou went away.

Simone glanced at him. Her voice crackled over the helmet intercom. "Are you all right?"

"Yes, are you?" He didn't meet her eyes.

"I am," she said.

Theo sweated. They followed the bumpy driveway over a rise and into scrubland. Suddenly the sky was big, big. Theo could no longer see the hotel or its lot or its slanted sign, dull in daylight. All he could see was the blinding blue sky and the slender path of the road and the approaching sands, creamy copper-gold. Minutes glided by. The sky and sand met so crisply that they could have been a painting. The heat was dry and unchanging. Theo felt it along the hairs of his nostrils, the prickle of his lips.

Up ahead, the driveway parted in a Y, each of its branches leading further into desert. A bamboo bike rack stood at the crossroads, half-submerged in sand—like something left over from a prior geological age. Simone brought the motorbike to a stop. YURTS, read the sign pointing left. CAMPUS, pointing to the right.

"Well," she said.

Theo's eyes alighted on a row of five leaning, wide-tired bicycles.

He got up from the sidecar, leaving his helmet, and wrenched a bike loose. Sand swished free from between the spokes. He gave the bike a bounce, squeezed the brakes. Simone watched him like a general appraising her weapon. "You want to go north?" she said.

"Yeah. Look around, find Lou."

"Sure that bike's okay?"

He wobbled a slow circle. He would not win any races with it, but the bike managed the terrain surprisingly well. He tried the bell. It was filled with sand. The sound it made was not unlike a whimper.

"What?" he said.

"You look so serious," she said.

He tried to flash a smile. "I'm sorry. I'm preoccupied."

She gunned her engine. "We can meet back at the hotel. Or call me if there's a problem."

"And you call me. If there's a problem."

She nodded. "I'll just shout through the heat."

"I'll be listening." His bell gave its whimper.

Simone made a sign in the air. "Good luck," she murmured.

"We'll talk later," he said, clumsily. "When we get back."

For many long minutes, Theo pedalled down the path. The asphalt was satin, silvery. Breezes had made small drifts at its edges. The heat seemed low and almost horizontal—at first it felt manageable, as if it could just be shuffled aside, replaced with something else. It was not replaced. It remained. *On the road to Lou*, he thought, with a mixture of wonder and uncertainty, sweating in his blue gingham shirt. He liked this slow, unwieldy bike. It was like cycling in slow-motion. It was like moving through time, from one second to another.

Then the road ended. There was nothing there, just the termination of the ribboned concrete, a neat line marking the beginning of a dune. "No doorbell," Theo muttered.

He pedalled off the asphalt and into the sand, his bike lumbering but able. Perspiration gathered at his temples and at the nape of his neck. One slaloming dune led to another, and to another after that. The clear, birdless sky. The dry, formless desert. The heat. He knew he was making progress because he could see the trace he was leaving behind him, like a single ski-track. He knew he was travelling in a straight line, more or less, ascending and descending with each slow slope. He knew these things, but as five minutes became ten, twenty, maybe longer, he knew them less and less. Perhaps he was slowing. Perhaps he was veering. Sand sifted and shifted through the bicycle's spokes, through its chain. He could not see any further than the next ripple of dune, or the last one. All he could hear was himself, his own bicycle and its movement through the sand, sounds almost silken, like a hairbrush through a woman's hair. Theo was lost, he realized. No evidence of yurts, road, facilities, anything made by human hands. Just the wordless Sahara, like something out of a dream. He imagined setting down the bike, trudging out into the wasteland. Advancing on hands and knees, like a one-panel cartoon. His stomach was like a knot of rope. He had brought a backpack, a little water. He stopped and sipped from the flask; he blinked and felt himself blinking. That is when you know things are going strange: when you feel yourself blinking. He felt the blink and then pictured himself doing it—as if there were now a second person, an observer watching a dusty cyclist drinking water, blinking. Theo blinked again. *Do I always blink like this?* he wondered. *This often?*

He wanted this journey to end. He wanted to arrive more than he wanted to stop, but there was no sign of his or any other destination. The air shimmered. He might never arrive, he realized. He had not given much thought to leaving the road. This was foolish, he saw now. He might die here. He said this aloud to himself, to the Sahara, which seemed like a single, vast room. "I might die here." He got back on his bike and pedalled hard up a dune, down it, then diagonally across to another, trying to cover more ground. The fat-tired bike moved slowly and Theo kept blinking and yet he did not want to panic. He thought of his family back home, roving through the history museum, and of his friends. He thought of the bright, blinding spotlights on the Knock Knock's stage. Laughter, the reassurance of other people's laughter, like a fortune you can't ever spend. Lou in a yurt somewhere. Simone on her Ural, daylit, rolling dice tests as she zigzagged through the sand.

Dice. Theo remembered his luck and reached for it, the box he kept in his jacket pocket. No jacket, no pocket. Or was it in his bag? It was not in his bag. He had not brought any luck. He had left it behind, at the hotel. The sun was unremitting, resplendent with indifference. Theo felt a low worry, deep and terrible, an intuition he did not wish to examine. He wiped his face. He kept going. What else could he possibly do.

He could turn back. He remembered this the next time he stopped. He was emptying the sand from his shoes, one then the other, and he looked back the way he'd come. The tire-tread was still visible, like a painted stripe. Perhaps it led all the way back to the road, intact. Perhaps it was already fading, like watercolour into paper. He stared at the sky, tried to evaluate the hour. It was not high noon. This was the extent of his knowledge. It was morning or it was afternoon, one of the two. He might have laughed but he did not feel like laughing. He dared not drink more water. The wind was billowing invisibly across the landscape.

A sound. From the whipping silence an interruption—steps, quickening. At first he imagined Lou then, with a pulse of dread, guards, soldiers, patrolmen. An unwitting rescuer, shaded and knowing. A Bedouin on a camel.

However, it was a fox. Blond as wheat, a desert fox darting over the bluff and descending peaceably towards him, half-stepping-half-slipping, leaving tiny sandy footprints. Its ears were huge and out-tilted, like downy satellite dishes.

The fox stopped some ways away, regarded Theo with frost-blue eyes.

"Hello." Before Theo had even finished the word the fox had turned and was scampering back up the dune.

Am I to follow? Theo wondered. At the top of the dune, the fox turned and regarded him once more. Theo gazed back.

Another sound. The fox's tufted outline dipped out of sight, restoring the desert's geometry, while a hum had begun to ripple across from the opposite slip face. Its source was even harder to recognize. A small object, partially black and partially chrome, vague as a mirage. When it finally drew closer Theo saw it was a flat metal tray, a sort of platter, with four outsized gray wheels. Its suspension dipped as it traversed the sand; somehow the platter remained level, as it was obliged to: it carried a drinking glass, part-filled with water.

Theo did not really have any idea what he was seeing. The robot halted just before his bike. It expelled a puff of steam. The jostled water glass steadied and stilled.

"Okay . . ." Theo said.

"*Salaamu aleykum!*" A mechanized and disarmingly cheery voice sailed up from what looked like a solar panel.

Theo swallowed. "Salaamu aleykum," he said. "Do you speak English?"

"Yes," it replied. "Welcome to the property of the Largo Living Foundation's Merzouga Clarity Retreat. May I offer you some water?"

"Thank you," Theo said. He paused, not knowing what he was pausing for.

The robot gave a little quiver of encouragement.

Theo crouched, picked up the glass, eyed it. It seemed fine.

It tasted warm.

"I'm looking for the yurts," Theo said.

"Why?"

"To see a friend."

"What is their name?"

"Louisa."

"Louisa Hval?"

"Yes."

"Is she expecting you?"

Theo hesitated. "Yes."

The voice crackled. "Please follow."

So the machine led him through the dunes, Theo riding his bicycle behind the foundation's rover, weaving between summits. For a long time there was nothing to see—just more sand, more sky, an empty glass swaying on a platter. Then Theo began to observe signs of life. Spindly cacti. Balls of animal dung, like gathered marbles. Beetles calmly teetering.

Theo was fairly certain the rover wasn't acting of its own accord—that it was essentially a remote-control car—but there was still something self-satisfied about it. It moved like a toddler who knows it is the leader. Theo pedalled and steered and sweated in its wake, scouring the horizon. The vision finally crept into view: a cluster of humped canvas yurts, like a congregation of tortoises.

Each of the yurts stood apart, in privacy. Together they resembled a stand of shrines, each one alone in its tranche of land. There was also a handful of gathering places, wooden benches, firepits, something that might have been a playing field. The tents' stiff canvas seemed untouched by the environment. All of the structures had circular openings, portal-like cedarwood windows, which could be loosened from inside. Through one of these openings, Theo saw a man brushing his teeth. Shiny roof panels reflected the sun. Theo had sweated through his shirt. There was a new aroma in the air. Citrus. Lime or grapefruit. This was where Lou had been living since the winter. Here in this summer camp or internment camp or crummy holiday site, with stalking big-eared foxes. The robot seemed as if it might glide away from him at any time, slipping under a canvas curtain. Was Z. Largo here, in one of the yurts? Was each of them occupied, or was this place almost empty?

The structures had no names above their doors, just symbols, like embroidered emoji; in fact they had no doors, just fastened cloth flaps. When the rover finally came to rest, Theo and his bicycle were in front of a yurt like any other. Its front flap lay shut. Its embroidered symbol was a green-stitched frog.

The rover had not spoken.

"Is this Lou?" Theo asked.

It was as if the thing's battery had run out.

"Hello?" he said.

"Louisa Hval," announced the robot.

Theo waited for something more to happen—for Lou to appear, for the robot to move away. But she didn't, and it didn't. The yurt's taut cloth seemed to tremble in the wind.

Theo put down his bike. He felt like he should knock, ring a bell. He moved to the yurt's closed doorway. He touched the canvas with his right hand. "Hello?" he asked into the canvas, across it.

He imagined he heard a sound from the other side. Lou's long-lost voice. Her voice saying, "Who's there?"

Or perhaps not.

"Theo," he said.

A movement inside, a change in the wind.

With his heart in his mouth Theo raised the canvas and when his eyes had adjusted he saw Lou. She sat in a chair, hands clasped in her lap. The yurt contained a twin-sized bed, a writing desk, a hotplate, a wardrobe, a bookshelf, a candle glimmering on a brass table. Lou was staring.

"Hi," he said.

She seemed absolutely speechless.

"Sorry," he said.

"How—" she began.

"I was nearby."

She had still not moved.

He said, "A robot brought me."

Lou was thinner than Theo remembered. Tanned, with longer

hair, a lighter gaze. She wore earrings. He did not remember earrings. Tiny, sparkling studs: had she always had them?

"Did you get my letter?"

"Which letter?"

Her eyes were robin's-egg blue, limned in silver.

"The one saying I was coming."

"Not yet."

He saw then the letters on her desk, the small pile of torn-open envelopes.

"You just flew to Morocco?"

He realized she seemed worried, almost frightened.

"Not to see you." He registered her confusion, shook his head. "I mean—it's a holiday. I'm here with friends. I wanted you to have your space. I didn't want to intrude."

"Yes," she said. "I'm sorry, I've . . . I owe you a letter."

"Were you meditating?"

"Yes."

"In a chair?"

"What's wrong with a chair?"

"I didn't know you could meditate in a chair."

"You learn something new every day, Theo Potiris," Lou said, but her voice caught at the end.

She was standing now. It was not as hot as he had expected because of the mirrored roof panels, ventings in the cloth and a device in one corner, like a white bowling-pin, which dispersed cool air. Theo discovered that he was experiencing a visceral sensation of relief. Lou was shielding her eyes with her hand, evaluating his profile.

"Come in," she said.

He did. The flap dropped closed behind him. "Hi," he said again, but as he spoke there was a shiver across his features, the kind of shiver that sometimes reveals a lie. The lie was not that he wasn't happy to see her; the lie was the tranquility he hoped to convey, the tranquility of that happiness. He was happy to see her but he was also apprehensive, and sad, and saddened by his apprehension, and he didn't know which feelings in which proportions.

They embraced. I remember her, he thought. The dimensions of her shoulders, torso, hips. He wasn't sure whether it was he who had taken Lou into his arms or she who had taken him into hers. *It was her*, he thought. *It was me*. He pressed his lips against her shoulder. He experienced the temperature of her body. A scent he had not known he knew.

For a little while they stood like this, embracing.

"I missed you."

"I missed you too."

When they stepped apart it felt like something had been mended.

"You're on holiday?" she said.

"Yes, but I thought . . ."

"You'd visit."

"I didn't know if it was allowed. You hadn't answered . . ." He caught himself.

She looked away. "I'm sorry. At a certain point I wasn't—I didn't know what to write." She was dressed all in white: white shirt, white pants, all linen. She took a white elastic from her pocket and used it to restrain her untangling hair. It made her seem more intent, as if preparing for a mission. He could see the outline of her bra through her shirt.

"It's been intense," she said, lowering her hands.

"But you're all right?"

"I am," she said. She tried to reassure him: "I'm good. I'm good, Theo. This has changed my life. It's just . . . It's a lot, you know?" She gestured at the room around them. "Living in the desert. Holding space. Studying, meditating, doing yoga. Listening to the others. Learning what I want, what I actually want."

"Changing," Theo said. He became aware that he was blushing. He couldn't say why.

"Changing," she agreed. Her tone was careful. She was using the softest version of her gaze and Theo was captivated by her—by this woman, her face, her body, or else by whatever it was she had found here, what she was carrying with her now. He was jealous of it, the clarifying thing she had found, and sorry he had not been present, or even requisite, for its discovery.

"That's good," he said, even though he wanted to say: You didn't have to change, you were perfect.

But she was not like Simone, whose contours had always seemed sharp; whose actions felt decided. Lou had suffered from an itchiness, not anxiety but discontent. It used to frustrate him. To Theo, Lou's grace had always seemed obvious: he saw it in the line of her leg as she dismounted a bicycle, in the way she held her face as she watered her plants. At the same time he recognized the arrogance of his frustration. It was not up to him how Lou understood herself. It didn't matter what he saw. Theo hadn't had a way to reach whatever burrowed itself in her heart.

This is something that often happens: we are insufficient.

"But what about you?" she said. "Are *you* okay?"

He swallowed. This small question disarmed him—the question, his journey here, all the secrets he was keeping back. "I'm fine," he said.

"Is the family . . ." She trailed off.

"We're all right." He looked at the candle, the shadow it left on the table. "I miss my mom," he said. He wasn't ready to look at Lou's face, to see what it was doing, and when the candle-shadow flickered he closed his eyes.

"I'm so sorry," she whispered, her chin now at his shoulder.

A beat later he opened his eyes, stared at the candle.

By and by she went to put a kettle on for tea.

"Mint?" she said.

He plunked down on the rug. He laid his hand over a woven eye. "Mint," he said.

He watched her from across the room, as she plucked peppermint from a green-glass vase. Each movement seemed distilled to its essential. She was happy, he realized. Peaceful, unhurried, happy. Not wounded or recovering, not tremulous or questing—happy. Here in the Sahara.

She asked, "Where are you visiting? For how long?" But Theo waved the questions off. He didn't want to dissemble, didn't want to tell the truth. Instead he talked about his family—Peter going patriarch, Hanna gone millionaire, the opening of the new location. "The old one's done at Christmas." He tried to seem indifferent.

"I think it's terrible," Lou murmured. She brought over the tea and they sat across from each other on the carpet. They raised their glasses. The liquid burned his lips but in his throat the heat became curative, fortifying.

"How long do you meditate every day?" he asked.

"Two hours."

"Two hours!"

"Not all at once. Three daytime sits. One in the night."

"Still," he said, wonderingly.

"It grew slowly. Ten or fifteen minutes to start. Group sessions are easier."

"I like to think I'm already an expert at meditating at night."

Lou laughed. He remembered her laugh: it came from deep, like ore from a mine. "Not sleeping," she said. "You set a timer for 2:30 in the morning. Zooey calls it dream-catching."

"I guess everybody needs a hobby," Theo said.

"Try it sometime. Maybe all your best jokes arrive while you're asleep."

"Maybe," he said.

She smiled. "But it's not *all* bodhi and dharma. There's more to do at the main campus. Ping-pong even."

"Ping-pong!"

"Only one table. They try to discourage anything too competitive."

"Ping-pong's cutthroat."

"Downright savage," she said. "So we finish a lot of puzzles."

"Do you think you'll come home soon?" He hadn't known he was going to ask.

She pressed her lips together.

"Unless you're becoming a nun."

The candle flame between them seemed solid, palpable, like a piece of the room.

She smiled. "I'm not becoming a nun."

"A desert nun."

"Not a nun of any kind."

"That's something at least."

"It's something," she said. "Have you become a vicar?"

That word, "vicar," perfect and random, cracked Theo up. Lou's hand, refilling their tea, wobbled a little. She tried not to show her grin, kept her gaze down, tucked a loose twist of hair behind her ear. Straightaway he saw it: he would stand up and go to her. He would forget the Black Cats' mission, tell her everything. He felt the carpet fringes in his fingers.

"Louisa?"

The voice came from outside. Loud, confident, clear as a waterfall.

Lou sat up, her expressions flashing so quickly that Theo struggled to read them.

"Yes?" she called back.

"Mind if I . . . ?" It was a man's weathered baritone, with an American accent.

Theo scrambled to his feet.

"Sure," she said. "I, uh, have a . . ."

"A visitor," said the man, entering. He was tall. Tall in a manner that emphasized itself, rendered itself conspicuous. A long neck and Adam's apple, handsome and clean-shaven, silver-blond hair kept short. A face of an indeterminate age—preserved and toughened by the sun. At first Theo didn't recognize him. Z. Largo always wore glasses in his photographs: small, round-lensed frames, which gave him a kindly affect. Here the man was barefaced, with an open, attentive bearing. The door flap fell closed. His eyes caught the candlelight—green heliotrope cutting straight through the room.

"You must be Theo," Z. Largo said.

Theo was caught off guard.

"Forgive me: I have a good memory for faces. I recognized you from one of Louisa's photographs."

"And you're Z. Largo."

"Call me Zooey." The billionaire's handshake was strong. It was supple. "When the bots first noticed you I thought, 'Here is one very lost tourist.'"

"You weren't wrong."

"We discourage visitors. However, exceptions can be made. Are you here alone?" The question had a challenge in it, the slightest metal.

Lou had just given Theo a fresh glass of tea. He hesitated, traded the drink from hand to hand.

"No?" Theo said.

"Right; I thought not. A woman on a motorbike?"

"We got separated," Theo said carefully.

Lou's eyebrows were raised.

"Yes, she seemed quite lost. I had her brought to campus."

"Who—?" asked Lou.

"A friend," said Theo. "You haven't met."

Z. Largo lifted the entrance flap. He smiled. "Maybe it's time to make some introductions."

:::

The three of them left on foot. Dunewalkers. A cluster of figures passing through the huddle of yurts, weaving a path through the rises. Lou and Theo's rapport had spoiled as soon as Z. Largo arrived, some flaw thrown into relief. Lou moved across the dunes with her head down, her fingers very slightly upraised—as if one hand might dart out and catch something out of the air, a seed-pod or an arrow. She seemed alert to everything, cocking her head at small sounds—wind on sand, distant bird-call—and at the same time tranquil, deliberate with her attention. Theo thought of the way a pencil-drawing, traced over and over, edges doubling, will seem *less* certain than it did at the start, less final. And Z. Largo was all ink, gold ink, striding like someone who understands a gospel, some secret message, and always knows where to place his eyes. The conversation was sporadic, but only Theo seemed discomfited by the silences.

Z. Largo's route took them past some kind of construction site— shrouded buildings, stacked cinderblocks, a discarded bulldozer on caterpillar treads. Bales of wire sat under a blue tarpaulin.

"What's that?" Theo asked.

"We're building a pool," Z. Largo said.

Like Lou, the businessman seemed untroubled by the sand—his stride was almost loping. Whereas Theo was scrambling, slipping, occasionally sinking to his knees; they stopped so Lou could help him up.

"I feel like I've forgotten how to walk," he said.

"It's just practice."

"And you don't lose your bearings?"

"I did at the beginning," she said. "I thought one day I'd wander into the desert, get swallowed by the sand. Never heard from again."

"She was a natural," Z. Largo said.

"It's like anything. Repetition, repetition. Subconscious lessons. The dunes don't move much, not usually. There's a way of walking. You get the knack."

In the open air Z. Largo was laid-back, amiable, smiling at Theo with perfect teeth. There was something disorienting about seeing him in the flesh—not just because he was famous but because he seemed so much more vivid than he did on the covers of magazines. Not just a voice on a podcast, arguing a point of policy—a real and booming presence, the ends of his sentences snatched away by the wind.

"You have to understand, Theo, the desert's a complex system," the billionaire said. "Top-down doesn't work. You can only truly learn it as you go, responsively. Intuiting through praxis. But I also always enjoy how little there is to *explain* about the desert." He held out his left hand, lifting it level to the horizon. "In a way it's self-evident. It is what it is, and as you see it."

"Apart from the mirages," Theo offered.

"Mirages are mistakes," said Z. Largo. "That's you making a mistake."

Theo narrowed his eyes.

"The topography can be a form of meditation," Z. Largo went on. "There is just enough to pay attention to."

"It's like washing dishes," said Lou. "Something for your body to do."

"A sop for the clamouring parts of your mind," Z. Largo added.

Theo wished they were still alone, he and Lou. He wished they had had time to remember how they used to talk to each other, the way it used to work. It *had* worked, hadn't it? Instead, the three of them moved together, eyes on the horizon. Was this what a clarity retreat was like? Lofty conversation between rested, reflective adults? Musing together in the white light of the Sahara? He studied the woman he had come here to see.

"It's like Plato says," Theo murmured. "'Happiness is not an animal you can catch.'"

The others nodded solemnly. Each of them in linen that billowed as they moved.

Theo tossed a handful of sand. He sweated in his gingham.

"How many people live here?" he said.

"At the retreat?"

"Yeah."

"Twelve, plus staff."

"Intimate."

"It's the desert," Z. Largo said. "It never gets very intimate."

"Too much sand?" Theo said.

"Too much sky," said Lou. "Have you seen the stars yet?"

"No. Last night there was too much moon."

"How long are you staying?" Z. Largo asked.

"Not long," Theo said.

"That's unfortunate," Z. Largo said. "This is a dark zone—maybe Louisa already told you. People travel from very far away to experience it. But it's not really apposite when the moon's out."

"Sometimes the stars are so bright they seem as if you could take them down," Lou said.

"The night would fall down around our ears," Z. Largo said.

The linen-clad figures shared a smile.

"Right," answered Theo.

They passed through more desert. Z. Largo broke into a well-rehearsed bit about the retreat and its aims, the frame of his intentions. "It began as a folly," he said, a "private hermitage" he'd visit sometimes to focus his mind. "I wanted to find a place far away from Cupertino and Sand Hill Road. A cabin, a refuge. Yet the landscape wanted more from me. It *demanded* more."

He decided the property would become one of his philanthropic works. "You may have heard," he said, "that I have committed to giving away the bulk of my fortune." Theo had heard—everyone had heard. When Largo announced a spending-spree the media duly trilled about it: AIDS research, mosquito nets, social housing, criminal justice reform, literacy . . .

Here in the sunshine, Z. Largo said he had borrowed his approach from business: to try as much as is feasible in order to see what sticks. While his peers obsessed over space travel, earth-to-orbit rockets, he gave aid, funded science, distributed vaccines; he even announced a plan to "save" journalism—independent fellowships for reporters, cost-of-living bursaries for the field's emerging hacks. Largo donated to the arts—eschewing ballet or opera company mega-gifts in favour of thousands of four-figure micro-grants, administered by app. Finally, he created the Largo Living Foundation, with a mandate to lobby for nirvana. "Our civilization can only ever make so much progress," he told Theo. "Little by little, we must evolve as individual human beings."

At first the foundation funded the development of meditation pro-grammes. It paid for schools and neuroscience, recruited movie stars as ambassadors for mindfulness, non-violence, the Middle Way. The foundation also maintained Z. Largo's property here. The Largo Clarity Retreat promised participants "time, space and resources to see more clearly," with workshops led by Z. Largo himself. Seekers applied from across the globe; those who were selected were hosted without charge.

Lou had never shown Theo her application. "I just tried to be me," she had told him, "for better or for worse."

Mere months later, Lou seemed accustomed to strolling beside the world's richest man. She did not appear encumbered by his status. She nodded along with his recitation, she smiled at his jokes, yet she never seemed overly reverent. She treated his pronouncements with a kind of affectionate forbearance. Theo wondered if it was a skill Lou had learned from being with him. He remembered writing to her about punishers. Had she taken this as an apology?

They crested another dune and at last the retreat's campus began
to come into view, one building then another, another, nearly a
dozen domes and cubes in steel I-beams and glinting frosted glass,
like a Mars colony. Each construction was linked to the others by a
raked pebble path; each had a cyan metal door, with Z. Largo's
symbol painted in white or vivid magenta. A few robots squatted
here and there, unmoving in the sand. Lou pointed out the theatre,
the conservatory, the dining hall—each another clean glass cube.
There was an air-conditioned dome called the Cold Room (containing wooden chairs and meditation cushions, in a circle), and the
Hot Room (the same, but sweltering, like a greenhouse). There was
an actual greenhouse: a pyramid disclosing the faint shapes of green
trees, drooping ivy. They toured the bathing facility—sauna, steam
room, saltwater bath—and the Practice Room, with a ring of bol-
sters, straps and yoga mats. Z. Largo led them both inside the
library, which was filled with bean-bags, desks and chairs, lamps
with amber shades. Volumes by Edward de Bono, Pema Chödrön,
Michael Harris, Thich Nhat Hanh, Michael Stone, Buddhists and
Taoists, plus ten tattered copies of Saint-Exupéry's *Le Petit Prince*.
Toured like this, the buildings brought to mind a fancy private college or the campus of an eccentric internet start-up. *Where is everybody?* Theo wondered. Sand sloshed in his shoes. As they left the
library he could feel the heaviness of his clothes, the bulk of them.
A young woman turned the corner of a building, appearing before
them on the path. Like the others, she was dressed in white, with
black hair held back in a knot. Her bearing had been peaceful, but
it stiffened when she glimpsed them.

Lou and the woman exchanged perfunctory waves. Theo smiled
politely. Z. Largo's back was to them, pointing out a set of solar

panels. The woman's gaze lingered there, on his silhouette, with a complicated expression. There was something covetous in it.

When she had continued out of earshot, Lou whispered, "That's Nikita. She's been here even longer than me."

At last they came to Simone's motorcycle and sidecar, parked in front of yet another cube. Z. Largo waved a keycard at a panel and a garage door juddered open, revealing a luminous hall, the sun grey-golden through smoked glass. A random array of objects crowded the floor: schoolroom chairs, embroidered cushions, modernist sofas, potted ferns, philodendrons and a sprawling fig tree, Moroccan carpets but also an empty canoe, a taxidermied hen, a balance-beam, an anvil, a ladder, a bowl of fruit beside a vintage Macintosh computer, a diction-ary as big as a sheepdog, a basketball, and an assortment of colourful geometric shapes, each one big enough to lean on—a shiny red prism, a white cylinder, an avocado-coloured cone. Theo couldn't see Simone anywhere. Then a thud and a creak and she emerged from an antique telephone booth. "Don't worry," she said, "I only made local calls."

Neither Lou nor Z. Largo acknowledged the joke.

"Hey," Theo said.

"Hey."

Lou stepped forward.

"This is Lou," Theo said.

"I'm Sally," said Simone.

"That's Sally," Theo repeated, nodding. His spirit felt aching, indigo, queasy.

"Nice to meet you," Lou said.

"And you've met Zooey?"

Simone sucked her teeth. "I think we talked via one of these." She gestured at a rover, on a rug.

"My assistants," Z. Largo said. His posture had changed since coming into the building. It was as if, encountering Simone, he had decided he neeed to wear a new and more capable shape.

"'Assistants,'" Simone repeated. "Yes. I'm Sally."

"Zooey. So good to be finally face to face."

Simone gave a curtsy. She did not seem quite capable of concealing her antagonism. "I like your pad."

"This is a Still Life Room." Z. Largo surveyed the miscellanea. "I encourage its visitors to imagine the world as a still life, objects in arrangements."

"Right," Theo said, feigning understanding. Lou let out a low laugh.

"I've built Still Life Rooms in fifteen cities," said Z. Largo. "It's a classroom that doesn't require any books. You hang around, you observe the arrangements . . . Eventually, intuitively, you apprehend the lesson. You recognize the way the assemblage is significant as well as pointless. That what seems posed might be random, and what seems random might be posed. The two are the same. And perhaps you take this message into other parts of your life."

One of the objects in the room was a smoke alarm—like a flat, white hockey puck. It chirped.

"Needs new batteries," said Simone.

"I used to live in Snowflake, Arizona," Z. Largo went on. "There was almost nothing to do. A church, a school, a market, a liquor store, a garage. The kids would go crazy, cause trouble. They threw live chickens over my fence, into the pool. So I built a cinema on Main Street. To entertain them. I ordered a brand-new projector, a popcorn machine. We inaugurated the building with *Moonstruck*. Everyone in town turned up, but the goal was to educate the kids. Indoctrination. I founded a youth film group. Free screenings, free tuna and ice-cream sandwiches."

"Tuna and ice c—?" said Theo.

"Tuna comma ice cream," said Z. Largo. "We showed movies by Kurosawa, Bergman, the Dardenne brothers. To introduce the children to new ways of seeing the world. A world beyond Snowflake."

"A true benefactor," said Simone. "A patron of the arts."

Z. Largo ran his tongue across his front teeth. "In any event, no soap. The chickens kept coming. I considered laying an ambush: a business of cameras, automation, current. But I have a hard-won disinclination towards the use of force. A dislike of unforeseen consequences. Whenever I am dealing with something nettlesome, I prefer a diversion." He looked at the back of his hand. "In the end, I pivoted. I bought an old furniture showroom, across the street. I ordered various goods online. A Sumatran corpse flower, a typewriter, a badminton racket, a grandfather clock. That kind of thing. My first Still Life Room."

"They must have *loved* that."

"In fact, Sally, it worked. Not for everyone, but for some. The ringleaders. Some people get so caught up with the *idea* of what they're doing, the *story* of it. When they let go of these stories, these expectations, they gain a clearer perspective on where they are. Living in Snowflake is like living anywhere; it's like living in any still life, any painting. Finally these young people looked around, chilled out, and became infected with some strange ideas. One of them turned to cartooning. One started writing screenplays. One designed an excellent emoji sticker set. They quit throwing chickens in my pool." Z. Largo smiled. The way he held his face let it seem open, unguarded. His green eyes seemed guileless. That judicious tone of voice. Yet his story was ludicrous. Was he a sage? Theo wondered. Or a fraud? He would probably make a good comic.

"Well anyway the phone booth's line is disconnected," said Simone.

"This is a retreat, after all," said Z. Largo. "We have to turn our backs on certain things." Then abruptly he raised his head; Theo had not noticed until now that he was wearing an earpiece. "Goodness, it's almost the hour of our group sit," he said. "Will you join us?"

"What's a group sit?" Simone asked.

"Meditation," said Theo.

"Oh," she said. "No. No—we have to go. We have a—a camel tour."

"Ah."

"We just dropped by for a visit. Theo wanted to see . . ."

"Lou," Theo said.

"Yeah," said Simone.

A basketball rested on the floor between them.

"When do you guys fly home?" Lou asked.

"Tomorrow," Theo said, and as he said it he wanted to hit the brakes—slow the encounter, stop. *Pause*: just for a split second, two breaths, enough time to say something final or restorative, something of substance, something definitive or brave.

The smoke alarm chirped.

Theo asked Lou, "Want to come with us?"

She hesitated. Theo felt himself beginning to blush again. That bare, pricking feeling in his cheeks; his uncertain smile. And then in a small, steady movement, Lou took Z. Largo's hand. She took it *there*, like *this*, intertwined fingers. The old man's palm in hers. For a heartbeat Theo imagined it was just a trick of the light.

No, not a trick.

His smile still flickered on his face.

"I can't," she said.

I'm retraining my hands, Theo thought.

The evenness in Theo's voice covered over the capillary feeling in his face: "It was very good to see you," he said.

He had not ended Lou's searching.

"We were overdue," she said.

She had not ended his.

"C'mon," said Simone, as if she were wrenching him out of one timeline and into another. "We should go."

Z. Largo shifted, panther-like. "Already?" he said. They had begun to walk—Simone, then Theo, then Lou and Z. Largo together. Through the still life, towards the desert.

Outside, Largo's rovers waited in columns on either side of the Ural. Simone had her helmet under her arm. "Thanks for your hospitality," she said, climbing on the bike.

Z. Largo rubbed his chin. "My pleasure," he said. "Trespassers are always welcome."

Lou looked from the motorcycle to Theo. "Sidecar?"

"Sidecar," he said, his voice thick.

"Delightful to finally meet you," Z. Largo said.

"Sure," said Theo. Lou was smiling. This was merely how she held her face as her eyes adjusted to the change of light. He kissed her once on each cheek, and he thought *good* and *bye*, like separate messages. The sky was blue and clouded, half-empty. "Take care," he said. He shook the billionaire's hand.

"Until our roads next cross," Z. Largo said.

There was a black speck high above them, a discoloration in the blue. A bird, or else a drone. Theo pulled on his helmet. Simone revved the engine. Theo wedged himself into the sidecar and Z. Largo raised his hand and Lou raised her hand and Theo clutched the handrail as the motorcycle jerked into motion, spraying sand. He turned to watch her as they went, tall Lou in white linen, her honey-blonde corona, a stranger suddenly. Serious and peaceful, that right hand raised, unburdened.

Z. Largo beside her, a concept fully formed.

Then the desert whipping past, glass buildings glinting like so many objects on a table.

The sun was raying all around.

CHAPTER FOURTEEN

"Did you find something?" Theo asked after a time, into the headset.

Her reply seemed as if it was coming from inside his head. "I am happy to report that the answer is yes."

"Yeah?" he said. It felt like surfacing.

"Yeah," she said. "The old man's goose is cooked."

:::

She had discovered Z. Largo's luck in broad daylight. Sitting on the dunes, barely concealed.

"Incompetence?" asked Suzy.

"Ego," said her sister. "He thinks his shit doesn't stink."

They were assembled in Simone's room, gathered around her mobile phone. The photos glowed like dreams. No patrols, Simone announced. No guard towers. Five huge chests under five massive tarps.

"Look," said JF, pointing at the machinery. "He must be building a new vault."

"He told me it was a swimming pool," said Theo.

Suzy swiped and zoomed at the images, trying to get a clearer look at the containers. Each had an inscription along one edge—blackened characters burnt into the wood. "Touchwood of Louisiana," Simone told her, exultant.

"It's got to be a trap," said Suzy. "How could it not be a trap? What else could it be?"

"A mistake," said Theo.

They had not expected this. *Sometimes we require high walls,* the inventor had written to Daniel. *Safeguards are easiest* en commun. Perhaps it was just a portion of the man's luck, the rest still secure. Perhaps the circumstances were temporary—a brief opening, a possibility.

"A swimming pool?" Suzy repeated.

Sebald was still in the city, awaiting word. The four other thieves were arranged across two double beds. A pair of bowls rested on a thin duvet—sand-coloured pistachios and their shells. The Gang studied Simone's photos, the construction mid-construction: half-finished walls, excavation pits. A future Olympic pool? A secret strongroom? Five lacquered wooden chests, each as big as a stagecoach. Dovetail joints, brass-stamped lids.

When Simone had reached the end of the campus driveway she had threaded among its buildings, throwing her dice as she went. No sign of luck, no sign of anyone. Eventually she circled beyond the campus perimeter, chugging up the dunes and coasting down their sides, growing a little discouraged. Still she kept up the dice tests. Z. Largo would not have been the first to bury his treasure.

She rolled her first sixes as she approached the construction zone. "The site didn't look like much," she admitted. The containers' blue tarps, battened-down against sandstorms, puffed in the wind, their edges trembling like prayer flags. Stacks of drywall and massive iron slabs, copper pipes, mounds of unmixed cement like sandbags for a dam. The place wasn't fizzing with good fortune—Simone didn't roll dozens of sixes in a row. But five sixes; then full quorum; and four; and again the full six. Results like this suggested luck was nearby—but shielded, suppressed, mirrored-in. She wasn't tall enough to reach the top of the chests; she ran her hands along their flanks, recorded their GPS coordinates, snapped shots.

She had been at the site for no more than ten minutes when a silver platter rose out of the sand. It happened when she was perched at a mid-slope vantage point, staring down at the containers. At first the object seemed like something alive: a surfacing turtle, a baby whale. Then Simone saw its tires, its axels. The rover's brushed steel shone dully in the sun. Simone put down her phone.

The rover merely sat there. A peaceful sentinel; a wordless signal that Simone was surveilled. After waiting a certain time, Simone released her motorcycle's brake and putted downhill. The rover did not follow but when she arrived at the bottom of the valley she noticed a movement in the distance. Another, second, robot had appeared, cresting the dune and approaching.

Simone considered her options. She could stay. She could flee. She could flip the machine with a well-timed kick. Were these things armed? Automated tasers and targeting systems? The swooping landscape, the barren sky: suddenly the afternoon had taken on an extraterrestrial cast.

"I wondered if you were already snared," she told Theo.

"'Snared'?"

"Rotting in a sandpit. Seduced by the enemy."

He snickered at this, shook his head, but there was a moment before she continued when he felt as if she was appraising him, eyebrows raised, pink lips thinly pressed. She hadn't asked about Lou and he hadn't volunteered anything. He wanted to keep Lou out of this.

In the end, Simone explained, she didn't kick any robots. By the time the second rover arrived yet another had appeared, emerging from the construction site. She reached into her bag and opened her little box of luck, spilling its sand into the bottom of the canvas, freeing its forces. Reinforcements.

The second rover chirped at her.

"Hello," Simone said, as if a cat had brushed against her.

"Salaamu aleykum," said the machine.

The third robot arrived, stopped, chirped. "Salaamu aleykum!"

"Hello," she repeated.

"Welcome to the Largo Living Foundation's Merzouga Clarity Retreat," said the first rover.

"Thank you."

"May I help you?"

"I'm . . . lost," Simone said.

"May I help you?" it repeated.

"I'm looking for my friend," she said. "He was looking for *his* friend."

"This is private property," said the second rover.

"Yes, I understand. We're just here to visit. We separated, because we weren't sure. We're looking for Louisa Hval."

"Please wait."

Simone pursed her lips.

"Hello?" The rover was speaking with a different voice now—a man's baritone.

"Salaamu aleykum," said Simone.

"You are lost?"

"Yes."

"It's either that or trespassing," said Z. Largo.

"I'm here with a man named Theo Potiris. He hoped to visit a friend of his who is here on retreat. Louisa Hval? We got separated."

"Is that so?"

"Yes," Simone said. She wondered if the rover was transmitting an image of her face. She furrowed her brow, attempted to convey dismay.

A long silence followed. It seemed once more that the rover had run out of juice. The second robot also said nothing, rocked back and forth on its wheels.

"Hello?"

"Please follow," the first rover said, and so she did.

Away from the chests' rippling tarpaulins, across the dunes, back to the campus and eventually to the raised garage door of the Still Life Room. Simone took her helmet, left her bike, stepped inside.

"That shithead locked the door," she said. "And left me there for hours. I peed in his ficus."

"Do you think he was on to you?" Suzy asked.

"No."

"No?"

"My gut says no," said Simone.

Suzy cracked a pistachio between her teeth, nodded towards Theo. "What about you? Do you think he smelled a rat?"

Theo stared towards the window. The desert beyond their room was slowly turning silver. He imagined Lou out there, sitting with her lover. He knew he was sad—but not for her, not even for himself. For their story put to bed. Why had he not seen the end sooner? It felt like an indignity that he had needed Zooey Largo to lean his head into the frame.

Simone touched his knee. "Theo?"

"No," he said. He took a breath, grinned. "No, the guy's got no idea."

:::

Over the course of that night, the No Name Gang hatched their plan. Diagrams on hotel stationery, satellite maps on laptops, calls to Sebald in Marrakesh. The group seemed energized by the nearness of their target—or else it was that Theo better understood their goal. A purpose beyond their purpose: to give all of Largo's luck away. Theo poured himself into the project with utter abandon, pretending to himself that nothing mattered more. He looked from Suzy and Simone to a suitcase on the floor, filled with small containers of luck. *We don't get to choose what we want*, he thought. *Only what we pursue.*

Given limited resources, the five of them privileged speed, simplicity. "Quick and dirty," Suzy said, turning the phrase to a mantra. They calculated for drag and torque. They had to act fast, before conditions changed, then slip away without scrutiny. Already something was quivering at the edges of the hotel staff's politesse: the Argo didn't often receive tourists so uninterested in helicopter trips or dromedary rides or guided tours to Berber villages. For reasons Theo didn't understand, Simone kept him as their point of contact with the Argo's personnel. He greeted room service, intercepted maids; he excessively hesitated over tips, mulling whether it was better to tip too much or too little, whether seventy-five dirham was likelier to safeguard or to doom them. Whenever he spoke with a local, Theo felt ungainly. Surely they could see through this gang of thieves. Had Largo already purchased their loyalty?

Late the next morning, Sebald arrived in a cloud of dust. It washed across the building like dragon's breath, blurring the trees. They stood together in the lobby, the concierge beside them. "What is coming?" he asked.

"Our friend," answered Theo.

The cloud of dust had a semi truck at its centre. The vehicle seemed oddly proportioned—flatnosed, trailerless, a drawing half-finished. Flawlessly black, as if swathed in dark velvet. The only signs of wear were the surfaces of the truck's studded desert tires.

Sebald stopped on the road outside the property. They went to meet him. Swinging down from the cab, the tall Sebald seemed like a rejoinder to Z. Largo, a mirror. He stood shading his eyes, squinting at the hotel's smudged neon signature. "It's me," he said.

Suzy took his bag. "Never any doubt."

That evening, as dusk fell, Theo and Simone returned to the patio. A pause before the final push. He had a plate of dates; she had the remainder of the raki. A few off-duty porters stood smoking near the driveway, their fezes stacked on a balustrade. They watched the guests through wraparound sunglasses.

Simone nudged him. "Say something."

"Going for a walk!" he called.

"Let's amble," she proposed, steering Theo away from the tables and around the building, under black-handed palms.

"Is this ambling?" he asked.

"Not quite. Ambling's in the hips."

"Like this?"

"Now you're skulking."

"Skulking!"

"You heard me. Relax your shoulders."

"I say skulking and ambling are the same thing. Skulking's just ambling after dark. It's a butterfly-moth sort of situation."

"You're nuts. Look: *this* is skulking."

"I see you've skulked before."

"Now relax your shoulders. Lift your head—there."

"Now I'm ambling?"

"You are."

They ambled for a little while.

"You know," he said, "you're the first person I've ever ambled with."

The path turned, the trees cleared; they emerged into a courtyard with a dribbling concrete fountain. Simone settled on a bench. She sipped from the raki, passed it to Theo.

"This stuff's better with water," he said.

She shrugged and took it back.

He took a date, chewed, spitting out the pit. The air smelled like toast. He waited, took another date. And another. Some flowers were growing on the other side of the courtyard, terracotta roses with heavy blooms. Petals were scattered on the pavement. He kept waiting for Simone to take a date but she was just sitting in silence. He took another, chewed. "Date?" he asked her.

She shook her head.

"What's wrong?" he said at last.

"I'm nervous."

"Don't be nervous," he said. "It'll go fine."

She inspected him. "How do you know?"

He shrugged. "How else could it go?"

"Things don't always turn out."

"That's true. But I have a feeling."

She narrowed her eyes. "A feeling, Theo? Or a hope?"

He drummed his fingers on the bench. The roses looked so heavy, as if they might lower their heads to the ground. "I can't always tell the difference."

She drummed her fingers too, a separate reasoned rhythm.

She said, "Don't be careless with your hope."

:::

They set off after midnight. The moon was gibbous, a token disappearing into a magician's palm. This time Theo could see the stars, all of them, as they glided onto Largo's property, following the driveway through the opening in the fence.

Simone, JF and Suzy were each on motorcycles. Theo rode sidecar. Sebald's tractor cab drew up behind them, a growling smudge in the night. With the arrival of darkness, each of Suzy's suspicions had been revived: of Theo, of Z. Largo, of their hasty, jury-rigged plan. "He just led you past the work site?" she asked over their headsets. "He just gave you the grand tour?"

But Theo was certain Largo had not taken him for a thief. They would rob him as he slept.

He sat next to Simone, a bundle of supplies at his feet: tape, water bottle, bandages, flashlight. Theo and Simone both wore black, two shadows clustered together. He nodded at JF as he drew alongside. *He looks so serious*, Theo thought. He wondered if he was wearing the same stern expression. The interior of his mind felt tugged between bravery and quietude. When he looked at the desert, the road, the steady horizon, the night seemed grave. His sand-smeared knees at his chin, his sand-smeared hands atop the sidecar's rail. His tender heart. But when he gazed at Simone he felt something different: the quest of it, the adventure, the glitter of the silver-dotted sky.

It was at least a mile from the highway to the dunes, across dusty scrubland. The premise of their operation was Largo's arrogance: he seemed to believe himself invulnerable and he didn't like to share. It had not escaped Simone's notice that Largo was overseeing his own security: the richest man on earth pottering around with an earpiece in, wasting time on petty trespassers. An army of sentries was only as useful as its master, and after sundown their master hit the sack.

"So when's bedtime?" JF had asked.

"What I can tell you," Theo said, "is that he dream-catches at half past two."

Crammed in the sidecar, Theo checked his watch: 12:26. Largo had to be asleep by now. That left them only an hour and a half to smash and grab; two hours tops. Not very long, but long enough.

Their caravan reached the end of the driveway. At the bike rack, where the road forked, they took neither branch. Instead they headed southeast, off-road, towards the stash's GPS coordinates. He glanced again at Simone, her hands on the handlebars. She wore gloves. They all did. Wise thieves leave no prints.

The work site came into view. Not a mirage—a gathering of structures, pallets of building materials, wind-whipped tarps. Sebald reversed on a patch of level sand, so the back of the truck was facing the darkened hill, the Touchwood chests, the "swimming pool" mid-construction. No sign yet of robots. They'd come soon, Theo knew—these systems seemed automated, inevitable—but the riders were counting on the protection of Largo's slumber. Worried that circumstances might change, they had decided to forego the prudence they had employed in Taiwan. "Fortune favours the bold," JF had said, in a tone that was more of a wish than a promise.

Now they parked and left their bikes. Sebald cut the engine, distributed supplies. The group fanned out, each of them hauling a large folded parcel, each heading for a different chest. In their spare hands they carried drills.

Theo's target sat on a diagonal, near the bottom of a dune. A sea-blue tarp had been nailed along the chest's seams, protecting the panels from sand and weather. A pile of bricks was stacked along one side, like armour. He stopped near a corner and laid the drill against the wood, where the tarp parted. He disengaged the safety. The heavy bit glinted silver-gold, like a rare coin, before he pulled the trigger.

Their drills punctured the silence of the desert basin. *Surely he'll hear us*, Theo thought, his confidence evanescing. *Surely he'll come.* The whine seemed savage, unforgiving. It seemed so loud. Theo's drill bit caught and skipped. He clutched the tool as tightly as he had ever clutched anything—as if that was all it took, holding on.

Still nobody came. He wanted to ask where the rovers were, why they hadn't come, but he didn't want to let himself wonder, either.

JF's drill was the first to pierce the wood. "Woohoo!" he shouted, syllables warbling across their headsets.

"Keep your *fucking* voice down," Suzy hissed.

Theo's drill was shuddering and shrieking in his grip. It bucked once. And died.

Meanwhile, sand was pouring out of the other four chests. The Gang was unfolding the bundles they had pulled with them from the truck: soft shapes that looked like tents or tarps but that were in fact puncture-proof foil totes, similar to the vinyl sack that had become their meteorite. They unfurled their vessels on the slopes, orienting the openings to catch the shushing sand.

Theo cleared his throat. "My drill conked out."

"'Conked out'?" Simone replied over headset.

"It's kaput. Something in the wood? Or maybe I fucked up somehow?"

"*Great*," said Suzy.

Simone had begun to hike down the hill towards him.

"Leave it," murmured Sebald. "We do not have time."

"We're not going to leave it," said Simone. She arrived at Theo's side. "You think there's something special about this chest? Another layer or something?"

"Maybe."

"Could be some kind of plating."

"Tied to an alarm?" asked Suzy.

"Or maybe it's nothing," said Theo. "Maybe the drill just went."

Simone blinked at him.

"Maybe?" he repeated, hopefully as he could.

"*Leave it*," repeated Sebald.

But Simone was hefting her drill. She brought up her free hand and closed it over the bit; a palmful of powder caught the light, scattering from her glove. "Second time's a charm," she said. She pushed the lucky point against the chest, beside his jagged first attempt. Theo felt a pulse of worry, like fresh heartache.

The tool whirred. It was a cutting sound, a sizzling sound. *VRRRRRRR!* and it was through. Simone pulled the drill away. Mirrored splinters fell at Theo's feet, and sand fell too, spilling from the hole. Simone helped him grab his tote and drag it into position, collecting their fortune. The rest of them watched silently. "Never any doubt," said Theo, looking around. For an instant he thought he saw the skidding slip of movement at the far edge of his vision—but no, nothing, just sand and sky. The stars sparkled coldly, their message not quite legible. Everything seemed bright and darkened at the same time, and the sounds were strange too: whispering sand, obvious and obscure.

"Did you hear that?" asked JF.

"Hear what?" said Simone.

"Like a voice. Maybe it was a bird."

"A bird in the night?" said Theo.

"This is taking too long," growled Suzy. She was scrambling up the side of a dune, to get a better vantage point.

"If they show up now we can leave with what we have," said Simone.

"Oh sure," Suzy said. "Meet you back at Le Black Cat."

"It's one in the morning," Theo said, trying to appease her anxiety. "Everyone's asleep."

"Robots don't sleep, they're insomniacs. Where are they?"

"Maybe Largo's do. Maybe he's taught them to dream."

"Maybe he's taught them to shoot us," said Suzy. "To zap intruders and turn them into rocks."

"It doesn't have to be either/or," said Simone.

"Enough," said Sebald. "Let's load the truck."

They worked together to lower the tractor bed's loading ramp, anchoring the vehicle in the dirt. A massive winch stood at the front of the cargo bed, just behind the cab; each of them threaded out a cable, dragging a tow cord across the sand basin. The lines were like knotted steel tightropes; each one clicked into a ring sewn into the side of a tote. The sand had stopped flowing now— even Theo's—and once the openings were sealed the totes seemed heavy as houses, immovable. Yet one by one, inch by inch, all the laden bags were wrenched towards the truck. The winch groaned as it heaved them into the cargo bay, where they slouched across each other like grubs.

It was a makeshift solution. But the Gang would have needed a crane to lift the massive Touchwood chests, and a bigger truck wouldn't have been able to navigate the dunes. Once the totes were secure, they didn't waste any time. Sebald climbed back in the cab while the others got on their bikes.

"Wait—"

They froze.

"Did you hear that?" JF asked, for the second time that night.

None of them had heard it.

"I think it was a bird . . ."

Sebald didn't wait. He brought the truck to life and sent it plunging back towards the road, over rippling terrain. The riders wove trails across his tire tracks, catching up and falling back, rearguards instead of scouts. Even from his sidecar, Theo could hear the truck's cables squeaking. Its cargo bumped and shifted. He kept imagining birds. Sebald was following his dash-mounted GPS, leading them northwest. Along a dune and down its slope— until at bottom he smashed straight into the bike rack. The sound of the collision was explosive—the bamboo structure bursting apart, crossbars windmilling into space. Something whistled past

Suzy's head and she tacked away, her bike listing as she dropped out of sight.

"Suzy!" called Simone, heading after her.

"I'm okay," Suzy answered, shaken.

Her motorcycle had steadied. The sisters drew even with each other and exchanged a look, their faces concealed behind dark glass.

Simone and Suzy accelerated, steering back to rejoin the convoy. Peering over the edge of his compartment, Theo pictured crouched shapes, a waiting army. *What would it look like if we were surrounded?* But nobody was waiting. The desert was still, eerily still, as if the whole place was unguarded. It didn't make sense, yet Theo didn't question it: he gripped the handrail, he hoped.

They had returned to the driveway, four black motorbikes and a hurtling truck. Another mile to the gate. The highest of the dunes was behind them now. Theo pushed his hands up under his visor, and rubbed his eyes. Totes sparkled silver in the back of the flatbed. One of them seemed to be expelling air—a ripple of pale steam, like winter breath. Theo watched it for a little while, the luck's curious exhalation—the way it ebbed and wafted, juddered with the movement of the cab. The plume was gradually growing thicker, like something material, and the tote was shifting with its breath, leaning into it, sloughing into the others beside it. *Sand*, Theo realized. *It's not breath it's* sand. Luck, pouring from a tear in the fabric. The bag had been punctured when Sebald hit the bike rack: now it stirred with every yaw and bounce, pushed by the weight of the totes around it. He turned and saw that Simone had noticed the puncture too, awe or dread in the way she held her black-helmeted head. The damaged tote was inching towards the edge of the cargo bay. It had dislodged the tote to its left, and a third one that rested on the others; after another buck of

the pavement Simone made a hissing sound. All three totes were teetering now, one overhanging the other and the first overhanging the
edge, dangling, not so much exhaling sand as spewing it, creaking on
its taut steel cord. It would drag the others after it. "What—?" said
Sebald, sensing something. The truck swerved and then came an ear-
splitting snap. The damaged tote fell free, skittering once, as the
broken cable whipped back. The truck swayed and coasted. Simone
pulled up hard, veering off-road, circling to stop beside the fallen loot.
It splayed in the dirt, like a giant's foil-wrapped corpse.

Everyone was shouting into their headsets—"We need to go!" "We
need to stop!" When Theo got out beside Simone, at first he didn't
know how to help. The gash in the side of the tote was almost a foot
wide, rough and tattered. Glitter spilled from the rip. Simone tore off
and dropped her helmet; she tugged at the torn edges of the cut to try
to close it. She was talking to him; he couldn't hear; he knelt, setting
his own helmet on the sand.

"It's luck," she repeated, voice hard. "Anything can happen."

Sebald had stopped the truck a little ways ahead, idling in the half-
light. "Leave it!" he shouted out his window.

"It's only the one rip," Simone said.

Suzy pulled up beside them. "One's too many," she said.

"We can't afford to leave it."

Her sister snapped up her visor. "No, we can't afford to get *caught*."

JF now, from his own bike: "Time, Simone."

She closed her eyes. "He ran straight into a fucking *bike rack*."

"We have to go."

Sand was running through her hands. "There's still time. We have
the spare cable . . ."

"We'd need a patch," said Suzy.

"Tape—we brought tape," Theo said, bolting to the sidecar. It reminded him of childhood: hurrying, hunting in the dark. "Here—" He raised the roll of duct tape like a torch, tossed it underhand. "Try to seal it, and I'll get the extra cable."

He began jogging towards the truck. He could see the cable in his mind's eye: untouched, undamaged, coiled at the base of the winch. One spare line for all the what-ifs.

JF came up beside him, visor raised. "Tape won't hold."

"We might get lucky."

JF rolled his eyes. Something was humming under the sound of the air and the engines, the pat of Theo's footfalls. Like a sharp breeze through reeds. Theo hadn't yet reached the truck when he understood it was a rover; he saw it coalesce out of the shadows like an inkspot gathering shape. The disc was bumping across the sand, moving at a rate that was difficult to assess—until it whizzed past him, shiny as a knife in the starlight.

Simone had glimpsed it too. She was standing with the roll of tape in one hand, its black tongue lolling, her knees slightly bent. Theo looked from her to the truck to the rover, feeling slightly nauseous.

"Get back on your bike," snapped Suzy.

The machine stopped in front of Simone and the tote. Two strands of tape clung lamely to the container's side, sand still sluicing through the gash. Everyone was appraising the geometries of their positions— Simone, the rover, the green Ural.

Theo edged towards the tableau. "Don't worry," he said carefully, "it's not dangerous."

"How do you know it's not dangerous?"

Theo moved like a man approaching a rattlesnake. "Salaamu aley-kum," he murmured to the machine.

It didn't have time to answer. Simone lunged forward—he saw her touch the pocket where she carried a little box of luck, before she kicked it. The toe of her boot sent it flying.

She yelled at him to get the cable.

Theo ran. JF and Suzy were both howling at them to get back on their motorbike. He reached the tractor bed and clambered up the side, hauling himself onto one of the still-secured totes. He scrabbled across the treasure and over to the winch; their extra cable was spooled at the base of the machinery, just as he had remembered. With the free end in his hand he wiggled back over the totes to the end of the flatbed, and rose to his feet.

Incredibly, Simone was nearly finished. Her patch was haggard, graceless, but it contained the tear, almost, with strips of matte black tape. For a moment Theo felt buoyed, exultant, until he saw the reason Simone was standing, the sand still seeping, her work incomplete. Two newly surfaced rovers, gyroscopes whirring, had pinned her in position.

Their menace was in their movements: like wolves, like sewing machines. One at a time they started forward, scurried back, spinning like bobbins. Another pair rose up from the ground—five rovers in total now, like eerie pedestals. Simone kicked one again, but this enemy was undeterred: flipped on its back, the four-wheeled platter was still a four-wheeled platter. It rejoined the swarm.

Theo yelled at them from his place on the trailer. "HEY!"—as if the machines were sheepdogs, easily startled. They swivelled to track his voice, then back to Simone, but in their hesitation she danced between them, outside the perimeter. Suzy tore through the area between Theo and the rovers, spraying sand. JF arrived from the other side. Each of them drew their own knot of rovers, yet the mass seemed undiminished. More machines had rolled in or lifted up; Simone was only metres from her bike, but a full column separated them.

"Scatter!" Simone shouted. "Split them up."

There was a lurch, and the truck began to move. For a moment Theo vacillated. Simone had taken off on foot, into the desert. Sebald was heading in the opposite direction, towards the gate.

When Theo jumped, he felt the end of the cable jerk out of his hand, dancing away.

He followed Simone across the sparkling floor.

The rovers duly scattered. Some were pursuing the runners, others the pair of motorbikes, while another group trailed Sebald and his truck. A chase in four directions, over the plain. Theo joined Simone near the ruined bike rack, where she stooped and picked up one of the bamboo poles. The others were now too far away to call to. The pole was light but strong, and taller than Theo—she began to use it as they ran, whirling around, beating back a rover. "Do you think we can outrun them?" she asked, breathless.

"No," he replied.

But as they reached the dunes—skidding down sandbanks, darting together and apart—their pursuers' numbers began to dwindle. A few of the robots they simply lost. Simone smacked some with her pole. Theo stomped one with a boot. Running atop a ridge, they could see JF and Suzy on the plain below, zigzagging separately through the scrubland, leading rovers in ever-complicating knots. Sebald's semi truck was cannoning towards the exit: it still seemed to be gathering speed as it swerved through the opening in the fence and onto the highway, engine howling.

On the pavement behind it, a chain of rovers stopped dead.

"They won't leave the property," Theo breathed.

The machines swivelled in unison, like a creature's compound eye. For a chilling instant Theo believed they were going to come their way—a dozen silvery coins—but instead the rovers streaked in the direction of the abandoned tote.

They're receiving orders, Theo thought. A beat later, their own pursuers seemed to receive the same instructions, dipping down the dune towards the remaining luck.

"They're letting us go," Theo said.

"Or something else is coming." Simone scrambled after them, down the hill. "Why would they be so quick to give up?"

"Where are you going?"

"I'm getting out of here."

He followed—skidding down the furrows of her footprints, flailing his arms, attempting to catch JF and Suzy's attention. But the riders didn't see them, or they decided they couldn't risk another foray: he watched as they looped around and followed Sebald out.

"We're just going to leave the luck?" he asked Simone.

"We can't carry it without the truck."

After Sebald's escape—and alone now, the two of them—Theo felt brazen.

"We can pack some on the bike," he said. "Load up the sidecar."

She stared back the other way. The tote was a dark hump, dimly visible, with the Ural beside it.

"Well?"

She looked at her watch. "It's too dangerous."

"The robots are clumsy. I could distract them—"

"He's *awake*, Theo."

He grinned, trying to catch her eye. "So it's a race."

"We're not playing a *game*, Theo!" she answered, suddenly furious. Then she was striding away—through the twisting coils of brush, low thorns. He let out a breath. Maybe the others were waiting for them on the highway, idling under a picture of two closed eyes. Maybe not.

Simone began to jog and he did too, each of them listening for rovers, voices, new threats. Every shadow looked like an enemy. They ran parallel to the driveway, well away from the tote and its guardians. The sky was clouding. More rovers could emerge around them at any time, rising like a cursed circle.

He listened to the rhythm of Simone's footfalls, her inhale and exhale. Her breathing was steadier than his, her footsteps lighter. Her bamboo staff cast the faintest, skinniest shadow. Dawn was lifting on the horizon, rose and pale sapphire, a blush of colour across the mountains. An early sunrise, he thought. He imagined a thousand rovers, skimming towards them. He imagined Largo—awake now, posture-perfect, seated in lotus in the Still Life Room. Aglow with fury. *To my betrayer*, he thought. *To my black-hearted deceiver.*

"He'll recognize the bike," Theo said abruptly. A thought out loud into air. "The Ural. He'll know it was us, Theo and Simone."

"Theo and Sally," said Simone.

"Yes," he said, as lights appeared.

Really they did not appear: they just made themselves more clearly known. What had come up like dawn—pinks and sliding blues— was actually police cars spilling down the highway, racing in from the east. They coiled through the entrance like jewels on an invisible thread. Everywhere the sound of sirens, foggy and keening.

Simone and Theo ran. Away from the sirens, away from the gate, into the no-man's-land abutting the fence. Sebald and the others had turned left as they departed, heading back towards the Dark Sky billboard. The police were coming from the other direction, klaxons wailing. Simone and Theo ran towards their friends, or where they imagined their friends might be, concealed on the other side of the barrier. They ran as if there were wolves chasing them. One formation of cruisers had unspooled down the driveway, towards the abandoned bag of luck; another bounced onto the grit, in pursuit of the runners. Whirling lights grazed their silhouettes: Theo felt spotlit, caught. The cars' white beams shone a straight course before them, like an electric path. Whenever the runners feinted, changing course, the police were still behind them, undaunted.

"Should we separate?" Theo shouted, but Simone did not hear him, or pretended not to. The police were too many, too quick. The wind brought with it the taste of the cars' exhaust, diminishing and grey. Largo's steel fence loomed beside them, too tall to climb—a line of smooth, slender-gapped metal panels. The landscape on the other side seemed to flicker as he ran, changing by degree, and then it wasn't changing any more, or it was changing less. Something occupied the side of the road, hunched in semi-darkness. He heard the truck's engine before he could make out their shapes: the riders, the semi. The police cruisers' beams caught the whites of Suzy's eyes, through the slats of the fence. How long would the others wait for them? Could they break it down, bust out?

Simone stopped running. Theo drew up beside her. The lights were painting colours on their bodies.

She knelt and peeled off her gloves. She took out one last pack of luck, dusting it over her hands and shoulders.

She was breathing hard. She didn't look at him.

Her bamboo pole lay beside her.

Theo swallowed. "Well," he said thickly.

Simone raised her head. Colours, shadows, shifted across her features. The night they had met, behind the Knock Knock Club, it had taken so long for him to make out her face.

"What will we tell them?" he said.

"Lie," said Simone.

"'We're tourists. Night hiking.'"

"Tell some jokes. You'll be all right."

"And you?"

Simone stood. "I'll be all right too." She picked up the piece of bamboo. The sirens had stopped.

"Nights like this," she said.

"Nights like what?" he asked.

The police cars were gathered in a semicircle, cutting off their escape. She shook her head, smiled.

"What?" he said.

"I can't do anything else," she said, as if she were quarrelling with something he had said. Though when he replayed it later he wondered if it was an apology.

Then she turned and ran. Towards the fence, tall dull metal, with her pole held out before her. She ran straight, heels lifted high. The tip of the bamboo kissed the hardpacked sand, then dug in, and she leapt. Or she was lifted. The bamboo bent impossibly. It unbent. Simone was curling through the air, thrown through it.

If she landed on the other side, he didn't hear it.

He only heard the pole as it fell—flimsy, hollow.

Sebald's giant truck as it roared into motion.

Policemen shouting.

Footsteps around him, and more shouting, voices in Arabic and French, as hands clasped his shoulders, seized his wrists.

As they pushed him towards a police cruiser, he saw that the stars were gone. The sky now seemed like so many he had known. But this is not so, he told himself. Each sky is different.

Sovrencourt

There are two kinds of policemen, and Benoît Sovrencourt understood this. There are policemen who solve crimes often and policemen who solve crimes rarely. This is not always a matter of wits, or of hard work, or of mere good luck. Some policemen have easy beats: they loiter at intersections, looking for jaywalkers; they trace embezzled funds through amateurs' bank accounts; they cradle TV remotes in their palms, skimming *forward* and *reverse* through department-store security tapes. Other policemen, policemen like Sovrencourt, have more difficult duties. They chase ghosts. They follow footprints that disappear. They look at empty spaces and imagine the things that once rested there.

Theo Potiris was not the ghost Sovrencourt had hoped to catch. Potiris was the one he had hoped would lead him to others. Immersed in one of his regular stakeouts, spying on the crew he called the Black Cats, Sovrencourt had observed a stranger with a cheerful face and tousled hair, sitting uncheerful, surveilling the gang's parked motorcycles. Who was he? Why had he followed Jean-François

Tanguay to the Black Cats' clubhouse, yet hung back, to peer through a window?

So Sovrencourt brought him in. Requisitioned an interrogation room at the local precinct, asked some questions. The man seemed totally clueless but also completely dishonest. He was hiding something, Sovrencourt was certain. He added him to a watch list and it was only a matter of weeks before the detective's suspicions were borne out. Despite Potiris's claims that he made his living (a) working for a certified forecasting association, the Rabbit's Foot SRK, and also (b) for his family's grocery business, the mathematician/grocer was soon spending whole days and nights with the Black Cats. These interactions extended well beyond normal business hours and often took place in the location's basement—an area suspiciously blank on the diner/hardware store's official plans.

Inspecteur Sovrencourt and the Agency were not concerned with the enforcement of petty city bylaws. They didn't care about the accuracy of blueprints. The Black Cats had first appeared on their radar years earlier, following a notorious incident at the Port of New Orleans. (A motorcyclist hidden in a shipping container, a fire at a warehouse, a yacht that was never found.) Their names next surfaced in the aftermath of an operation at Paris-CDG, where undercover police seized half a terabyte of records from a sky-to-sea chartered-cargo ring. Two officers were injured in that raid. Over the next six months, their financial unit flagged multiple tax irregularities—a succession of trails converging on one commercial address. Sovrencourt was brought in following a bank heist in Colombo. There was a later episode near Belfast. Yet whenever clues began to stack up, the sense of a mystery reaching conclusion, the trail would go cold. Once it was a security guard who forgot to replace a surveillance tape. Once, in Denmark, a freak snowstorm destroyed forensic evidence. Despite these misfortunes, or perhaps because of them, Sovrencourt had become convinced that the thieves' operations were larger, more wide-spanning, than the Agency presumed. He began to wonder about the arms trade. And also, naturally, drugs.

Until this summer, Sovrencourt's investigation had the standard staggered rhythm of contemporary detective work. He had never liked working with partners so he sat alone in his 1995 Buick Century, back-issues of *Nouveau Projet* and the *New Yorker* stacked on the passenger seat, observing Le Black Cat's front door in his rearview mirror. Police chatter rustled over the radio. From time to time his flip-phone rattled in the cup-holder, messages from colleagues at their desks. Sometimes he'd call them back. Sometimes he'd record somebody's arrival or departure on a yellow legal pad.

Other days Sovrencourt drove to the city's grandiose downtown library, claiming a desk in one of the reading rooms. He draped his overcoat on a brass hook; tilted the banker's shade; sat. He opened a secure connection on his notebook computer, browsing data from Agency partners. He examined the Black Cats' flight histories, speeding tickets, customs claims, potentially correlated police reports. Sometimes all it took to break a case was a trifling correlation, an unlikely coincidence: a gift. With his thumb on the ⌘ key, his ring finger touched *S*. A ruby sparkled.

Late one Sunday night, in an office hidden behind oak-panelled walls, a casino's chief fraud prevention officer showed Sovrencourt a series of surveillance clips, captured in the games room. A suite of familiar faces, under different wigs, watching the bounce of a phenolic resin ball across a roulette wheel.

In late July, Sovrencourt went to Zurich to present his findings to his superiors. They commended his work, assigned an additional officer to the case. The detective ate a plate of *geschnetzelte Kalbsleber* at a café overlooking the Limmat, drained a single glass of Petite Arvine. The following morning, after his red-eye touched down at home, Sovrencourt's cell phone shuddered with a notification. All five Black Cats had boarded a plane to Taipei.

Taiwan is not China, but this destination still posed challenges. It took days to obtain the proper clearances and by then he had given up any hope of having eyes on his targets. In a city of so many millions he ruled out a needle-in-a-haystack approach. Sovrencourt resolved instead to be ready for the next time.

Which explained what led to the arrest of Theo Potiris on the desert steppe of Merzouga, 250 miles southeast of Marrakesh. The Sûreté Nationale de Maroc had been uncommonly willing partners—their interest piqued by the entanglement of a certain billionaire foreign landowner. Unfortunately the Sûreté's zeal outstripped their competence, or else their interest in Z. Largo overwhelmed their attention to police work. When Sovrencourt and his deputy charged through the gates, sights set on the contraband, their partners at the scene either missed, or overlooked, the Black Cats' main party. Instead of apprehending five suspects, Benoît Sovrencourt was left with only one.

As Sovrencourt walked towards him across the sand, Potiris's expression had wavered between abject confusion and something close to awe.

Bonjour, Theodore, the detective said. Would you please come with me?

The early signs were good. In Sovrencourt's experience, the more docile a suspect the more likely a confession. At their first encounter, Potiris had been jumpy, squirrelly, weird. This time the man came quietly, neither panicky nor proud. He was polite, cooperative, thoughtful. This thoughtfulness, Sovrencourt realized later, should have been a warning. They sat together in the back seat of a Moroccan police cruiser, dawn bluing the edges of the sky. Giddy Sûreté officers had established the perimeter and now were swarming across the crime scene: cameras strobed at footprints, tire tracks; women in gloves and headscarves dusted the motorcycle/sidecar for fingerprints. One entire team was devoted to the contraband—cordoning off the site, documenting its position, preparing the material for transport. As his deputy moved among them, meticulous and confident, Sovrencourt was able to lean back in his seat and concentrate on Potiris. The man seemed melancholy. The rising morning light hadn't reached his eyes.

So, Sovrencourt said.

I'm on holiday, said Potiris.

Sovrencourt set his jaw.

It's such beautiful country, what I've seen of it.

Sovrencourt's lips curled. What exactly have you seen of it?

Less than I'd like.

He took him back to Marrakesh. Just the two of them, alone for the long drive. Sovrencourt thought that the story would come spilling out of him. Potiris was silent.

You understand we know everything, Sovrencourt said.

They had stopped at a roadside stand. Sovrencourt returned to the car with a pair of merguez sandwiches, two oranges, coffee. Potiris left his sandwich, began unpeeling the orange. The rind came off in a single supple spiral. Sovrencourt watched him slip a segment of fruit into his mouth.

Good orange, Potiris said.

Your friends have abandoned you, said Sovrencourt. You don't owe them anything.

The man continued eating.

Here's some advice, Potiris said finally, wiping his hands on his jeans. Not everything's a transaction.

Potiris refused to change his story. He had come to Morocco on vacation. He was travelling alone. Why was he in the desert? He was looking at the stars. As an alibi it was terrible. Hadn't Potiris known his seatmates on the airplane? What about his companions at the Argo, whom the hotel staff remembered well?

Fellow travellers, Potiris said. I can't recall their names.

The man did admit that he had met a friend at Largo's Clarity Retreat. We were catching up, he said. The woman's name came up empty in the Agency databank; Sovrencourt made a note to research further.

What about the motorcycle?

What about it?

It has a sidecar.

There was a discount on the rental so I took it, Potiris said. Will you make sure it gets returned?

After speaking to the rental agent, the deputy was certain Potiris had paid him off. But there was nothing to do about it. The agent described the matter as a simple rental, nothing special, and confirmed that Potiris came alone.

The real blow occurred when the lab results came back. By then they had returned home. Forensics had collected the contraband at the airport; thirty-six hours later the report came in. Sovrencourt stared at his phone in the foyer of the precinct. Negative for everything. Cocaine, meth, fentanyl, nothing addictive or hazardous, weaponizable—not even flammable. The tote contained sand. Pale dirt. Unusually high in feldspar. Traces of gypsum. Origins unknown.

He called the lab, practically yelling into the receiver. Sovrencourt, he said, mispronouncing his own name. He said it the way Americans would say it: *sovereign court*. He wanted to know if the powder could be a concealant, one substance disguising another. Or was it radioactive?

Forensics laughed. They suggested that he could use it for his beach-volleyball court.

Although Potiris was still in custody, without actual illicit goods it wasn't clear how—or why—Sovrencourt could keep him. It had already been two weeks. The detective went to see him in his cell, which Potiris shared with two other men.

It's sand! Sovrencourt said.

Potiris shrugged.

One of the other men laughed.

Later that evening, at a police facility south of the city, Sovrencourt washed all the worthless powder down a drain. Water slooped and sloshed across the surface of the sand; the detective, sitting on a plastic crate, held the hose in one hand.

Eventually they reached a representative for Zooey Largo. The businessman had no comment. He denied any involvement. He did not wish to press any charges.

Theo Potiris was set free.

During their final conversation—on a sunny Monday morning, their table scattered with the shattered remains of two croissants—Sovrencourt asked Potiris what he would do if he let him go.

Potiris seemed surprised by the question. He hitched forward in his seat, looking at his intertwined fingers.

Eventually, he said, I guess I'd get back to work.

CHAPTER FIFTEEN

Theo knocked on the hull of a watermelon. The sound was resonant, satisfying, perfectly pitched. "One of these days," he said, "one of these melons is going to knock back."

"Huh?" said Hanna.

"Take this." He plopped the melon in Hanna's arms. Its weight made the kid droop a little.

"Can I put it in the box?"

"Make sure it's balanced okay."

Hanna set the watermelon in place beside a bag of rice, a tub of feta, a bristling golden pineapple. A tray of veggie samosas lay plastic-wrapped beneath honey cake, blackberries, instant chicken noodle soup.

"Can you still lift it?" Theo asked.

Hanna tried.

"What else?"

His niece considered the contents of the box. "Nuts?"

"Good call."

They strolled towards the nuts.

The aisles of Provisions K were humming with the collective energies of a neighbourhood's Friday night. No, it wasn't as busy as it used to be—much of the new store's plundered clientele was never coming back—but now that the white, shining novelty of Provisions L had worn off, a surprising number of locals had fallen back on old habits. Familiar shoppers shambled through the produce aisle, squeezing hot dog buns, pondering small dilemmas (cheap/organic, crunchy/smooth). A small queue waited outside the closet of vinegars. Theo reached into a drum of almonds, drew out a scoop. Hanna had laid the cardboard box at her feet. "Bag?" he asked his niece, who proffered an empty plastic one. The almonds made a satisfying sound as they fell—something like riches, winnings. Hanna made an elaborate knot in the bag.

"All right," Theo said. "Toss in two bars of chocolate and then make sure it goes out tonight with the others. You have the addresses?"

Hanna rummaged in the pockets of her corduroys, held up the rumpled sheet of graph paper. Even from a distance, the sight of Minerva's handwriting brought a pang of emotion. It was like hearing her voice. *Remind me, Little Theo.* She was here in her way. She had never left.

Hanna raised her other hand, waving it before her. Somehow, mid-gesture, a stick of gum appeared at her fingertips. She placed the gum between her teeth, chomped.

"Thanks, Hanna," Theo said.

"You're welcome, Uncle Theo."

Theo walked back past the cheese counter, the misting produce cabinets, the un-eerie olive cart. He watched a woman filling a shopping basket with jars of sun-dried tomatoes, another plucking a sample of the store's house-roasted chestnuts. An announcement crackled over the PA, requesting help at the cash. Crossing paths beside the jams, Mo and Theo shared a complicated—and somewhat unsuccessful—high-five.

It was different here without Mireille and Eric. As Theo had taken back the reins at Provisions K, his sister and brother-in-law had decamped entirely to the new location. In retrospect, it should have happened years before: each of the Potiris children getting out of the other's way. Mireille and Eric seemed so much happier there. What they had needed all along, it seemed, was to build something new together. From time to time they'd leave the new store's petty business to João, or even to Maurice and Blake; Theo would climb upstairs for lunch and hear the two of them through the front door to their apartment, singing along to the radio.

Provisions K was altered by these absences, but unharmed. The departure of certain customary presences left more room for new ones, as if the aisles of the old store had grown wider somehow, or the light richer, wider-spectrum. Hanna still hung around, wise and changing, thirteen years old. One of the fish-boys had asked if he could open a smoothie counter. Theo didn't feel trapped as he swept corn silk off the basement floor, wrestled with a forklift full of Hallowe'en pumpkins. He felt practised. He took a deep breath. The air smelled of ground cinnamon, coffee, tomato vines, feta, and of the rows and rows of ripe Ataulfo mangoes, tidy in their boxes, like dragons' eggs still to hatch.

As ordeals go, Theo's jail experience had not been so bad. Part of this was privilege: a straight, white, law-abiding small businessman is not particularly vulnerable to the razor's edge of the criminal justice system. Moreover, there was the character of Inspecteur Sovrencourt, whose approach to detective work might be described as genteel. Yet Theo had also exhibited a surprising resilience to life behind bars. He would never have *said* that he had been preparing for an arrest on suspicion of membership in an international burglary ring. But in a way he had been. He liked routine. He could fall asleep anywhere. He was comfortable with strangers. He didn't mind being alone with his thoughts. And the twists and turns of recent months had imbued his character with a certain recklessness—the sense that *que sera sera* and, in fact, *que sera* was likely to be interesting.

For all of these reasons—in addition to his faith in others, naiveté, stubbornness, loyalty, a confused sort of heartache, a belief in honour among thieves, and his own self-interest—Theo patiently endured his days behind bars. He kept his secrets, trusting that the Gang's past caution would set him free. On the Morocco side the food was good: dates, crispy cumin pizzas, cakes with honey. Back home it was soggy cheese sandwiches, minestrone soup. He knew the sandwiches would be bad because they came wrapped in wax paper. There was a joke there, he thought: sandwiches in wax paper, that foreboding.

His fellow prisoners were cagey, pleasant, frequently depressed. Nobody ever asked what you were in jail for: they did it all with their eyes and ears, watching, eavesdropping, studying each newcomer. The faces of the accused were guileless, hangdog. They seemed guilty, not criminal. No switchblades or leather jackets, no heavyset men punching mirrors. Tax cheats, Theo decided. Counterfeiters. Small-time smugglers. In Marrakesh he met a man who had been arrested for running unlicensed tours of the medina. Back at home, he shared a cell with a guy who sold illegal replicas of brand-name espresso-pod machines. Everybody wanted to get along. Everybody wanted to get out of there. Those who snored apologized for snoring and nobody cheated at cards. The closest Theo came to an actually scary criminal operation was an *arancino*-shaped man who revealed that he "worked in cheese."

"You're a cheesemonger?" asked Theo.

"Not exactly."

"You make it?"

"No."

"All right," said Theo, worried he had asked too many questions.

"What I do is I help persuade stores that our cheese is the cheese they need to sell."

"Ah," said Theo, marvelling privately that he had at long last met a member of the cheese mafia.

"What about you?" asked the man. He leaned a mortadella-coloured elbow against the cell's empty hand-sanitizer dispenser.

Theo considered his words. He imagined this guy sauntering heavily through Provisions K's swishing automatic doors. His gaze swung past the rows of bunks, the card game, to the policewoman at her desk on the other side of the bars. "I'm thinking of opening a zoo," Theo said.

The cheese mafioso snickered. But he was staring at Theo now, eyes narrowed, as if he had recognized something there. Theo began to worry that the two of them had already met. Had they struck a deal together? Had Theo resisted his appeals?

The man said, "You're a comedian."

"Well," Theo said.

"No, I remember. Right? I saw you once at that club downtown. The Joke Barn."

"The Knock Knock Club."

"Yeah! I knew it! You were funny."

Theo gave a tight smile. He looked away, guarding his heart from this courtesy.

"You had this one about getting older," said the man, "how we're all just fucking idiots. 'Idiots getting wiser . . .'" He was nodding his head now. "Yeah, I remember! I quote you all the time. 'You were dumber yesterday than you are today.'"

Theo leaned his chin on his hand. "That sounds like me. A joke that isn't actually funny."

"No, it was the whole bit! It was like: we're all such fucking doofuses. As kids, as men—we're idiots. We only see it later. Or our girls see it." The man gave a low laugh. "'Don't be loyal,' you said. Loyal to yourself, I mean. 'Don't be faithful.' Your past self was *terrible*. Give it up already. Betray your fucking principles. I think you even said that: 'Betray your principles!'"

"Be a snake," Theo murmured.

The man guffawed. "Yeah! Be a snake!" He was smiling so wide. "You remember it. You made it look like you were just making it up on the spot. Fuckin' genius."

The cheese mafioso stared out into space, happily remembering. Theo looked at him and then looked away into the same empty air, as if he might see his past self there.

"And then I remember afterward this awesome astronaut went up," said the man.

Theo never heard from Z. Largo. Or Lou. Sometimes he thought about the billionaire's curiously harmless rovers, his oddly undefended chests.

He thought about Lou, and dice tests.

Theo didn't tell anyone he was in jail. When he got out of jail he went home. His welcome mat said welcome. His winter boots sat ready, outside his door, because it would be winter before long.

On his kitchen counter was a drawing Lou had made, blue ink on foolscap, a frog on a cross-hatched lily pad. He didn't throw it out, but he slipped it between the pages of a hardcover book, pushed the book onto a shelf, beside others.

When he went to Provisions L he learned that Suzy and Sebald had already come and collected everything from the supermarket basement.

"They said their institute found more storage space," Blake explained.

"Oh," Theo said.

"But don't worry," Blake added. "They paid through the end of the lease."

Theo nodded, staring across the cellar's empty concrete. A mirrored door leaned open.

"Did they leave me a note?"

Blake shook his head.

Theo clicked his tongue. On his way to daylight he passed Hanna—one earbud in, sitting on a box of boxes of cereal. She caught Theo's eye. "I told you they were dicks," she said.

Sometimes he wondered about them. He heard good news and he wondered. Climate stats. Homelessness rates. An unjust law overturned. A slumlord arrested, a sick kid recovering, a referendum going the right way for once—the arc of the moral universe bending a little truer, a little more steeply, as if it had been nudged. As if there were a little more fortune in the world, being passed around in mirrored parcels.

:::

Theo was standing at the register when his phone buzzed. He was trying to remember the code for peaches. "Esther," he shouted. "Peaches?"

"37121," she called back.

"That's apricots."

"It's peaches."

He punched it in, skeptical. The screen showed peaches.

"Why do I ever doubt you?"

"Patriarchy," Esther said.

Theo smiled, passed through the customer's peaches, his milk, his sprigs of mint. *A very particular feast*, he thought. As they waited for the debit machine, he checked the phone's screen. The text was from the Knock Knock Club:

you want to go up tonight? Annette wrote.

Theo had sent a text to Simone, once. No words—just a four-leafed clover emoji, jade-green.

The note underneath it read, *Message unread*.

He'd check it from time to time, like a charm.

Sometimes he'd bike past Le Black Cat, slowing at its low, smoked windows.

He never saw their motorbikes in their spots.

He always looked.

He did not resume his visits to the track.

The journey to the Knock Knock Club was part downhill and part up. These days the birds were gone. The roads always seemed clear. But at the club, everything felt the same. Getting up again, inside the spotlit circle, he was reminded how free it was up there. He held the mic to his lips, held it lightly. He had forgotten the forcefulness of the feeling he experienced when an audience began to laugh. The beginning of the laugh was what felt most important. The end of a laugh was its resolution, each ripple contingent upon that start. The way a laugh began and then unfolded: nothing, then something. The audience was quiet, they laughed, they listened, they laughed, they were quiet again. What would happen next? It could be anything.

Theo told stories, found punchlines, faltered, got lost—but he also repeated things now, tried bits he had stumbled onto before, last week or long before. Repeated them, revisited them, and in those revisitings discovered that he did not feel like a rerun, but in fact like a human being making progress, trying and retrying things, a procession of subtle revisions. The one about flooded basements. The one about snowplows. One about getting older; one about people who ride motorcycles; one about macaws in the flues. Ones about funerals, siblings.

It was work. It was sweeter than work.

Sometimes, for one of his bits, Theo would get a member of the crowd to flip a coin. He'd call it in the air. He was right half the time.

:::

A ceramic urn, filled with ashes, rested on the table beside Theo's bed. Its lid was smooth and almost completely flat. The glaze was matte, unornamented, faded alabaster. As time went by, Theo noticed the urn less and less. It was like his lamp, his charger cable, the photograph of his niece and nephews, the pile of unread books, a tarnished two-dirham coin. These objects had meant something or served a purpose; they might mean something still; they might yet be useful.

There was also a little box, slipped into the space between the books and the photo. It was roughly as big as a deck of cards, hard black lacquer with a copper clasp. At certain hours of day, at certain times of year, a narrow beam of sunlight would fall across the box and be cast right back, a patch of colour daubed on the wall.

Theo saw it once. He had just come into the room. The curtains were fluttering. He reached out with his hand towards the wall, ran his fingers over the spot of gold.

Light, just light, shining by chance.

Acknowledgments

Thank you to Meredith Kaffel Simonoff, for the force of her conviction and the depth of her belief.

Thank you to Anne Collins, who shaped this book with her intelligence and generosity.

Thank you to Tony Perez and Tin House Books, for all their care and fervour.

Thank you to Jan and Arlen Michaels, Robin Michaels and Daphne Elwick.

For advice, assistance and inspiration: François Vincent, Neale McDavitt-Van Fleet, Alexandre Lenot, Luc Mikelsons, Maryam Ehteshami, Catherine Leroux, Anna Leventhal, Melissa Bull, Jeff Miller, Elisabeth de Mariaffi, Emma Healey, Neil Smith, Vincent Morisset, Caroline Robert, Stephen Ramsay, Julien Lefort-Favreau, Anne-Renée Caillé, Basia Bulat, Mitz Takahashi, Adam Waito, Julian Smith, Angel Chen, Elisabeth Donnelly, Stu Sherman, Sugar Sammy, Shane Ward, Steven Hayward, Hamza Khan, Erin Wunker, Yung Chang, Ismail Elamroui, Yves Chiu, and the readers of Said the Gramophone. Thank you to Meg Storey, Doris Cowan and Elizabeth DeMeo. Evan Haldane conceived Sebald's formula for luck—and helped me imagine (and troubleshoot) the work of the Rabbit's Foot. Taso Erimos, John Crellin and especially Lar Vi consulted on groceries. None of my mistakes are theirs.

The Wagers is indebted to the many masterpieces of Daniel Pinkwater. Chapter Six lifts a passage from his book *The Last Guru*. I was also influenced by David Walsh's fascinating memoir, *A Bone of Fact*. And I am grateful for Marc Maron's matchless comedy podcast WTF—in particular his conversations with Adam Goldberg and Zach Woods, from which I borrowed anecdotes.

Special thanks to Michael Deforge, who designed the logo for Z. Largo's foundation, and to the writers and comedians who contributed jokes to Theo's monologues: Monica Heisey, Chandler Levack, Daniel Beirne and Mark Slutsky. They are all much funnier than this book.

This novel would not have been possible without Québec's public daycare system. I am also grateful for the support of the Conseil des arts et des lettres du Québec and the Canada Council for the Arts.

Long live Montreal's Café Felice, Café Olimpico, St-Viateur and Fairmount Bagel, Wilensky's, Delphi Variété, Royal Submarine, Chez Vito, Papeterie Zoubris, la Maison de l'Aspirateur, Euro deli Batory, Giovanni Clothes, Coiffure Mode Steve's, Dragon Flowers, Barbier Hollywood, Bar Exxxotica, Café Social, Monastiraki, Fruiterie Mile End, Serrano's, Capucine et Tournesol, Peinture Miller, J. Piché et Fils, Casa del Popolo, Bottines, Snack 'N Blues, Tapis H. Lalonde et Frère, and all the stubborn lasters.

To Thea Metcalfe and Miro: you reveal the world. Thank you.